*Juliana dipped her bare feet
into the hot spring and let out
an indulgent sigh. . . .*

"THIS FEELS WONDERFUL." SHE PATTED THE STONE next to her. "Take off your shoes and join me, Cole. I'm enjoying it too much not to share it with you."

Intrigued, Cole lifted an eyebrow. "I want to share in your enjoyment, Juliana, but I'm afraid of the consequences of our play."

"Consequences?"

He smiled slowly. "You're asking me to undress. Such a request will always have serious consequences. Are you certain you want me to?"

A soft gasp escaped her. She looked away, her cheeks rosy.

Cole stared at her profile. His conscience reminded him that she was an unmarried woman placed in his care by her trusting father. He should bundle her up and take her outside where William could vouch for their behavior. But another, more primal aspect of his personality urged him to indulge in the pleasure that the newly awakened passion in her eyes promised.

Keeping his attention on her, he removed his shoes and socks, rolled up his trousers, and dunked his feet into the spring. Deliciously hot water flowed over his skin, relaxing his muscles and drawing a sigh from him. "This does feel good," he admitted, shifting closer to her, bridging the distance between their bodies. "But I can show you something that will feel even better. . . ."

Books by Tracy Fobes

Touch Not the Cat
Heart of the Dove
Forbidden Garden
Daughter of Destiny
To Tame a Wild Heart
My Enchanted Enemy

Published by Pocket Books

My Enchanted Enemy

TRACY FOBES

SONNET BOOKS

New York London Toronto Sydney Singapore

This book is a work of fiction. Names, characters, places and incidents are products of the author's imagination or are used fictitiously. Any resemblance to actual events or locales or persons, living or dead, is entirely coincidental.

An *Original* Publication of POCKET BOOKS

 A Sonnet Book published by
POCKET BOOKS, a division of Simon & Schuster, Inc.
1230 Avenue of the Americas, New York, NY 10020

ISBN: 0-7434-1279-6

First Sonnet Books printing March 2002

10 9 8 7 6 5 4 3 2 1

SONNET BOOKS and colophon are trademarks of Simon & Schuster, Inc.

For information regarding special discounts for bulk purchases, please contact Simon & Schuster Special Sales at 1-800-456-6798 or business@simonandschuster.com

Book design by Kris Tobiassen
Front cover illustration by Lisa Litwack;
photo credit: Jeremy Walker/Gettyone.com

Printed in the U.S.A.

for my niece Anne-Marie, with love

Prologue

❦

Shoreham, England

A CHILL WIND BLEW ACROSS THE HILLS. IT WHIS-
tled through the branches of a gorse bush, ripping away
dead leaves, and twisted around saplings that shivered in
response. Salt tinged the breeze, drawn up from the
ocean just beyond the cliff, and a layer of mist floated
close to the ground. The mist glowed pale with moonlight. Ghostly figures seemed to dance among its currents. On another day, the old gypsy woman might have
said a quick prayer against the devilish currents in the
air, but tonight, she heard only the shouts of those who
would see her dead.

She crouched among several iron crosses erected
upon the cliff. The crosses formed an ancient place of
worship far more holy than the church erected in the
center of the hamlet, and far less demanding on the
pocket. In the past she'd felt safe here.

Tonight, though, she suspected the crosses might well
mark her grave.

Cold from the ground seeped through her bare feet
and into her bones, making them ache. And yet, a terrible magic in her burned like a fire in her veins, magic

that she'd never really learned to control. Always she kept it leashed, for fear of what it might persuade her to do. But tonight . . . tonight, the magic frightened her. Like a beast locked in a dungeon and rattling its cage, it demanded vengeance.

It demanded release.

Excited bellows split the night. The Englishmen were much closer now.

And they were many.

She could hear them beating the bushes with sticks, trying to find her people, the gypsies who knew of their sins.

The rest of her tribe had run alongside the cliff. They'd tried to help her, the wise one who could bless and curse, heal and make sick. But she'd felt her heart squeezing uncomfortably in her chest, and knew she would only slow the ones who might survive, so she'd insisted they try to escape, while she bought them time by cursing the Englishmen for their sins.

An orange glow rose up over the hillside, from the direction of the approaching mob. Shadows danced among the old Celtic crosses, forcing her to duck behind the largest one. Moments later, the first torches came into view.

Her breath coming in quick gasps, she clutched the cross so hard that her knuckles shone white. Inside, the magic raged. A tendril of hair brushed against her cheek. She realized that her hair had begun to stand on end. In the past, she'd managed to control the magic inside her with the help of the Sea Opal, a powerful jewel that had blessed her tribe with good luck for many a century. But now that the Sea Opal had been stolen, she had no such assistance.

The Sea Opal. How foolish they'd been to lose it! And yet, how could they have protected *anything* from such a determined and accomplished thief?

Lips pressed together, she recalled the stringent methods they'd adopted to guard the opal: She'd carried it in her very own wagon, and one of her nephews had always remained outside the wagon to guard her. Still, the thief had possessed the instincts and grace of a cat, along with the morals of a jackal. He hadn't hesitated in clubbing her nephew over the head, and then nearly strangling her to death before stealing the opal from its velvet-lined box. No doubt he thought he'd killed her, but she'd lived, and caught a glimpse of his face.

And yet, despite her hatred of the thief, she fully understood why he hadn't been able to resist the Sea Opal's lure. It glowed with a rare bluish opalescence, as though lit from within. Strange patterns twirled and danced within its depths. Never since had she seen such a jewel, one that had the power to drive thought from a mind with its beauty. Sometimes she even fancied that something lived within the opal, a presence trapped forever inside its hard walls, able to communicate only by changing color and swirling like the currents and eddies that washed up on shore.

How many people had died fighting over this jewel?

Ilona suspected their number was legion.

Hateful slurs against the gypsies echoed in her ears. She cringed. The thief, known as Anthony St. Germaine, who thought a mongrel was more deserving of respect than a gypsy, topped the nearest hill with his compatriots and lurched her way. The whole of them were drunk with righteousness and desperation.

Her heart contracted, hard, in her chest. A pain shot through her left arm. For a moment, her old bones refused to move, and her gut twisted horribly with the thought that she might remain frozen behind the cross while her enemies staggered by and went after the rest of her tribe.

Then, Ilona lifted her chin and forced the pain from her mind. She *would* save them, her Elena and Stefan and Walther, and all the others who needed her now. She stood up, knee joints creaking, and with her shoulders as erect as she could make them, walked directly into the field before the mob, setting herself in their way. They didn't see her at first; perhaps her form was lost among the shadows. Rather, they continued forward, yelling and shouting to God for assistance in ridding their land of gypsies, their humanity replaced by blood lust.

When they came within fifty feet, someone finally noticed her.

"What is this?" the female voice shouted, allowing Ilona to identify her as St. Germaine's wife, known for her charitable efforts in the hamlet. "Have we finally found one of the gypsy jackals?"

"Aye, it's a dirty piece of scum," another voice crowed. This time Ilona recognized St. Germaine's voice. "Let's see why it isn't running away from us like the rest of them."

Surging forward as one, the thief, his wife, and their clan held their torches high over Ilona, illuminating her fully.

"Look at her clothes," a different female voice said, her tone hushed. "They flap as though caught in a wind."

A new wariness invaded the crowd. While St. Germaine and his wife stepped close to Ilona, the rest hung back. Ilona knew that the magic that flowed through her was beginning to materialize in various ways outside her body. Still she fought to contain it, for her magic could be a fearsome thing.

"You have taken something very precious from me," she said in a thready voice that was better suited to the gypsy language. "It is called the Sea Opal. Return it to me now, and I will spare your lives."

The mob froze at her words. Silence reigned. Then, suddenly, one of the white men laughed. Others joined in, until the hills fairly shook with laughter. St. Germaine stepped forward amid the tumult, his bearded face aglow with torchlight, and held a bluish jewel up high for her to see.

"Is this what you seek?" he asked, his tone triumphant.

Ilona trembled. "Return the Sea Opal to me, and I'll spare you."

St. Germaine dropped the Sea Opal back into his pocket. "I will never return it, old witch."

"She *is* a witch," the thief's wife accused, her voice clear and strong. "An abomination in the eyes of God, who must not be tolerated. We must rid our land of this canker before it destroys us utterly."

Hoarse shouting erupted from the crowd.

Ilona groaned. All of her life she'd avoided deliberately calling upon the magic, knowing it acted unpredictably and often brought more trouble than relief. And yet, she'd never had a more dire need of it than now. She would have to risk calling upon it, if only to save those she loved.

Narrowing her eyes, she drew some figures in the air, her gnarled old fingers moving as gracefully as a ten-year-old's. Her knuckles stopped aching as she first directed the magic to her fingertips, and then through them to the Englishman who stood closest to her.

"Snakes," she hissed at him.

Eyes wide, the man she'd cursed lurched backward. He pressed a hand against his stomach. Evidently he'd already felt a twisting in his stomach.

Gasps replaced the laughter from a mere moment before.

St. Germaine drew himself up to his full height. "In the name of God, gypsy, you will be punished."

Ilona kept her attention on the man closest to her. "Punish me," she told him, her voice wavering, "and you will *all* have snakes."

Sweat broke out on the cursed man's forehead. His hands curled into claws, he began digging at his midsection. "There's something inside me," he panted. "She put something inside me. It hurts." He looked around wildly.

For a knife, Ilona thought. Men cursed with snakes often tried to cut their own insides out to free themselves from the painful coiling. If they could be kept from gutting themselves, they'd recover before sunrise.

If.

"Do you see, thief, what I can do to you?" she crowed, suddenly feeling powerful for being able to control the magic just this once. She hoped the rest of her people were far enough ahead to avoid capture.

"I fear you not, old gypsy," St. Germaine declared. "I *will* be rid of you."

Without warning, he ripped a woolen cloak from around his shoulders, strode up to her, and wrapped her in its rich folds, trapping her arms at the sides of her body. Then, before Ilona quite knew what was happening, the crowd had caught her up and was carrying her atop their shoulders, like a sheep destined for the slaughterhouse.

"I forgive you, and may God forgive you as I do," she cried.

But even as the words emerged from her mouth, she knew she didn't mean them, for her love for Elena and Walther and Stefan and the rest of them was so great that she could never forgive any atrocity perpetrated against them. In fact, if these Englishmen hurt anyone in her tribe, she would happily allow the magic free reign, to perpetrate any evil it wished.

They jostled her roughly upon their shoulders, one of the hands supporting her ramming into her spine and another pounding against her ribs. The indignity of it was far worse than the pain, and a new beast began to twist within her gut, this one full of both magic and rage. A traditional and very old gypsy curse came to her lips, and she shouted it aloud, earning another brutal jostling but also some small satisfaction.

Idiot Englishman, she thought.

Suddenly, the mob slowed, then stopped. The ones carrying her shouted and released their hold on her. She dropped heavily to the ground. When she glanced upward to see what had made them shout, she could not stop the cry that emerged from her own throat.

They were all here, their faces illuminated by torchlight: Elena, her long black hair flowing unbound to her waist and her dark eyes flashing with fear; her grandson Stefan, his head held proudly as he faced those who would kill him. The other gypsies stood farther back, their faces not quite visible, but Ilona knew who they were.

Her loved ones.

They all stood at the very edge of the cliff. Some fifty feet below them, the ocean pounded against the cliff wall. If the Englishmen forced them back any farther, they would fall.

The mob fell silent. Ilona could feel the tension gathering in the air. Death was very close now.

"Let them go," she screamed, "or I will curse you and your loved ones, and you will prefer hell itself to life!"

"Be quiet, gypsy witch," the Englishman nearest her commanded.

Rage brought darkness to Ilona's field of vision. Her head began to ache. The tight mental control she held on the magic inside her began to scatter.

St. Germaine withdrew a sword from a scabbard at his side. The metal along the sword's edge glowed in the moonlight like silver death. He leveled it against Stefan's midsection, and pricked her grandson with its tip. Blood bloomed bright red on Stefan's shirt.

"Move backward, jackal," he declared, "or I will skewer you on the spot."

Stefan didn't move. His eyes flashed. Ilona saw the impotent anger in them. Her heart seemed to shrivel and die within her.

"Kill me, English pig," Stefan challenged.

"No!" Ilona shouted.

St. Germaine narrowed his eyes. He flicked his sword until its point rested against Stefan's throat. "Move backward," the thief repeated.

A great stillness came over the gypsies.

Her grandson shuffled backward. Chuckling, the thief

gave him a little push. Stefan's screams as he fell to his death in the ocean far below chopped through the silence like an ax.

Ilona gasped. The last of her determination to hold the magic at bay crumbled. Darkness grew in her mind, becoming thick, deep, without mercy.

She would see them dead, or die herself.

A predatory smile stretching her lips, she freed the beast from its cage in her mind. Immediately a fire spread through her veins, one so hot she thought she might be burned alive.

Let the Englishmen see what evil really was!

"Move backward. All of you," St. Germaine demanded, and transferred his sword point to Walther. The gypsy became as still as a statue.

Elena's face twisted with fear for her husband.

The cloak holding Ilona immobile began to smoke. A blue glow began to flicker eerily against the face of the man who held her prisoner. Grimacing, he stepped away from her and the cloak fell away. Ilona realized *she* was the source of the glow.

She smiled, baring every one of her decayed teeth.

The man made the sign of the cross upon his chest.

St. Germaine dropped his sword from Walther's throat and turned to stare at Ilona. "You are the devil," he breathed.

Ilona offered him her most vicious grin. Feeling like a thundercloud so burdened with rain that it must explode and crash and strike the land with lightning before drenching it in rain, she stared at the thief from the corner of her eye. The smile slipped from her lips, replaced by a frown of concentration. She would use the spell of the sea people to punish them. The spell would force them and their descendents to live in the ocean as *nagas*: half-human, half-dolphin creatures. Such a fate, in Ilona's estimation, was far worse than death itself.

"Your legs shall be taken from you," she intoned, feeling the magic leap toward the thief, "and you will have fins, and over your skin shall loathsomeness creep."

St. Germaine began to shake, and the sword he still held began to shake with him. Ilona knew he was fighting against the effects of the spell. He was, she acknowledged, very strong; but no match for the beast.

"Witch," he growled in a tortured voice, his free hand spasming around the Sea Opal.

She narrowed her eyes. He *would* return the jewel to her. "Come here."

His right leg flailed toward her, like a puppet's, obeying her command. The rest of him stayed still. Uneasiness filled her. She'd never met a man with such a skill at resistance. Perhaps the magic of the Sea Opal was strengthening him.

"Give me the Sea Opal," she commanded.

Veins popping out on his forehead, he slowly raised the hand that held the jewel. She too, lifted her hand, intending to pry the opal from his fingers, when suddenly he stiffened as though his heart had clenched.

"Never," he hissed, and before she knew what he was about, he jerked his hand upward and threw the opal. Like a shining star it arced through the air, glittering in the moonlight, and disappeared over the side of the cliff with her Stefan.

Ilona froze. Something like an iron talon seized her insides. Dear God, she'd never get the jewel back now. The good luck that the Sea Opal had brought would reverse, and her family would be forever cursed with calamity. The desire to drop to the ground and curl up into a ball grabbed hold of her. She fought it away, instead feeding the rage that swelled anew inside of her. The beast screamed in response. Aware that she had never commanded a stronger magic than she did at this moment, she directed an onslaught at the thief that no human could endure.

Immediately his eyes became unfocused. His sword dropped to the ground, apparently from nerveless fingers, and his mouth opened slightly.

She frowned, her pleasure in seeing him beaten gone. She'd lost the Sea Opal.

Even so, she focused her magic upon the thief's wife. "And the ocean shall become the coffin in which you are bound, and the sunlight shall be withheld from your eyes, and your house will become mine."

The woman uttered a tiny sigh and allowed her hands to drop to her sides. Her eyes became wide and blank. She was weak and contemptible.

Ilona's lip curled. One by one, she stared at the rest of the Englishmen who had killed Stefan. "And all nourishment that passes your lips shall taste of salt, and you shall be held as evil from all men."

The men were now completely still. They'd dropped the hoes and rakes and torches they'd been carrying. The clothes of a few men caught on fire. Ilona knew the sea would put the fires out soon. Jaw clenched, her head throbbing with the effects of magic, she intoned, "As long as our gypsy blood remains pure, my curse shall endure."

The gypsies teetering near the cliff's edge uttered a collective sigh, reminding her of their presence.

"Move away from the edge. Quickly," she muttered to Elena, who staggered out of the way. The rest of her people followed, stumbling, their faces like pale moons in the darkness.

Ilona focused on Anthony St. Germaine. She looked through him, seeing him as he truly was for the first time: A thief from the East End of London who had made his fortune by stealing from others; a man without any family other than his wife and whose friends remained loyal only as long as he continued to offer them food and shelter. Disgust for him twisted her lips. "Go as you've been bid."

His eyes wide and unblinking, he began to walk toward the cliff. Without missing a beat, he reached the edge and moved forward until he disappeared into the night, with nary a sound.

Elena made a soft noise, like a sigh.

Her pulse racing, Ilona drew a figure in the air before the thief's wife. "Go."

With the shuffle of a blind woman, the thief's wife walked forward until she, too reached the edge of the cliff. Then, silently, she stepped over the edge and dropped from sight.

Ilona smiled. The St. Germaines were no more.

One by one, Ilona walked St. Germaine's friends and servants off the edge of the cliff. She savored the darkness that filled the place where they'd stood as they disappeared. And once the last of them had gone, she staggered and collapsed to the ground. Now fully satiated, the beast within her grew quiet.

She thought it very likely that she would die. Soon.

Someone grasped her hand.

Ilona looked up at Elena. She thought she saw censure beneath the horror and worry in the younger woman's eyes. "I haven't killed them, child," Ilona managed to whisper. "They've joined the *naga*, the sea people. Leviathan is their god now."

"The Sea Opal," Elena whispered. "The ocean has swallowed it."

"We must get it back," she panted, the life in her body slipping away. Her hair, which the magic had stood on end, settled gently against her shoulders. "Elena, promise me you will get it back."

Elena gripped Ilona's hand. "I will try, wise one. I will try."

One

❧

COLE STRANGFORD PUSHED HIS MAGNIFYING spectacles up onto his forehead and stifled a sigh of exasperation. A few feet away, his uncle Gillie was fiddling with the coiled copper tubing that fed oxygen into an iron compressor tank, his movements clearly calculated to draw Cole's attention. Gillie had entered the laboratory some five minutes before, but Cole had pretended blindness to his presence, wanting to finish work on his oxygen compressor. Unfortunately, though, Cole was beginning to realize that he'd have no peace until he entertained his uncle's latest complaint, whatever it was.

"Don't touch that," Cole barked.

Gillie jumped, his fingers dropping away from the tubing as though it had scorched him. His grizzled eyebrows rose as he looked at Cole. "So, you've finally noticed me."

"I noticed you from the start, Uncle. I was hoping you'd go away if I ignored you. I'm in the middle of an experiment, and it's a very important one. Please come back later."

"I have important news for you," Gillie said, a hint of wariness entering his gaze as he examined the copper and iron apparatus strewn about Cole's worktable. Without warning, he changed the subject. "What exactly are you working on?"

Nonplussed, Cole returned his attention to his newest device. "An underwater breathing device. Tell me your news later. I'm busy."

"An underwater breathing device? What for?"

"So I can dive in the sea without having to come up for air," Cole informed him, his focus remaining on the small iron cylinder that was supposed to compress the oxygen he would breathe underwater. At the moment, the tank was leaking oxygen copiously and absorbing heat, creating a skim of frost on its surface. "Once I have it working, I'll be able to carry the tank with me when I swim underwater, and take breaths from it when I need to, rather than come to the surface. I should be able to stay underwater for at least an hour at a stretch."

"I think I like your diving bell better."

"You didn't *dive* in my diving bell," Cole grumbled. "You don't know what it was like to come to the edge of a new, unexplored portion of sea floor, only to be strangling on stale air and have to rise to the surface. Perhaps if you'd worked the pump that supplied the diving bell with air a little more vigorously, I wouldn't be here right now trying to invent a replacement for that pump and for you. Now, go."

"Your pump was at fault—not me."

"The pump was fine."

"And your air hose became kinked, cutting off your air supply."

"I saw nothing wrong with the hose."

Gillie shrugged. "At least you're no longer trying to rid the world of chamber pots. *That* was an experiment I'd rather not repeat."

Cole lowered his spectacles to the bridge of his nose and peered at his uncle. "Aren't the wash closets I installed a far cry above an outhouse?" At Gillie's unwilling nod, Cole smiled in satisfaction and pushed his spectacles back up. "Obviously you prefer my wooden privy to a hole in the ground, so stop complaining and leave me to my work."

"I *would* leave you, if I hadn't such pressing news. Don't you have even a minute to spare?"

"The Royal Oceanographic Society has invited me to demonstrate my diving suit with its breathing apparatus at their next meeting," Cole informed him. "Not only is that meeting less than six months away, but a gentleman named William James is working on a similar device of his own. If I want to gain an advantage over Mr. James and receive credit for this invention, not to mention contracts from the Royal Navy, I'll have to hurry."

"Cole, what I have to tell you is far more important than any invention," Gillie insisted.

Cole noticed with some annoyance that his uncle had donned his finest afternoon jacket. As Gillie normally spent his afternoon in a waistcoat with his shirtsleeves rolled up, Cole assumed that they were expecting guests. He groaned at the thought of having to abandon his compressor tank and entertain. "Is someone coming to visit?"

"Two very special people are on their way to Shoreham, even as we speak," the older man confirmed. He drew a piece of parchment from his vest and placed it on an old wicker side table Cole had rescued from the attic in Shoreham Park Manor. "Do you remember the woman I spoke of several months ago, the one whom I thought might make you a good bride? Well, her father has written. He looks kindly upon a match between you and his daughter, and has accepted our invitation to come and visit. He and his daughter should be here tonight."

Cole felt his gut tighten. "Tonight? Good God, man, you might have given me some warning."

"The mail coach broke its axle, or some such nonsense," Gillie explained. "Otherwise we would have received the letter sooner."

Cole stood up and moved away from his work table, toward the window that offered a view of Shoreham Park Manor. A faint sense of dread was seeping through him. He had spent all of his one-and-thirty years as a bachelor, and though he knew he was long overdue, he still hadn't gotten used to the idea of tying himself down with a woman. After all, with research and experimentation, you could predict the behavior of most inventions. No amount of research and experimentation, however, could predict the behavior of any woman. Nevertheless, he understood the necessity of marrying a proper gypsy bride, and knew that he had to do his duty at some point.

Cole, Gillie, and the rest of the Strangfords were members of a gypsy bloodline that had once been the finest in all of England. They'd known wealth, prestige, and magnificent fortune until centuries earlier, when they'd lost the Sea Opal, a fabulous jewel that supposedly brought good luck to whomever possessed it. Since losing the opal, the Strangfords' luck had taken a terrible turn for the worse.

In an effort to return to that shining place of good fortune, the Strangfords had exchanged their wandering for permanent residence at Shoreham Park Manor, an estate close to the place where they'd lost the Sea Opal. To a man, their descendents had searched for the Sea Opal . . . without any luck. As a result, the family had been forced to wallow in catastrophe and had long ago lost much of their prestige in the gypsy community. Cole hardly even considered himself a gypsy anymore. He and his ancestors had forgotten so many of the old traditions, and become so gentrified, that they bore more resemblance to country squires than true gypsy wanderers.

Sometimes, in the darkest hours of the night, he lay in bed with a sense of failure eating away at him like acid. Even with all of his inventions and determination, he hadn't detected the slightest glimmer of that sainted family jewel on the ocean floor. Usually he managed to console himself—temporarily, at least—with the knowledge that while he hadn't found the Sea Opal, his quest had led him to invent several devices that had improved living conditions at Shoreham Park Manor. Still, he believed that only the recovery of the Sea Opal would banish the dark cloud that hung over his family's head, and had confirmed this notion by spending some time researching the jewel's history and learning that it had brought good fortune to all of those who had ever owned it. Not surprisingly, he'd discovered that those who had owned the jewel and then sold it suffered a string of disasters, just as his own family had experienced. As a man of science, the whole idea of a jewel controlling fate seemed ridiculous to him, but he simply couldn't discount the evidence.

His mood souring at the thought of marriage, Cole took off his spectacles for good. He walked over to the window and stared out across the green lawn, his gaze unfocused. Unable to think of a single avenue of escape, he eventually turned back around to stare at his uncle. "You haven't given me much time to prepare for her arrival."

Gillie swung his thin, wiry form into a wicker chair. "We have an entire day before she arrives. What sort of preparations must you make? Zelda will manage all of the household details, and I'll take care of everything else."

Cole gazed around the room he'd used as his laboratory for well over a decade. The bottom floor of a windmill, the room contained junk he'd scrounged—like old copper wash pans, lampposts, and wagon wheels—as well as machines he'd constructed but had found no use for. He tried to imagine what sort of impact a wife might have on this room, and in his mind's eye, he saw his laboratory swept clean and decorated with lace and flowers.

He frowned. For years he had fought with his elderly aunt Pesha and cousin Zelda, in an effort to keep them from "straightening up" his laboratory. The thought of having to start all over again with a wife nearly made him ill. "I have to prepare myself for the possibility of marriage and all of the duties and obligations the wedded state entails."

"Don't worry about marriage. Just take an hour or so to practice being agreeable, and you ought to be more than ready for her when she arrives."

"I don't know about this. I don't appreciate the idea of some skirt turning my life upside down. Do you think she'll insist I give up my inventing? Because if she does, we're finished."

Gillie didn't answer, preferring instead to stare at the shards of a looking glass Cole had broken the week previous and had yet to sweep up.

Cole walked over to the oversized wooden gears that spun in response to the windmill's turning. Some of the gears lay on their sides, and others sat straight up, and eventually they all connected to a spindle that turned a leather belt. All of that power forced water through the pipes he'd installed between the windmill and Shoreham Park Manor, and the sound of the gears creaking and water rushing through the pipes was like music to his ears. The hot and fresh water piping system was one of his finest inventions, supplying Shoreham Park Manor with hot and cold water on demand, and heat in the winter.

"I'm a mechanically minded man," he told Gillie. "When I'm not diving, I spend my time in this laboratory. I won't tolerate a woman sticking her nose into my business here, or trying to tie me to her apron strings."

Gillie sighed, loud and long. He shook his head, in the manner of an old schoolmarm. "Cole, you are a very difficult nephew."

"Difficult? Not at all. I just don't want to marry."

"I'll give you three reasons as to why you ought to seriously consider marrying immediately," Gillie replied. "First of all, are you forgetting how you signed the entail on Shoreham Park Manor some ten years ago?"

"How could I forget? Father threatened to cut off my allowance unless I signed the deed of settlement."

"Then you well remember that the entailment requires you marry and produce a proper Romany heir by age six-and-thirty, in order to continue to draw income from the estate." Gillie lifted an eyebrow. "I expect your father's old barrister friend in town,

Sedgewick, is eyeing you rather carefully right now. He was damned close to your father, and wouldn't hesitate to send a letter to the Crown if you ignored the rules of the entailment."

"Old Sedgewick is a blighter," Cole muttered, leaning down to adjust the nozzle on the billows beneath the hot water holding tank, so that more air flowed through to fan the coals.

Gillie resolutely ignored Cole's comment and leaned forward slightly. "Secondly, we need to preserve the family name."

"Ah yes, the sainted family name," Cole muttered.

"There are only four of us left, Cole, and of the four, you're the only one young enough to produce an heir. If you neglect your duty, the Strangford family name will fade from the earth for all eternity."

"I wonder if everyone will breathe a sigh of relief once we're gone, considering our ill fortune."

Gillie shook his head. "Ill fortune or not, there's something comforting in the notion that even while my body turns to dust, the name of my family remains on the lips of the living, as the Strangford heirs go forth in the world."

"If we truly want to preserve the family name, we have to find the Sea Opal. And to find the Sea Opal, I have to extend the amount of time a man can spend underwater. To that end—" Cole leveled a pointed glance at his iron compressor tank.

"All right, then; let's discuss the third reason why you must marry. In my mind, this is the most important reason." Frowning, Gillie looked at him expectantly.

"You're referring to the sea people?"

"I am indeed."

Cole nodded solemnly and grew quiet, an old, familiar uneasiness twisting through him. Gillie, too, was silent, as if in deference to the seriousness of the topic.

Many centuries ago, when the Strangfords were at the height of their power and prestige in the gypsy community, an Englishman had come to their encampment and stolen the Sea Opal from them. The thief then chased their gypsy tribe and drove their leader into the sea. Cole's ancestor, a witch named Ilona, had cast against the thief the most powerful spell any gypsy witch knew: that of the *nagas*, or sea people, to stop the slaughter.

From that day, the thief and his people were forced to live in the ocean as half-dolphin, half-human creatures, and they'd taken the Sea Opal into the water with them. Since the lore surrounding the spell of the *nagas* suggested that the sea people could walk on land for brief periods of time before the magic forced them back into the ocean, Cole's ancestors had lived in a constant state of alert since the casting of the spell, and considered every outsider with a very sharp gaze.

Cole had learned of this story at a very young age. He'd been taught to believe in the sea people and had grown up doing so, even though he'd never seen one of them or knew anyone who had. Now, as an adult, he would tell anyone who asked him that he believed the old tales, just as he believed in God and all the saints, and in the inalienable right of all men to be free.

Privately, however, he had his doubts about the sea people, due to the lack of scholarly evidence documenting their existence. Indeed, he sometimes thought that the sea people had become a crutch, an explanation for the hardships the Strangford family had suffered, and an offering of hope for deliverance. Essentially, if the sea people existed, then the Sea Opal probably existed, too; and it followed that the Strangfords could improve their lot in life if they simply recovered that maddening jewel. If the sea people didn't exist, then their bad luck was simply fate that couldn't be controlled and had to be endured.

But these doubts he didn't express aloud, and sometimes even refused to admit to himself, for he'd spent most of his life diving and searching for the Sea Opal. If the sea people didn't exist, and the Sea Opal didn't exist, then he'd basically wasted his entire life chasing rainbows. He would dearly love to find one of the sea people, even though he was supposed to consider them his deadly enemies. Proving their existence would validate his entire life.

Just as the silence between them began to feel uncomfortable, the older man spoke. "The fact that you're the last living male heir to the Strangford estate makes you very vulnerable. Once you're gone, the sea people will have no opportunity to breed a child with Strangford blood. In effect, you're their last chance."

"You're worried that one of their women might seduce me and ultimately set the entire clan free."

"Basically, yes."

Cole leveled a frown at his uncle. "We may not have all that much to fear from the sea people. No one has ever documented their existence. Perhaps they all died at sea directly after the gypsy witch cursed them."

"Oh, they're around," Gillie insisted. "They're just very subtle. I think they hide their existence with the hope that we'll let down our guard. Indeed, I've heard tales through the years of their ability to walk on land for a brief time, so I wouldn't be surprised to hear that several Strangford men had narrowly escaped being seduced by a sea maiden without even knowing it."

Cole nodded. *Seduction.* That was the name of the sea people's game. They knew that they could break the spell cast upon them by seducing a male Strangford gypsy and breeding a child with gypsy blood. So far, they hadn't succeeded, and it was in Cole's best interests to ensure that they never broke the spell, for the sea people had promised to drive all of the remaining gypsies off a cliff should they ever emerge permanently from the sea.

"Why do you suppose marriage will protect me?" Cole asked. "Do you think I'm so green that I'd fall prey to a sea maiden, should she try to seduce me?"

"A sea-woman is tricky," Gillie warned, his voice low. "She's so beautiful that she blinds a man to her true nature when he first looks at her. And don't forget, she will do anything to break the curse that binds her and her people. No intimacy is out of the question; a man must be strong to resist. It helps if he has a wife and children to keep his thoughts occupied."

Cole raised an eyebrow at Gillie. "I've reached one-and-thirty without falling prey to a sea maiden, Uncle. I think I can be trusted."

"You're making light of a serious situation. Our ancestors knew how dangerous they are."

"Our ancestors, the devil take them, received far too much pleasure from dictating how people should live," Cole muttered.

One of the first of the Strangford gypsies, a venerable old man who had taken over leadership of their gypsy tribe after the witch Ilona had cursed the sea people, was the origin of all the traditions and customs designed to keep the Strangford men from being seduced. According to that great Strangford, a man shouldn't swim alone in the ocean, ever. Not for any reason. Nor should he wander the hills above the cliffs alone at night. Furthermore, lovemaking outside of marriage or infidelity, even with a light skirt, was punishable by immediate banishment, and a bride had to be splashed with seawater before marriage. Seawater, it seemed, forced the sea people to give up their temporary human form, which according to legend they somehow managed to attain, and return to their true, if unnatural, form.

For centuries these rules had been enforced by the tribal elders. Today, however, they were mostly ignored, except for the bridal seawater ceremony. The sea people hadn't shown themselves for a long time now, and Cole supposed his family had recognized the old traditions as foolish.

Cole's thoughts drifted toward his bride. Just what sort of woman had Gillie found for him this time? The kind who would tolerate being splashed with seawater? He hoped so. Some five years ago he'd recognized the necessity of marriage and charged his uncle with searching for suitable brides, as was the gypsy custom for marriages of convenience. He'd told Gillie he didn't care whom he married, as long as the woman met a few small criteria . . . including an easygoing temperament and a fine set of legs that didn't turn into a dolphin's tail.

His thoughts on the qualities of a perfect bride, Cole said, "I hope this newest find of yours is more attractive than that last one. Tell me where you met her, and what you remember of her."

Gillie rubbed his chin in an attitude of great thought. Still, his eyes remained shuttered, allowing Cole not the slightest clue as to the nature of those thoughts. As Cole waited for his reply and the silence between them lengthened, he began to wonder why Gillie was so reluctant to speak. Could his latest potential bride have more in common with a toothless hag than an eager, dewy-eyed innocent?

"How old *is* she, Gillie?" Cole asked, suspicion hardening his voice.

The older man shrugged. "My memories aren't as sharp as they once were. Old age can take a man's wits away, you know."

"Your wits are as sharp as a sword."

His eyes wide, Gillie raised his hands in a defensive gesture. "I simply can't remember."

"Can't remember, or won't? I haven't forgotten Sashina, Uncle. I recall very well how you tried to persuade me to look past her limp and her warts, and consider her fine baby-making potential. Sashina didn't stay more than a day, and neither will this woman if she bears any resemblance to her."

"If I could remember her age, I'd tell you," the older man insisted.

"It shouldn't be so difficult to remember a woman's age, particularly one you're trying to marry me off to. Are you certain you've met her?"

When Gillie didn't respond, Cole narrowed his eyes. "You've never even met this woman, have you?"

Gillie's eyebrows drew together in an expression of irritation. "Bringing you to the altar has proven a difficult task, Cole. And with our bad luck hanging over our heads, potential brides aren't exactly beating down the door. Even worse, I've had to look for Romany women who wouldn't mind settling down in one place for the rest of their lives, and there aren't many of them. I wish you would be a little more thankful for my efforts."

Cole sighed. "All right, so you've never met her. Considering my ill luck, she'll probably be about a century old and toothless."

"Please, bear with me," Gillie pleaded. "At least I'm trying."

"I know you're trying, Uncle. I'm trying also—to be appreciative. Still, we've been in this game for five years now, and so far, it's been nothing but a disaster. Even the most intrepid brides are frightened off by the inevitable calamities. And it's hard for me to be thankful when you're so damned zealous about marrying me off. I feel more like a prize stud than a man."

"Stud you are, but with the wrong women," Gillie announced dourly. "I know about your visits to town and a certain widow."

"My visits to Shoreham are my business," Cole informed him.

"Just don't get her with child, by Christ," the older man muttered. "If you put a babe in any woman's belly other than a Rom, you'll create an impure child and set the sea people free."

Sighing, Cole swallowed his exasperation at having his private life pried into over worry about the sea people, however legitimate, and tried to give his uncle some reassurance. "I haven't seen Charlotte Duquet in over a year."

Gillie nodded, then fell silent.

Unwillingly, Cole recalled the brides who had come to inspect him and his home in the past, and then left before an engagement could be announced. He knew his appearance hadn't put them off—physically, he passed muster, according to his various women friends. He certainly possessed no shortage of social graces and, while he wasn't the wealthiest man living in the south of England, he had inherited a fine old estate on which he lived quite comfortably. He wasn't a demanding man, either, content to putter about in his windmill and explore the nooks and crannies beneath the sea for the Sea Opal.

What had driven them from the manor and his side was the Strangford family ill fortune, which often showed itself as a series of horrendous incidents. Despite all of their assurances that they could remain strong in the face of any sort of disaster, they'd eventually turned tail and run.

A feeling of helplessness came over Cole. He leaned toward a beat-up wicker side table, picked up a jug, and poured a few fingers of whiskey into a cracked tumbler. "I don't think you've told me my intended's name. What is it?"

"Lila Whitham," Gillie said, his voice glum. He, too, picked up a glass.

Cole lifted the jug and filled Gillie's glass.

Gillie took a sip, and then whistled appreciatively. "That's a fine whiskey."

"It was tucked away in a dusty corner in the cellar." Cole lifted his glass and took a healthy swallow. The whiskey burned its way down his throat before settling into a warm pool in his stomach. "Zelda found it."

The older man shook his head. "That woman has a nose for liquor. It's going to land her in a grave one day."

"Never mind Zelda. Tell me what you know about my bride," Cole urged.

"Well, Zelda is the one who brought Lila Whitham to

my attention. Lila used to be a Pritchard before she married Joseph Whitham, and Zelda has a friend who lives in Buckland Village, the same village the Pritchards call home. This friend of hers attended Lila's wedding, and says that Lila's first husband died—of old age, in fact."

A *widow*, Cole thought, nodding slowly. The idea appealed to him. Although dewy-eyed innocents were more attractive than hags, their simpering and foolishness could drive a man mad. He would rather have an experienced woman as his bride, one who would know how to please him without being told, and one who wouldn't be shocked if he pleased her in all the ways he knew of. "How long ago did she lose her husband?"

"Many years ago. She's more than ready to remarry."

"Is she attractive?"

"According to Zelda, passably so."

Cole narrowed his eyes. "Zelda would consider a tree stump attractive. Does she meet the other criteria I've given you?"

"Such as?"

He made a spreading motion with his hands. "Is she wide hipped, with large breasts?"

"Her figure is ample," Gillie allowed after a lengthy pause.

"Were there any children from the first union?"

"One, who has since died of the fever."

Cole nodded, sympathy for his faceless bride creeping through him. The woman had clearly suffered during her life. "Does she possess manners? Stamina? Strength? Is she healthy? How skilled is she domestically?"

Another silence ensued.

At length, Gillie cleared his throat and answered, "She is from a very good family."

"Something about your expression isn't inspiring any confidence in me."

The other man shifted on his chair. "From what Zelda recalls, she commanded a high bride price when she married the first time."

"You and I both know that bride price has nothing to do with attractiveness. Do you remember Stanka? Her bride price was so high we had no hope of meeting it, and she was built like a horse, with a horse's face, too."

"Ah, but she made a delicious stew, no? Beauty can't be eaten with a spoon."

Cole sighed. He placed his glass on his work table, stood, and walked to the window. When he stared out, he saw not the sun-dappled lawns of Shoreham Park but the wrinkled face of a woman old enough to be his mother. So, his would-be bride was both old and ugly, and probably fat, too. God help him. "How in hell am I going to get her with child?"

"You've never shown any hesitancy with women before."

"That's because I usually pick my women for myself."

"You pick light skirts who prefer whiskey over tea."

A quick smile curved Cole's lips as the old, wrinkled face he'd been imagining sharpened into the features of the widow Duquet, with whom he'd had a brief affair. "I pick women with good sense, you mean. Besides, I happen to like red hair."

"Mrs. Whitham has brown hair, not red," Gillie informed him. "I hope you like brown hair, too. What will you do to court her?"

"Court her?" Cole shrugged. "I haven't thought much about it."

"Well, let's think *now*. Will you ply her with wine, cut

roses from the garden for her, take her dancing on the patio, under a moonlit sky? I can help you with all of these things, and more. I have many ideas."

"Wine? Roses? Dancing? Are you mad? No one could possibly consider my union with Mrs. Whitham a love match, so why should I pretend otherwise? I plan to assess her suitability as a bride by testing all of those criteria I mentioned to you before. Her domestic skills are of much more concern to me than her reaction to a bouquet of flowers."

Gillie shook his head. "You sound as though you're proposing twelve labors for Hercules. What will you have her do, slay the lion of Nemea? Or behead the Hydra? If you want her to marry you, Nephew, you must court her in some small way."

"I have no time for courtship."

"Let me offer you some advice. Do what you must to get her to the altar, and then put a babe in her belly. Once she's expecting, the babe will take up her attention, and you'll be free again. And we can't dismiss the chance that you may fall in love with her. Wouldn't that be a capital development?"

"I won't fall in love with her," Cole informed him, frowning. "I have no time for love and its intricacies. Can you think of a larger waste of my time?"

Gillie shrugged. "Yes. But it doesn't matter what I think. It's what *you* think that counts."

"Exactly." Cole's frown grew lighter as he began to plan out in his head how he would put his potential bride to the test. Quickly he decided to send Zelda out to visit this friend of hers in Buckland Village, and leave the household management to Mrs. Whitham, to assess her domestic skills, manners, disposition, and suitability.

Something impinged on the edge of his consciousness, some wariness without origin. Reluctantly he put his plans aside and scanned the hills and woods surrounding Shoreham Park. While his ears heard naught but the sounds of his aunt Pesha and cousin Zelda puttering about the house, and the low neigh of a horse in the stables; and his nose detected not the slightest hint of smoke or other fragrant harbinger of disaster, his gaze sharpened on the ocean that lie beyond the hills.

There he found the source of his discomfort.

The ocean, an angry gray, tossed restlessly. The whitecaps on its surface were clearly visible from his vantage point. He had trouble finding the place where the sky met the ocean, for the portion of sky nearest the horizon was a charcoal-colored bank of clouds marching quickly toward land. The contrast between the hazy blue skies directly above Shoreham Park and the darkness of the approaching storm roused fresh uneasiness in his gut.

"Uncle, come over here and look at the sky," he urged.

The older man joined him at the window, and then whistled through his teeth. "It's been a long time since I've seen clouds that dark."

A strange premonition grabbed hold of Cole. His attention locked on the approaching storm, he couldn't rid himself of the feeling that change was coming on swift—and perhaps even spurred—feet. On the whole, he wasn't opposed to change; it brought freshness to old ideas. But this time, instinct told him that the storm he was about to face might not just bring freshness.

They were in for a rough ride.

Two

THE CLOUDS ABOVE SHOREHAM PARK CHURNED angrily, dropping sheets of rain onto the stately old manor, and lightning flashed intermittently, illuminating its chimneys, parapets, and oblong windows with a ghostly luster. Out beyond the castle, past the hills and cliffs where the ocean met land, a roaring wall of water rushed into the beach and grabbed bucketfuls of sand before receding again. Thunder blasted the land with a deep, rumbling vibration; and when combined with the roar of the waves, even the loudest voices faded to nothing.

Dressed in a shift, Juliana St. Germaine lay upon the shore just beyond the ocean's reach. Every bone in her body felt either bruised or broken. The waves, which were cresting at well over eight feet, had tossed her relentlessly during her entire journey into shore. Even now that she was safely on shore, they lapped at her skin, trying to draw her back into their cold and dark depths.

Drawing in great gasps of air, she pulled herself a little farther away from the shoreline. Her lungs burned almost as badly as her skin, which felt flayed raw from saltwater. Despite all of these discomforts, however, she felt none of the fright that another woman might have experienced after an extended stay in the water, without a boat or raft, during a storm. Indeed, she knew only irritation at the rough ride she'd experienced and the effort it had cost her to avoid being tumbled by the waves. The ocean simply couldn't drown her, and she knew it.

She listened over the noise of the storm-lashed waves for the sound of her brother George's voice. Her legs were itching terribly, and she fought the desire to scratch them, knowing that the sensation would pass even as the rain washed the salt water from her skin. Slowly she pushed herself up on her elbows, then into a sitting position, where she could examine her newly formed legs.

Her eyes widened as she looked at her feet first, then at her calves and thighs. Her legs were long and slender, the ankles nicely turned. George had told her that these were the kind of legs that the men who lived on land noticed, and considering her purpose, she was very glad she possessed them.

Strident thunderclaps overhead grabbed her attention. The storm was a bad one, reminding her she had to get up and get moving. Here, on land, she didn't feel as safe as she did in the water. And while she and George had waited for a storm such as this before beginning their mission, so they could emerge from the sea without worrying about someone strolling along the shore to spot them, it was a dangerous sort of atmosphere to linger in.

Sand was clinging to her skin, but she barely noticed the gritty sensation as she went from a sitting position to kneeling, and then to standing on her shaky legs. In front of her, perhaps ten feet beyond the edge of the beach, granite cliffs reached high above her, their faces pockmarked with indentations and small caves carved out by water. In the largest and best-concealed of those caves, one that French smugglers had once used to hide their finest bourbon, George had stored a change of clothes during a scouting mission two weeks previous. She knew that the first step in their undertaking was to retrieve their clothes, and looked upward, scanning those cliffs for any signs of George.

She saw only an undisturbed vista of gray stone. Apparently George hadn't gone for their clothes. Then where was he? Still out in the ocean somewhere?

The first tendrils of anxiety slipped through her. "George," she shouted.

Only the wind answered.

Her worry growing, she hurried down the beach, looking along the shoreline for some sign of her brother. All the while, the rain and wind thrashed around her. Soon she began to feel very cold. Numb, in fact. Her teeth started to chatter. She glanced down at the long, close-fitting silk shift that she wore while living beneath the sea. Though it concealed her curves well enough, it was designed specifically for wearing beneath the water and did little to keep her warm. George or no George, she knew she needed those fresh clothes hidden in the cave. A quick dip in the cave's hot spring, she thought, wouldn't do her any harm either.

Buffeted about like a piece of chaff caught in a whirl-wind, she struggled toward the cliffs and scanned their surfaces for the small, almost invisible path that led up to their storehouse.

"Over here, Juliana!"

The shout sounded more like a murmur beneath the fury of the downpour, but Juliana heard it nevertheless and spun around. When she saw her brother George approaching, two rolled-up bundles of clothes in his hand, she was torn between bewilderment, relief, and the peculiar brand of frustration that all siblings tend to feel for each other at some point or another during their lives.

They'd agreed earlier that George would wait for her before trying to retrieve the clothes, so that they might support each other while climbing the cliffs. Indeed, they were supposed to be a team, follow the plan, and discuss any changes to the plan together before acting on them. George, however, had chosen to ignore the rules they'd agreed upon. Granted he had more experience as a landwalker than she, but that didn't mean he should pretend she didn't exist.

He crossed the distance between them, stumbling only a little. When he reached her side, he put his hands on her shoulders and turned her to face him. "Are you all right, dear sister?"

"I'm wet and cold," she informed him in clipped tones.

"And otherwise?"

"I haven't broken anything, if that's what you're asking."

"Very good." His tone all business, he threw her the smaller bundle.

She caught it and unwrapped it, finding a fresh shift, an embroidered peasant's dress, stockings, and shoes within a cloak. Quickly shrugging the cloak around her shoulders, she hid the rest of the clothes beneath its folds to keep them from becoming damper. Then she examined her brother's face for bruises.

His bright blue eyes were shadowed as he stood there, unblinking in the rain, his brown hair plastered to his head in an unflattering way. He'd pressed his lips into a tight line, in the manner of someone determined to succeed even though the notion of success brought little pleasure. While she wasn't expecting him to be a pattern card for gaiety, she nevertheless wished he might display some enthusiasm for the fight.

George, she thought, took little joy in anything lately. She suspected that he'd begun to lose faith in the idea that someday, they would be free of the gypsy's curse.

Her gaze dropped lower and she discovered his feet remained bare. He evidently hadn't yet covered up his underclothes with the clothing they'd hidden in the cave. Satisfied that he remained unharmed, she leveled a frown in his direction. "You're lucky you didn't slip off of those cliffs and break your neck. Why didn't you wait for me? We could have climbed them together and supported each other."

"I'm fine, aren't I?"

"By the grace of God." She pulled her cloak tighter around her shoulders. "We had a plan, remember? We said we would do everything together, until circumstance forces us to part."

"The situation called for improvisation," he explained. "The storm was a lot worse than we'd expected. We washed up on shore farther apart than we'd planned on. When I couldn't find you right away, I went for the clothes, so we wouldn't freeze. And I must tell you, the cliffs were slippery. I didn't want you to risk yourself climbing them."

"So you were protecting me. Coddling me. Eh, George?"

"Protecting, perhaps. After all, I am your big brother. But I wasn't coddling you at all."

"You're only older than me by two years. That isn't a very long time. And you must understand that we're equals on this mission. I will not be protected and coddled, even if you do have more experience with land-walkers."

"Let's not stand in the rain and argue," he said over a particularly loud clap of thunder. "I saw a niche between some fallen boulders not far away. We need to dress."

"Fine."

She followed George about a hundred yards down shore, to the point where the cliffs started tapering off, then into a stone shelter of sorts, formed by three boulders which had tumbled from above. There, they both began to shrug into the rest of their clothes, beneath the privacy of their cloaks.

As they dressed, the silence lengthened between them, and Juliana got to thinking. She remembered how anxious she'd been when she couldn't find her brother, and how very important their task was, and how they had no room for mistakes. She also recalled the way her brother had taken matters into his own hands, all in a bid to "protect" her. The more she thought about it, the more annoyed she became.

"Is this how it's going to go, then?" She finally asked, unable to stay silent any longer. Frowning, she yanked on a moist wool stocking. "Are you going to be changing our plans at a moment's notice without consulting me first? Because if you are, I'm returning home. I won't be party to a fool's mission."

"Juliana . . ." he muttered, fumbling under his cloak with a waistcoat that was no doubt as wet as her stockings.

"Don't 'Juliana' me." Eyeing him narrowly, she fastened the peasant skirt around her waist. "You're not working alone this time. We agreed that we're a team, with both members having equal say."

"We're a team. I promise."

"Every decision is a joint one, then, from now on. As we originally agreed." Juliana gave him another very pointed glare before focusing on putting those hard, uncomfortable devices called shoes onto her feet. "We both have very specific goals which we'll meet only if we cooperate."

"I have every intention of cooperating *and* succeeding over the next few months," he replied as he tucked his linen shirt into his waistband. "We're charged with breaking the curse, and that's exactly what we're going to do."

Juliana watched as he shrugged into his jacket, astonished as always by the transformation wrought by clothes. Suddenly he looked exactly like every other landwalker she'd ever encountered. And why shouldn't he? They had once been landwalkers, too, and still would be if that evil gypsy witch hadn't cursed them to live out their lives in the ocean, as sea people.

"God curse the gypsies," she muttered.

George nodded. "Amen."

Her frown growing deeper, she finished dressing herself, and then wrapped the cloak closer around her body even as she armored herself in righteous indignation. Perhaps the trick they planned to play on the gypsies wasn't particularly honorable, but the gypsies hadn't acted honorably toward the St. Germaines, either. In fact, they'd consigned the St. Germaines to a living hell, so she certainly didn't intend to pamper them in return. Rather, she would do whatever was necessary to break the gypsy's curse, even if it meant she had to seduce a gypsy and produce a child of impure blood.

And that was exactly what she planned to do—seduce one of the fiendish gypsies. The man who she'd set her sights on, Cole Strangford, was the youngest remaining member of the tribe who'd cursed them. If he died and the gypsy family line died out while still pure, then she and her descendants could look forward to an eternity beneath the ocean waves, with no hope of returning to land to reclaim their heritage. Therefore, her effort to seduce the gypsy, no matter how distasteful, had to be her very best.

Fully clothed, she turned to face George and realized he, too, had finished donning his landwalker attire.

"You look very dashing, George," she said, and she meant it, too.

"And you, little sister, are a perfect bride."

She wrinkled her nose at him. "Please, don't remind me."

His tight-lipped frown smoothed out a little. "Shall we start our walk into town? Mr. and Mrs. Wood will be waiting for us there."

Juliana glanced at the rain that slapped at the sand a few feet away. It seemed to be slowing down a little. Indeed, the sky had lightened from dark to light gray. "I suppose we must."

He grabbed her arm and steered her out into the rain. Immediately the wind clawed at her hair and cloak, but now that she was fully dressed, it didn't seem quite so strong. Grateful for her brother's body, which sheltered her from the worst of the downpour, she huddled next to him as they walked along the shoreline, and then onto Brighton Road, which led into Shoreham.

His step was measured, and his mien, solemn. She knew he regarded their assignment with the utmost seriousness. Because his talent in resisting the transformation from sea person to landwalker allowed him to move among the landwalkers with the least chance of detection, he'd performed many missions for the sea people over the years. He'd gone everywhere, from Constantinople to Madrid to the Spice Islands, trading treasure the sea people had found in shipwrecks for land, building accounts in various banks, and slowly building the sea peoples' fortune in preparation for the day when they emerged permanently from the sea. Always he did his best, and never once had he complained; and yet, Juliana couldn't help but wonder if he were becoming tired of wandering and fighting. Sometimes he looked so drawn, so pale and beaten, that he frightened her.

It gave her all the more reason to want to break the gypsy's curse.

"Shall we go over the particulars of the plan again as we walk?" George asked after a while.

She nodded. "We might as well make sure we've got our facts straight. Tell me first about the woman you're going to meet. She's Cole Strangford's future bride, no?"

"She is. Her name's Lila Whitham and, according to Mrs. Wood, she's a widow. Strangford's never met her, of course. But Strangford's uncle has exchanged letters with the widow's father, and they've agreed to bring the widow and Strangford together, to discover if a marriage of convenience is a possibility between them."

"Only they won't be meeting each other, they'll be meeting us."

"Exactly. In their letters, they agreed that Strangford would go to Buckland House to stay with the widow's family, the Pritchards. We, however, sent Strangford an additional letter explaining that the Pritchards preferred to journey to Shoreham Park. And so, Strangford thinks Mrs. Whitham is coming to *his* home to visit him, and Mrs. Whitham thinks Cole Strangford is coming to *her* home to visit her."

Juliana lifted a brow. "Why didn't we simply send Mrs. Whitham a letter, explaining that Strangford no longer wished to consider her for marriage? Why must you travel to her house as Cole Strangford?"

"The answer's simple enough: to prevent word of our scheme from getting back to Strangford."

She frowned. "Could you imagine what would happen, if after you'd left Buckland House, she came to Shoreham Park Manor looking for you? How would I explain my deception to Strangford?"

He nodded. "Every plan must have an exit strategy, a way to get out without getting hurt. If our deception is discovered, we'll rely on a man named William James to explain ourselves. Mr. James is an inventor who is competing with Strangford in creating a diving suit, and we'll simply say that you cozied up to Strangford in order to spy on him for Mr. James."

Shuddering, Juliana couldn't imagine having to go through such a scene. "Please, George, make certain that Mrs. Whitham wants nothing to do with Cole Strangford."

"You can depend on me, dear sister."

"Good. Then I can remain unencumbered as I maneuver my way into marriage with Strangford."

Her brother's face darkened. "This isn't the way I would have it, Juliana, were there any other choice. You should have a lengthy engagement, followed by a marriage with long strands of white pearls and a glimmering dress. Instead, you'll have to settle for a quick marriage to a man you don't love."

She placed a placating hand on his arm and took big steps in an attempt to keep up with his stride, which had lengthened. "George, if I don't sacrifice myself in this way, then we'll likely remain as sea people forever. You and I both know that Cole Strangford is the last of the gypsy witch's line. If he dies without producing an impure child, then we'll never have another opportunity to break the curse."

"I know you're right. I still wish we had another alternative."

"There are no other alternatives. Think of this as a marriage of convenience. My honor will be protected. And if all goes as planned, we will all be free of the ocean before the year is out."

"And I shall personally bundle you off to safety, away from Strangford." He sighed. "To think that I allowed you to volunteer for this. I, of all people, should have known better. I must be mad."

"Maybe we both are mad. Or maybe we understand that we're the only ones of our kind with a chance at succeeding on this mission. Even from childhood, you and I have always been able to resist the transformation the longest. Most of us transform from legs to fins the moment we come in contact with saltwater."

The downpour had settled into a soft mist. Suddenly Juliana felt stifled. She threw her hood back, allowing the brisk sea breeze to play with her hair. "Our resistance to the transformation is the key to our success."

"I hope so, Juliana," her brother said fervently. "I truly do."

* * *

GEORGE ST. GERMAINE SHEPHERDED HIS SISTER
down High Street, the most prominent road in the little
town called Shoreham. To his left, the River Adur
flowed its final few hundred feet before opening up into
the ocean, and on the other side of the river, Shoreham
Beach beckoned with a showy drift of pink and white
flowers among pebbles. Up ahead, fishing boats with tall
masts were bobbing gently on the river, their hulls safely
tied to the wharves that protected them.

He glanced toward the western horizon. The rain had
stopped and the worst of the storm clouds had fled out to
sea, allowing the setting sun to paint the sky with an
orange and red glow. A youth was already beginning to
light the oil lamps that lined High Street, and George
figured they only had a few minutes before the heavens
grew completely dark.

Two fishermen were still working on their boats,
cleaning the decks and otherwise putting them to bed,
and a few street vendors lounged against brick walls that
formed a sail house and fish shacks, no doubt hoping to
sell the last of their wares. Otherwise, the town was
mostly empty, its good citizens having gone home for
their evening supper and prayers.

George couldn't have been happier with the situation. He didn't want anyone noticing his and his sister's passage through the streets. Small townsfolk had a
way of remembering very particular details about
strangers, and he didn't want even a hint of mystery
surrounding this day or the next, when Juliana would
arrive in Shoreham as Lila Whitham, Cole Strangford's bride.

The smell of offal was strong in the air. In fact, the odor was downright terrible, suggesting meat and vegetables that had gone bad. But there was also a nasty undertone to the stench. A glance at the ditch that lined the side of the road confirmed that the townsfolk used the ditch to hold their sewage. Not for the first time he wondered how landwalkers could stand to live in such conditions. Filthy, they were.

At times, he wondered why in God's name he was working so hard to become one of them.

George felt his mood slipping as his thoughts traveled down this well-worn path. That was the conundrum in his life, the realization that had made things so difficult for him these last few years. His travels had shown him that landwalkers weren't at all admirable. They lied, they stole from each other, and they killed. He'd seen endless starvation, diseases, and suffering. And yet, here he was, locked in a battle to free the sea people from the gypsy's curse, so they might return to their natural form.

It just didn't make any sense.

Sighing, George glanced at Shoreham Park Manor, soon to be his sister's home. The estate was at least a few miles from town, but because of its location, one could see it from just about anywhere. The windmill situated near the edge of the cliff added an unusual dimension to the estate, and Cole Strangford, the eccentric inventor who lived there, supplied the townsfolk with plenty to gossip about. From what George had heard, the man was constantly installing odd contraptions that made a lot of noise and smoked, while serving no real purpose. And when he wasn't fooling with his machines, he was in the ocean diving.

George permitted himself a small smile. He knew exactly what Strangford was looking for . . . the Sea Opal. He also had a pretty good idea the gypsy would never find it. George's ancestor Anthony St. Germaine, the thief who had originally stolen the Sea Opal from the gypsies, had picked a secret cave deep within the ocean to conceal the jewel in. He'd explained the cave's location to his family, and then left their small community to take the opal to its hiding place.

He never came back.

Others went to the cave to look for him.

They never came back either, though the badly decomposed body of one of Anthony's rescuers eventually surfaced nearby.

As the centuries passed, men and women who thought themselves capable of handling whatever that cave held went there to retrieve the sea opal.

They were never seen again.

And so, the Sea Opal still rested in that hidden cave, the one surrounded by darkness and fish that couldn't tolerate sunlight, but no one dared go there, because anyone who tried to enter the cave, died. Indeed, the entire area was now forbidden to all sea people, in an effort to protect them from whatever menace lay in wait for them in that corner of the ocean.

Although Juliana had been preparing for this assignment for years, it pained him greatly to see her put herself in harm's way. He felt responsible for her, as their father and mother had passed away long ago. Indeed, Juliana had been so occupied with learning the ways of the landwalkers in order to succeed at marrying Strangford, that many of her friends had drifted away, leaving him as her only true confidante. And yet, she had her own mind and ought to be respected for the choices she made, even if he didn't wholly agree with them.

His hand grasping hers, he turned right onto Church Street and hurried past the Thomas Macy Warehouse and the Mitchell & Sons Candle Factory.

"How much farther?" Juliana asked.

George hesitated in replying. A man with a wheelbarrow was creaking toward them. Once the man had passed by with a load of mackerel, he spoke.

"The inn is around the corner. Mr. and Mrs. Wood will no doubt have dinner waiting for us."

She sighed. "That sounds heavenly."

George glanced sharply at her. Not often did he hear his sister's voice fade with exhaustion. "Would you like to stop and rest?"

Her brilliant hazel-yellow eyes wide, she returned his gaze, and slowly one of her eyebrows went up, as if to chastise him for staring. "I may be female, George, but that doesn't necessarily mean I'm weak."

His attention settled on the light purple shadows beneath her eyes. "You don't want to rest, then?"

"No. I thought you said you weren't going to coddle me."

Her tone told him quite clearly that she thought him a complete idiot.

"I wouldn't dare coddle you, Juliana. Forgive me for showing you some compassion. From now on, we march onward without pause, just like the Regent's finest soldiers."

She snorted. "You are a trial."

"And you, my dear sister, are a pain in the arse."

The words between them, while fairly stringent, were spoken with affection, and he knew that she had nothing but the highest respect for him and his accomplishments. He, too, felt the same way about her, and was very proud of the woman she'd become. Juliana had a habit of championing difficult causes, and no one had worked harder than she to keep the sea people positive and hopeful that the gypsy witch's curse might soon be broken. An idealist, she was very kind, and special, and fine-looking for a woman, too. Still, he couldn't help but wish she wasn't so stubborn and competitive. He supposed they shared those particular traits, but sometimes, it made it difficult to get anything done.

Both of their stomachs were rumbling by the time they reached the Topping Tavern, a clapboard-style inn that an aristocratic lady had once described as "simply topping." And yet, as the fates would have it, they ended up waiting another thirty minutes before settling down at the inn where the Wood couple awaited them. Before they could sneak across the road and make their way quietly into the inn, a cavalcade of high-sprung carriages pulled into the carriage yard outside the inn. By the look of them, they carried only the wealthiest citizens, who were no doubt on their way to Brighton and the Royal Pavilion.

He and Juliana stayed in the shadows and watched until the last of them had unloaded their well-dressed passengers and parked in the carriage yard. Dispassionately he assessed them. This is what the sea people would become, once they left their homes. They would trade their current homes—shipwrecks scattered about the ocean floor—for only the finest of castles and manors. He himself had insured their fortunes by trading and selling the booty they'd rescued from the bottom of the ocean. He'd even bought certain royal favors and an aristocratic title or two. And yet, while he saw differences between the wealthy and the average landwalker, the wealthy often had their own set of vices that made them far worse than average.

"Are you coming, George, or are you simply going to stand there woolgathering all night?"

Juliana's whisper pulled him away from his thoughts. He spared her a dry glance, and then pulled his hood over his head and forward to conceal his features. With his sister following close behind, he walked past the lantern and stocks near the inn's entrance. Before he could open the front door, however, she stopped him with a hand on his arm.

"How safe is it in the tavern for us?" Her voice was very low, and she chewed on her lower lip. "After all, we've been putting ourselves to a lot of trouble to avoid being seen, and now we're going to barge into a crowded dining room. Is this wise?"

He studied her for a moment. "In order to remain undetected, one has to play to the audience's expectations. The people in a tavern expect to see other travelers, and won't think twice about seeing us, two cloaked strangers stopping off for a rest before continuing on the morrow. On the other hand, we had to be careful earlier because of the people around us. A village matron on her way to the cold spring, for example, might remember two cloaked strangers, if only to alleviate the tedium of her day with a prime piece of gossip she might share later."

He started to move forward, but still, she held him.

"Are you certain?" she asked.

"Quite. What's wrong?"

Lower lip caught between her teeth, she turned her attention to the door. "I'm frightened."

He stared at her, knowing how much it must have cost her to make that admission. Suddenly, he realized what the inn's front door must represent to her. Once she crossed that threshold, and met with Mr. and Mrs. Wood, their plan would be set fully in motion. Entering the tavern signified a commitment to their mission and to her eventual marriage to the gypsy. Who could blame her from hesitating?

He pulled her aside, into the shadows, and spoke urgently. "If you want to return home, Juliana, tell me now, because unless you're completely committed to seducing and marrying this Cole Strangford, we will fail."

She frowned. "Marriage is not a trivial commitment."

"No, it isn't. Even so, from what I've heard, Cole Strangford is not as terrible as some of the gypsies we've investigated in the past. While the other Strangford men we've observed over the years just haven't been good candidates, Cole Strangford is the first one to display some honorable and gentle qualities. He'll give you a good home and children to love."

"I know this intellectually, but I can't seem to feel it inside." She briefly rested a hand over her heart before dropping it back to her side. "I suppose part of me is wondering if there is any way to avoid this ordeal."

"I wouldn't blame you if you went home. In a way, I wish you would. By marrying Strangford, you're sacrificing yourself, even if it is for the good of all the St. Germaines. And I don't want you to sacrifice yourself, no matter how much we all stand to benefit. You're my little sister, damn it, and I want the best for you, not to mention how much I'm worried about you."

"I know, George." She shook her head. "I'm not certain if I'm strong enough to fool this man into believing

I'll make him a good wife. How can I possibly forget that his ancestor—a gypsy witch—damned the St. Germaines to an eternity in the ocean?"

"I want you to go home," he said suddenly, surprising even himself.

Her eyes dark, she met his gaze head-on. "If I go home, who will take my place? Who is of the right age, and can resist the transformation long enough to convince the gypsies we aren't sea people? Who, in other words, has the slightest chance of breaking the gypsy witch's curse other than me?"

He looked away. He didn't have to answer. She already knew the answer.

No one.

That was the problem, the sticking point that neither of them could maneuver around.

She placed a gentle hand on his arm. "Let's go inside. I'm ready."

"I'm proud of you, Juliana." Taking her hand in his own, he led her into the tavern.

A blast of warmth from a fireplace along the far wall assaulted him, along with the smells of ale, charred mutton, and wet wool. Oil lamps brightened the interior with a smoky glow, illuminating people of all shapes and varieties who quaffed pints and ate trenchers of meat and cheese. Fortunately, no one marked their entrance. Rather, the group of aristocrats who were spilling out of a private dining room had captured everyone's attention. Quickly he pulled Juliana into a dimly lit corner and scanned the room for Mr. and Mrs. Wood.

The Woods were the latest of a long line of faithful retainers who had been in service to the St. Germaines, both before and after they had become the sea people.

Though the Woods knew the St. Germaines' secret—that they lived as sea people—they remained loyal to the St. Germaines, partly because the St. Germaines paid them very well, but mostly out of respect for their employers. Ironically, the Woods had no permanent home, instead wandering from town to town as the St. Germaines needed them to . . . just like gypsies.

Juliana saw them first. She tugged on his sleeve and murmured, "Over there."

He followed the direction of her gaze and saw the older couple, dressed in sturdy blue woolen clothing that would garner no attention. At that moment, Mr. Wood looked his way, and George nodded slowly. Mr. Wood's eyes widened with recognition. He said something in his wife's ear. When he returned his attention to George, his face had sharpened somehow. He gestured toward a short hallway with stairs.

Juliana, at his side, answered Mr. Wood with a nod of her own.

The couple disappeared into the hallway and up the stairs.

George followed them, keeping his head low and making certain Juliana did the same. In short order they were up the stairs, and then Mrs. Wood whisked them into a room with two cots and a large window that offered a view of the stars.

Mr. Wood shut the door behind them. For a moment, they all looked at each other, and then Mrs. Wood crossed the room and dropped into a curtsey before Juliana. "Miss Juliana, it is good to see you."

"And you, Mrs. Wood," Juliana replied, returning her curtsey with a smile. "You and Mr. Wood are well, I trust?"

Mr. Wood offered Juliana a bow. "Very well, miss, thank you, though I hope you won't mind if I say that you look as though you need a rest."

"Not at all, Mr. Wood. These legs of mine are bothering me terribly." Juliana collapsed on one of the cots.

Mrs. Wood clucked sympathetically as she knelt at Juliana's side. "Let me take your shoes off for you, you poor girl. Mr. Wood has already ordered dinner. It should be along soon."

"Thank you," Juliana said, her tone full of gratitude. "You're an angel."

While Mrs. Wood fussed over Juliana, George took Mr. Wood aside. He pulled a string of pink pearls from his waistcoat pocket and handed them to the older man.

Mr. Wood whistled low, between his teeth, attracting the attention of the women. Juliana stood, despite her complaints of aching feet, and joined the two men, as did Mrs. Wood. The older woman took the pearls from her husband and examined them with a critical eye.

"They're from a shipwreck off the coast of Japan," Juliana informed them. "I hope they're to your liking."

"Aye, they're very fine," Mrs. Wood pronounced, a gleam in her eye. "What else did you find in this shipwreck?"

Juliana smiled. "Goblets of carved jade, ivory, and pearls for the most part. I think you'll be pleased with them."

"You and your brother are very good to us," Mrs. Wood said, her face wreathed in a smile. "I wonder if wine still tastes like wine when drunk from a jade goblet."

"Now, Martha, don't start thinking about jade goblets. We have work to do," Mr. Wood reminded his wife.

Mrs. Wood sighed. "A tricky piece of work, if you ask

me," the older woman pronounced. "Are you certain, Miss Juliana, that you wish to marry?"

"I must, Mrs. Wood. Cole Strangford is the last of his line capable of producing the child we so desperately need, one of impure blood. God forbid, if he dies without having children, then the sea people will remain forever in the ocean."

"It seems a crime," the older woman stoutly declared. "You have a right to happiness, Miss Juliana."

"I *will* be happy, once the St. Germaines return to land."

Mrs. Wood's eyebrows drew together. She turned to George. "I can't help but worry about your sister, Mr. St. Germaine. Are you certain you will keep Strangford's true bride's attention occupied, so she doesn't interfere with Miss Juliana's marriage?"

"I'll keep Mrs. Whitham very busy," George promised, though he silently wondered, like Juliana, if he could be convincing in his pursuit of the Whitham woman. He decided to pose a question of his own. "Are you certain Juliana's identity won't be questioned when she arrives at Shoreham Park Manor? How much does she look like Strangford's bride?"

"Other than those eyes of hers, she'll do," Mrs. Wood remarked.

Everyone turned to glance at Juliana, who sat quietly on the cot. Meeting their gazes head-on, she silently dared anyone to say something about the odd color of her eyes, a hazel green that was more yellow than green. George had been tempted to say many times that her eyes weren't hazel green, but were yellow, and that "hazel green" was just a way of trying to make something that looked unusual seem normal. Juliana, however, had made it clear that she didn't want to be known as the girl with the yellow eyes, so George just cleared his throat and said, "Very good."

"I went to Mrs. Whitham's village and spent some time there, finding out about her family and getting a gander at her when I could," Mr. Wood piped in. "For the most part, our girl could pass as Mrs. Whitham. She's much younger than Mrs. Whitham, though, so Mrs. Wood and I suggest we introduce Juliana as her sister, to explain the age difference. We can feign confusion over the letters that Strangford's uncle and Mr. Pritchard exchanged, and say that we thought Strangford wanted to marry the younger daughter, not the older one."

"Does Lila truly have a younger sister?"

"Indeed she does. The girl is in a finishing school in Ireland. Her name's not Juliana, though. Rather, she's called Anna. If the difference in names is called into question, we can say that 'Anna' is a pet name for 'Juliana,' though I don't believe this will become an issue for us."

George nodded. "That sounds like a good solution." He transferred his attention to Mr. Wood. " You have enough information about Mrs. Whitham's family to convince Strangford that you're her father?"

Mr. Wood nodded vigorously. "That I do."

George turned to Mrs. Wood. "I'm assuming that you have enough information about Strangford's family to convince Mrs. Whitham that you're his cousin Zelda."

"I've investigated Zelda Strangford thoroughly, and can relate some persuasive facts about the family," Mrs. Wood said with some authority.

"Excellent," George said. "My sister and I, as you know, have spent several years studying the gypsy culture. We've also familiarized ourselves with the Strangfords and Pritchards, who for various reasons have traded many of their traditional gypsy customs for more English ones. Perhaps we might all spend some time reviewing these facts together."

"We'll spend the next several hours memorizing the details," Mrs. Wood agreed. She waved toward three trunks in the corner. "Also, those trunks contain everything both of you will need in terms of clothes and accessories."

George nodded. "Very good. You've also purchased carriages for us, yes?"

"We have one for you, to take on your trip to meet the real Mrs. Whitham, and one for Juliana, to take up to Shoreham Park Manor," Mr. Wood confirmed. "Juliana's is outside in the carriage yard, and yours is hidden in the forest some miles away." He took a breath, then added, "Yesterday when I arrived, I spread the word that I was Mrs. Whitham's father, and intended to bring my younger daughter to Cole Strangford on the morrow."

"Why don't we get started with the Strangford family history, then," George said, and glanced at his sister. She smiled from her perch on the couch, her long chestnut hair curling past her shoulders to settle around her waist, her eyes alight with eagerness; and suddenly, she seemed so very young and vulnerable to him that something tightened within his chest and he knew without a doubt that this would be the last time he'd see such untouched innocence in her face.

Three

❧

COLE STRANGFORD WAS IN HIS LABORATORY, fitting new iron rivets to his oxygen compression tank, when Gillie barged in and told him to make himself presentable.

"Aunt Pesha has just returned from town," the older man informed him. "She says that a young gypsy woman is just now leaving the Topping Tavern with her father. They're bound for Shoreham Park Manor and should be arriving within minutes. I suggest a change of jacket."

Cole carefully set the oxygen chamber on his worktable and glanced down at his tweed coat. He brushed at a few holes created by sparks from a fire. "Must I be on hand to greet her? Can't you just take her to her bedchamber and tell her to rest from her journey? I'm very close to making the compressor work, Uncle. I can't desert my laboratory now."

Turning his attention from his jacket to the compressor, Cole adjusted the width of the copper coils within, making it tighter, so the oxygen would have more time to travel through the coils and contract. At the same time, he examined the compressor, confirming that the machine was creating not even the slightest amount of friction. Experience had taught him that oxygen was a highly combustible mixture, and at the moment, he could smell oxygen in the air. Evidently he had a leak somewhere—

"For God's sake, Cole, first impressions are everything," Gillie badgered. "Don't meet Mrs. Whitham in a ratty old coat."

At Cole's lack of response, Gillie began to shrug out of his own coat, made of superfine wool and significantly more presentable than Cole's. "We're not of the same size," he declared, pulling his arms out of the sleeves, "but at least you won't look so beggarly—"

As he pulled the coat from his shoulders, a gold-toned snuffbox fell from his pocket. Cole watched the snuffbox's descent to the cobblestone floor, a silent prayer forming on his lips even as oxygen wafted in his nose. With lightning reflexes he grasped the knob to the compressor, determined to shut off the flow of oxygen, but before he could even turn the knob an inch, the snuffbox hit the stones.

A spark, created upon impact, flew upward.

At the same moment, Cole turned the knob to the off position.

Still, some oxygen remained in the air.

The gas ignited with a muted puff, producing a brief yet powerful fireball that exploded in Cole and Gillie's faces before traveling upward to blast against the ceiling. Both men shouted, and Gillie fell backward against a chair. Cole quickly felt his face to make sure he still had eyebrows. Gillie, shaking his head, stood again, and glared at Cole.

Slightly stunned, Cole returned his uncle's gaze. The

older man's face, neck, and chest were covered with black soot. His gray hair, which normally hung down over his forehead, was blown backward as though caught in a mighty wind. Cole had a pretty good idea that his own face looked very similar to Gillie's.

He glanced down at the jacket in Gillie's hand. It appeared untouched by the explosion.

"May I still have your jacket?" Cole asked.

Gillie's expression grew dark. He looked from the jacket, and then to Cole. Without speaking a word, he handed the jacket to Cole.

Cole took it. "Many thanks, Uncle."

Gillie opened his mouth, and then closed it. Just as Cole began to think he was safe, Gillie opened it again. "You aren't ready to marry. You don't deserve a wife. My God, man, you'll kill any wife who dares to marry you within six months. I'm going to tell that poor woman that she should turn around and hie back to town as fast as her horses will take her."

Cole thought for a moment, searching for the right sort of reply, one that might smooth his uncle's feathers. Before he could find it, however, the door to his laboratory creaked open and Aunt Pesha entered, a crocheted shawl wrapped around her stooped shoulders.

"What are you boys doing?"

Cole and Gillie looked at each other, but neither man ventured a reply.

"Didn't Gillie tell you that your guest has arrived?" the old lady demanded. "Try to summon some enthusiasm and come to the house at once." She paused to squint at Cole and Gillie. "What is that on your faces? Mud?"

"It's soot from an experiment gone wrong," Cole explained. "Tell me, Aunt Pesha, what you think of my intended. Is she mannerly? Presentable?"

"I don't think you'll find cause for complaint. I can't say the same for her."

"Can you elaborate a little more on her appearance?"

The old lady shrugged. "She isn't what either of you imagined. There's been a mistake of some sort."

"A mistake?"

"Come to the house and see for yourself," Pesha told them. Without clarifying further, she turned around and left the laboratory.

Cole followed his aunt, with Gillie close behind. The threesome began walking across the lawn toward Shoreham Park Manor. Cole noticed a barouche in the carriageway in front of the manor, the intricate carvings on its wooden panels indicative of a well-heeled family. Apparently their guests were wealthy. But what was wealth, other than an excess of money? It didn't guarantee good breeding or pleasant manners.

Gillie glanced his way. "I wonder why Aunt Pesha thinks there's been some sort of mix-up."

"We'll soon find out."

"In any case, this is a fine kettle of fish that you've gotten us into. Now we have to greet Mrs. Whitham looking like a couple of circus performers. Mistake or not, we'll be lucky if she doesn't run off at her first glance at us."

"I thought you said I don't deserve to be married."

"Don't be ungracious," Gillie barked.

Cole shrugged. He withdrew a square of linen from his pocket and wiped his face. The linen came away dark with soot. Once he'd done all of the repairs possible, he handed it to Gillie, who mopped at his own face.

"I should have expected this," the older man said as they followed their aunt's diminutive form across the lawn. "Of course we'd experience a calamity at the worst possible time. It's the Strangford ill fortune at work. Perhaps we ought to sneak around to the servant's entrance and into the kitchen to clean up before meeting your bride."

Cole shook his head. "I don't consider our scruffy appearance ill fortune at all. This, Uncle, is one of the best ways to assess my new bride. I'm not interested in marrying a woman who'll shrink at the sight of soot on a man's face. If she marries me, no doubt she'll be seeing a lot of soot on my face. And so, I'd like to know right now if she judges people solely by their appearances. If she does, then she's not for me."

"There's a pig pen over the hill," Gillie muttered. "Why don't you go and roll in it?"

Cole laughed. "If I thought Aunt Pesha wouldn't grab my ear and attempt to haul me along, I might."

Muttering blandishments, Gillie walked faster and separated himself from Cole by a few feet. Thus, in a line they made their way to the manor's front door, Gillie and Cole trailing behind their Aunt Pesha like two worn-out soldiers following a determined, if tottering, general who wore a lace cap.

On the porch, Aunt Pesha paused, her rheumy eyes squinting at Cole. "I've kept them waiting in the parlor while I went to retrieve you from that laboratory of yours, so be nice, boy."

Cole offered his aunt a quick bow. "I promise to remain at my most charming."

At his side, Gillie snorted.

Quietly the threesome entered the front hall of Shoreham Park Manor. Cole paused once within, and took a deep breath, trying to work up the nerve to go and view his intended, while Gillie and Pesha forged ahead. They'd almost reached the parlor door when they realized Cole was no longer by their sides and turned around.

"What's wrong, Cole? Aren't you coming?" Pesha asked in her shaky voice.

Cole nodded but didn't move. Instead, he glanced around the front hall, seeking comfort and strength in the familiar. Dark woods lined the walls and cases full of trophies and other odds and ends lay scattered about beneath a ceiling sporting heavy oak beams. A massive hearth took up the far wall, and a winding staircase with a wrought iron handrail led off into the nether regions on the second floor. Though he found the decor quite masculine and pleasing, he knew enough about women to suspect his potential bride would judge it dismal and medieval. Would it be enough to put her off?

Probably not.

Disappointed, he motioned to his elderly escorts to go into the parlor. "Go ahead, I'm coming."

Eyeing him distrustfully, Gillie preceded him into the parlor. Aunt Pesha tottered in next. Cole listened for Zelda's footsteps, thinking that his elderly cousin should be along also to greet their guests, but then he remembered he'd convinced Zelda to visit friends of hers in Buckland Village, the small town where Mrs. Whitham lived with her father. Squaring his shoulders, he entered the parlor and took up post next to Gillie.

His two guests faced him. A small elderly man stood by a settee, and next to him, a woman sat upon the settee's velvet cushions, her sky blue skirt and petticoats spread out around her. She stood as he entered.

Cole's gut tightened instinctively. He blinked and, for a moment, forgot that anyone else was in the room.

The first thing he noticed were her large eyes, eyes the color of the sun rising over the ocean, deep yellow with hints of blue and green. Like the sun which banished a cold and dark night, her gaze gently warmed his blood and promised a new day. She didn't look away from him, just regarded him calmly, and he discovered that he was staring at her with something close to wonder.

Most people probably wouldn't think of her as beautiful at first glance; her eyes were set far apart and her nose hadn't that patrician nobleness that was de rigueur for all English beauties. Still, the more he looked at her, the more he realized that she was actually very pretty, with perfect skin, full lips, and a wild mass of wavy chestnut hair that fought the chignon it had been wrapped in. In fact, her profile had elegance and character, making her interesting to look at and suggesting a lively personality.

His gaze dropped lower, and he noticed her arms and neck had a certain coltish quality, a long-limbed delicateness that hinted at both strength and vulnerability, while her breasts appeared full and tempting. A low-cut blouse, waistcoat, and gypsy skirt with many petticoats hid the rest of her, but he knew without having to lift her skirts that her legs would go on forever.

She was sensational.

Cole shook his head. He could see the mistake clearly. As much as he would enjoy making love to her, she wasn't made for having babies; no, hers was a body designed for male enjoyment without the trouble that babies brought. He glanced at Gillie and noted bewilderment on his face, too. Only Aunt Pesha seemed unfazed, perhaps because she'd had a chance to talk to the chit and sort the matter out.

His heart beating faster, he returned his gaze to the woman near the settee. This one he'd enjoy keeping as a mistress. Unfortunately, though, he needed a wide-hipped matron for a wife. He wondered why she was here, rather than Mrs. Whitham, the widow he'd agreed to consider.

Aunt Pesha tottered into position between himself and the sylph, and then performed the introductions. "Miss Pritchard, may I present Mr. Cole Strangford, and Mr. Gillie Strangford."

Cole bowed, thinking that "Miss Pritchard" was very far from the widow he'd expected.

The sylph inclined her head in acknowledgment.

"And to you, Cole, I present Miss Juliana Pritchard of Buckland Village; and her father Mr. Joseph Pritchard of the same."

Curtseying, Juliana lowered her eyelashes demurely.

"Delighted," Cole managed. "I trust your journey was without mishap. Why don't we all make ourselves comfortable?"

"Thank you," Juliana said, and they all seated themselves.

Her father cleared his throat. "I can see from my brief talk with your aunt that there has been some miscommunication between us. My heartfelt apologies for any confusion . . . but I thought that you wished to consider wedding my daughter Juliana, not my older daughter Lila, Mrs. Whitham. I suppose I misread the invitation you sent us."

"We *had* intended to invite Mrs. Whitham," Gillie admitted. "While Miss Pritchard would no doubt prove a delightful addition to anyone's family, her older sister seemed more suited to the lifestyle Mr. Strangford pursues. Still, now that you're here, perhaps we could—"

"I'm an inventor, with a particular interest in deep-sea diving," Cole cut in, with real regret. "When I'm not diving in the sea, I'm in my laboratory. In fact, you can see the results of one of my experiments on my face." He offered the girl and her father a slight smile, which they didn't return. More slowly, he continued, "Miss Pritchard, you are rather young, and if I might say so, quite handsome. If we try to make a match of it, I'm afraid you might end up feeling cheated. You see, a woman like yourself needs a devoted swain who will spend his hours at your feet. I assure you, I am not that man."

At his side, Gillie stiffened. Cole knew without asking that his uncle wished him to go through with the match even though he'd gotten the wrong sister. He ignored Gillie.

"Thank you for being so honest," she replied softly, her voice light and musical.

He sighed, feeling much like a fish who had just spit out a hook. "You deserve the chance to be happy."

Nodding sorrowfully, her father said, "While I don't blame you, Mr. Strangford, I must say that your rejection is a disappointment."

Juliana placed a hand on her father's arm. She looked downward, her lashes thick and dark against her white skin. Cole thought he saw a sheen of moisture in her eyes. He silently groaned at the thought of a weeping female in his parlor.

Gillie gripped his arm in what felt like an eagle's talon. "Cole, may I speak to you outside for a moment?"

Cole bit back the vehement *no* that threatened to escape him. "Of course." He offered Juliana and her father a polite smile. "We'll return in a moment. Until then, Aunt Pesha, would you see to our guests' comfort?"

"Go on, go talk to Gillie," his aunt ordered in a disgruntled tone. "I'll have Cook make up a tea tray and bring it in."

Cole bowed, excusing himself, and followed Gillie into the hall. The older man cornered him in a little nook that was out of their guests' earshot, and began his entreaties.

"Cole, they've made a long and arduous journey to meet us. Since they put forth such a great deal of effort, I think we ought to reciprocate by at least considering the idea of marriage to Miss Pritchard. In fact, I can't believe you're hesitating. She is easy on the eyes, and appears good-natured . . . good God, man, for once Lady Luck has smiled upon us. What else could you want in a wife?"

"Lady Luck never smiles on us. That's why I'm so worried. Exactly what sort of trial does Miss Pritchard have in store for me? And as far as my criteria for a wife are concerned, I want many things—none of which she seems to satisfy."

"Give me an example," Gillie challenged.

"Well, I want a wife who can bear me children. After all, if I remain childless and someone informed the Crown that I was neglecting the rules of Shoreham Park Manor's entailment, I might find myself penalized."

"How do you know Miss Pritchard won't bear children? Her sister proved fertile enough."

"Did you look closely at her? She's as slender as a reed, with hips more suited to a boy. You and I both know that birthing a child would prove difficult for her. And she's young, Gillie. Young women want a lengthy and back-breaking courtship, which I am simply not interested in giving her. I'll only make her unhappy. I need a practical, older woman who won't expect me to write poetry praising her beauty."

"You're judging her without really knowing her," Gillie pointed out. "Maybe she *is* practical-minded."

"Even if she is, she can't have the experience I need in a woman." At Gillie's raised eyebrow, he clarified, "I want someone who is willing and able to keep the household running smoothly, without my constant interference. As I spend most of my time in the laboratory or diving beneath the sea, I also want a wife who can represent me in town when necessary. This girl is too young to assume such responsibility."

"Again, you're making assumptions. Why not give her a chance?"

Cole switched tactics. "Let's forget about Miss Pritchard for a moment. Don't you think it a bit odd that we ask for Mrs. Whitham, and get the younger sister instead? My instincts are telling me that something's not right."

"As long as she's Romany and not one of the sea people, who cares?" Gillie replied. "I've had a damned difficult time finding a bride for you, Cole. If you turn Miss Pritchard away, you'd better have a very good reason for doing so."

"What if she and her father are working some sort of fancy dodge on us?"

"A fancy dodge? For what reason?"

Cole shrugged. "I don't know. I can't think of a reason. Still, something isn't right."

"I'll tell you why you're feeling this way: You simply would prefer to remain a bachelor. You've avoided the yoke of marriage and would continue to do so forever if it weren't for me. Cole, you have to give her a chance."

He sighed. "All right. You've worn me down. I'll ask her to stay on, so we can get to know one another."

Gillie nodded eagerly. "Tonight, at dinner, we'll question them to find out a few particulars, and hopefully that will put your suspicions to rest. We can even steer the discussion toward issues of health and childbearing, to see what your intended is made of."

Mouth quirked, Cole shook his head. "That ought to be enjoyable."

"And after dinner," the older man continued, "we'll have our special ceremony, to make certain she's not one of the sea people. Hopefully by tomorrow, you'll feel more amenable to a match with her."

"We'll see."

Smiling, Gillie patted him on the shoulder. "Let's go and give them the good news."

Despite his answering frown, Cole did indeed feel more comfortable with the idea of considering Juliana Pritchard for marriage. All of Gillie's arguments had made sense, and she was handsome. When they reentered the parlor and his gaze fastened on her oval face with its shining yellow eyes, he felt even more at ease with the notion. Therefore, it was with a great deal of consternation that he observed her father stand upon their reappearance and inform them that he and his daughter would leave Shoreham Park Manor immediately, rather than inconvenience him further.

Gillie immediately rushed forward to Mr. Pritchard's side, his hands making placating gestures. "Oh, no, sir, Mr. Strangford and I wouldn't hear of it. You must stay on. In fact, Mr. Strangford and I have agreed that we would like to continue as we'd planned, with Miss Pritchard taking Mrs. Whitham's place."

Juliana's eyes widened, and her father placed an arm around her shoulders. "Oh. I see," Mr. Pritchard said.

Cole nodded, his attention remaining on Juliana. "I would be delighted to have Miss Pritchard's company for as long as she wishes to stay."

She glanced at him, her gaze straying from his eyes to settle upon other portions of his face, as though she were a physician performing an examination. "May I have a moment to speak to my father in private?"

Cole stiffened, hearing the consternation in her voice. Why was she looking at him like that? She'd seemed eager enough before, when he'd been hesitant, but now that he was willing to consider marriage to her, she acted as though he were a toad wallowing in a brackish pond. "Of course you may speak to your father. Feel free to step into the hallway. My uncle, aunt, and I will await you here."

Their answering smiles clearly forced, the sylph and her father made their way out into the hall.

As soon as they left the room, Gillie shook his head. "Couldn't you have shown more eagerness? You're acting like a king who's bestowing favors on well-behaved subjects."

"Would you rather I gush over them, and give her false ideas of what she might expect from me as a husband? Honesty, I tell you, is a better approach in these situations."

Aunt Pesha tottered over to him, a silk handkerchief in one hand. "Never mind your manners, boy . . . I say it's your looks that have given her a turn. You'll be lucky if she decides to stay even a day."

Eyebrows quirked, Cole wondered what his aunt was talking about. While no one would confuse him with Lord Byron, he wasn't hideous either. When Aunt Pesha handed him the handkerchief, he was still at a loss, and began to stuff it into his pocket.

"Wipe your face, for Heaven's sake," Gillie hissed. "Quickly, before they come back into the room."

Suddenly he understood the reason for that earlier look of consternation on Juliana's face.

The soot.

He shrugged and returned the handkerchief to Aunt Pesha. "I stand by my earlier statement."

Pesha reluctantly took the handkerchief, and even tried to dab at him herself. Cole shooed her away, just as Juliana and Mr. Pritchard returned to the parlor. Cole studied her, trying to see her answer in her eyes, but saw only a brilliant golden touched with green.

"My daughter and I have talked the situation over, and we've decided to stay for a bit," Mr. Pritchard announced to the room in general.

"Though we're not making any other promises," the sylph added ominously.

A beat of silence passed, during which everyone in the room betrayed some emotion. Gillie's shoulders slumped—with relief, no doubt, while Aunt Pesha smiled foolishly and made a comment about enjoying the prospect of a young woman's company. Mr. Pritchard appeared stiff, perhaps with wariness, and Cole, despite understanding the necessity of his immediate marriage, knew a burgeoning sense of doom.

"I *am* delighted," he lied, determined to see this thing through, if only to produce that heir he needed.

Juliana smiled tentatively at him, those eyes of hers

glowing at him, and a hot flush swept through him, surprising him mightily. Suddenly he decided that it might behoove him to do a little courting, just in case she turned out to be suitable.

"Very good, then." Gillie glanced around the room. "I see that Cook has yet to bring our tea. Why don't I show you to your rooms, and bring your tea services directly there, so you might relax in comfort and privacy before dinner?"

Juliana transferred her smile to Gillie, who blinked in response. "That sounds lovely."

Moments later, Cole watched Gillie escort his intended from the room, and after they'd left, his gaze strayed toward the horizon visible beyond the window. This time, he saw not black clouds, but soft yellow light from a fading sun, where the sky met the sea. The color reminded him of Juliana's eyes. Would she prove as benign as a setting sun, or would dark clouds suit her better?

Soon, he would know.

GEORGE SWAYED FROM SIDE TO SIDE AS HIS carriage bumped its way up the carriageway to the country manor called Buckland House. As he examined the building he would call home for the next few weeks, he idly decided he approved. Constructed of brick and timber, it possessed a welcoming front porch with two wrought-iron benches and several colorful gardens beneath casement windows, suggesting a gentleman's country home. He could see a kitchen building behind the house, with an outline of an oversized fireplace, and a fenced-in herb garden where hollyhocks lifted their faces to the sun. Stables formed an orderly row out further behind the house, and a fenced-in meadow enclosed several cows that grazed contentedly.

He sighed with pleasure, the scene a sharp contrast to one of his previous visits to the west of England, when he'd been scouting the Pritchard's location. He'd stayed for weeks in a farmhouse-turned-inn that was practically windowless. Daily he wallowed in conditions of disrepair, overcrowding, and the absence of sanitation. After a time, even his nightly trips to the ocean hadn't made him feel clean. Even so, he'd kept mostly to the dark, breathing in stale air and drinking polluted water, and sat himself in the inn's dining room. There he'd found out as much as anyone could about the Pritchards, from a few locals who liked to talk more than they liked their ale.

At least his stay at the Pritchard's cottage would prove more comfortable and, with a little luck, equally as successful.

Next to him, Mrs. Wood chatted happily about wild roses that grew over a fence and a mock orange that was swaying in the breeze. He said nothing, allowing his co-conspirator to ramble on while he studied the place, committing certain details to memory. He could never tell when such knowledge would become useful. It might even save his life one day.

When they arrived at the front porch, an elderly man came from around the kitchen garden to greet them. Assuming the old man was Mr. Pritchard, George exited the carriage and helped Mrs. Wood down. Silently he reminded himself to call Mrs. Wood "Zelda," as their scheme required.

"Good day to you," Mr. Pritchard said. "You must be Mr. Strangford."

George offered him a sharp bow, his gaze missing nothing. The man wore a jacket of superfine wool, its quality good but not outstanding. A few briars clung to his trousers, suggesting he had just come back from a walk in the meadow. He'd brushed his hair back from his forehead in a casual style and wore heavy sideburns as favored by country gentlemen. The Pritchards, he thought, were prosperous gypsies but not wealthy.

"Good day to you, sir," George replied. "I am indeed Cole Strangford, and this is a cousin of mine, Zelda Strangford."

Nodding, Mr. Pritchard led them toward the front door. "My wife, Mrs. Pritchard, passed away a long time ago, God bless her, otherwise she'd be here to greet you; and my younger daughter Anna is at a finishing school in Ireland. Lila is out picking flowers, so I'm afraid 'tis only me available to welcome you to Buckland House."

"That's quite all right, sir," George said, already aware that Mr. Pritchard had sent his youngest daughter to finishing school. He'd also heard that Lila Whitham, Strangford's intended, lived here at Buckland House permanently, having returned to her childhood home after losing her husband and daughter.

Mr. Pritchard went inside, and motioned them to follow.

"Shall I go and fetch Lila?" George promptly offered.

"Now, Cole," Mrs. Wood scolded in a motherly tone, "you cannot go and fetch Mrs. Whitham. You haven't been properly introduced."

Her father lifted a pipe from a side table and stuck it between his lips. "We don't stand on ceremony here. Go on, Mr. Strangford. You'll find Lila in the meadow behind the house, past the hedgerow. It's my hope that you can talk her out of joining that convent of hers."

Convent?

George swallowed, and struggled to keep the shock out of his face. No one had ever mentioned that Lila Whitham was considering locking herself away in a nunnery. Even so, the knowledge didn't change anything for him. He wasn't really interested in convincing Lila to marry him; rather, he simply wanted to distract her while Juliana completed her mission in Shoreham. "I had no idea Mrs. Whitham felt a calling of that nature."

Her father shrugged. "She's lost her husband and daughter. I don't think she wants to take any more risks."

George nodded. "Thank you for telling me, Mr. Pritchard."

Summoning his courage, George walked back out the front door and past the kitchen. He skirted around the herb garden and exited to the fields beyond. He hadn't gone very far before his hair became warm with sunshine and his body grew sticky beneath the layers of clothes he wore, while splashes of delicate blue and yellow flowers swayed in his wake. He looked up at the blue sky, and for a moment, it shimmered like the waters far south of England, where tiny fish swam and the ocean felt warm. Yearning gathered in him, for the swift flowing currents that swept him effortlessly along, and for the other creatures who would play in the sea with him.

"God help me, I want to go back," he muttered, his voice so raspy he barely recognized it as his own.

"Go back where?" a feminine voice asked.

George blinked and opened his eyes. He felt a slight jolt as he focused on the woman in front of him. She was older than he by several years—he could tell by the tiny lines that fanned out from the corners of her eyes. Her hair appeared as fine and light as wheat, and her skin had the pearlescent glow of a conch shell found on the shores of the Spice Islands. A large floppy hat shadowed the expression in her green eyes; nevertheless, George sensed a deep calmness in her, and something else, something he had a difficult time identifying. He wanted to describe her strange quality to himself as honesty, but he sensed a sharp edge to that truthfulness, as if it were the kind that hurt. It wasn't honesty so much, he finally decided, as a penetrating discernment.

This one, he thought, saw lies easily.

"Go back where?" she repeated, again in a soft voice that belied her piercing gaze.

"To the sea," George said quickly, in a tone that matched hers.

Abruptly he felt that his playacting might prove more tricky than he'd anticipated. He realized now that he couldn't just trot out facts from Cole Strangford's past; surely she'd detect a wooden quality in his delivery. If, however, he mixed in incidents from his own life, incidents he could explain to her with some passion, she just might believe him.

"Do you love the sea?" she asked.

"I do." He offered her a bow. "I am Cole Strangford, and I assume you are Mrs. Whitham."

She studied him for several heart-stopping seconds, and just when he thought she would call him a pretender, she smiled. "You're correct, Cole Strangford. I *am* Lila Whitham, but you may call me Lila. Now tell me why you love the sea so much."

George felt a queer stirring in his gut. He looked at her again, seeking the reason behind the feeling, but saw only calm green eyes. Taking her arm, he offered her a smile of his own as he led her deeper into the meadow, and began to tell her about the sea's ferocity, its energy, and light, and life.

Four

❦

AFTER THE ELDERLY GYPSY MAN CALLED GILLIE had shown her to her bedchamber, Juliana had spent the several hours unpacking with the help of a dark-eyed young maidservant. The maidservant had talked her ear off about Cole Strangford, taking the time to describe each one of his strange inventions before mentioning that her employer had a love of diving and the sea. Juliana had listened, of course—no opportunity to gather intelligence could be ignored—but learned nothing new. She'd studied Strangford as part of her training for this mission, and much of what the maidservant had said was common knowledge anyway.

Her mind on Strangford, Juliana had later enjoyed a light lunch and then lay down on a fluffy bed with a lace canopy and damask coverlet. She would have very much liked to nap, because she knew she would have to swim later in the ocean while most landwalkers slept. Still, thoughts of her future husband kept her wide-eyed. He had a dark charisma about him, and this made her uneasy, because she didn't want to feel any interest in Cole Strangford. She didn't want to see him as anything but a means to an end, and had one purpose only here on land—to take advantage of him and break the curse. It would be much easier to trick an evil ogre than a normal man who possessed a flair for invention and a love of the sea, one who seemed as reluctant and uneasy about marrying as she.

That, in fact, had been her overall impression of Strangford—that he didn't want to marry. As soon as she'd gotten over her surprise at the soot coating his face, and the attractive features behind the soot, she'd noticed his ambivalence. At first, his eyes had glowed with male admiration for her, and she'd experienced a completely disconcerting and unexpected tingle at that glow. But then, he'd apparently changed his mind, and started explaining why she was unsuitable, even though his eyes had continued to tell her that no one else would do.

A smile formed on her lips. He *had* proven interesting.

Even so, she reminded herself to guard her heart, because her mission here on land called for her to betray him completely and utterly, by marrying him under false pretenses and having his child for no reason other than to break the curse. Her task could only become more difficult if she allowed herself to feel anything other than detachment.

Her smile faded. A cold sensation gathered in her midsection. She reminded herself that many people were counting on her to succeed. Not only had the gypsy witch sent all of the St. Germaines into the sea, but several family friends and retainers as well. Only a fool, she told herself, would waste time lying on a bed and making herself sick. She ought to be surveying the area, planning escape routes, and such. And so, feeling grainy-eyed but determined, she left her bedchamber and took some time to tour Shoreham Park Manor.

She had a very good reason for planning out an escape route. Later that night, and indeed every night, she would have to sneak out to the ocean to swim, or suffer a slow and painful dehydration that in extreme cases could lead to death. If she wanted to leave the house in the dark without stumbling around and possibly alerting someone to her skulking, she had to know the path leading to the front door intimately. Generally, this was the first task that any sea person on land performed, regardless of circumstances.

Moving quietly and keeping to the background, she inspected the dining room, salon, parlor, billiards room, study, kitchen, and music room, all the while conscious of the fact that she hadn't even left the first floor. Carefully she noticed the pitfalls on the way to the front door and, by the end of her impromptu tour, the amount of space landwalkers used for the daily task of living had amazed her.

She and her family hadn't nearly so much room to move around in. They lived in a shipwreck some twenty-eight miles off the south coast of England, near the Scilly Isles. The string of a hundred forty islands were a death-trap for sailors, but a boon for the sea people, who had settled in the many wrecks to form a town beneath the waves. Juliana's particular wreck was called the HMS *Association*, which had gone down in the early eighteen century and boasted an iron cannon and silver coin in endless quantities. There, bathed by the Gulf Stream, treated to dramatic coral reefs and sea life both temperate and tropical, she'd grown up with her family and spent almost every day wondering what it would feel like to live on land all the time without fear, rather than in unsatisfying little segments where every moment was fraught with worry, that someone might discover her secret.

Now, as she completed her tour with her route to the front door firmly in mind, she decided to go outside where the air wasn't so stuffy and the atmosphere so drab, and finish plotting out her course to the ocean. She made her way to the center hall, and just as she grasped the doorknob, the front door opened and the old gypsy man walked in.

"Oh, hello Miss Pritchard," he said, his tone nonchalant. "Did you enjoy your nap?"

"I couldn't sleep." She eyed him carefully. His appearance was so opportune that she suspected he'd been waiting for her. "I've decided to take a walk, instead."

"Would you like some company?"

"No, thank you. I'd prefer to walk alone, and clear my mind."

His eyebrows gathered together in an expression of concern. "Alone?"

"Yes, please," she told him firmly.

"Have we done anything to upset you?"

"Not at all."

"Miss Pritchard, all of us are very happy to have you here. I hope you're not considering leaving."

"Your hospitality has been exceptional, Mr. Strangford. I plan to stay on for a while."

"Good." He patted her awkwardly on the arm. "I'll leave you to your walk, then."

Summoning a smile, she moved off onto the lawn, leaving the old gypsy staring after her. A moment later, he began walking toward the windmill, which stood near the edge of the cliff. With a quick step, she left him behind and headed to a spot some distance away, where the cliffs offered a good vantage point of the sea.

The sea called to her like a lodestone; she could imagine in her mind the thousands of beautiful creatures hidden by just a few feet of water, treasures that dazzled the eye. Idly she wondered if Strangford, when diving, ever took the time to admire the beauty beneath the sea, or simply focused on his search for the Sea Opal. Aware that she ought not to indulge herself in this way, she nevertheless couldn't seem to stop herself from imagining how it would feel to take his hand, dive with him, and show him fantastic sights that landwalkers had never seen before.

A flash of movement near the windmill caught her eye and pulled her from the fantasy just as she'd decided that giving him this joy would feel very good indeed. Two figures in tweed were standing outside of the windmill. *Strangford and Gillie*, she thought. Evidently, while she'd been standing here staring at the ocean and mooning about, Gillie had marched straight over to Cole and informed him that she was out walking alone.

Cole returned his attention to Gillie and said something. Gillie answered. While she couldn't make out their actual words beneath the sound of the wind, which whistled through the boulders and stalks of grass, she could detect the tone of their words, and they both sounded angry. Then, the older gypsy threw his arms upward in a theatrical show of annoyance and she knew the two were at odds over her. In fact, she suspected that Gillie had asked Cole to join her on her walk, and Cole had refused. Clearly the older gypsy had thrust himself into the role of matchmaker.

She frowned, wishing she stood close enough to overhear the substance of their argument. And yet, before she had even begun to wander in their direction, her gaze on the ocean and her attention on what they were saying, Cole stomped back into the windmill and slammed the door, leaving Gillie outside.

The old gypsy began walking in her direction. She allowed him to catch up with her, and then offered him a pleasant smile. "Hello, Mr. Strangford. I hope all is well."

Gillie returned her smile, though his looked strained. "He and I have made an art form out of disagreeing. Please don't allow our arguments to trouble you."

"Where did he go?"

He shifted from one foot to the other. "Back into his laboratory. He works inside the windmill, you see, which generates power for him. He's in the middle of a very important experiment; otherwise, I'm certain he would have joined you," he said, confirming her suspicion.

"An experiment? Of what sort?"

"He's building a cylinder that holds compressed oxygen, which he plans to take on his dives with him, to allow him to stay under water longer."

Juliana lifted an eyebrow, feigning surprise. She knew very well what Cole was working on. "How unusual."

"Mr. Strangford has invented many unusual devices. Useful devices, too."

"Does he mind visitors?" she asked. She wondered if he planned on diving with this iron lung of his near the Scilly Isles. The last thing the sea people needed was a curious landwalker exploring their underwater homes. Perhaps she ought to investigate while she was here. Sabotage might even be in order.

"He wouldn't mind *you* visiting," the old gypsy assured her. "Cole would enjoy sharing his work with you."

"Are you certain?"

"Yes. I'll walk you over to his laboratory."

Juliana nodded and, together, they began walking along the cliffs. Her gaze continually straying to the slate-gray water below, she took deep breaths of salty air and couldn't stop herself from commenting on the beauty of the cliffs as they merged with the sea. Their jagged surface was full of nooks that no doubt hid all manner of seashore birds and other creatures, reminding her of a coral reef she'd once explored in the Pacific's tropical waters. "The cliffs *are* beautiful," Gillie agreed with an expression that suggested he would fall in with just about anything she said. "Very picturesque."

"Everywhere I see sky and water." She watched as a seagull soared by, caught up in a current of wind. "I love the openness of the place."

"So does Cole. He loves this old estate and the grounds that go with it. He wouldn't leave it willingly, I assure you."

Silently she mused that *her* ancestors hadn't left willingly, either. "What was Cole like as a boy?"

"He had more curiosity in him than any boy had a right to," Gillie replied with a chuckle. "His mother used to call it an infernal curiosity, because it was always getting him into trouble. He liked to take things apart to see how they worked, and then either she or his father had to put things back together."

She smiled. "He sounds like he was a handful."

"More than a handful, I assure you." The older man shook his head. "Cole's father—my brother, in fact—had a spyglass which he used to watch the ships out at sea.

One day Cole got his hands on it and had the spyglass in pieces in less than a half an hour. He left the lens in the sun, which refracted and intensified the sunlight. The lens was shining on his sleeve, but Cole didn't realize it, and soon he'd set himself on fire. That's how his father found him—yelling and rolling on the ground, on top of broken pieces of spyglass. Needless to say, it wasn't a very happy day for Cole, though he laughs about the incident now."

"What happened to Cole's father and mother?"

Gillie sighed. "His father died of a heart condition almost fifteen years ago, and his mother went less than a year afterward. She caught the ague and by all rights should have recovered . . . but she didn't fight it. I don't think she wanted to live without her husband."

"They must have loved each other very much."

"That they did, Miss Pritchard."

A few beats of silence passed, in deference to the memory of Cole's parents. Then Gillie asked her if this was her first visit to the south of England.

"My family is much like yours when it comes to traveling," she murmured, trotting out a piece of Pritchard history she'd memorized. "We've left Buckland House only rarely. The so-called gypsy trait of needing to constantly take to the road and find new adventure has never been very strong in us."

"Why travel, when your home has all that you could ever want?" Gillie agreed.

Their arrival at the windmill saved Juliana from a reply. They paused outside and watched the windmill's blades turn with deep, bellowing creaks. A sense of power clung to the building, and it almost seemed to quiver from within, as if intending to explode in a moment's notice. Juliana had once swum near volcanic vents in the South Pacific that had quivered and creaked in just the same manner, and shortly after she'd left the area, they'd spewed super-hot water and killed every living thing within reach.

Gillie opened the door for her and ushered her inside. Juliana stopped short upon entering. Amazed, she tried to take it all in. Broken wagon wheels hung from pegs on the walls. Old plowing equipment formed a pile in the corner. A giant billows, powered in some way by the windmill's blades, fanned air on a coal fire beneath a metal tank. She could feel the heat from the coal fire on her face, even from where she was standing.

The metal tank, she noticed, was hooked up to all manner of pipes. The pipes, in turn, funneled water from a well in the ground, whisking it off to destinations unknown and making a whooshing noise in the process. Gears made of wood and easily the size of a table creaked as they spun on their spindles, all of them meshed together and performing some grand purpose that she couldn't quite decipher.

She allowed her gaze to drift toward the chipped oak worktable and the man who stood behind it. He apparently hadn't noticed her yet, his attention fixed on a small copper canister and a helmet with a glass faceplate. He was fiddling with some sort of hose attached to the canister, his fingers long and sure. The hose, she saw, connected the canister to the helmet. Juliana had the idea that this must be his diving suit, which would increase his diving depth.

Still, she was more interested in the man than his invention, and took advantage of his inattention by studying him.

He wore his hair long and brushed back, other than a few thick black waves that fell artlessly over his forehead, giving him a disheveled look. Clearly unaware that she was observing him, his face appeared relaxed and natural, his eyes the color of the sky at twilight and framed by lashes dark and thick enough to make a woman jealous. He had a strong chin, and dark brows, and a nose and cheekbones that made him look like an aristocrat from some romantic country.

Her gaze dropped lower. He'd rolled up the sleeves of his linen shirt, displaying powerful forearms, and wore his tweed waistcoat unbuttoned, revealing trim hips. She guessed that he had a lean and strong body that utilized every muscle, probably from his diving. The black cravat at his throat, which he'd loosened, allowed a few curls of black hair to show, confirming that he was a fine specimen of manhood. Still, he managed to appear well-built and confident without oozing masculinity as some of the men in her acquaintance had, and she knew that she would have to be very, very careful not to become enamored with the gypsy who had the blood of witches flowing through his veins.

A peculiar fluttering commenced in her midsection. She took a quick breath.

Gillie, at her side, cleared his throat.

His expression annoyed, Cole looked up at the door and focused on the two of them.

Juliana felt her cheeks heat.

Gillie cleared his throat again. "Cole, Miss Pritchard was out walking alone—" he paused to give the younger man a meaningful glance "—and decided to come over to the windmill with me, to view your work. Would you mind taking some time to show her around?"

Suddenly she felt very awkward. "If my timing is poor, I can come back later—"

Cole sighed. "No, no, your timing is fine, of course I'd be more than happy to explain what I'm working on."

Gillie gave an approving nod. "I'm going to return to the manor, and see that a proper dinner is prepared for you both. I'll return to tell you when it's ready."

"Gillie," Cole warned, "don't put yourself to any . . . trouble over dinner."

"It's no trouble at all," the older man assured them, smiling, then made his escape.

Cole sighed. "God only knows what sort of dinner he'll have in store for us."

She lifted an eyebrow. "Whatever do you mean?"

"My uncle Gillie is determined that we'll make a match, regardless of how we feel about it, and will probably attempt to plan some intimate affair that neither of us will feel comfortable with."

"Our situation is rather tricky, no?" she asked with a smile designed to disarm him.

He returned her smile, his teeth white and even in his tanned face, and her heart did a little jump in her chest. "Yes, it is and will be, at least at first," he agreed. " I think we can ease the situation by not concentrating so much on marriage, and instead becoming friends. What do you think, Miss Pritchard?"

"I would like to become friends, Mr. Strangford."

"In that case, why don't you call me Cole, and I'll call you Juliana."

"Very well, Cole."

His smile widened. "Welcome, Juliana, to my workroom. It's here that I spend most of my time, working on various devices designed to improve life at Shoreham Park Manor. This is my most recent device." He motioned her over and directed her attention toward his worktable.

"Is it a . . ."—she pretended to think for a moment—". . . an underwater breathing device?"

His eyebrows rose. "You've seen an apparatus like this before?"

She laughed. "No, not really. Your uncle Gillie told me about it."

"What did he tell you?"

"Only that you planned to use it to breathe under water while diving."

He nodded. "It should allow me to stay under at least an hour."

"How does it work?"

"Well, the canister you see is full of oxygen, and that little brass fitting at the top of the canister is a regulator, which allows only a certain amount of oxygen to flow through the hose to the helmet. Once I've strapped the canister to my back, and put the helmet on along with the rest of my diving suit, I ought to be free to move about at will, at greater depths than I've ever managed before."

Lower lip caught between her teeth, she narrowed her eyes. She didn't like the looks of the thing. With it, he could easily reach some of the wrecks that the sea people lived in. "Where did you acquire a canister of oxygen?"

"The university at Edinburgh, in Scotland. They're conducting diving experiments of their own. I often exchange notes with a few professors there. Indeed, the Royal Oceanographic Society is extremely interested in my device, as is William James, a competitor of mine. Mr. James and I are both working on the same sort of invention, and the Royal Navy plans to reward a contract to whomever produces the first and best working underwater breathing device."

"Hmm." She nodded slowly, remembering George's mentioning William James, the gypsy's competitor. "I can see why you're so focused on completing your device, Mr. Strangford."

"Call me Cole," he reminded her.

She smiled. "I've never met a man who liked to dive to the bottom of the sea. Have you been diving for long?"

"Since childhood. I've searched old wrecks to see what I can salvage. I know from various accounts that there are other wrecks out in deeper water I can't possibly reach without some sort of breathing aid. I'd like to create something that will allow me to get at those wrecks."

Casually she ran a finger along the brass regulator. Discreetly she pushed against it. The thing didn't budge. "What sorts of treasures have you recovered?"

"Coins, mostly. Some pottery and naval equipment. A few Spanish doubloons once." He lifted an eyebrow. "Please don't touch that. It's difficult to adjust."

She moved her fingers away from the regulator, and focused her attention on the mask. It was a gruesome piece, designed to turn its wearer into a google-eyed beast. Idly she ran a hand across the faceplate. *Solid glass*, she thought. "Where do you usually dive?"

"When I was younger, I explored the reefs just off shore from Shoreham. Recently I spent some time in Cornwall. I'd like to get out to the Scilly Isles at some point, too. The shoals around those islands have lured more than one ship to its grave."

She nodded, her worst fears realized. "And you think this copper lung of yours will allow you to reach them."

He abandoned his regard of the breathing apparatus to view her fully. "I do. What about you? Have you ever tried a bathing machine, or taken the waters in some other way?"

She hesitated for one split second, and then shook her head. Casually she allowed her fingers to wander toward the regulator valve again. "My parents never considered bathing attire proper for young ladies to wear, so I never even attempted a bathing machine."

"There are many health benefits to taking the waters," he told her.

"I have no desire to flail about in the sea, weighed down by wet wool and battered by waves that seek to drown me."

"I agree, the bathing attire most matrons consider proper would as soon drown a person as allow them to derive any benefits from the water. I, personally, never wear those striped suits that men are expected to cover themselves with."

"What do you wear, then?"

"Breeches." A sudden smile curved his lips, and he added, "Or nothing at all."

She sucked in a quick breath, then fought to regain her composure. At last, she raised an eyebrow and managed to say in cool tones, "I suppose you don't visit very many public beaches. Or find yourself arrested quite frequently."

"I take the waters on the beach just below Shoreham Park Manor. It's quite private. If I could suggest some modified bathing attire for you, something that wouldn't weigh you down, would you like to learn how to take the waters?"

She swallowed. "Well, no."

He stared at her, his face darkening somehow, and she knew she'd disappointed him. "Why not?" he finally asked, one eyebrow lifted.

"Because it *isn't* proper," she invented.

His gaze became assessing. "So, you're a very proper young lady, then. Am I right?"

Again, she hesitated. What did he want in a wife? Someone with "propriety" for a middle name, or a more adventuresome spirit? She'd heard that most men wanted wives that would enhance their status and reputation during the day, while showing a little inventiveness at night, so she decided to be a little of both. She could only try, and see how he reacted, and then adjust her attitude as necessary.

"Of course I'm very proper, Mr. Strangford. All well-bred young ladies are. And yet, I must admit that at times I long for a little impropriety in my life. I know it's terrible of me to say such a thing, but if we're to become friends, we must share confidences, no?"

"Yes, we must." He pushed back from the table and fixed an unwavering gaze on her, his blue eyes searching her face. She felt naked beneath his scrutiny.

"In that case, isn't it your turn to share a confidence with me?" she asked.

"What would you like me to share? Or, should I say, what would you like to know about me, Juliana?"

She thought it over. There were a lot of things she could have asked him, and many things she wanted to know. Did he like her? Was he, at present, still considering marrying her, or just going through the motions to satisfy his marriage-happy uncle? And what, exactly, did he think of the sea people? But all of these questions seemed fraught with danger, so instead she offered him a puzzled expression and said, "I do have a question that's been nagging at me. Are you sure you don't mind me asking?"

He tensed a little. "Not at all. Friends share confidences, remember?"

"All right, then. I hope you'll answer me truthfully."

"I promise. Ask me anything, Juliana."

She paused, enjoying the suspense she'd built up between them; and then with a quick little breath said, "Why did you have soot on your face when we met?"

His eyes widened. Clearly he'd expected something more probing, more difficult for him to answer. Then he laughed, low in his throat. "I don't quite know what to expect from you."

Smiling, she lifted an eyebrow. Inside, however, she began to think that Cole Strangford liked cleverness in a woman. That could very well be his weakness. "Well? Why did you have soot on your face?"

"That's easy. An experiment I was conducting went sour, and the oxygen canister I'd been pressurizing blew up in my face, leaving me sooty."

"Do you greet all of your guests in such a manner?"

"Ah, I see you *are* a proper young lady. No, I only greet my important guests that way."

She acknowledged his teasing with a smile. "You promised to tell the truth, Cole."

He rolled his broad shoulders in a shrug. "All right, I'll tell you why. But first let me explain something else to you. Quite frankly, I don't always walk around this manor in a presentable state. I'm an inventor first, and a gentleman second. I need a wife who understands this, and won't fuss the moment she sees a speck of dirt on my lapel. And so, I decided to meet you in my less-than-presentable state in order to see if the soot would frighten you away; for you see, Juliana, I don't want to marry you if you're going to hold me up to some strict gentlemanly standard."

She bristled. "Many women consider gentlemanly conduct a sign of respect."

"A man who is constantly on guard to observe the niceties of gentlemanly conduct is a man who has no time to relax."

"I can understand that," she allowed. "But if you're an inventor first and a gentleman second, where does husband fit into that list? Before inventor, or after gentleman? The truth, please."

"I won't mislead you—I don't know where it'll fit. Are you still interested?"

Nonplussed, she avoided answering his question. "Why do you want a wife, Cole? Clearly you're not looking for companionship."

"I need an heir by the time I'm six-and-thirty," he told her baldly. "I'm one-and-thirty now. That gives us five years, dear Juliana, to satisfy the entailment on Shoreham Park Manor and avoid future complications."

A slight flush warmed her cheeks. She swallowed. "I see."

"And what about you? Why do you want to marry?"

"All young ladies want to marry."

"Why do you want to marry *me*?"

"Because you possess all of the qualities that are considered good in a prospective husband: wealth, prestige, and a fine old estate."

He laughed. "Prestige? That's an interesting word for it. I might have called it notoriety."

"What do you mean?"

"Are you telling me that you haven't heard about the Strangford family ill fortune?"

She thought about the best way to reply, and decided to remain as honest as she could. "I have heard some."

"Good. It'll be easier on both of us if you've agreed to this arrangement with prior knowledge and acceptance of possible difficulties. Are you superstitious, Juliana?"

She tilted her head in a noncommittal gesture. "Sometimes."

"Do you believe in gypsy witchcraft?"

"I think gypsy witches have existed," she allowed, while inside she groaned.

"Well, there are some darker aspects to my family history that may alarm you. You may have heard that I have a witch for an ancestor. In fact, the story is true. My ancestor Ilona was a *shuvani* who had a special talent for making people act in the way she wanted them to act. Some say that she's responsible for our ill fortune."

"How *ill*, exactly, is your fortune?"

He smiled ruefully. "Everything that can go wrong often seems to. Summer storms almost always bring lightning strikes that set something afire. Our horses go lame with more frequency than anyone else's. Moths get into the linen despite the blocks of cedar we set inside the cupboard. My canisters explode, leaving me with a coating of soot on my face."

"These sound more like annoyances than catastrophes."

"For the most part, they are. What sets us apart from other families, though, is our frequency in experiences. They happen far too often. And so, I must ask you again: Given your knowledge of the Strangford ill fortune, why do you wish to marry *me*? You're an attractive woman,

Juliana. Surely you've had someone special in your life before me."

"I'm afraid I did have someone special in my life before you." She swallowed, in what she hoped was an obvious fashion, and prepared to recite another little piece of Pritchard family history that she, George, and the Woods had concocted. This particular story was untrue, but she didn't think they stood any chance of being found out, because the Pritchards would never admit this publicly, and probably not privately, either. The story itself didn't reflect well on her, but it certainly explained why she would agree to marriage with the King of Ill Fortune. She prayed that it didn't put Strangford off completely. "You may not appreciate this bit of knowledge. I'm going to tell you anyway, though, because you have a right to know, and I'd rather you hear it from me than someone else." She affected a look of worry. "Do you have any idea what I'm speaking of?"

He appeared mystified. "Not at all."

"Well, when I was much younger—sixteen, to be exact—a few of the wealthier young men in Buckland Village, who had become officers in the army, came back from the Continent. They were on leave from His Majesty's cavalry, and attended many of the summer fetes thrown by village families."

"So?"

She allowed her shoulders to droop. "One of the men had a charming manner about him, and focused his attentions on me. Soon, I fancied myself . . . in love. Aware of my father's intention of settling a thousand pounds on me every year past my twenty-first birthday, he convinced me to elope to Gretna Green with him.

My father caught us before we could marry, but I fear the escapade tarnished my reputation rather badly."

"I'm so sorry," he murmured.

"I was foolish, and terribly young. I hope you won't hold my indiscretion against me."

"And yet, you still long for impropriety," he pointed out, echoing an earlier statement of hers.

"I do, but my experience with the young officer has tempered the emotion. Now I understand that love is a reckless emotion that only leads to trouble. At this point, I much prefer a marriage of convenience, where all expectations are placed on the table well beforehand. Even more importantly, I know my union with you will make my father happy, and after causing him so much misery, his happiness is a priority of mine. So why not consider you?"

He nodded. "Well, this has been a productive conversation. Now we both know where we stand. I like that, Juliana."

A small sigh escaped her. Obviously he hadn't minded the notion that her reputation might be a bit tarnished. Things couldn't have been going better, she decided. "I'm pleased to hear it."

He stood, stretched with lithe grace, and then gestured to some of his devices that lay scattered about the room. "I suppose I should give you that tour I promised you, before my uncle announces dinner."

Her gaze slid back to that underwater breathing apparatus. She wondered if she could find a way to sabotage it, for the notion of Cole Strangford meddling around the Scilly Isles in a diving suit positively terrified her. Perhaps tonight, when she snuck out to the ocean, she'd detour to his laboratory and see what could be done.

"Your uncle is very much involved with all of the household activities," she remarked. "Is your staff very small?"

"I employ a cook, a few maidservants and footmen, and a butler named William. Uncle Gillie, my aunt Pesha, and a distant cousin of mine named Zelda handle most of the other activities."

She nodded, thinking that Mrs. Wood was masquerading this very minute as Zelda, while George worked his magic on Lila Whitham. She dearly hoped George was having some success.

"Does a small staff bother you?" Cole asked, drawing her away from thoughts of her brother.

"No. I'm not in favor of keeping a large staff simply to impress the neighbors. I'm certain you employ all that you need. I haven't met your cousin Zelda yet, by the way. Will I see her at dinner tonight?"

"Unfortunately, no. Zelda is visiting a friend. She plans to return before you end your stay with us, however, in order to meet you."

"I've been looking forward to meeting her."

"You may already know her. She, in fact, is the one who alerted my uncle to your sister's marital availability. An acquaintance of hers, a Mrs. Howe, lives in Buckland Village and knows of your sister."

"Buckland Village, you say?" Juliana interrupted, a sinking feeling in her midsection.

He nodded. "Isn't your home just outside of Buckland Village?"

"Yes, it is." Her stomach contracted to a cold ball of dismay. "Isn't that a coincidence. I had no idea that your family had any ties to Buckland Village."

He eyed her closely. "You look pale. Is something wrong?"

"I'm feeling a bit faint." She pressed a hand against her forehead. The room was all but spinning around her. "Your laboratory is very warm. I believe I should go back to my bedchamber and lie down."

His expression became concerned. "Forgive me for standing here, talking your ear off while I should have offered you a seat. I'll take you back myself."

Juliana didn't argue with him. She wanted to return to the manor as fast as possible, so she might pen a letter to her brother, informing him that a significant leak had just sprung in their dam of lies. If this Mrs. Howe ever communicated to Zelda that "Cole Strangford" had visited Lila Whitham, she and George were finished. Thankfully, the real Zelda Strangford had apparently gone out of town and couldn't receive any letters from this Mrs. Howe until she returned. Nevertheless, she decided to write her brother about the situation. Forewarned, she mused, was forearmed.

Cole took her arm, his grip firm yet gentle, and drew close to her, his touch making her shiver with pleasure despite her anxiety. His body easily dwarfing hers, he led her out of the windmill, across the lawn and into the manor. Once they'd reached her bedchamber, he released her, the clean scent of him—salt, lime, and soap—lingering in her nose. Still, her worry over this latest complication didn't allow her to enjoy his closeness as much as she might have otherwise, and she all but sighed with relief when he stepped back from her.

He studied her with blue eyes that seemed to miss nothing. "Will you be coming to dinner?"

"Oh, yes," she assured him, certain she'd have finished writing her letter within the hour. "I simply need a small rest. Where and when does your family usually gather for dinner?"

"We meet in the salon, at about a quarter to six o'clock."

She gave him a small nod. "Until then, Cole."

"Have a good rest," he murmured in reply, then turned on his heel and left her to admire his broad shoulders and trim hips as he walked away.

Five

COLE LEFT HIS UNDERWATER BREATHING APPARA-
tus behind and retreated to his bedchamber about an
hour before dinner to change into more formal attire. He
wasn't usually that particular about dressing for dinner,
but tonight he wanted to impress. He'd already done a
smashing job of explaining to Juliana that he would
occasionally need a respite from gentlemanly behavior.
Now he needed to show her that he could be very much
a gentleman when the situation demanded it, because at
some point during their talk in his laboratory, he had
decided that Miss Pritchard might prove a desirable
addition to his household, and feared he might have
painted himself in too negative a fashion for any woman.

He faced the looking glass in his bedchamber and tied
his cravat into the Oriental style, a simple, elegant knot
that he favored for formal occasions, and then shrugged
into a jacket of black superfine wool.

"Well done, Cole," a crotchety old voice said behind
him. "She won't be able to resist you tonight."

Cole spun around. "Please close the door, Uncle
Gillie. From the outside."

Cackling, Gillie advanced into Cole's bedchamber and slung himself into a chair. "So, what do you think of our fair Miss Pritchard so far?" His gaze roved over Cole's evening attire before returning to his face. "Obviously, at the moment, you're favorably inclined toward her."

"Do you always go where you're not wanted?"

Gillie laughed again. "Confess. You like her."

"She has a certain charm that I can't deny," Cole admitted, turning away from the looking glass.

"She's a beauty, Cole, and you're damned lucky she's willing to consider you."

He shrugged. "She's clever and witty. Her mind travels down paths I don't expect. She definitely keeps me off balance, and I find that aspect of her more intriguing than any else."

Gillie shook his head. "If you say so . . . though a pretty smile helps, in my opinion."

"You're far too interested in giving me your opinion on this matter," Cole accused. "In fact, you're far too involved all around. You've gotten her here. Now let me take over and do the courting."

"Oh, so you're courting her now, eh? I'm delighted to hear it."

"I'm courting her because she has possibilities. If you keep pushing, though, I might grow tired of the two of you, and send you both packing. What were you thinking earlier, to bring her into my laboratory? You know I don't want a woman poking around my equipment."

Gillie shook a finger at him. "I brought her to your windmill because I'm trying to set the proper tone between the two of you. You spend a lot of time in your laboratory, and since the two of you need to be together, she'll have to become accustomed to the laboratory, too."

"That remains to be seen."

The older man's accusing expression gave way to curiosity. "Did you two get along after I left?"

"We had a long talk. About many things, my inventions included."

"You interrogated her, you mean."

"No, we *talked*," Cole corrected him. "She did show a gratifying interest in my work. Perhaps she was a little too curious, though. She kept touching the regulator valve on the oxygen canister. I thought she might break it."

"You said you like cleverness. You have to take the good with the bad. Would you rather she be as dumb as a post, and never show the slightest interest in your work?"

"You're an annoying old hen."

"And you're a pigheaded youngster." Gillie shrugged. "So, she was clever. What else did you find out about her?"

"She doesn't like the sea, and never learned to take the waters. Her father didn't see bathing attire and machines as proper."

"Her father was zealous in protecting her reputation. I see that as a positive sign."

"I find it disappointing." Cole paused to place a watch fob in his waistcoat pocket, then continued, "You know how much I love the sea. I would have liked to share my enthusiasm with my wife."

"Well, you can't have everything. Wouldn't you rather have a proper wife than a hellion?"

"She apparently was a hellion at one time," Cole revealed. "Ran off to Gretna Green with a cavalry soldier just after her sixteenth birthday. Her parents caught her before she could spend the night with him and destroy herself utterly, and later they tried to cover the incident up, but evidently enough of the story leaked out to make her a less than desirable commodity on the marriage mart."

Gillie nodded sagely. "That explains it. Surely nothing else would convince her to consider *you* for marriage."

"She appeared worried about my reaction to her past," Cole added, moving toward the fireplace mantel and leaning against it, now that he'd finished dressing. "Quite frankly, it doesn't bother me at all. You know how much I dislike a simpering female who demands love sonnets and expects some poor fool to ride around on a white charger, dressed in armor. This one has loved and lost, and now she carries those lessons with her. A marriage of convenience is all she wants."

"She does seem to have the proper attitude," Gillie remarked.

"From that perspective, she's perfect—completely dispassionate and practical-minded," Cole agreed. And yet, even as the observation left his lips, he realized the notion didn't bring him the kind of satisfaction he thought it would. In fact, he felt rather out of sorts. And though the feeling contradicted everything he'd convinced himself of regarding marriage, and everything he'd said to Gillie, he couldn't deny it.

Gillie motioned expansively from his chair. "She apparently has a healthy constitution."

Recalling the way his tour of the windmill with Juliana had ended, Cole said, "I'm not certain of that. Earlier she nearly swooned from the heat beneath the hot water tank. I had to escort her back to her bedchamber for a nap, lest she collapse."

The older man made as if to stand. "Good God, man, why didn't you tell me Miss Pritchard is sick? I would have sent for the physician immediately."

Cole leaned forward and restrained him with a hand. "Sit down, Uncle Gillie. I didn't say she was ill, I said that the heat had made her feel faint. I'm certain she's fine now. But I have to wonder what will happen when the summer temperatures rise. Will she swoon in the middle of a fete?"

"Why not escort her to a couple of the dances in town, and see what happens?" Gillie asked. "You could also take her to Shoreham's dinner and theatrical production, the one that the orphanage hosts as a fundraiser. There she'd meet Shoreham's most influential citizens."

Cole nodded slowly. "The fund-raiser is a capital suggestion. I'll ask her if she'd like to attend this evening, as soon as I've explained the courting ceremony to her."

A second passed while both men looked at each other. Gillie shifted on his chair. Cole felt similarly uncomfortable. The courting ceremony was just a fancy name for the seawater test, where all prospective mates stood ankle-deep in seawater to ensure they were human. In the past, the women who had experienced this ceremony found it engaging and romantic, and never had any of the prospective brides transformed into one of the sea people. Cole hoped Juliana Pritchard didn't prove to be the first.

Tension invaded his body at the thought of the sea people. He abandoned his slouch on the fireplace mantel and moved toward the window, which allowed a generous view of the ocean.

Gillie cast a worried glance toward the window, too. "You've spent some time with her, and spoken in depth to her. Do you think we have anything to worry about regarding the courting ceremony?"

"Are you asking me if I think she's one of the sea people?"

"Is she?"

"If I thought she was, I wouldn't be entertaining her in my home. Even so, there's always a chance she could be hiding her true identity, but I don't see what that would gain her. As a sea person, she would surely know about the courting ceremony, a ceremony which reveals all sea people, and must realize that her ruse would be discovered rather quickly."

"She seems too sweet and gentle to be one of those cold-blooded fish," Gillie remarked.

Cole nodded. "I think the chance that she's a sea person is very remote."

Still, he felt uneasy.

Gillie glanced toward the clock Cole kept at his bedside. "It's nearly half past five o'clock. We should go to the salon and wait for Miss Pritchard."

Cole cast a critical eye over his uncle's attire. The older man still had on the jacket he'd donned in the morning, which sported a distinct layer of dust. "After all of the grief you've given me over my appearance, you dare to go to dinner dressed in your day clothes?"

"I'm not going to dinner . . . with you. Pesha, Mr. Pritchard, and I are going to sup in the salon. Juliana will be your only companion, outside of William."

Eyes narrowed, Cole tried to fathom the twinkling he saw in Gillie's eyes. "Where, exactly, are we going to dinner?"

"You and Juliana will be enjoying a variation on *le déjeuner sur l'herbe* . . ."

"Lunch on the grass? Have you gone mad, uncle?"

"She loves the cliffs," the older man said. "She told

me so while we were walking to the windmill. So I arranged for a picnic in the meadow, near the edge of the cliffs. I couldn't think of a better place for you both to enjoy your first meal together."

Cole narrowed his eyes thoughtfully.

Gillie gave him a knowing look. "You may not share a love of the sea, but you do have one or two things in common, eh?"

"Perhaps."

"Indeed you do. She loves the openness of the cliffs, and the brilliant view they afford her . . . much the same way you feel about them."

"That's an important point, Uncle Gillie, to know. And yet, while I appreciate all you've done to assist me in retaining my inheritance, once we've completed the courting ceremony and determined that Miss Pritchard is not one of the sea people, I'll ask you to put your matchmaking cap away and allow me to forge a relationship with her in my own way."

The older man stood rather hastily. "Well, I guess I should be going now."

"Uncle Gillie, I'm asking you kindly to stop interfering."

Heading for the door, Gillie winked at him. "Enjoy your dinner."

Sighing, Cole watched the door shut on the older man's retreating form. His uncle, clearly, was hell-bent on having him married and would stop at nothing to see the deed done. Heaven only knew what sort of machinations he and Juliana would have to put up with until they announced their engagement.

Cole shook his head. His uncle was a rather large pill to swallow. Even so, he shouldn't forget that all of his uncle's schemes were rooted in a desire to help. And, he had to admire Gillie's inventiveness. The man ought to try his hand in the windmill laboratory, to see what sort of devices *he* could invent. Sudden affection overcame his annoyance for Gillie and he allowed himself a small grin. In his youth, Gillie had always been like a second father to him, dispensing advice and intervening on his behalf when he'd gotten himself into some scrape or another. He also supposed he'd filled an emptiness in Gillie's own life, as Gillie had never married or had children. Now, they'd become more like the best of friends, fully informed and accepting of each other's bad and good habits.

His mood improved, Cole took one last look at himself in the looking glass and, satisfied that he appeared his best, left his bedchamber. Shortly thereafter he entered the salon, whose celery-green damask walls were bathed in the soft orange glow of dusk. He immediately focused on the window that presented a stunning panorama of the cliffs and the sea beyond; but he wasn't so much interested in the view as in the woman who stood within its frame.

She stood in profile, looking out to the sea with an intense expression of yearning. Immediately he wondered why. A question he couldn't suppress echoed in his head, and he forced himself to listen.

Was she one of the sea people?

He grew very still, his heart beating harder, and tried to determine if she represented danger. He reviewed everything Gillie had told him about her, and everything she'd told him herself, and couldn't recall anything at all that might be setting his instincts off. Then he stared at her delicate profile and unlined brow. She appeared so guileless that he didn't think her capable of deception even if her life depended on it.

Clearly he was seeing monsters where there weren't any. His lips curved upward at his own folly.

There were other explanations for that look of hers, he reminded himself. Hadn't she told him that her father had never allowed her to take the waters? He wondered if she regretted her father's decision. Would she agree to learn to swim, if he offered to teach her? Looking at the tender bloom of rose in her cheeks, he decided that he'd enjoy watching a frilly piece like Juliana Pritchard frolic in the waves.

Quietly he stepped into the salon. She still hadn't noticed that he'd entered the room, and he took the opportunity to study her further. She was stunning, he realized anew, with dark brown brows winging back from her eyes and thick, lustrous chestnut hair. She'd donned an ankle-length sea-green gown, its long, loose sleeves tied at the wrists with velvet ribbon. The antiqued frill at her bodice permitted him a view that suggested her breasts would fit perfectly into his palms. A hot tightness invaded his gut at the notion.

He allowed his gaze to rove downward, noticing that her gown clung to her curves past her waist, then flared out near her ankles, reminding him of the foam atop a wave. Delicate ivory slippers encased her feet, matching her fashionable apron of antique lace. And yet, despite all of these virginal clothes, he detected a sensuality in the way she gently smoothed her gown and ran a hand over her shining chestnut hair. Indeed, her seductive quality was all the more potent given her air of innocence. Though he doubted very highly that she was one of the sea people, she nevertheless possessed the beauty of a sea siren, capable of bringing a man to his knees with a single wave of her delicately wrought hand.

Abruptly he wondered if her little escapade to Gretna Green with her unnamed soldier had lost her more than her reputation. How could any man resist the opportunity to steal a kiss from such a woman, if not more? Surprised at the sudden flare of jealousy in his midsection that the thought had incurred, he cleared his throat and acted as though he'd just entered the salon.

She spun around, the sunset behind her now and painting an orange glow around her. He caught his breath at the dewy-fresh picture she presented, one enlivened by those yellow eyes of hers. Of all the women he'd dallied with over the years, none had been so young, or bright, or as desirable as Juliana. She was like a gold coin laying on the ocean floor, winking in the sunlight and catching his eye with her brilliance and promise.

"Good evening, Mr. . . . ah, Cole."

He walked toward her, took her hand, and kissed it, keeping his lips an inch or so above her skin as was proper. Still, he wanted to bend his head closer, to touch her wrist with his mouth and feel her pulse quicken beneath his lips. "You look sad, Juliana."

She sighed and turned slightly to face the ocean again. "The sea is so beautiful, no?"

He, too, looked out the window. "Why does that make you sad? Because you've never been able to truly enjoy it by letting the waves caress you?"

"I'm not sad, Cole. I'm simply thinking about how far away from home I am."

"You're only about a week's journey away from North Wales."

"Sometimes a week can feel like forever."

He frowned, unhappy to think of her as longing for her home. "But your father is here."

Her brow furrowed for a moment, then cleared. "Yes, he is."

"Does that knowledge not bring you any comfort?"

"A little," she said.

Mystified by her attitude, he tried to fathom the secrets he fancied had darkened her yellow eyes to gold. "Is there someone you would rather have not left behind at home? A certain officer, perhaps?"

Again, her brow furrowed, as if she hadn't any idea of whom he spoke; and then she laughed, the sound both carefree and very feminine, and going straight to his head. "Of course not, Cole. I haven't left anyone behind that I wish for."

He smiled and held out his hand. "Forgive me for prying."

She allowed him to enfold her hand within his own. Her bones felt very fragile in his grip, and her skin soft and warm. A charming scent clung to her, something like wildflowers, and he breathed it in deep, wondering if she would taste as sweet as she smelled.

She smiled at him, her teeth very white between rose-pink lips.

"Let me take you to dinner," he said gently.

"Shouldn't we wait for my father and the rest of your family?"

"They aren't coming with us. Rather, they'll sup in the dining room."

"We're dining alone?"

"I'd like to dine alone," he told her in a low voice, noting how her lips parted slightly at his admission, "but for propriety's sake, we'll bring a chaperone. My butler William is very discreet."

The roses in her cheeks bloomed even pinker. "Where are we dining?"

He smiled. "Gillie has prepared something very special for us. Come." Without waiting for her reply, he urged her gently toward the hall, and then out the front door, where William was waiting for them.

His gaze averted from Cole and Juliana, William gestured with a hand toward a table set up near the cliffs. The table, which was covered with a white tablecloth, held a pile of silver dishes that glinted in the sunlight.

"Your dinner awaits you," William informed them solemnly.

Juliana was looking at the table with wide eyes.

"Very good, William," Cole said, enjoying her surprise. He noticed that her breasts were heaving slightly, and silently admitted that Gillie knew what he was doing when he set out to pair a couple up. Now he only had to pray that some chance disaster didn't befall them and send Juliana packing.

"Cole, this is . . . delightful," she breathed.

"Delightful for both of us." Leaving William behind, he led Juliana across the lawn. "My uncle Gillie has the heart of a romantic. He arranged for us to spend time alone together at dinner, and I for one highly appreciate the opportunity."

"While I was on my way to Shoreham Park Manor, I tried to imagine what it would be like to meet you. I wondered what you would do, and what I might look forward to. But my day has gone far better than I expected."

"You had such a poor opinion of me?"

"I'd heard about two other ladies who'd come here to

Shoreham Park Manor over the years, to see if you and they suited. I'd also heard that they'd left in a hurry. Naturally I wondered why, and suspected you might have something of an ogre in you."

"An ogre." He smiled. "When you saw the soot on my face earlier, you probably thought your suspicions confirmed."

"I'll admit to being curious about it, but I also found you had many other, ah, redeeming qualities and I quickly realized you weren't an ogre at all, but just, perhaps, a little cranky."

His smile widened. "How could you have found any redeeming qualities in me, after such a short meeting between us?"

The flush in her cheeks, which had faded into a soft bloom, pinkened to a deeper hue again. "Well, ogres are ugly, and you're far from unattractive."

He knew she was attempting to compliment him, and the awkward way in which she was doing it endeared her to him. "Thank you, Juliana. I'm pleased that you don't find me completely ugly, considering we're contemplating marriage between us."

She looked down, her eyelashes very dark against her cheeks. "I wasn't absolutely certain that you wanted to consider me at all. You seemed so . . . well, unhappy about me replacing my sister."

"I'm a bachelor, set in my ways," he told her, his tone low and reassuring, "and you gave me quite a surprise. Do you recall the warning I gave you earlier, that my manner may not always be what you deem proper?"

She nodded. "Yes, I do."

"If I seem gruff, it's only because I haven't had a woman in my life for a long time," he said, pushing the memory of his affair with Charlotte Duquet from his mind. "You'll have to be patient with me."

"I *will* be patient, Cole." Without warning, she grasped his hand, her movement so obviously unplanned and heartfelt that he wanted to draw her close against his body.

Fighting the urge, he guided her to her seat and helped her sit down, then releasing her hand regretfully, he folded his large frame into a chair opposite hers. For several seconds, he said nothing, preferring to commit this moment to memory, as his first dinner with his possible wife. She, too, remained quiet for reasons unknown, but their silence was companionable and he felt himself relaxing, even as a pleasant anticipation of the evening ahead built inside of him.

The table and chairs Gillie had brought out to the cliffside, he noticed idly, were some of the finest the Strangfords possessed, as were the glass goblets, plates and salad bowls Gillie had chosen for their dinner. Sparkling like red rubies in the waning sunlight, the dishes were relics from a Great-Great-Grandfather's time and had been sitting in a glass case in the dining room for many years. Someone had placed a large bowl of cherries on a platter, and filled a compote dish with strawberries, carrying through with the theme of red . . . a color of desire, of passion, and of boldness.

Cole hid a smile at the notion and lazily surveyed the porcelain pitcher that presided at the center of the table. It contained an artful arrangement of red cockscomb and very fragrant roses whose scent lay heavily on the air. A salty tang drifting in from the ocean gave that scent a fresh, clean element that reminded him very much of Juliana. He wasn't quite sure why he kept thinking of her whenever the sea came to mind, and as he glanced out at the place where the sky met the ocean and saw that mist had blurred that horizon, he admitted that his own instincts about Juliana were equally as blurry.

In any case, the courting ceremony later should resolve all of his doubts.

Juliana, he saw, had picked up a knife and was examining it with a curious air. It was a fine piece, Cole thought, with its intricately carved ivory handle that matched the rest of the silverware which had been in the Strangford family for generations. William must have polished the embossed silver platters and bowls that they only used on special occasions, and placed them on the table, too. On the whole, the effect was both sumptuous and intimate, and Cole knew his uncle was trying to impress Juliana with the Strangford family wealth.

"May I begin serving you, sir?" William asked, appearing out of nowhere.

Cole looked at Juliana. "Are you hungry?"

"Very," she told him, a sensual lilt to her voice.

He swallowed, his focus narrowing in on her, looking into her delicate, arresting face.

She smiled at him with a suggestive innocence.

For several moments, she was all that Cole could see, hear, and smell. He lost himself in her. A relentless need to possess her made his nostrils flare.

"Sir?" William murmured.

Cole shook his head and collected his wits. "Yes, William, you may begin."

His attention resting on Juliana, he tasted each of the dishes William placed on his plate—pheasant pâté, roasted tarragon chicken, and potato salad. Juliana, for her part, took small, ladylike nibbles of the chicken and salad, bypassing the game pâté. Their gazes met at several different moments, but oddly, Cole suddenly found it difficult to find a topic of conversation to share with her; he couldn't seem to drag his focus away from her lips and how full and wet they looked.

As the silence continued, he became more uncomfortable, and attempted a few lame sallies about the weather that she hardly responded to before returning her attention to her plate. At length, he realized he could have made her uneasy. He was behaving like a randy goat and knew it, and she probably knew it, too. She couldn't help the fact that she had a body designed to make a man's mouth water, eyes that warmed his blood to the boiling point, or the kind of face a man would think of when making love to his wife.

He had to break the growing tension between them, so he put his fork down and selected a raw carrot from the stack of cut vegetables. Using his fingers, he dipped it into the herb sauce and crunched it in his mouth. He knew his action was unorthodox and very improper for formal dining, and that's exactly why he did it. He wanted to replace the sensual awareness between them with surprise, shock, disapproval . . . anything would do.

She looked up from her dinner at the sound of him eating. A smile lifted her lips. She didn't seem shocked at all. Following his example, she abandoned her fork and selected a raw cucumber. Her gaze locked with his, she dipped it into the sauce, slipped it between her lips, and then chewed with obvious relish. When she finished, she licked her fingers, outdoing him on the impropriety scale.

He stifled a groan and forced himself not to display any other signs that her action had affected him, but inside, his blood surged hot through his veins.

A platter of Cantal and Port du Salut cheeses sat near the middle of the table. Cole reached for it, and William moved forward to help, but Cole gave the footman an imperceptible nod. He knew he was damned near lost to his body's impulses. He was also damned near to not caring anymore. William, a smart man who often found a few extra sovereigns in monthly pay, bowed slightly before backing away from the table and moving several feet away, to sit beneath a tree. There, the footman picked up a stick and a knife, and began whittling, leaving Cole and Juliana virtually alone.

Juliana noticed the footman's retreat but she didn't remark on it, instead chatting with him on pleasant, yet inconsequential topics. Her lack of objection over William's retreat surprised but pleased him. He'd thought he would have had to murmur some reassuring words, but instead he grabbed the platter of cheese and offered it to her. She picked a piece of Port du Salut from the platter and ate it slowly, following it with a sip of the Beaujolais William had poured for each of them before retreating to his tree. Cole did likewise, making sure to refill both their wine glasses. Then, over the next several minutes, he continued the small talk with her as they ate slices of cheese, strawberries, and cherries, watching as the fruit stained her lips a luscious red.

Their inconsequential chatter lightened the mood between them considerably. And yet, Cole's inner tension still grew with each moment they spent together. When they finally began to eat the last course, an apple gâteau with fresh cream, he found his hunger had only grown—for her. He glanced at William, and saw that the man had relaxed into a reclining position, his hands behind his head. Cole suspected the footman had gone to sleep, and knew he could expect no help curbing his carnal appetites from that quarter. The only alternative left was to end their dinner soon, before he was tempted to do something he'd later regret.

But first, he had to broach the subject of the courting ceremony.

"Juliana," he murmured between mouthfuls of apple gâteau, "you mentioned that you had heard about two other Romany ladies who'd come to Shoreham Park Manor, and then left without becoming engaged to me. Did you happen to also hear of the Strangford's courting ceremony?"

Her brow furrowed. "No. I don't think I've ever heard of such a thing. Is it a Romany tradition, or is it peculiar to your family?"

"The ceremony has been part of the Strangford family for many generations. In essence, we tie a love knot while standing in the sea, to ensure that we remain in each other's hearts forever."

"Why must we stand in the sea?"

"The Strangfords have a deep connection with the sea," he told her. "Centuries before, when we lived in Italy, we lived along the coastline near Genoa and made our fortunes fishing. When the fish became scarce, we sailed from Genoa to England, and settled in houseboats along the coastline. We became gypsies who wandered in boats and made our living catching fish and salvaging valuables from shipwrecks.

"At some point, my ancestor salvaged a beautiful jewel, called the Sea Opal, from an ancient vessel. The Sea Opal brought him great luck. His fortune grew and he became wealthy enough to call Shoreham Park Manor his home."

"I remember you mentioning the Sea Opal before," she said.

He nodded. "It's responsible for the Strangford family bad luck. When the sea opal was stolen, and later lost to the sea, ill fortune began to haunt the family. The Strangfords have ever since been trying to find the opal in the shoals and coral reefs, with the hopes that its recovery might stem the minor catastrophes that have plagued us over the years, but we haven't discovered it yet."

She lifted an eyebrow. "You *do* have a deep connection with the sea."

"The courting ceremony is our way of paying homage to the sea, while also blessing a new relationship."

"What a lovely thought. How far will I have to stand from the shoreline?"

"Not too far. I'll be there with you."

"I never learned to swim," she reminded him. "I can't go in any further than ankle-deep."

"Don't worry, Juliana; the courting ceremony doesn't require one to go in deep, though I'd like to teach you how to swim some day, if you would agree to try—"

"Cole, there's something I haven't told you," she said suddenly.

Something in her voice gave him pause. He braced himself. "All right. Tell me now."

"There is another reason why I never take the waters. While it's true that my father thinks the activity improper for all well-bred young ladies, he also fears the sea, as do I."

"Why?"

"When I was much younger, we took my older sister Lila to a finishing school in Ireland. On the way home, our ship became caught in a storm and capsized. For hours Lila, my father, and I clung to a wooden crate and prayed for rescue. A fishing boat eventually saved us, but from that day forward, my father would not allow either myself or Lila to place even one toe into the ocean." She pressed a hand against her brow. "My heart pounds even today when I think of it."

Cole stared at her for a moment, seeing the pain in her eyes, before speaking in his most understanding voice. "I can see how difficult that time was for you. I promise that I'll make certain you step into the water no deeper than your ankles."

"Thank you, Cole."

Again, he noticed a pinched look around her mouth. He stood up and held out his hand, trying to focus her mind on something other than her accident. "Walk with me, Juliana."

Her lower lip trembled as she took his hand and allowed him to lead her away from the table. Hand in hand, they strolled through a meadow toward the cliffs, and then stood together to look out at the sea. Abruptly he realized she likely didn't want to see the ocean at all, and steered her in another direction, toward the garden out behind Shoreham Park Manor, which Aunt Pesha tended.

While they walked, he admitted to himself that he'd spent a good deal of the evening torturing himself, by thinking about how delectable she was and how much he'd like to kiss her strawberry-reddened lips. If she'd had even the slightest inkling of where his thoughts had lingered most of the evening, she probably would have quit Shoreham Park Manor immediately, preferring to marry a gentleman rather than a rutting boar.

Disgusted with himself, he nevertheless pulled her closer and noted how she didn't fight him at all, and actually moved in a few more inches herself. This, he thought, was exactly the sort of thing that made him forget himself. Determined to get some use out of the evening, he did his best to ignore the view that his height and her lacy bodice allowed him, and embarked on a new tactic of conversation.

"Do you like children?" he asked, as they meandered past a bed of sea thrift.

"I adore children." She gripped his hand a little bit harder.

His heart responded with a quickened beat. He fought to keep his own grip unchanged. "Do you have a lot of nieces and nephews?"

"No. Lila's daughter was the only niece I ever knew. She died, poor thing, of the fever. Still, I often involve myself in charity work at Buckland Village, and I enjoy working with children the most."

"I'm so sorry about your niece. Too often, one chance disease or another gets a foothold in a family, and then the suffering never seems to end. Do you have many aunts and uncles?"

"Just two. Large families were never very much in fashion at Buckland House. Fewer children allows one to focus more attention on the sons and daughters one *does* have."

"How about you?" he pressed. "Do you wish for a big family, or a small one?"

"I'd like at least four children." She paused to peek up at him from beneath her lashes. "I think I would enjoy that very much."

He smiled in reply. "I'm glad to hear it, for I too want several sons and daughters."

Her step slowed as they passed a bench nestled in a patch of lavender. A breeze blew through the stalks of purple flowers, sending their soothing fragrance into the air. "May we sit down, Cole?"

"Of course." He watched as she sat on the bench, fluffing her skirts around her, and then settled next to her. She sat so close that he could almost feel the heat from her body. Suddenly he felt dizzy, almost giddy with need for her. At the same time, he became angry with himself, for having so little control over his body. He'd been in the company of beautiful women before, and they hadn't produced this kind of effect in him. But something about Juliana was drawing a response from him like he'd never felt before.

Perhaps they were meant for each other. It could be as simple as that.

"I'd like to introduce you to several different people in town," he said, his voice sounding shaky in his ears. "This year's fund-raiser for the local orphanage might be the best event for us to attend, to allow you to meet the town elders."

"Shoreham has an orphanage?"

"We take in abandoned children from all of the counties in the south of England," he confirmed. "If you'll agree to attend with me, I'll have William purchase tickets for us."

"What sort of event is it?"

"Usually it involves a dinner and a theatrical production, held at a volunteer's home."

Next to him stood a statue of cupid carrying a shell. Water gushed from the shell, forming a fountain that sprayed a mist on the yellow roses at its base. Juliana leaned over him to better view the roses, and then she exclaimed over their beauty, saying that the water droplets on their petals looked like diamonds on yellow silk. As she did so, her breast pressed momentarily into his arm, and the image of Juliana naked except for diamonds around her throat and wrist, reclining on yellow silk that perfectly matched her eyes, formed in his mind.

He swallowed. "Do you think you'd like to attend the fund-raiser?"

She touched a rose petal with one finger, then looked at him, wide-eyed. "They're so soft."

Desperately he continued. "Would you like to attend the fund-raiser with me?"

"Of course I'll attend with you. I can think of no better way to spend my evening than on a charitable cause."

He didn't quite hear what she'd said. "If we attend, you can see whether or not you like Shoreham and its townsfolk. And if you enjoy children, you'll likely have quite a bit of fun watching the theatrical production, for the orphans are traditionally involved in the planning process and often come up with ingenious ideas."

She placed a warm hand on his arm. "It sounds lovely. I would very much enjoy attending."

"You will?"

She laughed. "Of course. Perhaps I'll even offer to help with the planning."

His eyes widened. "Your offer is very gracious, and I'm certain they would very much appreciate your help. Thank you, Juliana. I don't quite know what to say."

Leaning closer, she gazed at him, her expression very warm, and yet vulnerable somehow. "You don't have to say anything," she said, her voice barely a whisper.

Cole knew at that moment that he was going to kiss her. Any sort of restraint he'd been harboring melted at the sensual vulnerability in her eyes. Some sane portion of his mind reminded him that he barely knew Juliana Pritchard, but he dismissed the notion, a captive of his own burning need for her. He tilted his head to just the right angle, so he might gently press his lips into hers.

Her eyes narrowed a little, as though she was trying to see directly into his soul. Without warning, she lifted her hand and ran two fingers down the side of his face. His skin tingled where she'd touched him, and he lowered his mouth to hers, his blood surged through his veins, demanding that he take what he'd wanted so badly from the moment their dinner had commenced.

She closed her eyes and slipped her hands behind his neck to urge him downward; still, he continued to gaze at her as he took her mouth, noticing the porcelainlike quality of her skin and the red fullness of her lips before he pressed his own lips against them. As their lips touched, he groaned deep in his throat, for she was soft, just as a woman should be, her softness reminding him of other parts of her that would no doubt prove even more silky.

At first, their kiss was hesitant, almost like a question. Quickly, though, he felt her lips widened slightly, and he reacted instantly by pushing his tongue past them to taste her fully. She groaned against his mouth and wound her arms around his waist, giving herself fully to the kiss, and he abruptly understood that Juliana was the kind of woman who would rejoice in the pleasure love-making could give her, rather than look upon it as a dis-tasteful duty.

He tangled his tongue against hers. Her mouth, he thought, tasted the same way she smelled—fresh and sweet like wildflowers—and he found himself licking at her tongue, the roof of her mouth, her teeth, just as a bee dips and dives for nectar. She responded with another low moan, and ran her hands over the planes of his chest and shoulders, paused to knead his forearms urgently before traveling lower, to his midsection. For one startling moment, he thought she might fondle his erection, which had become so engorged with blood that the need for release twisted like a knife in his vitals. But she shied away, instead lifting her hands to wind them into his hair.

Nearly shaking, he grasped her around the waist and slid her into his lap. Then, the barest hint of a sigh escaping his lips, he lifted his mouth from hers, and then glanced around the garden to make certain they weren't being observed. When he looked back at her, she was watching him from beneath her lashes, the look both shy and sultry. A slow exhale of breath passed her lips, and she moved her hands gently, teasingly back to his chest. She hesitated for several seconds before slipping them between the buttons to touch his bare skin.

He encouraged her boldness by planting a swift kiss on the top of her head. "Don't be afraid, Juliana," he whispered.

A shaky sigh passed through her. Her side pressed against him, she rested her cheek near his neck. Her skin felt soft, like rose petals. He could feel each of her breaths as she unsteadily drew them in, and when she looked up at him, he focused on her mouth, her lips wet and red and bruised-looking from his kisses.

For several thrilling seconds he considered freeing her breasts from her bodice. He could only imagine how silken they would feel, and how their pink tips might tempt him. And yet, the image of her father kept intruding on the fantasy, and finally he gained control of his runaway impulses. Breathing heavily, he berated himself for taking such liberties with her, and told himself he couldn't possibly indulge any more without having Mr. Pritchard after him with a pistol.

When she leaned forward to kiss him again, he turned his head slightly. "No, Juliana. We can't. Not yet."

"Don't you like me, Cole?" she asked, moving her mouth blindly until her lips were against his.

"I like you very much," he said, his lips forming the words while brushing against hers. "But I won't dishonor you."

With a little groan, she pulled away from him and looked at him with golden eyes that suddenly seemed shadowed by darkness and mystery. Her pupils, he saw, were large and dark, and her body quivered in his lap; and he knew that she wanted him equally as much as he wanted her. The desire to kiss her again was very strong. Still, he needed to offer her the respect she deserved.

"I don't consider your kiss a dishonor," she whispered huskily, her fingers idly playing with the buttons on his shirt.

"Well, it could lead to dishonor." He moved her off his lap. "Didn't you learn this with your cavalry officer?"

She looked at him sharply, clearly surprised by the vehemence of his tone. Hell, he'd surprised himself with his bitterness, too. He didn't know why the mere mention of this cavalry officer had tied his gut into a knot.

"My cavalry officer kissed me once, too," she admitted, roses blooming in her cheeks. "I didn't enjoy his kiss as much as I did yours."

He cupped the sides of her face. "But he *did* stop after the first kiss, no? Don't lie to me. I don't wish to discover the truth on our wedding night."

"I've been truthful with you." She brushed a finger across his cheek, the caress sending shivers throughout his body.

"And now I'll be truthful with you," he told her. "I don't think I've ever kissed a woman on the first day I've met her. With you, though, I simply couldn't resist. Without a thought for consequence, I gave in to my impulses. I apologize for my behavior, and hope you won't think ill of me for it."

"My own behavior has been as bad as yours," she murmured, her eyes wide and clearly looking to him for reassurance. "But I, too, feel the strange, undeniable attraction between us; and while I might have found the strength to resist another man, I knew before I kissed you that you'll most likely be my husband, and that no other shall ever kiss me again. And so, justifying my actions in that way, I surrendered to weakness."

He summoned a smile, though his body pained him terribly. "We should return to the estate. You are willing to participate in the courting ceremony, no?"

"As long as you don't ask me to walk into the sea any further than ankle-deep, I'll participate."

"Good." He held out a hand.

She allowed him to clasp her hand within his own, and they began walking back to the manor.

"How long will the ceremony last?" she asked.

"It will be over very quickly," he reassured her, silently hoping that the seawater didn't end their budding relationship.

Six

JULIANA HELD TIGHT TO COLE'S HAND AS THEY walked across the lawn toward Shoreham Park Manor. She felt dizzy—her head was swimming with what had just happened between them. She'd intended to walk a careful line between innocence and seduction, one designed to tempt and intrigue him, while not giving him any reason to question her identity as the vulnerable and naive younger sister of Lila Whitham. And yet, the moment their lips had touched, she'd felt a sizzle between them that had shocked her, and she'd lost all of her fine resolutions and forgotten all of her schemes in an unexpected storm of need and desire.

She swallowed and reminded herself that she could want him . . . that wanting him was good, in fact, considering the nature of her task. She could even like him—and she did. He was clearly a good and honorable man who was loyal to his family and would no doubt make a fine husband. But she couldn't allow it to progress any further than that. If she fell in love, she might be tempted to compromise her mission, and reveal the truth to him rather than betray the man she loved. Such a course would put her people's future in jeopardy, consigning them all to an eternity in the sea.

Squaring her shoulders, she began to breathe deeply, but in an unobtrusive fashion so Cole wouldn't notice. She also started to focus on her senses—to recognize what she was smelling, feeling, tasting, hearing, and seeing—so she might close off each of those senses when the time came. In order to delay the transformation from taking control of her, she had to be supremely aware of every function her body was performing, and focused enough to keep those functions from changing as the gypsy witch's curse dictated.

They walked up the front steps into Shoreham Park Manor, through the main hall, and into the salon where Cole's uncle Gillie, his aunt Pesha, and her own "father" awaited her. Cole released her with a smile, and they all began to chatter—all but Juliana, that was.

After a short time, Mr. Wood sidled up to Juliana and searched her face. In a soft voice that no one could overhear, he said, "Is everything going according to plan?"

She answered in an equally low voice. "Yes."

"Are you ready for the courting ceremony?"

She nodded.

"Good, because the others are beginning to notice your detachment."

His statement jolted her out of the peaceful state she'd worked herself into, and for the first time she realized Gillie, Pesha, and Cole were all sending curious and worried glances her way.

"Let's begin the ceremony now," she said, breathing

deeply, trying to remove them from her awareness without appearing too withdrawn.

Mr. Wood needed no more encouragement. He placed an arm around Juliana's shoulders and spoke to the room in general. "I understand there is a courting ceremony we're to participate in. Perhaps we ought to get the ceremony underway, so we might retire for the night. The day has been a long one, and I fear my daughter is growing tired."

"Oh, of course, you must be exhausted, dear," Pesha exclaimed as she tottered across the room to Juliana's side. "Why didn't I realize it sooner?"

Juliana summoned a smile. "Regardless, I am looking forward to the courtship ceremony. Cole has explained it to me, and it sounds like a delightful tradition."

The elderly woman turned to survey her two younger relatives. "Gillie, retrieve the ink. Cole, do you have a piece of ribbon?"

While Gillie ran to do Pesha's bidding, Cole withdrew a scarlet ribbon from his pocket.

"Very well, then," Pesha said, taking the ribbon from Cole. "Cole, would you please escort Miss Pritchard and her father down to the beach? Gillie and I will join you shortly."

Cole nodded and offered an arm to Juliana. Mr. Wood took Juliana's other arm and, escorted on both sides, they left the manor and climbed into a phaeton waiting for them near the front door. As they set out, Juliana talked only enough to allay Cole's suspicions, preferring to concentrate on the mental preparations she needed to survive the ordeal. Thankfully Mr. Wood kept the conversation on desultory topics that didn't require a good deal of thinking, and in this manner, they drove down a carriage path that clearly hadn't enjoyed much traffic and reached the beach a few minutes later.

Pesha and Gillie joined them shortly thereafter in a smaller gig of their own. With Cole's assistance, the elderly pair climbed down from their perches and they all walked to the edge of the sea. Careful to keep her slippers from touching the water, Juliana glanced up and down the coastline and saw nothing other than sand, rocks, and waves. When she looked to the top of the cliffs, however, she could see the windmill's blades turning slowly as they gathered up the air and converted it to power.

"Cole, take Miss Pritchard's hand," Pesha urged, and Cole obeyed, clasping Juliana's palm in a warm, firm grip that completely disrupted her concentration.

Juliana fought for control of her wayward senses. Her stomach was roiling with tension and anxiety. This was the moment she'd been dreading, the one that the sea people's future hinged upon. She had to outwit the gypsy's curse, and forestall the transformation, but she couldn't do so without her mind's total commitment to the task, for she'd discovered some time ago that if the mind decided something, and the mind was strong enough, the body would follow along.

The wind was whipping about her, pulling tendrils of hair from her chignon and snapping them against her cheeks. Her breathing very slow now, she dismissed the low bluster of the wind and the tiny stings on her face. Rather, she focused on Cole, seeing him but not really paying any attention to him.

Pesha handed Gillie the scarlet ribbon. Shoving the ribbon into his pocket, Gillie took Cole's and Juliana's hands in his own and led them to the place where the water met the sand. Juliana allowed not the slightest amount of panic to invade her mind as the first eddies of water touched her slippers. Her breathing didn't even increase slightly as the seawater soaked through her slippers to settle against her feet.

"Welcome, both of you, to the courting ceremony," Gillie said, his gaze fixed unwaveringly upon her.

Juliana's feet began to itch. Ruthlessly she ignored it, just as she ignored the strange restlessness building deep in her gut, one that would become worse the longer she defied the gypsy's curse. In her mind, she saw her heart beating, her lungs filling with air, and blood rushing through her veins. She forced their patterns to remain calm and unchanged.

Gillie transferred his attention to Cole. "Here, in the presence of the sea, which has given us life and made our fortunes, you begin your journey to discover if love can blossom between you and Miss Pritchard."

Cole nodded solemnly.

"And here, in the presence of those who will become your new family, you begin the same journey," Gillie murmured to Juliana.

Juliana nodded, aware that Gillie was studying her closely. She knew the reason behind his intense scrutiny—he was waiting to see how the seawater would affect her—but didn't allow the knowledge to bother her. She couldn't afford to break her concentration.

Gillie urged them further into the water. She felt water slosh over the tops of her slippers, through her stockings, and soak into her calves. The itching in her feet intensified and spread upward to her knees, while her toes grew numb. Inside her, the restlessness built; she could only liken the sensation to the way one might feel after sitting in a chair for a week without moving. She could imagine that in such a case, the need to stand, to run, to shout would eventually became more vital than the will to survive. Such was also the way with the gypsy's curse. Ultimately she would die if she continued to refuse her body's desire to become of the sea people. God willing, the ceremony wouldn't last that long.

Gillie released Cole's hand, and then released Juliana's hand. "To help you both on your journey, we will create a knot, to tie your hearts together."

The older man pulled the ribbon from his pocket and spread it out on his palm. He then solemnly accepted a quill from Pesha, and offered it to Cole. "Write your name on the ribbon, please."

Cole grasped the quill and scrawled his name onto the ribbon. Once he'd finished, he handed the quill to Juliana.

Her eyes unfocused, Juliana took the quill from him and stared blindly toward the scrap. The itching had reached her waist now, and restlessness was gathering like a scream in the back of her throat. She wasn't going to last much longer. Panic was knocking at the door in her mind, and pretty soon, that door would swing open.

"Now it's your turn, Miss Pritchard," Gillie murmured. "Inscribe your name on the ribbon."

Seawater sloshed against her thighs. Each grain of salt felt like a tiny creature trying to burrow into her skin. She stiffened.

"The tide is coming in," Mr. Wood remarked. "Shouldn't we move toward the shoreline? One stray current and my daughter could be pulled out into the waves."

"We're almost through, Mr. Pritchard," Gillie said. "Juliana, will you please inscribe your name?"

Her throat dry and her hand shaking, Juliana made a mark on the ribbon.

Gillie squinted at her handwriting. "Perhaps you should try again, Miss Pritchard. This is somewhat difficult to read."

Mr. Wood tried again. "My daughter and I were once in a boat accident. She and I have many bad memories regarding the accident. I do believe we are upsetting her by forcing her to stand in the waves—"

"Get on with it," Cole urged. "We need not keep Miss Pritchard in this cold water forever."

Eyebrow lifted, Gillie examined Cole for several seconds before continuing with the ceremony. "Very well, then. Now I will tie the ribbon around your wrists, linking you together for all of eternity."

Juliana grasped Cole's right hand with her own. She said nothing, and didn't even smile. She couldn't. She'd never felt such intense agony before. She could no longer control her breathing. Her heart was racing in her chest. Tears began to run down her cheeks. She was going to swoon.

Pesha's eyes welled up, too. Clearly the older woman thought the ceremony had touched Juliana's heart.

"Where the sun goes up, shall my love be by me. Where the sun goes down, there by her I'll be," Gillie sang, his expression softer, more trusting as he wrapped the ribbon around their wrists.

Juliana swayed slightly on her feet.

Mr. Wood grabbed her arm to steady her.

The moment Gillie finished tying the ribbon, Cole moved behind her and supported her with his body. "I know you're frightened," he whispered softly, as he led her out of the ocean. "It's over."

Gillie and Aunt Pesha smiled approvingly and let them go without interfering. Mr. Wood offered Juliana a satisfied nod. Juliana knew she'd won, that she'd forever laid to rest their fears that she was one of the sea people, and that one of the most difficult aspects of her mission was completed. The notion did little to ease the agony she was still feeling.

Cole untied the ribbon as soon as they reached the sand. She clutched his arm and leaned heavily upon him. "I'm sorry, Cole. I don't mean to act childishly, but the memory of that day is so strong in my mind—"

"Shh. Don't apologize." He handed her up into the smaller of the two gigs parked on the carriage path. "You've had a long and difficult day. I'll bring you home."

New tears formed in her eyes at his kindness, even as the itching and restlessness receded to a tolerable point. She uttered a heartfelt sigh as they drove back up the carriage path and to the front entrance at Shoreham Park Manor. After they stepped down and Cole handed the gig over to William, he placed an arm around her waist and half-carried her up to her bedchamber.

She felt so wonderful with his arms close around her that she didn't want him to release her or to leave. Still, she knew he'd do both; propriety had left him no other choice. And so, he gently pulled his arm from her waist and offered her a slight bow. "Good night, Juliana."

Summoning a smile, she wiped at her cheeks to remove the last trace of tears. "Thank you, Cole. For everything."

A spark flickered in his eyes. "I assure you, it's my pleasure."

She grew warm inside. "Until tomorrow."

Before he could respond, she slipped around the edge of her door and closed it, leaving him standing outside. Then, her heart pounding and her nerves afire from the day's stresses, she pressed her back against the door and crossed her arms over her breasts. A curious mixture of emotion swept through her—jubilation, sadness, satisfaction, anticipation—and she knew that she'd found something today, and lost something as well. She'd found a man who could arouse her soul in a way she'd never expected, and she'd lost her belief in her own invincible strength, because her very attraction to him had weakened her and made her question her own goals.

Her fingers fluttered to her lips. They still felt bruised from his kisses.

This, she thought, might possibly prove one of the most enjoyable assignments she'd ever known.

COLE SHUFFLED THROUGH THE PAPERS ON HIS desk. Bills of sale, receipts from local craftsmen, monies paid out to the household staff—they all needed to be recorded in the accounting books. He hadn't been able to sleep earlier, so he'd come down here to the study, to take care of this tedious task that he usually put off because he detested it so much. He should have realized that thoughts of his prospective bride wouldn't allow him to concentrate on income and expenses any more than they'd allowed him to sleep.

A glance at the clock on his desk confirmed that the time had slipped past midnight.

Sighing, he shuffled the papers around some more, and then stood, stretching. If he couldn't sleep, and couldn't work on the books, what was left? The glitter of moonlight on the carpet, and the memory of how warm and inviting the sea had felt earlier during the courting ceremony, reminded him that he hadn't gone diving in a long time, his hours spent mostly in his laboratory trying to perfect his underwater breathing apparatus. The ocean no doubt looked beautiful tonight with a full moon in the sky, why not take a swim? At least it would tire him out, and it might even make sleep possible.

Thus decided, he left his study and stopped long enough in his bedchamber to grab a blanket, and then made his way through the house to the front lawn. The walk down the carriage path to the shoreline took him longer than it had earlier when he drove in the gig. He didn't care—he enjoyed the night smells and sounds, and the pale glitter of moonlight that turned everything to silver. The ocean roared dully as the breeze swept through the sea thrift that grew on either side of the path, blowing past him with a clean, haylike scent and depositing a salty tang on his lips and skin, and he knew a sudden sorrow that he'd allowed so many weeks to pass without taking advantage of the peace and purity that the sea offered him. His laboratory was hot and stuffy, and he began to think that perhaps he'd become stuffy, too, so involved had he become in his determination to create an underwater breathing apparatus that worked.

His mood becoming thoughtful, he came to the end of the carriage path and walked onto the sand. Silently he acknowledged that, barring any major complications, he would most likely marry her if she would have him. She may not possess all of the criteria he deemed necessary, but he felt more alive in her company than he had while with any of his previous potential brides, and he supposed that had to count for something.

Once he'd drawn close enough to the edge of the water, he took off his clothes and placed them atop a boulder, so they wouldn't get wet. Then he waded into the sea, enjoying the way the water felt as it washed over his bare skin. It now felt cold to him, enough to raise goose bumps on his arms and legs, but also silky and invigorating. Taking a deep breath, he glanced up at the sky. Wispy, nearly transparent clouds drifted across the heavens, creating a hazy corona around the moon and the brightest stars. He found the effect quite beautiful.

Quietly, he surfed over the tops of the waves until he was about chest-deep in water. He stopped there, and treaded the surface, his focus on the windmill. It sat on the top of the cliffs, its blades turning slowly, relentlessly. A warm light glowed from within, and Cole could see a shadow moving around inside.

William, he thought. *Cleaning up after the day's work.*

The footman was just about the only one Cole tolerated in his laboratory. William had brains and a deft touch, and had proven many times over his ability to organize and straighten up a mess. An irreverent thought suddenly struck Cole, and he smiled. Too bad William wasn't a woman, or he might have married the fellow.

He turned his back on the laboratory and dove through a wave that threatened to break on him, relishing the way the foaming whitecap swept across his body before continuing its journey on to shore. For several minutes he continued to challenge more waves, and exercised every one of his muscles. Once he felt pleasantly spent, he floated on his back, allowing the moonlight to shine on his face and paint the water on the surface of the sea a few shades lighter. It was in this comfortable and peaceful position that he heard a muted splash.

Immediately he lifted his head up. The splash had been a large one, suggesting a big fish or dolphin, although dolphins usually didn't come this close to shore around here. He began to tread water again, his gaze sweeping across the surface of the ocean. All at once, he saw a furrow in the water, as though something sizeable was swimming just beneath the waves. It had to be a dolphin, he mused, and continued to tread water, though he made his movements small so he wouldn't frighten it away. Delight filled him at the thought of observing this rare visitor to the Shoreham coastline.

A roiling wave began to build several feet beyond him and out to sea; as it drew closer to him, it grew in height and he knew he'd have to dive through it or suffer a pounding on the head. Just as the wave reached him it crested, and he jumped off the seafloor and through the wall of water, looking toward the dolphin as he did so. It, too, chose to jump the wave, and what it revealed to him as it took flight made his heart pound hard in his chest.

It wasn't a dolphin at all.

It was a woman.

The night was too dark for him to make out any distinguishing features on her face; he could only see long wet hair of an indeterminate color that hung down over her shoulders and curled around her breasts, which glowed full and pale in the moonlight. He saw the small, dark peaks of her nipples just as the wave swallowed him up and he came out the other side.

His mind raced, even while warmth flooded his gut at the unexpected and stimulating sight. Could one of the women from Shoreham have come down to the sea for a nighttime swim? Even as the notion occurred to him, he dismissed it. Females simply didn't swim. They generally weren't strong enough to negotiate the waves while dressed in the bathing attire that propriety demanded; and if they entered the waters dressed in any other way, they not only endangered themselves but risked utter ruin.

Another thought occurred to him, and his gut grew cold. Could he have run across one of the sea people?

He sunk down into the water to his chin, so only his head was showing. Then, eyes narrowed, he scanned the surface of the water for the female swimmer. Again, he saw the furrow of her passage some fifty feet away, and he knew that she was staying underwater far longer than a normal person could manage. He remained very still, and watched as she swam toward a boulder. As soon as she drew close to the boulder, she propelled herself out of the water, flinging her hair back as she did so and sending up a spray of salt water.

Cole's mouth went dry. He stared at the perfect form of her breasts, at the hard little peaks of her nipples, and the wild hair that flowed around her face and shoulders, just like the waves from which she'd come. His gaze traveled lower, and he saw that just below her navel, her skin became darker, grayer, reminding him of a dolphin's sleek hide.

Realization flooded him.

He'd finally found one of the sea people.

He trembled.

And yet, his trembling had little to do with the cold. Desire for her burned like fire through his veins, giving him a rock-hard erection. He remembered his uncle's admonition that a sea maiden was so beautiful that a man could think of nothing but possessing her, and now he knew it to be true. She looked perfect yet flawed, untouchable yet so terribly vulnerable, a mythical creature he longed to possess but could never capture. He was helpless in the face of her enchantment.

Though part of him understood that he was acting foolishly, and dangerously even, he could only think of cupping her breasts in his palms and licking the salt from her lips and nipples. Ever so quietly, he began to swim in her direction. He wondered if perhaps he were dreaming.

Painted silver with moonlight, she grabbed her long hair with both hands and lifted it up to the nape of her neck. She stretched, elongating her body, the movement so sensual that Cole sucked in a breath.

She froze for one split second, and then released her hair, spinning in his direction at the same time.

He froze, too, and treaded water.

Suddenly, she dove under the waves. He saw the ocean roiling in a furrow that was coming toward him. His heart began to beat madly in his chest. He took quick, gasping breaths and realized that she *did* frighten him. Quickly he swam away, but she was faster, and he saw the tip of her tail crest the water as she drew abreast of him, seemingly swimming with him for several seconds before diving down into the water to disappear for good.

As soon as she had gone, his longing for her overcame his fear, and he dove under the water, too, but could detect no trace of her. For several minutes he surfed the waves, hoping she might come back, but eventually he became aware of a bone-deep chill and knew he had to go back to shore.

His heart still beating hard, he made it back to the beach and grabbed his clothes. Quickly he put them on while scanning the ocean, looking for a telltale furrow that would suggest she'd come back. The ocean, however, remained as still as glass, other than the waves which rolled in, and he knew that his once-in-a-lifetime encounter with her had ended without him satisfying the desires she'd magically aroused in him. Feeling like he'd squandered a precious opportunity, yet knowing he'd more likely escaped a terrible fate, he trudged back up the carriage path and into Shoreham Park Manor.

The way to his bedchamber led past Juliana's and, guided by an instinct he didn't understand, he stopped once he reached her door. Frowning, he touched the doorknob, then let go.

His fingers came away wet.

He grew very still.

Abruptly his gut felt hollow.

He tried to fathom what it meant.

She couldn't be one of the sea people. Not Juliana. She wouldn't have managed the courting ceremony otherwise. And yet, he had to know. His grip firm, he clasped the doorknob and turned it.

The door swung inward on her bedchamber.

Cole took a step inside, his gaze riveted on the four-poster bed near the window. Moonlight flooded the bed, revealing Juliana dressed in a thin cotton shift and tangled in a lace coverlet. With her eyes closed and her hair in a neat braid, she looked as blameless as a newborn babe.

He took another step into the room, determined to touch her hair to see if it felt wet. He just couldn't tell from looking at her whether or not she was faking; and yet, when she uttered a muted sigh and turned over, he hesitated. She certainly appeared to be sleeping—she took deep and regular breaths, and she'd flung her arms outward in a completely unselfconscious position. What if she really was asleep, and he woke her? How would he explain his presence in her bedchamber?

Cole shook his head. She wasn't one of the sea people. How could she be?

His unusual experience this evening, and the rush of conflicting emotions it had brought him, had made him overly suspicious. Softening inside at the sight of her innocence, he backed out of her bedchamber and closed the door. Moisture could have made the knob wet, he told himself. Humidity lay heavily in the night air. Or she could have had a bath earlier.

Cole hesitated near the closed door. Now what was he supposed to do? In no way would a decent sleep come to him now. Sighing, he headed back down to his study, resigned to a night of brooding over the sensual creature he'd encountered in the waves.

A WEEK HAD PASSED SINCE GEORGE HAD ARRIVED at Buckland House. Ever so carefully, he'd spent those days pointing out incompatibilities between himself and Lila Whitham. She'd even added to the list with a few of her own. And yet, she still hadn't asked him to leave, and he didn't know why. The fact that he was *glad* she hadn't sent him packing left him even more confused.

Now, as he sat with her in the conservatory attached to her father's home at Buckland House, he admitted to himself that he was enjoying his conversations with her far more than he should. And yet, he couldn't seem to stop himself from taking such inordinate pleasure in her company, so he simply surrendered to the moment and told himself that he would remain safe as long as he allowed himself to feel nothing more than admiration for her.

A table set with a silver tea service stood in front of them. Fading sunlight penetrated the windows held in place by swirls of wrought iron painted white and created patterns of light upon the potted palms and miniature orange trees that grew with lush abandon around them, while a delicate blossom fragrance perfumed the air.

George, however, had little interest in the beauty around him. His attention remained locked on the beauty sitting next to him. They were supposed to be taking tea, but as usual, had gotten involved in a spirited conversation—this time regarding living conditions in the poorest sections of London, and how they might be improved given the proper legislature.

"My late husband held a seat in the House of Commons," she told him. Her eyes, which had been bright with ideas, suddenly glistened with moisture. "He had always been so interested in improving the lot of those less fortunate than us. He managed so much good in his lifetime. I often think about him. Indeed, I wish I were more like him."

George placed his hand gently over hers. He tried to think up something clumsy to say, so he might secure her disgust, but he just couldn't bring himself to hurt her. Not this time. Not now. "You are beautiful, Lila, on both the inside and the outside. I wish I were more like *you*."

Her expression softened. She turned her hand over so that their palms were touching, and entwined her fingers through his. When she spoke, her voice was very gentle.

"We haven't really talked yet about why you've come to Buckland House."

He nodded. "I know."

"You're here to see if marriage is a possibility between us."

"I am." Tightening his fingers around hers, he forced himself to say, "We seem to have our share of dissimilarities, no?"

A quick smile curved her lips. "We do. Personally, I find differences interesting."

"I do, too." The words were out of his mouth before he could stop them.

"But I have to be fair to you, Cole," she murmured, her smile fading. "My husband was quite a bit older than me, but I loved him well. When I lost him, I never thought I'd be the same. And when I lost my little Sarah . . . it was like someone had cut my heart out of my chest. I'll never stop grieving for her, and when she died, I promised myself that I would never love again. *Never*."

George nodded. He heard the suffering in her voice, and his stomach tightened. He wanted to enfold her in his arms. Instead, he simply said, "I understand."

"I don't think you *do* understand, Cole. I am telling you that I will never love you, regardless of whether or not we marry."

He stared into her eyes, which appeared as green and mysterious as a primordial forest, and blurted, "I want to make you happy."

Immediately he cursed himself for such a foolish and unproductive sentiment. What the hell had gotten into him?

"I don't want happiness. I'm no longer capable of love," she said softly. "Indeed, I plan to give myself to

God. There is a convent not too far from here, and I think I could live comfortably with other like-minded women. I'm entertaining you now only because I promised my father to do so, in exchange for *his* promise that if we didn't suit, I would go into the convent."

"Why would you give yourself to a God who has taken those you love best away from you?"

Her eyes darkened. "I won't question His way."

"The priesthood is a calling," George murmured. "One shouldn't really question or interfere with a man's decision to become a priest; and I believe a woman's desire to devote herself to God is the same. . . ." He trailed off, the encouragement he'd prepared to give her toward becoming a nun getting stuck in his throat.

"And your point is?"

Rather than tell her he thought she'd be wasting her life when she was clearly made for light and love and happiness, he gazed at her for a long time. The memory of their most recent walk through the meadow, the one where she'd laughed at something he'd said and intoxicated him thoroughly, played through his mind. A sudden impulse overwhelming him, he stood up and kneeled at her side. He cupped her face with both of his hands and kissed her, slowly, opening her lips and dipping his tongue inside her mouth to taste her.

Lila pushed away from him, gently, her hands on his shoulders. "What are you doing, Cole?" she breathed, her eyes very wide.

He didn't reply. Rather, he slid his hands downward, over her shoulder blades and along her arms, and then around her waist. He gathered her close to him and kissed her again, and she struggled in his embrace, but he only held her tighter. Her resistance weakened, and her mouth began to respond to his, her lips opening and her own tongue touching his own, carefully, shyly. His heart pounded with triumph and desire as she confirmed his suspicions that while she said she'd never love again, deep inside she yearned to laugh, and to love.

Suddenly, she pushed him hard, sending him off balance so that he fell backward, against the floor. "What in heaven are you trying to do? I'm going to a convent."

Fighting a smile, he regained his feet and returned to his chair by the tea service. "My apologies if I've abused your feelings, Lila, but I simply wanted to see how set you are in your plans to devote yourself to God."

"I am *very* devoted," she told him, a spark lighting her eyes. "You go too far, sir."

"I think I haven't gone far enough," he murmured, smoldering inside. For the first time, he realized he'd truly annoyed her. He wondered if a few more stolen kisses might be just the way to persuade her to send "Cole Strangford" on his way. If he continually took liberties with her, considering her determination to join a convent, wouldn't she eventually become disgusted with him?

He would just have to try, and see.

Seven

JULIANA SHIFTED ON HER SEAT IN THE GIG THAT William was driving for her, and glanced idly at the waves that were passing by at a fast clip on the left. They were heading for tea with the elder ladies of Shoreham who sat on the board of the Shoreham Orphanage. At the tea, Juliana planned to offer her assistance in preparing for the dinner and theatrical production, which was evidently a staple of the annual event.

Mrs. Morris had sent the invitation to tea a week or so ago, and Juliana had accepted with alacrity, seeing the tea as a way to not only ingratiate herself with the town's leading women, but also to display a charitable touch that Cole could not help but appreciate in a wife. Earlier this afternoon, she'd dressed her very best in order to make the best possible impression upon them. Her gown, a fine muslin decorated with rosebuds, fell in soft waves from her breasts, and a chip bonnet covered her hair, both of them finely tailored and giving her a measure of confidence.

She clasped her gloved hands around her reticule, her mind turning from the upcoming meeting to the pattern her life had settled into over the last couple of weeks.

She woke, ate porridge and coffee, explored the estate, had tea and scones, dressed for dinner, ate beef or chicken, and then retired to the salon. Bed followed shortly thereafter to end a leisurely day.

Normally she didn't mind predictability or patterns, at least for a time—they allowed the mind and body to rejuvenate. And yet, here at Shoreham Park Manor she took exception to each day's predictability, because it didn't include Cole. Just as he'd warned her, he'd kept his nose in his windmill laboratory during the day, and while he later joined her for dinner, they had no opportunity for intimacy the way they'd enjoyed on their first night.

Overall, she found it terribly frustrating.

Part of the problem, she admitted, was of her own making. When he'd gone into his laboratory the morning after she'd arrived, and discovered that his underwater breathing apparatus no longer functioned, he'd taken it into his head that someone had sabotaged it and then spent many hours trying to fix it. She, of course, *had* sabotaged the apparatus, in an effort to slow his effort to explore the sea near the Scilly Isles, but she hadn't counted on him ignoring her completely in his attempt to fix it.

Now she was left with the onerous task of regaining his attention. Perhaps if she joined him for a swim in the ocean he might take notice of her. He'd certainly noticed that first night.

She grimaced and put the idea right out of her head.

Good heavens, she'd been so lucky that he hadn't managed to trap her and reveal her identity as one of the sea people. Since then she'd been much more careful during her evening forays to the sea, making certain that she remained quite alone and undetected, even if part of her did wish for Cole as company. Her cheeks still grew warm at the thought of him seeing her naked, and she became positively hot over the eyeful she'd received when passing him beneath the waves. He'd been completely nude, too—and quite aroused.

Today, she decided impulsively, she would invite Cole to join her on a long exploration, and see if she couldn't urge their relationship a few more paces down the road to marriage.

Moments later, William pulled the gig up in front of a brick town house and stepped down from the driver's box, scattering her thoughts. She eyed the carvings on the building and its great oaken door, and saw wealth. The impression did little to shake her confidence, because wealth had little to do with the ability to detect lies—and she did plan on feeding these poor women a whole plateful of lies.

And yet, while her confidence remained strong, she still felt slightly disgusted with the position this assignment had put her in, as the supreme lie-teller. She didn't much enjoy lying, and far too often found herself in the position of having to do so. She supposed she could ultimately lay the blame at Cole's ancestor's door, for cursing her to become a creature that no one could understand and many would hunt.

William lifted the knocker and banged on the oaken door for her. Moments later, the door swung inward and a man dressed in a navy blue uniform motioned her inside. Leaving William outside to make his way around to the servant's entrance, she allowed the servant to escort her into the hallway.

"Good day, miss," he said in a sonorous voice, after introducing himself as Childers, the butler. "You must be Miss Pritchard. Mrs. Morris has been expecting you."

She nodded. "Indeed, I am Miss Pritchard."

"Allow me to show you into the drawing room. Mrs. Morris will be with you in a moment."

"Very well." A few butterflies flitting about her stomach despite her intention to remain cool and confident, she preceded the butler into the drawing room and immediately found herself dazzled by gold. Childers disappeared to find his mistress, and she took a moment to gawk. The windows, she saw, were swathed in royal blue draperies fringed in gold, and gold damask covered the couch and settee. A cabinet sporting inlaid gilt and a half-moon table of rosewood stood against one wall, while a white marble fireplace in the classical style dominated another. Gilt mirrors above the fireplace and sofa contributed to the general lightness of the room.

Moments later, Mrs. Morris entered, followed by two other well-dressed women.

"Hello, Miss Pritchard, I am Mrs. Morris," the first woman announced, her gray hair piled so high on her head it nearly resembled a pompadour. She indicated the other two women with a no-nonsense hand gesture and continued, "This is Mrs. Duquet and Mrs. Hobbs."

Both women murmured greetings. Then Mrs. Duquet, who possessed the unmistakable panache of someone with French ancestry, examined her shamelessly, while Mrs. Hobbs, her shoulders curving inward, regarded her without much enthusiasm.

"Thank you very much, ladies, for inviting me to tea," Juliana said, curtseying. "I've seen some of your lovely town since I've arrived, and I'm looking forward to hearing the history behind it."

"And we're looking forward to knowing you better as well." Mrs. Morris gave her a kindly smile. "We've been wanting to meet the lady who has captured Mr. Strangford's heart."

Juliana blushed.

"Why don't we sit down," Mrs. Morris suggested, and they all complied, Juliana selecting a straight-backed chair upholstered in blue velvet. Mrs. Morris sat on a settee, and Mrs. Hobbs positioned herself on the couch, her arms crossed over her breasts. Mrs. Duquet, for her part, sprawled on a loveseat, her very casual—almost scandalously casual—position indicative of a woman who routinely got her way, and who had grown used to acting poorly whenever she pleased, while expecting that bad behavior to be forgiven because of her beauty. Juliana disliked her instantly.

Moments later, a maidservant dressed in a gray uniform and frilly white apron entered with a silver tea service. The maid poured each woman a cup of tea and took the lid off of pots of cream and jam, and a plate of scones. Following Mrs. Morris's cue, Juliana helped herself to a scone and spread the confection with cream and jam. She was unable to do more than nibble on it, though. Her stomach was tied into knots with worry over making the proper impression.

"So, Miss Pritchard, tell us about yourself," Mrs. Duquet said with a challenging glint in her eye. "What is your home like? And how long have you known Mr. Strangford?"

Mrs. Hobbs sucked in a breath, perhaps at the directness of Mrs. Duquet's last question. Juliana sensed that it was indeed the last question that interested Mrs. Duquet the most. She shrugged and answered the first question, spending a few minutes explaining the Pritchard family history. While she prattled on, the other women sipped their tea, their eyes revealing nothing.

After she'd finished, Mrs. Duquet raised an eyebrow. "How long have you known Cole Strangford?"

"I knew of Mr. Strangford through a mutual acquaintance, but we've met only recently," Juliana admitted.

"I heard, gel, that you were his fiancée," Mrs. Morris said.

Juliana discerned a mixture of generosity and interest in the woman, and relaxed a little. "I'm not his fiancée. My father and I are simply visiting with him."

Mrs. Morris nodded, her expression bland. "I see."

Juliana eyed her closely. Clearly a lot of gossip had been circulating about her visit with Cole, and she didn't doubt that the facts had been greatly embroidered to provide more entertainment value. Such was often the case with gossip. Heaven only knew what these women were thinking in regards to her lengthy visit with Cole.

Juliana knew she should try to befriend these women. If the local dragon ladies accepted her, Cole would no doubt look more kindly upon her as a wife. At the very least, a friendship with them couldn't hurt her. But before she could make allies of them, she had to dispel the rumors surrounding her visit with Cole. "Might I trust you ladies with a confidence?"

Mrs. Morris and Mrs. Hobbs nodded their heads *yes*, while Mrs. Duquet simply stared at her.

Juliana lowered her voice and leaned closer to the threesome. "Mr. Strangford and I *are* considering becoming engaged."

Mrs. Morris's brows drew together. "How is that possible? You said yourself that you've only just met Mr. Strangford."

Juliana nodded. "'Tis true that Mr. Strangford and I are newly acquainted. But you see, the Romany have marriage customs which are somewhat different from traditions you may be more familiar with. Unlike conventional marriages of convenience, where the bride and groom are often well acquainted before marrying, it isn't unusual for a Romany bride to meet her groom mere weeks before the marriage. Now that isn't to say that the Romany eschew love matches—there are plenty of those—but in cases where the bride's and groom's interests are being served without the complications of love, they often get right down to business."

"I can appreciate that notion," Mrs. Morris observed, real warmth entering her voice. "We need *that* kind of attitude for the orphanage fund-raiser."

"The orphanage fund-raiser?" Juliana asked, her head tilted with interest. "I've heard a lot about it from Mr. Strangford. We both plan on attending."

"Before you can attend, we must find a volunteer who will lend us his house," Mrs. Hobbs informed her mournfully. "This year we're having a hard time of it. The lady who'd originally volunteered to lend us her home has decided to extend her stay upon the Continent, and no one else has agreed to volunteer in her place."

"How terrible," Juliana pronounced.

"It is possible that we'll have to cancel the fund-raiser this year," Mrs. Morris confirmed.

Juliana chewed her lower lip. A plan was occurring to her. "I understand from Cole that you're all on the board of directors for the orphanage."

Mrs. Morris nodded. "We are."

"It was my intention during my visit with you today, to offer my assistance in planning and running the fund-raiser," Juliana said. "But now, it seems that you may not need any help at all, unless you can find a place to hold the fund-raiser."

"We're trying, gel, we're trying," Mrs. Morris assured her doggedly.

"Perhaps I can convince Mr. Strangford to have the fund-raiser at his home." Juliana held her breath and waited for their reactions.

Mrs. Duquet was the first to speak up. "I sincerely doubt Mr. Strangford will agree to such a plan. I've asked him myself many times to volunteer, and he routinely told me no, with a variety of excuses. I hardly expect *you* will fair any better."

Juliana eyed the other woman closely. Clearly Mrs. Duquet disliked her, and she disliked Mrs. Duquet. Sometimes relationships just worked out that way between people—they simply didn't mix. And yet, she'd begun to think Mrs. Duquet's dislike of her ran at a personal level.

Was it possible that Mrs. Duquet was jealous of her?

The more Juliana thought about it, the more her guess appeared right. She could only wonder about the claim Mrs. Duquet thought she had on Cole. What sort of intimacy had existed between them? Did it still exist? Her gut began to burn at the thought. "I can only try, Mrs. Duquet."

Mrs. Duquet snorted.

"Now, Charlotte, don't be so quick to squash Miss Pritchard's plan," Mrs. Morris chided. "We are in no position to ignore any possibility, and if Miss Pritchard thinks she has a chance to convince Mr. Strangford, we should bless her for trying."

Mrs. Duquet's smile was bitter. "All right, Elizabeth, we'll allow Miss Pritchard to try. I think we should also accept her offer of assistance. If Mr. Strangford agrees to hold the fund-raiser at his house, who better to help organize the event for us than Miss Pritchard? Indeed, we should spend the remainder of the hour discussing our expectations with Miss Pritchard, so she understands what she's getting herself into. What do you say, Miss Pritchard? Can you stay a bit longer?"

"Of course," Juliana said warily. She had a feeling Mrs. Duquet was going to make her life very difficult if she could. *Expectations?*

Mrs. Morris pulled on a bell cord. "Let's get right down to it, then. I'll order some more tea."

Over the next hour, Mrs. Duquet explained to her in superior tones that any fund-raiser, in order to raise money, had to demonstrate the merit of its cause. Therefore, one of the purposes of the orphan's fund-raiser was to show how very loveable and worthy of additional funds the children were. The dinner and theatrical production, she said, was a way to showcase the orphans' meager talents while promoting their image of poor waifs who could one day grow into successful members of society if only given the chance.

Her head spinning, Juliana tried to memorize all of the requirements, though she hadn't the slightest idea how she could help to satisfy them. Mrs. Morris then called her a good gel and told her they'd check back with her soon, to see how successful she'd been in convincing Cole to host the fund-raiser. Once back in the gig, with William behind the reins and Mrs. Morris's elegant town house fading in the distance, Juliana faced the fact that her assignment to win Cole Strangford's hand in marriage and have his child had just become immeasurably more complicated.

* * *

GEORGE SAT IN AN OPEN-AIRED GIG WITH LILA behind the reins and secretly admired the very pretty picture she presented. The large, floppy hat was gone, replaced by a chip bonnet trimmed with tiny rosebuds made of satin; and her white muslin dress made her look fresh and far younger than her four-and-thirty years.

Somewhat desperately he urged himself to explore more of her personality, and find another thing she enjoyed, so that he could profess a dislike for it.

"How do you like village life?" he asked, as they drove alongside a picket fence, the horses moving at a stately pace. The previous day, she had offered to take him into town, and while he didn't particularly want to parade around Buckland Village as Cole Strangford, he couldn't think of a reasonable excuse to give her. In the end, he decided that the risk of being identified as an imposter in a sleepy little place like Buckland Village was negligible.

She glanced at him cautiously. She'd been giving him a lot of cautious looks lately, ever since he'd tried to seduce her in the conservatory. And although he'd vowed on that day to continue his campaign of seduction, he'd found himself treating her honorably since then. Lila simply had some quality that demanded respect from him.

"Oh, I'm quite content with a bucolic existence," she admitted, her voice soft and unassuming. "And I believe Buckland Village to be one of the prettiest in all of the south of England. We should arrive there shortly, and I think you'll agree with me once you've seen it for yourself."

"How do you know it's the prettiest? Have you traveled a lot?"

"Once, to Ireland, to take my sister to her finishing school. We rode by carriage to Liverpool, and then took a steamship to Ireland. The trip, in fact, was very difficult for me. I found that the constant rocking I had to endure in the long carriage ride, followed by the steamship ride, made me ill. I don't wish to repeat it." She slanted a look at him from beneath the brim of her chip bonnet, one that made his heart race. "And you, Mr. Strangford? How extensively have you traveled?"

George cast his thoughts back over Cole Strangford's history, and remembered that several years before, the gypsy had paid several visits to a university in Edinburgh, Scotland. "I often visit Scotland. Indeed, I enjoy traveling very much, and especially enjoy sea voyages. You've heard of my passion for diving?"

"No, but I suspected as much, given your passion for the sea. When you describe the sea to me, I can tell you're just as familiar with the ocean floor as you are with your own home."

George swallowed. "I suppose my gypsy blood is always encouraging me on to a new adventure."

"I, too, might be inclined to seek adventure, had I not a predisposition for carriage sickness."

He tried to mold his face into a sorrowful expression, but suspected he looked more dismayed than anything else. "'Tis a regrettable incongruity between our characters, no?"

She fixed her attention on the road ahead, and urged the horses into a faster trot. "Regrettable indeed."

The remainder of their trip passed in silence. George fought the desire to squirm in his seat, and admitted to himself that this assignment had proven—and would continue to prove—far more difficult than any he had ever undertaken before. The constant lying was bothering him, though God knew he'd had to lie before and hadn't felt bad about it. As one of the sea people, he'd learned to lie to landwalkers at a very early age. One might even say that lying was a matter of survival. So why was he so uncomfortable with the tales he spun for Lila Whitham, and with his effort to convince her to discard the idea of marriage to him?

Maybe her quiet faith in God had gotten to him, a faith that remained strong despite all that He had taken from her. Perhaps her purity and innocence, which persisted regardless of her experiences, had left him feeling like a heel. Most likely, though, her vulnerability had affected him; for every once in a while he caught a flash of deep pain in her eyes, and he knew she was thinking about the husband and child she'd lost.

"Here we are," she said, jolting him from his thoughts.

She had pulled the carriage up to the village center, a cobblestone square that possessed a well, a few benches, empty stocks, and a gaggle of matrons out for a stroll.

She offered him a smile. "Would you care for a walk, or would you rather we drive?"

"I'd prefer to walk." He stepped down from the gig and tied it to a post, before moving around to the driver's side and handing her down. "I'd like to find you a lemonade," he couldn't help from saying. "You must be parched."

"How very nice of you, Cole, to be so solicitous."

Silently he told himself to stop being so solicitous.

Once he had helped her down, he offered her an arm and proceeded to guide her along the street, past the general store and local tavern. Several times they stopped for introductions, much to his dismay, but no one seemed to recognize him or care all that much about him, and so eventually he relaxed and enjoyed the sunshine and the company of a pretty woman.

About an hour later, as he and Lila were heading back to the gig, he espied a woman walking determinedly toward them.

"Mrs. Howe," Lila murmured softly to him. "The town gossip. If we walk fast enough, we may outpace her."

George shuddered at the sight of the woman, a welldressed matron who'd scraped her hair back from her face and tied it into a severe chignon. The style accentuated her long nose, a perfect feature for a gossipmonger. He increased his stride, and Lila followed suit, but Mrs. Howe seemed determined to have her quarry and cornered them just as they reached the gig.

"Good day to you, Mrs. Whitham," Mrs. Howe said. "I see you're out for an afternoon stroll."

"Yes, we are," Lila agreed, her tone patient.

The woman transferred her attention to George in an expectant way.

Lila sighed deeply. Then, with a visible effort, she managed a smile. "Oh, how thoughtless of me to forget introductions. This is Mr. Cole Strangford, of Shoreham Park. He and his cousin are here visiting my family."

"Did you say Mr. Cole Strangford?" Mrs. Howe asked in a coy manner. "Very pleased to meet you. I hope you enjoy your visit with the Pritchards. Our dear Lila is such a gem."

"She is indeed," George agreed, having no other option.

Mrs. Howe lifted an eyebrow. "Are you related to Zelda Strangford?"

He stiffened. "Well . . . yes, I am. She's a distant cousin of mine."

"I've been expecting her for a visit. I thought she would be staying with me, but it sounds as though she's elected to stay with your family, dear," the woman said, her attention switching to Lila. "Tell her she must come see me at once."

Lila nodded. "I will."

George tightened his grip on Lila's arm. His mind was spinning. When had Mrs. Wood been in contact with the town gossip? Why had she agreed to visit Mrs. Howe? He was going to have to remind Mrs. Wood that as long as she was masquerading as Zelda, she had to keep as low a profile as possible. "Please excuse us, Mrs. Howe. Mrs. Whitham and I have been walking for some time, and I'm afraid we're both in need of some rest. We ought to leave for Buckland House immediately."

"Of course, Mr. Strangford. Please stop by soon with Lila."

"At our first opportunity," he promised, and then steered Lila toward the gig. Silently he wondered if the worst had happened—that someone who could pierce his disguise as Cole Strangford, and Mrs. Wood's disguise as Zelda Strangford—had stumbled upon their deception.

"I didn't know that my cousin had an acquaintance in Buckland Village," he managed to say with some calmness while they walked, though inside he felt drawn as tight as a coil.

Lila lifted an eyebrow. "I had no idea, either. Mrs. Howe never mentioned knowing her."

Her reply did little to cheer him. He helped her in, hopped into the driver's seat, and set off at a fast pace. As they drove back toward her home, cold gathered in his gut, and he couldn't rid himself of the feeling that their scheme had already begun to unravel right before his eyes.

Eight

COLE STRANGFORD WAS CAREFULLY TWISTING a piece of heated copper pipe, a replacement part for his breathing apparatus, when suddenly it snapped in two.

An hour's worth of work. For nothing.

"Bloody hell!"

He pushed the piece of copper aside and stared blankly at his work table. He wanted to sweep the entire apparatus onto the floor, but the knowledge that he'd be helping the swine who'd damaged his equipment stopped him.

Cole sighed deeply and turned away from his work table. He didn't feel like working on the damned thing anymore. In fact, he hadn't had much interest in any of his devices lately. His focus had turned toward discovering the identity of the intruder who had broken into his lab, and why that person had ruined his breathing apparatus. Not a soul inside Shoreham Park Manor had escaped his questioning, but much to his chagrin, he stood no closer to finding the culprit than he had two weeks ago when he'd first discovered the destruction.

Everyone he'd talked to had no knowledge of the incident, including Juliana. He also knew first hand where she'd been—in bed sleeping. He supposed she could have been faking sleep, but he didn't think so. He remembered quite clearly her deep breathing and soft dream-sighs. In any case, she just didn't have a reason for destroying his equipment, especially not if she were considering marrying him, and wanted to cultivate his good regard.

No, Juliana wasn't at the root of his troubles.

He thought it more likely that the sea maiden he'd seen had something to do with it. The fact that he'd seen such a fantastic sight on the very night that his apparatus had been sabotaged was no coincidence. Perhaps the sea people feared his device and had moved against him.

Suddenly uneasy, he took a deep breath.

"Cole, are you in there?" a sunny voice called out. His door opened and in walked Juliana, her hair shining like chestnuts in an errant ray of sunshine coming through the window. Dressed in a patched skirt and apron, and her hair tied back with a single sky-blue ribbon, she had a fresh-faced, country appeal.

Cole glanced at the sizeable muslin bundle she carried under one arm. "Are you going somewhere?"

"*We* are going somewhere." She linked her arm through his and tugged him away from his work table. "Come with me, Cole. I'm tired of sitting around in that old home of yours. I want to go for a long explore."

He looked back helplessly at his half-finished breathing device.

"You've done enough work for one day. Please come," she urged, smiling appealingly at him.

Something inside him melted. He didn't really want to work on the damned device anyway. "Where do you want to explore?"

"Oh, I don't know. Why don't we walk along the shore? The cliffs are very pretty, particularly when the sun is going down."

"But the sun isn't going down," he pointed out. "It's early in the afternoon."

"By the time we're ready to turn around, the sun *will* be setting."

He smiled. "You're planning a very long explore."

"Are you worried that I may tire you?"

"Not at all. I was more worried that you might grow tired before we're able to return, and then I'll have to carry you."

She narrowed her eyes. "Cole Strangford, I am more than capable of a lengthy walk. What do you think I'm made of? Fluff?"

His smile widened into a grin. She was a fiery one, this little gypsy from Buckland House. "I don't know what you're made of. Why don't you show me?"

Chin rising, she nodded. "I'd be more than happy to. I've brought something for us to eat, in case we become hungry."

She patted the muslin bundle she was carrying. He held his hand out to take it from her, but she misread his gesture and slipped her hand into his. As soon as he felt her warm skin against his own, he felt a rush of need, one that he quickly squelched. At the same time, he berated himself for acting like a damned greenhorn, or a virgin about to land his first woman.

"To the shore we go," he murmured and, hand in hand, they left the windmill.

William was waiting for them just outside. Cole felt a rush of disappointment as soon as he saw the footman, even though he knew how necessary William was in preserving Juliana's reputation. He consoled himself with the idea that the footman was very smart and extremely discreet, and would retreat as necessary to give them some degree of privacy.

"I asked William to come with us," Juliana murmured. "I also asked my father, but he was unavailable."

"That's too bad. I would have enjoyed your father's company." Cole nodded to the footman, who offered Cole a dignified bow in return.

The threesome started down the carriage path to the beach, Cole and Juliana leading, with William strolling some twenty feet behind them. A breeze blew softly at their backs, making Juliana's hair flutter around her face and plastering her skirt to her legs. He slanted an admiring glance her way while they talked about inconsequential matters, such as the time they could expect high tide and speculation about the darkness far away on the horizon, and whether or not it meant a storm.

He told her about Gillie's romantic meddling and his determination to see them married, and they both laughed a little about this. Indeed, he liked to hear her laugh. Some women in his acquaintance possessed a harsh, braying laugh that grated on the ears, or a high giggle that sounded forced; but Juliana had a soft, husky laugh that seemed to come up from deep within her, lighting up her face and bringing a golden sheen to her eyes, showing an inner beauty that the casual eye might miss. Over the next several minutes, he made several comments about silly things designed to amuse her, just to hear her laugh some more.

When they reached the shoreline they began walking east, past the lower sections of cliffs. Cole positioned himself next to the water, which occasionally lapped over his feet. Juliana kept clear of the sea, however, complaining that the water was so cold it numbed her toes. Amused at her display of feminine weakness, after her earlier feisty challenge to "see what she was made of," he brought the conversation around to the subject of Buckland House and her life there as a child.

"Tell me more about your childhood in Wales, Juliana," he urged. "I want to know more about you. Why did your family forsake the traditional gypsy tradition of wandering, and decide to settle down in one place?"

Her gaze on the sand before, she began to speak in halting tones. "My family once traveled about the countryside with other gypsies, in brightly painted carriages. We cooked over campfires and somehow scraped together an existence. As you must know, however, the outside world does not look kindly upon us, and petty local officials harassed us relentlessly."

"The *gaje* can be single-minded in their persecution," he agreed.

"*Gaje?*"

He tilted his head and looked at her oddly. "That's right, *gaje*. Englishmen. Anyone who isn't Romany."

She laughed nervously. "Oh, of course. *Gaje.*"

"So, you were persecuted," he said, helping her pick up the thread of their conversation again. He thought it somewhat strange that she wouldn't recognize this most basic of Romany words. "Is that why your family settled down?"

"Yes, we gave up the old ways because we became tired of missionaries infiltrating our camp and forcing us into religious conversion. Buckland House became our haven, where we could live peacefully and gain respectability in the eyes of society, despite our gypsy blood."

"I hear Buckland House is a profitable old estate. How did your family come by it?"

She hesitated, slanting him a look from beneath her eyelashes, and he immediately prepared himself for a revelation he probably wasn't going to appreciate.

"I don't know how much you've heard of my family history, Cole," she murmured, "but we do have a somewhat scandalous past. My grandmother was an extremely gifted woman. She had a way about her, a certain joie de vivre that one couldn't quite describe, and many men desired her. Eventually she settled with the man of her choice, though they never married. Her paramour, a gentleman of some stature, gifted her with Buckland House."

Cole nodded, well able to believe in her grandmother's ability to instigate desire in a man. Obviously the trait had been passed down to Juliana. "That's quite a gift."

"Perhaps not. Unfortunately, at that time Buckland House had fallen nearly to ruin. My grandmother never lived there, preferring her warm carriage to a drafty, leaking hall. My father, however, objected to being called a 'gypsy problem,' and decided to settle into Buckland House. Eventually he restored the estate to the point where it became profitable. Money often buys friends, and at length we were absorbed into society, losing almost all of our gypsy identity in the process."

"Settling down into one place seems to have that effect," he agreed. "When you live somewhere long enough, eventually you begin to act like your neighbors, right down to your speech, accent, and mannerisms. My family has also forsaken many of the old ways for more conventional traditions."

"It is a shame, no?"

"In a way. I don't like to think of the Romany as a people disappearing forever like an over-hunted species, but at the same time, my days are very comfortable. Why fight society, when it can give you so much?"

"I think we should be true to ourselves regardless of the cost. If I'm Romany, then I should embrace the Romany ways no matter how much I'm persecuted."

He shrugged. "Some costs are simply too high. I want my sons to have as many opportunities to succeed in this world as I can offer them, and they'll have more opportunities as Englishmen than as gypsies."

"Don't you think your sons will always feel a sense of incompleteness, by forsaking their heritage? People who are divided can never be happy."

"Perhaps I ought to allow them a chance to choose."

"I hope you *will* give them that freedom, Cole. The ability to make a choice is a precious one. Not all of us can make choices. Indeed, some of us are forced to endure lives that are unnatural and inherently wrong."

Eyebrow quirked, he studied her. "I almost feel as though you're speaking from personal experience. Do you wish your parents hadn't given up the old ways?"

She laughed, though the sound was a harsh one. "Indeed. I would love to go back to the way my family once lived."

The unexpected vehemence in her voice silenced Cole. He'd obviously touched on a sensitive subject for her, and unfortunately he held the opposite opinion.

"This is a subject you and I will never agree on." Suddenly out of sorts, he focused his attention on the waves that crested onto the sand a few feet away. "I don't mind being 'absorbed' into English culture. Sometimes, when you mix two metals together, the resulting metal is stronger than either of its constituents. In my opinion, we're stronger and more apt to survive if we try to fit in with those around us, and consider our Romany heritage an additional strength we can draw upon, but not an identity we hold exclusively."

Her grasp on his hand tightened. "Perhaps you're right."

He turned to stare at her, surprised at how easily she'd given in. Could he have overestimated her passion for Romany heritage and traditions? Or had he misunderstood her entirely? "Right or wrong, it's a difficult subject," he murmured, and she had no reply for him.

For the next several minutes they walked quietly. Her mood became pensive, and she looked out to sea frequently before focusing on the cliffs next to them, which were growing increasingly taller. Cole sensed he was losing her in some obscure way and drew her closer to him. At length, he decided some light conversation was in order.

"Did you take long walks at Buckland House?" he asked.

"Why do you ask?"

"We've been walking along the beach for almost an hour. Other women of my acquaintance would have been pleading to turn around by now. Evidently you're used to taking long walks."

A wry smile curved her lips, and while he didn't know why she felt his assessment ironic, he welcomed her smile.

"Oh yes, at Buckland House I walked everywhere. My home is near a sleepy little village without a lot of entertainment, and to amuse myself I explored the woods surrounding us. How about you, Cole? Do you want to turn around?"

Amused that she would tease him with that same question, he offered her a grin. "Not at all."

"Good. Let's continue on, though I admit the scenery is becoming somewhat monotonous. Why don't we meander around the cliffs for a while?"

He lowered his brows. "The cliffs are dangerous, Juliana. I don't think we want to stroll along the ledges. Besides, I don't think William would appreciate it. He's been lagging further behind with every minute we continue on."

"William can stay on the beach," she informed him. "Besides, a true adventure requires some danger, though the cliffs don't appear all that difficult to navigate."

"Nevertheless, they conceal many pitfalls just waiting to turn a pretty little ankle like yours."

"Oh, pshaw." She wrinkled her nose at him, then broke free of his grasp and began to climb on the lowest ledge.

"Juliana," he warned.

"Come with me, Cole," she sang out, her mood obviously improved now that she had embroiled herself in a risky activity. Mentally he filed away a note about this aspect of her personality, certain that it would get him into trouble more than once if he married her.

His smile slipping into a frown, he ran over to William, who was just catching up with them. "Miss Pritchard has the notion to climb the cliffs. I'm going to follow her, but for safety's sake, I'd like you to stay here."

William nodded. "As you wish, Mr. Strangford."

As the footman settled down against a boulder,

clearly thinking he would be there for some time, Cole followed Juliana's path and climbed onto a ledge, noting the pebbles and loose debris piled on its surface. He climbed faster to close the distance between them, in case she fell. "Juliana, be careful," he called out. "I don't like how these ledges appear, like they're ready to crumble at a moment's notice. Make sure your footing is firm before you place any weight on the ledge—"

"Don't worry, I'm being very careful." Just as she finished the sentence, her left foot slipped and a tiny gasp escaped her. Acting on instinct, he jerked forward to grab her, but she recovered quickly and moved forward, leaving him waving at air.

"That's it," he growled at her as she scrambled further up the ledge. "I won't be responsible for you breaking your neck. We're going back down."

"Cole, look," she called out. "A sea cave. Should we explore?"

"Snakes live in sea caves," he warned, at the same time trying to remember if this was the cave he'd once explored as a boy, the same one that had held a nest of brightly colored snakes. "Don't go in there."

She laughed. "Do *all* caves have snakes in them, or just this one?"

"All caves." He tried to quell her good humor with a frown. "Let's go back home."

"Oh, Cole, you're acting like an old woman." She disappeared behind a boulder that partially blocked the entrance to the cave.

Climbing more quickly to catch up with her. "Juliana, are you all right?"

A second later he rounded the boulder that blocked his sight of her and saw for himself that she was, indeed, just fine. The cave didn't go very far into the cliffs; rather, it appeared to be a niche in the rock, deep enough to allow some sea thrift to grow in the crevices and sand to collect along the floor, but not dark and narrow like a conventional cave. Abruptly he recalled cooking some freshly caught fish over a campfire with Gillie in this place a long time ago.

Juliana sat upon another boulder, her picnic bundle still held beneath her arm, her skirts spread around her in an attractive way. She looked very young to him in that moment, and very desirable.

"I don't see any snakes," she said, smiling.

He frowned. "I think I'll lead from now on, before you break that slender neck of yours."

"You'll lead us back down to the shore," she charged. "You're not a very courageous explorer, Cole." And with that sally, she was off her boulder and continuing down the trail ahead of him.

Groaning with frustration, he started off behind her. "At least give me the bundle."

"Very well." She placed it on a boulder she was passing, and then pointed at a dark section of the cliff wall. "Look, another cave."

"What luck. Another cave."

Pausing long enough to give him a put-out glance, she continued her trek up the ledge.

Cole judged the distance to the beach below him to be about twenty feet. "Aren't you at all nervous? Look how far we've climbed."

"I don't look down."

"Are all of your 'long explores' this dangerous?"

She didn't answer. Instead, she paused at the entrance to the second cave she'd found and peered inside.

"Something smells terrible in there. I don't think we should go in."

"No, we shouldn't," he agreed as he reached her side. "It's time to turn around. Going down the ledge will prove more difficult than going up, and the path becomes much steeper from now on, if you'll notice."

"Why do you suppose it smells so bad?" she asked, as if she hadn't heard him.

He sniffed the air, and caught the unmistakable scent of decay. "An animal of some sort—a seagull, possibly— might be using the cave as a home." Deliberately he lowered his voice and added, "or maybe it contains the body of a smuggler, who died guarding his treasure."

Her eyes lit up. "There are smugglers in these parts?"

Enjoying her almost childlike fascination, he nodded. "The coastline around Shoreham has several small harbors. In fact, if you'll look down, you'll see that we have a natural depression right below us that could be used as a harbor for a small ship. French ships used to come into this area during the Revolution to deliver various forbidden goods—brandies and wines, mostly."

"Maybe we'll find a smuggler's cave," she breathed.

"Maybe we'll kill ourselves doing so," he countered, seeing now his mistake in fanning her interest in smugglers. "We should go back, Juliana."

But she wasn't looking at him, and didn't seem to be paying attention to him at all. Instead, her gaze was locked on another section of darkness on the cliff face. "Over there. Do you see it, Cole? It looks like another cave."

"There are many, many caves in these cliffs, and all of them probably smell." He paused to touch the cliff face next to them. "Do you see the moss growing on the rock here? This kind of moss grows in fresh water. Evidently this portion of the cliffs is full of water, and water means crumbling, unstable rock."

She trailed one finger through a rivulet of water running through a nook in the cliffs. "The water feels warm."

"I've heard there's a few hot springs in the area, though I've never found them." He shrugged. "More likely, sunlight has warmed it."

Her eyes wide, as if he'd said something of great import, she fixed her gaze on the cave above them. "I think we should go explore that one."

Gently he took her arm. "Enough, Juliana. You've proved your strength to me. Now, I want you to humor me and climb down."

"Just one more cave, Cole. Please? Then I promise I'll follow you home," she pleaded with a little flutter of her lashes. "If this next cave doesn't have any animals living inside, why don't we stop and eat? I'm famished."

He caught his breath and said nothing, wanting to tell her *no* but unable to, not in the face of her potent feminine wiles.

"Please, Cole," she said again, nearly begging now.

Tension invaded his body. He imagined her pleading with him for more intimate favors. Silently damning himself for his weakness, he gave in to her. "All right, we'll explore one more cave, but then you must agree to climb down."

At his words, she smiled brightly; and before he quite knew what she was about, she leaned forward and pressed a soft kiss against his mouth.

He stood utterly still, stunned and hungry for more. Before he could muster his wits enough to react she'd begun climbing again, to what he swore would be their last and final cave.

AFTER HIS DISASTROUS MEETING WITH MRS. Howe, the town gossip, George brought Lila back to her home at Buckland House and immediately sought out Mrs. Wood, with whom Mrs. Howe had apparently made friends. He couldn't understand why Mrs. Wood had been so foolish as to cultivate a dangerous woman like Mrs. Howe; but the damage was already done, and now they simply had to figure out how to salvage the situation.

He surreptitiously followed Mrs. Wood to her bed-chamber, where she went to rest before dinner. All the while he worried about Mrs. Howe and wondered how tenacious the woman was. Usually the gossipy types were beyond compare when it came to ferreting out scandal. If Mrs. Howe sensed something unusual about himself and his cousin Zelda, would she pursue it, or let it drop?

His gut roiling, George knocked on the door.

Dressed in a lace cap which hid her gray hair and sim-ple white gown, Mrs. Wood opened the door, grabbed him by the arm, and whisked him inside. "Mr. George," she whispered, "whatever is the matter? I've been sens-ing a thundercloud on the horizon ever since you and Mrs. Whitham returned from town."

"Thundercloud is an apt description." He moved past her into the sitting room and began to pace, his hands fas-tened together behind his back. "Did you know that Mrs. Howe is perhaps the largest gossip in all of Buckland

Village? What were you thinking when you agreed to visit the woman?"

"Visit? Mrs. Howe? I don't believe I've met her."

"You must have. She claimed that you had promised to visit with her, and when I told her you were staying with the Pritchards, she demanded you come for an afternoon visit at the very least."

Mrs. Wood pressed her fingers against her lips in a thoughtful manner. "What does she look like?"

Quickly George described her long nose and sharp gaze.

"I'm sorry, Mr. George, but I don't recognize her," she said once he'd finished his description. "I've been very careful to limit my exposure to Mr. Pritchard and his daughter, just as you asked me to. I've never driven to Buckland Village, and I certainly never promised to visit Mrs. Howe."

George eyed the older woman, assessing both her manner and the ring of sincerity in her voice. At length, he nodded, satisfied that Mrs. Wood was telling the truth. And while he was glad she'd followed his instructions, her compliance made the problem more knotty. The roiling in his gut grew more nauseating.

"How, then, does Mrs. Howe know Zelda Strangford?" he asked.

Mrs. Wood's eyes became very wide. "Heaven help us, Mr. George, could they be acquainted in some way?"

He began to pace again. "I don't know. It's possible, although I can't believe the investigation on the Strangfords could have missed a fact like this. Our research on the family is long and detailed."

"What *exactly* did Mrs. Howe say about her so-called friend Zelda Strangford?"

"Mrs. Howe explained she'd been expecting a lengthy visit from Zelda. She seemed disappointed over the fact that Zelda had elected to stay with the Pritchards, and demanded I tell Zelda to come see her for an afternoon."

"Mrs. Howe is a gossip, no?" Mrs. Wood asked.

"According to Lila, nothing escapes the woman."

"Well, then, perhaps she manufactured her friendship with Zelda in order to extricate some useful gossip from the situation. How else do women like her know so many secret details about things that don't concern them?" Mrs. Wood, clearly warming to her theory, nodded once for emphasis. "Women such as she have reputations for possessing loose lips. Smart people don't share any sort of information with them. But a gossip loves to talk, and so must no doubt resort to all sorts of trickery to uncover *on-dits* that might garner a few scandalized hisses from the few friends she has."

George thought it over. "You have a point, Mrs. Wood."

"I'd wager that Mrs. Howe was simply throwing out an acquaintanceship with Zelda like a fisherman throws out a hook," the older woman continued. "She hopes I'll be polite enough to discover if I really do know her, to avoid insulting a friend—and when I do, she'll reel me in."

"That could be true. It very well could be," he said, his gut settling down. The alternative—that the sea people had missed such an obvious and dangerous relationship as the one between Mrs. Howe and Zelda Strangford was simply unthinkable. "I did ask Mrs. Pritchard if she'd heard of any relationship between Zelda and Mrs. Howe, and she said that as far as she knew, they hadn't met. So perhaps we're worrying about nothing."

"In any case, I'll avoid the woman at all costs. And if she comes knocking on our door, I'll plead a headache and refuse to receive her," Mrs. Wood promised. She raised one gray eyebrow. "How is your task proceeding? Has Mrs. Whitham come any closer to declaring that the two of you won't suit?"

He shook his head. "My constant attempts to point out our incompatibilities have yet to put her off. Perhaps deep inside she's been harboring some doubts about entering the convent, and is using me as an excuse to delay taking orders."

"Well, you certainly seem to be working hard at it."

"Why, of course I am. I've no desire to linger here in Buckland House, especially now," he said, but wondered if he'd told the truth. That was the hell of this assignment. He liked Lila Whitham. He enjoyed spending time with her, and felt very uncomfortable in the role of insensitive oaf, because he wanted her to think well of him.

Mrs. Wood lifted an eyebrow. "I agree. The sooner we leave Buckland House, the better."

"Mrs. Wood, I apologize for doubting you, and taking up so much of your time when you should be abed. I'll see you at dinner."

"Don't trouble yourself, Mr. George," the older woman assured him. "I believe all is going to plan."

Nodding, George slipped out of her bedchamber and made his way back to his own, a finger of unease sliding down his spine despite Mrs. Wood's wholly reasonable explanation for the town gossip's behavior. He fervently hoped Mrs. Wood was correct in her assumptions; and yet, he knew that even a crack as minor as this in their disguise, particularly this early in the mission, boded ill for all.

Nine

JULIANA SCRAMBLED UP THE CLIFF FACE, LEAVing Cole to follow, his heart in his throat over fear of her falling. He noticed that the ledge was becoming damper and more slippery as they drew close to the cave, and he also realized that this last opening in the cliffs was a large one. She apparently noticed this, too, and suspected that she thought she'd found a bona fide smuggler's cave, because she began climbing faster. Pebbles fell toward him in her wake.

"Slow down, Juliana," he called out. "The ledge is extremely dangerous."

Much to his relief, she did heed his warning and proceeded at a more careful pace. Even so, Cole regretted agreeing to explore this final cave. His desire for her had silenced his common sense and had made pleasing her more important than insuring her safety. He didn't often display this kind of poor judgment.

Good God, he mused, he was putty in her hands. All she had to do was flutter her lashes at him, and he immediately sat back on his hind legs and begged for treats from her like a damned mongrel. Is this what marriage had in store for him? A series of poor decisions made in an effort to secure his place in her heart, and in her bed?

He groaned.

"This one appears fairly deep," she said as they approached the cave opening. Carefully she sniffed the air and announced, "and it smells better. Let's go inside."

"Juliana, wait." He lifted a hand to grab her arm, but again he was grasping at air. She had already disappeared into the cave's interior.

His jaw tight, he also walked into the shadows. Immediately a musty smell surrounded him, and he heard a bubbling noise similar to the sound of water rushing through the piping system he'd installed at Shoreham Park Manor. The cave, he realized, had a ceiling almost eight feet high, and measured equally as wide at the mouth. Though it narrowed ahead, it seemed to widen once beyond a large boulder sitting in the middle of the cave. Juliana was circling around that boulder.

"Are you afraid of bats?" he asked loudly. "If so, I suggest you walk with care, because a cave this size is guaranteed to harbor hundreds, if not thousands of the creatures."

"I don't see any bats." Her voice had a thread of excitement running through it. "However, I do see something far more interesting."

Cole hurried toward the boulder Juliana had disappeared behind. A soft, warm mist began to surround him. He noticed the temperature inside the cave rose considerably as he moved deeper into its interior. Within moments he was working himself around the boulder, which had a coating of slimy moss upon it. Once he had passed the boulder, however, he grew still. There, in the middle of the cave floor, water bubbled up from a crack in the rock. The water sent fingers of steam into the air.

A hot spring, he thought, bemused.

"Isn't it fabulous?" she breathed.

Slowly he circled the pool. It appeared rather deep in the middle. "I can't believe it. A hot spring."

"There's something else," she murmured, pointing.

He gazed in the direction she'd indicated and observed several rotting crates. "I'll be goddamned," he muttered, and strode over to the crates. Shaking his head in disbelief, he yanked a few pieces of rotting wood off the crate and discovered rows of corked jugs.

"Is it smuggler's brandy, Cole?" Juliana asked, pressing her body against his back.

For once he managed to disregard the feel of her against him. Instead, he pulled out one of the corked jugs and examined it for writing of any kind. He found nothing. His curiosity raging, he tried to pull the cork out, but couldn't get a solid enough purchase on the jug, so he set it on the floor and kneeled next to it. Holding the jug between his knees and balancing one hand near the jug's neck, he grasped the cork with his free hand and pulled with all of his strength.

A popping noise suddenly filled the cave. Cole nearly careened backward with the force of his effort. Cursing silently, he righted himself and picked up the jug. A quick sniff confirmed what Juliana had suggested.

Smuggler's brandy. Or, more specifically, French bourbon.

"Well, Cole? What is it?" Juliana stood at his side, her hands clasped together. She nearly vibrated with excitement.

Shaking his head, he set the jug on the floor. "It does appear to be smuggled bourbon."

"How remarkable!"

"It is indeed. I never fancied myself a treasure hunter, but we appear to have stumbled upon an extraordinary find indeed." He grinned at her. "We're extremely lucky."

And yet, even as he said the word *lucky* he knew he was anything but. The coincidence of their stumbling upon bourbon and a hot springs boggled his mind. How in hell had they managed such a feat, given the ill fortune his family seemed to attract? The chances of finding a cave such as this were practically nil . . .

His grin faltered. Sudden suspicion filled him as he remembered how insistent Juliana had been in going on a long explore to the cliffs, and then how she'd risked life and limb to coax him up to this cave. If he didn't know better, he'd almost think that she'd purposefully led him here. Logically, however, he knew that she couldn't have known the location of this cave before coming here with him. She had lived all of her life in Wales, and this was her first visit to Shoreham.

He supposed he just ought to accept the fact that for once, Lady Luck had decided to throw him a bone.

"We should stay here, Cole, and eat lunch," Juliana urged.

"Are you certain you want to? We haven't much light. In fact, it's little better than twilight in here, and rather musty."

"I can't think of a better place for us to eat. We also should celebrate our finding the treasure, don't you think?" She took the bundle from him and placed it on the floor, out of reach of the hot spring's spray. Then she moved back to his side to grasp both his hands. "If this is a harbinger of things to come, I'm ready to marry you tomorrow."

He laughed, though he grew warm inside at her pronouncement. "Ill fortune is more my style. Perhaps you're responsible for our good luck."

Shadows filled the cave, making it difficult for him to see nuances of color, but he could almost swear that a blush darkened her cheeks.

"I don't think it's me," she murmured. "In any case, why question the reason behind our discovery? Let's simply enjoy it." With that bit of advice, she picked up the jug, hefted it to her lips, and took a swallow.

Shocked, he stared at her.

At once she began coughing and choking. Her eyes watered. She damned near dropped the jug. Only his quick reflexes saved the jug from breaking on the rock floor.

He set it down carefully and then eyed her.

"Are you all right?"

Wiping at her eyes, she clutched his arm. "I had no idea . . . I thought it would taste like wine . . . my apologies . . ."

Laughter built in his chest. He managed to keep it inside. "Sit down, Juliana, before you fall over."

Humbly she obeyed.

He, too, sat near her and grasped the picnic bundle. "I'm all in favor of celebration, as long as we remember that we've a long walk back to the manor. Also, we can't forget about poor William, stuck sitting in the sand with only the sea for company."

"Stop talking, Cole, and open the bundle. I'm hungry."

"I'd better feed you, then." Smiling outright, he opened the bundle and brought out several smaller muslin-wrapped bundles. Opening each of them, he placed various mouth-watering edibles before her: lobster on toast, bread stuffed with cold meat salad, curried chicken drumsticks and tiny lemon tortes. Without silverware, they were forced to eat with their fingers, and Juliana showed great abandon in doing so, picking up pieces of lobster toast and licking her fingers once she'd finished with them.

Cole ate more slowly, not so much interested in the food as in watching Juliana. His eyes hooded, he noticed how she wasn't afraid of a little dirt, or of flouting convention. Overall, he didn't like fussy women, and had long been of the opinion that squeamish behavior in public translated into squeamish behavior in bed. Juliana didn't seem to possess any of those qualities.

His mouth suddenly dry, he picked up the jug and took a swallow. Quickly he realized from the way the bourbon burned its way down his throat before settling into a warm pool in his stomach that it had been fermenting in the cave for a long, long time. Very strong, yet smooth and fruity, it tasted like pure heaven. A woman who rarely drank, he mused, would be mightily affected by even the smallest swallow.

"Lord, it's hot in here," Juliana murmured, and took off her tattered apron. She began to unbutton her embroidered bodice, but he stayed her with a hand on her arm.

"Are you certain that's wise?" he asked.

She gazed at him with yellow eyes that appeared preternaturally light in the cave's shadows. "I trust you, Cole."

He dropped his hand away from her arm. "Maybe you shouldn't."

Visibly swallowing, she abandoned her attempt to unbutton her bodice, and instead loosened the neck of her linen blouse beneath the bodice.

"Eat, Juliana," he murmured.

Her gaze sliding away from his, she lifted a piece of lobster toast to her lips and chewed more slowly, more thoughtfully.

"Aren't *you* going to eat?" she asked at length.

"I'd rather watch you," he replied, the bourbon burning in his gut like fire.

Her gaze locked with his. A spark flared in her yellow eyes. She made as if to grab the open jug of bourbon.

Again he stopped her with a hand on her arm. "No, don't. It's too strong."

"I'll do as I please, Cole Strangford."

"I'm responsible for your safety—"

"But you're not my jailer," she interrupted. "Or my father." She lifted the jug to her lips and took a ladylike sip. This time, she didn't cough or choke, but her eyes watered. He could only imagine the sort of effect the bourbon would be having on her. It had damned near made him giddy, judging by the pleasant hum that had invaded his system.

"We have a long walk and a steep climb back to Shoreham Park Manor," he reminded her. "We ought to be leaving soon, before the sun goes down."

"Oh, we've some time yet," she insisted. "We still haven't finished our lunch, and besides, I'd love to stick my toes into that hot spring. I have to confess that my feet hurt terribly from our long walk."

Fascinated by the notion of seeing her naked feet and ankles, he offered no objection, instead taking another swig of bourbon. Against his better judgment, they spent the next several minutes indulging in the remainder of their lunch al fresco and a few more mouthfuls of bourbon. When they'd finished, however, and Juliana reached for the jug, Cole kept it out of her reach.

"You've had enough," he told her.

She shrugged and began to fold up the pieces of muslin scattered around them. Cole watched her closely, noting how her folds seemed smooth and straight. Clearly she wasn't at all used to bourbon or any sort of hard liquor, and yet, she still appeared poised. He thought her ability to hold her liquor rather remarkable, given that a raging fire was flowing through his veins. Still, when she stood and walked over to the hot spring, he noticed a wobble in her step, and realized she was very much feeling the effects of the bourbon.

"Time to revive my feet," she announced, and sat down to remove her slippers and stockings.

Swallowing, Cole watched these preparations, aware of how finely turned her ankle was and how delicate the bones in her feet appeared. Once she'd finally bared both her feet and dipped them into the hot spring, she let out an indulgent sigh.

"This feels wonderful." She patted the area of stone next to her. "Join me, Cole. I'm having too much fun not to share it with you."

He lifted an eyebrow at her invitation. It sounded innocent enough, but there was a certain smoldering look in her eyes that heated his blood. He remembered her story about the soldier she'd nearly run away with. Perhaps she did have a wild streak running through her, one she tried to hide, but one that came out in certain circumstances.

He shook his head, thinking about how he'd been sorely tempted ever since he'd met her—more so than any other female in his acquaintance. And somehow, he'd given in to those temptations despite his resolution not to. If he didn't know better, he'd think he was being seduced.

Being seduced . . .

Intrigued by the idea, he moved closer to her. "I want to join in your fun, Juliana, but I'm afraid of the consequences of our play."

"Consequences?" Wide-eyed, she offered him a guileless look.

He smiled slowly. "You're asking me to undress. Such a request will always have serious consequences. Are you certain you want me to?"

She lowered her gaze from him. "Cole, I just want you to enjoy yourself."

"I think you want more than that." Keeping his attention on her, he removed his shoes and socks, rolled up his trousers, and dunked his feet into the hot spring. Deliciously hot water flowed over his skin, relaxing his muscles and drawing a sigh from him. "I wonder how it would feel if we were to . . . bathe in the hot spring."

"But we haven't any clothes to change into."

"We could bathe naked."

A soft gasp escaped her. She looked away, her cheeks rosy.

Cole stared at her profile. His conscience reminded him that she was an unmarried woman placed in his care by her trusting father. He should bundle her up and take her outside where William could vouch for their behavior. But another, more primal aspect of his personality urged him to indulge in the pleasure that the smoldering look in her eyes promised.

"Have you ever seen a naked man before, Juliana?" he murmured.

She looked up at him. "No."

He gazed at her for a long time, thinking about that cavalry officer of hers. "Are you certain?"

She nodded and smoothed her skirt with trembling hands.

He shifted closer to her, bridging the distance between their bodies. Before he knew what he was doing, he'd tilted his head and pressed his mouth against hers. He kissed her, hungrily, his passion for her drowning out his gentler instincts, and he pushed his tongue into her mouth. Her lips were slack, maybe with shock, but when he began to stroke her tongue with his own, she put her hands on his shoulders and pushed away.

"Cole, I'm nervous," she whispered breathlessly, her eyes very wide.

"Do you want to stop?"

She hesitated, then shook her head *no*.

He kissed her again, wrapping his arms around her lithe body and pressing her backward until she lay upon the rock, with the waters of the hot springs about a half inch deep beneath her. She struggled slightly in his embrace, but he held her tightly, and her struggles became weaker until she began to respond to him and her arms encircled his neck. Shyly her tongue darted into his mouth and tangled with his, before exploring the surface of his mouth, his teeth, tasting him.

He pressed his body against hers, leveraging himself on an elbow so he wouldn't crush her, and started to plant tiny kisses on the corner of her mouth, along her jaw, and then down lower, toward her breasts. Deep in the back of his mind, he knew that this might have been the wrong thing to do, and that his behavior was far from gentlemanly; but the feel of her body beneath his and the hunger in her kiss made it easy to forget all of that. He popped the buttons on her bodice and loosened the strings of her blouse to bare her breasts, then sucked hungrily on their coral tips, drawing a gasp from her.

"Oh, Cole," she moaned, her fingers buried deep in his hair.

Tasting her on his lips, he abandoned those coral tips which had hardened beneath his tongue, and shifted his weight until he'd straddled her, his knees pressing into the rock on either side of her hips. He dragged his lips upward, across her skin, until they rested on hers again. She whimpered, her body straining upward and brushing softly against his erection, teasing him, setting him afire.

He kissed her mouth, pushing his tongue deep inside, and then kissed her nose, her cheeks, her chin, her forehead, her eyelids, until he'd branded every patch of bare skin on her face with his mouth. He cupped her breasts in his palm, enjoying the rounded fullness of it, even as her fingers found his waistcoat buttons and began undoing them one by one.

"You're so beautiful," he murmured.

Instead of replying, she leaned upward and nipped at his earlobe with small, white teeth. Shivers washed over him, and seemed to settle into his loins. His erection throbbed with need, and he knew she could feel it pressing into her belly through the heated fabric of his trousers; but he didn't expect the sudden fluttering of her fingers across it, nor the sudden dip of her hand beneath his waistband as she caressed him with a feather-light touch. He caught her gaze and held it, and he saw the need in her eyes, the newly awakened desire that didn't care about conventions or morality or reputation. He could see how badly she wanted him to possess her, and the knowledge damned near maddened him.

He kissed and caressed her breasts again, then blew softly on her nipples until she whimpered and thrust them toward his lips in silent supplication for more kisses. At the same time, she began thrusting her hips in earnest against his erection. Every time her hips brushed against him, jolts of pleasure nearly scorched him with their intensity, and water from the hot spring splashed over him. He felt that familiar building-up sensation deep in his gut. Quickly he moved off of her, before he ended the pleasure between them prematurely, and positioned himself on his side, so that he faced her.

"Cole," she whimpered, "don't stop."

"I'm not going to stop, sweetheart," he promised huskily, and yanked off his waistcoat. Impatience forced him to pop a button on his shirt as he pulled that off, too. Juliana loosened the fastener on his trousers and slipped her hand inside fully, flexing her fingers around his throbbing erection. With a delicate motion, she fluttered her fingers across the head of his erection before she began to pull on him, bringing him even closer to the edge.

"Ah, God," he muttered, and held her hand still before his release came too soon. Determined to bring her to the edge, too, he pushed his hand beneath her skirt to caress her moist recesses. She arched her body and pushed into his palm, seeking more. When he touched her and felt how wet she was, how ready for him, his erection became almost painful in its need for release.

He slipped one finger inside her hot moistness, earning another whimper from her. Breathing heavily now, delighting in the way she rocked her hips against his hand, he slid his finger in deeper . . . until suddenly, he hit an obstruction. The meaning behind this obstruction was unmistakable. His intense desire became tempered with an abrupt sense of accountability.

Juliana Pritchard was pure in the truest sense of the word.

"Cole, please," she moaned, and again he began to tease her with his finger, slipping it inside of her before withdrawing again and tracing little circles around the center of her pleasure, his touch as light as a butterfly's wings.

When her hand began to wander toward his groin again, he coached her softly on how to please him, and she followed his instruction, sliding her hand into his trousers, and cupped the head of his shaft before enclosing it in her fingers. Her fist moved up and down the length of his erection, and he muttered incoherently, his own teasing motions between her thighs growing more urgent.

She rocked and bucked against his hand, and she sought to draw him back between her legs by pulling gently on his shaft. Her meaning was clear. She wanted him to possess her as only a man could possess a woman. Cole groaned, but held his ground. He would have dearly loved to satisfy her, but he found that despite the deep pleasure she was giving him, he couldn't. The discovery of her innocence had changed something for him. For all of her passionate ways, she was truly an innocent, and he didn't want her gaining that sort of knowledge until her wedding night.

"I need you closer to me," she whimpered, her hand jerking convulsively on his shaft.

He leaned down to nuzzle her neck, his entire erection a mass of tingling pleasure that seemed on the verge
of exploding. Even as he was breathing heavily against
her neck, he pressed his palm into the curls between her
thighs, and slid his finger into her, and drew circles
around the little nub of her pleasure until she began to
pant softly, her hips thrusting uncontrollably and rhyth-
mically in a way which told him she was near to release.

Then, with a small moan, she began to thrust very
quickly against his hand. Immediately he slid his finger
inside her, filling her as much as he dared without com-
promising her virginity, and her heated moistness
clenched around his finger. She tensed with a small cry,
and moaned his name, her fist on his erection tightening
involuntarily, bringing him indescribable pleasure and
not a bit of pain mixed in.

He moaned. The burning sensation that seemed to be
centered around his erection became a hot wave which
rushed through his body, and he tore his shaft from his
trousers. Eyes squeezed shut, he surrendered to blinding
pleasure that had him shaking before it left him spent,
empty, his muscles like jelly as he fell on his side to lie
next to her, the water of the hot springs lapping gently
against his arm.

He gathered her close. She sighed and, lying on her
back, cuddled into his side. Several minutes passed during which neither he nor Juliana did anything other
than hold each other. He couldn't help but think how
good, and how right she felt in his arms. Never had he
felt this way with another woman, and he wished the
moment would go on forever. Nothing, however, lasted
forever, a notion he confirmed with a glance toward the
front of the cave. The outside light had faded, darkening

the interior of the cave as well and suggesting they'd been picnicking for a long time. Soon, they would have to leave, or they'd have a rescue party from the manor after them.

He transferred his attention to Juliana, prepared to say as much, when suddenly, he thought he saw disquiet in her eyes. He propped himself up on one elbow to look closely at her.

"Are you all right, sweetheart?" he murmured against her ear.

She offered him no reply. Instead, she kept her gaze fixed on the center of the hot spring, which bubbled up from a crack in the rock.

Uneasiness brought a frown to his lips.

Obviously the situation between them had now become sticky. He knew he should propose marriage. And indeed, the question hovered on his lips. Still, he couldn't quite bring himself to utter it. While Juliana was perfect for him in many ways, something was holding him back. An instinct of self-preservation had sealed his lips, and he didn't know if unconsciously he still wanted to preserve his bachelor status or if his instincts had sensed something that his logical mind couldn't. He had to admit, a few strange events had occurred since her arrival, such as the destruction of his breathing apparatus and the sighting of the sea maiden, not to mention Juliana's odd lack of knowledge regarding gypsy culture.

"Juliana," he murmured, "is something wrong?"

She rolled onto her back so she could face him, and traced the planes of his jaw with a delicate touch. Still, she remained quiet.

He brushed her hair back from her forehead. Concern filled him. "Tell me what bothers you."

"Cole, did I please you?" she asked suddenly, her gaze fixed on his lips.

A smile curved his lips upward. "Very much so. Did I please you?"

"Yes," she said, though the tone of her voice suggested that perhaps she wasn't completely telling the truth.

Partly amused, and partly offended that she would question his manhood, he flicked a finger across the tip of her nose. "That doesn't sound like a very confident yes. You were less than satisfied?"

She sighed. "You showed me something that I never knew could exist between a man and a woman. The pleasure was, well, indescribable. But I thought . . . I mean, I'd heard that a man usually . . . well, what I'm trying to say is that I'd heard when a man joins intimately with a woman—"

He nodded, relieved that she hadn't considered his performance lacking. "I know what you're trying to say. We didn't make love in the fullest sense of the word. Does that bother you?"

"I just thought that perhaps I didn't please you."

"You pleased me mightily," he insisted. "I don't think I'll ever think of lovemaking in the same way again."

"Then why didn't we make love fully?"

"Well," he said slowly, "what happened between us here today isn't perhaps the most honorable thing that I've ever done. You're an unmarried young woman, and though I couldn't deny the need between us, I didn't want to take your, ah, virginity. I shouldn't have taken advantage of you. What I *should* do is offer you my hand in marriage."

"Don't apologize for this afternoon," she whispered. "Don't cheapen our first time together."

"Oh, sweetheart, I don't mean to cheapen what happened between us today, but by the same token, I don't want to cheapen you, either. We should marry."

She frowned. "I can't say yet for certain if I want to marry you, Cole Strangford, and since you didn't take my virginity, there's no reason for us to rush to the altar. I suppose I should be thankful for your restraint."

"It was damned difficult to come by," he admitted, doing his best to hide the surprise that had filled him at her declaration. He'd thought she would demand marriage after their intimacy. But no, apparently she didn't consider him a prize at all. He assessed her with new enthusiasm.

"I expect we've left poor William outside for too long," she murmured, and sat up.

He stood, and helped her to her feet. "I don't want this afternoon to end."

"Neither do I," she said, shaking out her skirt. "Still, it must."

"Unfortunately," he agreed.

Aware that she'd taken control of the situation in a subtle move, he grabbed her bodice from the floor and smoothed the wrinkles from it before handing it to her. "Thankfully your bodice isn't too wet, though I'm not certain what advantage that offers you, because you're soaked to the skin, as am I."

A laugh escaped her. "What will your footman think?"

"William won't even notice," he assured her, and helped her shrug into the garment, before adjusting his own clothes.

She fastened her blouse, slipped into the bodice, and squeezed the water from her hair before re-coiling it onto her head in a loose chignon and securing it with an ivory stick. Struck by the grace of her movements, he stared at her without being consciously aware of it until she cleared her throat and lifted an eyebrow.

"Are you ready, Cole?"

Feeling like a fool, he nodded and offered her an arm. She placed her hand in the crook of his elbow and, together, they walked out of the cave.

Twilight greeted them. William was standing in the sand far below. Cole waved to the footman, to capture his attention, and William waved back. Beyond William, the ocean surface appeared as smooth as glass and reflected the dusky glow of twilight.

"This explore has definitely been my longest," Cole remarked, hoping that Mr. Pritchard wouldn't take exception to their lengthy absence. "And my most enjoyable."

"Mine, too." She stopped to take his hand and hold it tight. "I hope we can explore again soon."

He squeezed her palm gently. "We will, sweetheart, I promise you that."

Juliana stopped to pull her skirts closer to her body, so she might navigate around an outcropping of rock. As she did so, Cole noticed a little furrow in the ocean, a place where ripples of foam marred its flat surface. About fifty feet out to sea, the furrow cut quickly across the water, suggesting that something big was swimming beneath the waves.

He froze, his attention locked on the swimming creature. "Do you see that?"

Juliana grew still as well. She glanced at him, then looked out to sea, following the direction of his gaze. "See what?"

"That furrow of foam cutting across the ocean surface," he murmured. Images of the sea maiden he'd encountered in the water some two weeks before formed in his mind. Excitement filled him. "What do you suppose it is?"

Eyes squinting, she stared out at the ocean. "It has to be a dolphin. There are probably a few others nearby. They usually swim together, in families."

He looked at her with interest. "How do you know so much about dolphins? I didn't think you had much to do with the ocean after your boat accident."

"Well, I, ah . . ." She waved her hand at him, as if she couldn't quite find the right answer to his question.

He wondered why she was floundering, but didn't pursue it. The furrow had caught his imagination. "Perhaps it's something stranger than a dolphin. I'm going to try to catch it."

"It could be a shark," she offered.

"Or one of the sea people," he breathed. "Let's go."

She didn't move an inch. Rather, she stared at him with wide eyes. "One of the sea people?"

"Go," he urged.

Saying nothing, she turned and began to pick her way down the path, moving much more slowly now than she had before. After almost a minute of this went by, Cole suspected she was deliberately trying to obstruct him.

He cast a worried glance out to sea. The furrow was still there, moving in random directions, like a sea maiden frolicking in the waves. He came up right behind Juliana and urged her forward. "It's her. I know it is. I'll have to move quickly if I'm going to catch her."

"Catch *who?*"

They had almost reached the bottom. The rest of the ledge, he saw, would be easy for her to finish. Carefully he maneuvered around her and completed the walk to the shore with her behind him.

William was waiting for him when his feet touched the sand. "Are you ready to return to the manor, Mr. Strangford?"

Cole shook his head. "Not yet. Keep an eye on Miss Pritchard for me, William. And when we get home, if anyone asks, you stayed with us throughout our entire walk."

The footman nodded. "As you wish, sir."

Cole filed a mental note to put a few extra sovereigns in William's pay this month. "I'm going for a quick swim." He began shucking his shoes.

"Yes, sir."

Juliana reached the shore a moment later and strode over to him. "Cole, what are you doing?"

"Going for a swim."

"Fully dressed?"

"There's someone I want to meet."

She lifted an eyebrow. "Why? I thought these sea people were your enemies. How do you know they even exist?"

He paused. He knew very well that they existed, but if he admitted to seeing a sea maiden, would Juliana think him mad? He decided not to find out. Even so, she deserved as honest an answer as he could manage, so he thought about it for a minute before replying, "Logic tells me that the creature swimming out there is a dolphin. And yet, the most important inventions were born through intuition rather than logic. In essence, sometimes it pays to chase rainbows."

"And if you find one of these sea people, what will you do?"

He smiled. "I don't know. Introduce myself, maybe? Ask her kindly to return the Sea Opal to me?"

Juliana looked away. "I'll wait here for you."

He glanced out across the ocean. The furrow was still there, although it had moved down the coastline some. He had to move fast or the creature would move too far away from him.

He took off running and hit the water at full stride, splashing through the surf until the water had become deep enough for him to dive. The ocean felt ice-cold. He let out a little gasp and began swimming vigorously in an effort to warm his muscles. When a wave crested on him, he dove through it, salt stinging his eyes and sand boiling past him in a rush of water. As soon as he surfaced, he gauged his distance to shore. He didn't want to drift out any further than fifty feet, or he might miss the creature beneath the waves.

Soon, his muscles began to burn with effort. He didn't care. He felt incredibly alive in that moment, and savoring every moment of the chase. Slowly he drew closer to the furrow, and saw a gray tail crest the surface of the ocean before sliding beneath the waves again. A *dolphin's tail*, he thought. But that didn't mean he was chasing a dolphin. He thrust his arms through the water more quickly and kicked as hard as he could. Just a little further, and he would reach her. Remembering her perfect face and figure, he smiled.

Up ahead, the furrow petered out to nothing.

Cole stopped swimming and treaded water. He scanned the ocean surface. Confusion brought a frown to his lips.

She'd disappeared.

He continued to tread water and spun around in all directions. She must have gone deep, he thought. He just needed to wait a few more seconds, and she would come up again.

The ocean surface, however, remained undisturbed— even after a full minute.

Disappointed, he glanced toward the shoreline.

And discovered he had drifted out to sea far more than fifty feet. Indeed, he had drifted more like fifty yards. Uneasiness settled into his gut. Christ, he had a long way to swim in.

A small figure on shore was waving at him.

Juliana, he thought. She was trying to alert him to the danger he'd placed himself in. Well, luckily for him, he was a damned fine swimmer. He had lived near the ocean all of his life and spent most of his free time diving. He knew the water well, and didn't fear it.

He faced the shore and started swimming.

Soon his arms began burning. He ignored the sensation and kept moving. And noticed something very odd.

Even though he was heading toward shore, he seemed to be moving farther out to sea. In fact, waves were forming and cresting perhaps twenty feet to the right and left of him, but directly around him, the water appeared very smooth, almost as if he were swimming in a river within the ocean.

Sudden realization left him stone-cold.

He was caught in a rogue current, one that pulled everything that stumbled into its path out to sea.

And he'd already exhausted himself.

Panic filled him. How in hell had he managed to find a rogue current? This shoreline hadn't seen one for years now. Christ, what bad luck. Remembering the advice his grandfather had once given him, he began to swim parallel to the shore rather than straight in. No one could fight a rogue current head-on. It was just too strong. You simply had to try to swim out of it, to either the left or right, and pray that it wasn't too wide.

For what seemed like an eternity, Cole swam in what he thought was a direction horizontal to the shoreline. He kept glancing at the beach, trying to gauge whether or not he'd come any closer. And while he seemed to have made some progress, he just didn't know if he'd made enough. His muscles were screaming, and water was starting to wash over his head. He realized what that meant. He had started to drown.

He was going to die out here.

The thought came out of nowhere, and yet, it had the ring of truth to it. He couldn't believe it was actually going to end like this. As another wave washed over him and he gasped a huge mouthful of water, he understood that he'd played the wrong cards this time. He shouldn't have chased that dolphin. Juliana was right. He was mad, mad . . . and soon he would be dead.

He gave up swimming and concentrated on attempting to keep his head above water. He knew there was no one nearby to save him, and yet, a fierce will to live forced him to stay afloat as long as he could. Again he thought of Juliana. They could have had something special between them, he felt certain of it. Maybe if he just hung on . . .

Another involuntary swallow of water a few seconds later had him retching. His head went under water. It took him a few hard kicks before he surfaced again. He hadn't very many kicks left in him. His legs and arms, which had felt on fire a while ago, were now becoming numb and cold.

Drowning, he mused, wasn't too bad a way to die.

He went under again. He considered deliberately sucking water into his lungs, just to end it quickly and peacefully. His mind, he realized, was growing fuzzy, just like his vision. He couldn't really see anymore. A rainbow of colors had formed behind his eyes—probably from lack of oxygen.

"Always chasing rainbows," he whispered.

It was his last coherent sentence.

Ten

HER HEART GROWING COLD IN HER CHEST, Juliana watched as Cole swam directly into a rogue current. Did he understand the danger he'd just placed himself in? Should she be worrying?

She strode over to William, abandoning the girlish act in favor of quick action. "How well does Mr. Strangford swim, William?"

"Very well indeed, miss," the footman said.

"Look out there," she directed. "Do you see where he is? He's stumbled into the middle of a rogue current. They're very difficult to swim out of, and they'll take you a hundred yards out to sea before they let you go. Is Mr. Strangford that good of a swimmer?"

William's brow creased. He squinted, staring out at Cole's form. "He was practically born in the ocean. He can swim circles around even the dolphins."

Juliana lifted a brow. She refrained from pointing out that he wasn't swimming a circle around the dolphin he was chasing. "Have you ever become caught in a rogue current?"

"He knows what he's doing, miss. Don't worry."

"Nonsense. If that man isn't in trouble now, he will be shortly," she pronounced.

The footman glanced at her for several seconds before looking back out to sea. Juliana could sense his surprise. "How well do you know these waters, miss?"

"Better than you'll ever know, William," she couldn't help herself from saying. Silently she acknowledged that there was another reason she didn't want Cole to die: He'd come to mean more to her than she'd thought possible. "Do you swim?"

William had grown very still. He was staring out to sea. Juliana followed his gaze, and saw that Cole had stopped swimming and was just treading water. He was growing smaller as she watched. The current was taking him out.

"I don't swim, miss," the footman finally said, his voice trembling, "but I wish I did. I believe you're right. Mr. Strangford is in trouble."

Juliana grabbed William's shoulder to steady him. "William, is there anyone within a reasonable distance who might be able to help us?"

"He's gone under, miss." The footman's gaze was locked on the sea. His face had grown pale. "I don't see him anymore."

"I need you to go for help, William," Juliana told him in a voice that shook. What she really needed was to get rid of the servant, so she could do what had to be done. "I'll stay here and keep an eye on him. Look, he's come back to the surface."

And indeed, Cole had resumed treading water, though Juliana suspected he had only a minute or so left before he went under for good. Her mouth dry, she took William's arm and urged him toward the path that led to the road. "Run. Find help. The faster you go, the better a chance Mr. Strangford has."

His head bobbing in a nod, and his eyes as wide as saucers, William turned and fled up the path. Juliana waited until he had gone out of sight, and then began stripping off her clothes in a frenzy. She knew she was taking a huge risk by allowing the transformation to take place. If Cole recognized her as one of the sea people, she would fail in her mission. And yet, what other choice did she have—let him drown? She simply refused to allow this complicated man, who fell prey to doubts and chased rainbows and tried so hard to be noble, to die.

Completely naked, she waded into the water. As soon as the saltwater touched her feet, they began to itch. Juliana allowed the sensation to wash over her. In fact, she welcomed it, and urged it to spread and intensify. Normally, she would wade slowly into the ocean, so that her transformation would progress in a slow fashion, without shocking her system; and by the time she'd walked into water about waist-deep, her legs had become a dolphin's tail. From there, she'd swim sedately into the depths.

Now, she didn't have that kind of time. Moving quickly, she raced into the sea and dove in, immersing her limbs in saltwater and crying out as every fiber in her body simultaneously reacted to the water. Restlessness spread through her and she thrashed helplessly in waist-deep water, the pain of the transformation a bone-deep ache that she had to tolerate, because her body had left her no other choice.

Her legs pressed against each other seemingly of their own accord and her skin began to itch. She didn't need to touch her legs to know that her skin had grown tougher, yet smooth, with a rubbery feel. Back arched, she smothered a moan as her spine elongated and became more supple, able to twist back and forth in a way that would propel her quickly through the water. Muscles grew where before, there had been none. Her feet stretched and spread, then flattened to form a tail, her toes becoming webbed and then dissolving into a silver dolphin's tail.

Feebly she splashed in the water, which foamed and boiled around in her response to the magic that was transforming her body. Her eyes started to itch, too, as a protective membrane covered them. Unable to do anything else, she rubbed at them. She felt hot all over, as though she'd caught the ague, and then she felt ice-cold; and for a second she needed to vomit. She began to shiver uncontrollably, her body trembling so hard that she thought she might shake herself into a hundred pieces.

Teeth shattering, her mind nearly beyond the point of thinking, she squeezed her eyes shut and prayed for it to be over soon. Still, her body contorted and her bones popped and muscles formed in record time. Deep inside, she felt burning as her lungs changed to filter oxygen from water, and all of her organs twisting and reforming to withstand the increased pressure under water. Through it all, the itch and heat increased until it became something very close to agony. A howl built behind Juliana's lips.

And yet, just when the pain became too much to bear, it started to melt away.

Convulsively she twitched her tail. The water around her stopped foaming.

She had become one of the sea people.

Her body felt warm all over and incredibly invigorated. She flicked her tail again and darted effortlessly through the currents, her hair floating sensuously behind her. At the same time, she drew seawater into her lungs and absorbed oxygen into her system, while her heart sent blood to the very ends of her fingers and toes. Sometimes she thought that the transformation from landwalker to sea person must feel much like being born. No wonder babies cried at the moment they entered the world—it hurt so darned much.

Usually after the transformation she frolicked a bit, enjoying the feel of water rushing past her skin and the freedom of being able to dive deep and explore a very different world from the one above. This time, however, she could only think of Cole. Her heart pounding, she propelled herself forward with her tail, and held her arms tight to her sides to reduce the water's drag on her progress. From what she recalled, she should find the rogue current just ahead, and then to locate Cole, she only needed swim out to sea in the current.

Within seconds she felt the rogue current enfolding her in its cool embrace before sweeping her away from shore. She scanned the waters around her for Cole, darting to and fro in the current in search of him. As horrible as the thought was, she hoped he had fallen unconscious. That way, he wouldn't see who rescued him. And yet, she didn't think it would be that easy. Cole was a fighter. It would take him a long time to surrender to the ocean.

Far in the distance, she heard a dolphin's cry. She suspected that same dolphin had accidentally lured Cole into the water before continuing on its way down shore.

Silently she bid the dolphin a good journey and rippled through the water, her tail a flash of silver behind her. Her anxiety grew as the seconds passed and she didn't find Cole.

Could he have sunk downward already?

With a tremendous thrust of her tail, she rushed down into the depths beneath the rogue current and searched for him. A few dogfish glanced at her with serene expressions, their interest in anything other than predator or prey nonexistent, but otherwise she saw nothing.

Inside, she trembled.

She didn't know how, or why it had happened, but Cole had touched her on some primal level. She remembered what he'd said about chasing rainbows, and a sob caught in her throat. He wasn't the ogre she'd been expecting, but an attractive man with both admirable and frail qualities, one who could make her laugh, and annoy the devil out of her, and bring her exquisite pleasure.

At another time, she might have smiled tenderly at the memory of his worrying over her safety, and his determination not to take advantage of her. He'd surprised her by resisting her seduction for so long, and once he'd finally capitulated, the passion that had blossomed between them had shocked her mightily. But she couldn't love him. She could never love him. She was his Judas, his betrayer, and when he finally discovered her treachery he would loathe her.

The problem was, she suspected she was already falling in love with him.

A flash of white among the strands of seaweed on the ocean floor caught her attention. She rushed downward and discovered Cole, floating, his eyes open and a few bubbles of air escaping his lips. Terror grabbed her by the throat, making her want to choke.

He had drowned.

And yet, when she grabbed him around the waist and shot toward the surface, he blinked at her.

The relief that rushed through her veins was so potent she nearly let him go. Somehow, she held on. They crested the water, but he remained listless in her arms, and she could tell he wasn't breathing. Kicking her tail hard to keep them both afloat, she started back toward the shore, wondering all the while if he'd recognized her, or if he was in a state of semiconsciousness, unable to make sense of what had happened to him.

She dearly hoped it was the latter.

Grasping his large form in her arms, her heart beating close to his, she swam over to a rock that stood about twenty feet from the shoreline. At high tide, the sea covered the rock, but now the tide was going out, leaving the rock as a safe, if temporary, haven for a landwalker. With a great gasp of effort she hefted him onto the rock and turned him onto his back. His face looked pale, and his lips almost purple. His heart, she noted with alarm, beat very slowly.

Fluttering her tail back and forth to keep her upper body thrust out of the water, she pushed on his chest with her palms. As soon as she saw a gush of water escaping his mouth, she turned him onto his side, so he wouldn't choke. Five times she did this, until suddenly he started coughing.

At the sound, a muted cry of triumph escaped her. This time, at least, they'd cheated death. Now she had just to dry off her tail and return to human form before either he regained full consciousness or William returned with help.

Almost giddy, Juliana dove into the water, arching her back at just the right angle to avoid hitting the sandy bottom. She swam up the coastline for at least a hundred yards before shooting in toward land and getting stuck in the surf where it rose about a foot high. Expertly she rolled her body the rest of the way in, until she was completely clear of the water, and waited for the evening wind to dry her and transform her tail to legs.

A WARM, SINFUL WAVE OF DESIRE PASSED through George's body. He was leaning on the balcony of his bedchamber, looking out over the meadow where Lila so often lost herself in a sea of fragrant blossoms. The entire house was filled with the flowers she picked, and George had begun to think of her as a flower herself. Now, as he sat there watching her among daisies and Queen Anne's lace and goldenrod, he found himself imagining how she would appear undressed, with two daisies covering her nipples and a bouquet of Queen Anne's lace and goldenrod fanning out across the curls between her legs.

Thoughts about Lila had really been getting to him lately. She was so good, so noble and just, and so bloody sensual that he couldn't seem to help himself from thinking of her in various naughty circumstances. He supposed it had something to do with the fact that he now knew Lila had enjoyed making love very much, and missed the sensations that came along with intimacy; and that these urges put her in direct conflict with her desire to devote herself to a godly existence that stood beyond reproach. She was a sleeping beauty who needed a solid, lengthy round of lovemaking to wake her up.

And George wanted to be that man.

Still, Lila had given him little opportunity to act on this new plan of his. Every time he managed to find her alone, she raced into the house; whenever he spoke to her of intimate topics she brought in her desire to join a convent and become a nun. George found it incredibly frustrating. He wished she would either give in to him, and satisfy the raging desire that plagued his daily existence, or tell him to leave her home, and free them both from this silent battle they'd locked themselves in.

Cursing softly to himself, he left his bedchamber and made his way down to the meadow where he knew he'd find Lila. Once he'd walked close enough to her to see her, he spied on her for a minute or so, enjoying watching her graceful movements and the very feminine task she'd involved herself in. Then, unable to prevent himself from staying away any longer, he finished the walk toward her and sat nearby on the grass.

"Good morning, Lila," he murmured, noticing the bluish shadows under her eyes. Pangs of guilt bit into him. He knew he'd put her in conflict with herself, and was ultimately responsible for those shadows beneath her eyes.

She jumped, and threw him a flustered look before moving as if to stand.

He stayed her with a hand on her arm. "I just want to talk to you, Lila."

"I must go," she insisted, but made no effort to shrug him off.

He lifted his eyebrow. "I had no idea you were such a coward."

"I'm not a coward."

"Then why do you run away every time you see me?"

"Because you frighten me."

"It's not my intention to frighten you. Please sit down."

Her gaze not leaving his, she sank back onto the grass. "We are very close to home, and I know my father is nearby, wandering in the woods."

"Why do you tell me this?" He allowed his hand to slip from her arm. "Do you think I plan to ravish you?"

She swallowed. "You aren't the most noble of gentlemen."

"Ah, but what have I done, outside of steal a few kisses? Isn't a man who is courting a woman supposed to do exactly that?"

"I don't want you to court me."

"Then why don't you send me on my way?"

"Because I've promised my father I would consider you for marriage," she said softly, her shoulders drooping. "He won't send me to the convent if I dismiss you too quickly."

"We've been together for a few weeks now. Surely even he would agree that you've considered me long enough. Why don't you tell me the real reason why you haven't asked me to go?"

Her breathing quickened. She looked away. "'Tis as I said. My father . . ."

He nodded and plucked a long stem of goldenrod, noticing how much it looked like a feather duster. "I think you're dissembling, Lila, but I won't press you on it."

"May I ask *you* a question?"

"Go ahead."

"Why do you stay here at Buckland House when you know I don't want to marry you, and I'll never love you?"

"It would be ungentlemanly of me to declare you undesirable and end our visit. Just as a gentleman never breaks an engagement, I can't leave until either you or your father tells me to go."

She sighed.

"Since we are stuck with each other, why don't we enjoy ourselves?" he murmured, his gaze locking with hers.

"It wouldn't be right—"

"The way I feel about you, Lila, is very much right." He lifted the piece of goldenrod he'd been holding and brushed her cheek with it, leaving a trail of yellow dust on her skin. "And I think you feel the same way about me."

"Then why don't you propose to me, and see how I reply?"

He said nothing. He couldn't propose to her. He wasn't Cole Strangford, by God. Instead, he dragged the goldenrod down across her neck. He could see her pulse pounding in her neck and knew her body was just as tight with desire as his own. She'd left the pelisse she'd donned over her sprigged muslin gown open, leaving him free access to her more forbidden parts.

"Cole, please, don't . . ."

"Don't what?" He drew the goldenrod lower and teased the tops of her breasts. A golden trail of dust soon decorated them, and George imagined dragging the flower across her nipples and gilding them in the same fashion. Too bad her bodice covered them.

Lila remained absolutely still while he played with her. He fancied she even stopped breathing. Inside him, desire raged and he knew that despite their close proximity to her home, he was going to reach forward and free her breasts from their muslin confines.

Without warning, she stood up. "I have to go."

"Lila," he pleaded. "Stay with me."

"I cannot!" She whirled on her heel and ran into the house.

He stood quickly and followed her into the entry hall, catching a glimpse of her skirt as she finished climbing the staircase and rounded a corner on the second floor.

She was going to her bedchamber.

He took the stairs two at a time. The sound of a door slamming rang out ahead of him. He walked quickly down the hallway and stopped before her bedchamber. A quick turn of the doorknob confirmed that she'd locked it.

Shamelessly he crouched down and peered into the keyhole.

She was standing near the bed and struggling with her pelisse. After a brief tussle she managed to yank it from her body, and left it rumpled on the bed. Then, fanning herself with her hand, she began to pace back and forth across the room. Abruptly she stopped before her looking glass and stared at herself, her hands drifting upward to curve around her breasts before settling on her throat. Her expression suggested she didn't recognize the woman looking back at her from the looking glass.

George straightened. He'd seen enough. A slow smile curved his lips.

Soon, she would either send him along or surrender to him, and though the first result was more in line with his mission, the second result would please him the most.

Eleven

TWO WEEKS LATER, COLE SAT AT HIS WORK-
table in his laboratory, staring at his breathing apparatus
but not really doing anything significant with it. He
wasn't even thinking about it. Instead, memories of a
bright yellow gaze and smiling rosebud mouth had filled
his mind.

Sighing, he recognized the fact that Juliana's presence
in his life had changed everything for him. No longer did
he really want to spend his days cooped up in his laboratory, though he did so anyway, out of a sense of duty and
a dogged determination to finish the diving apparatus
before William James finished *his*. He wanted to be the
one to find the Sea Opal, and he needed the tank of
compressed oxygen to do so, though he didn't look forward to diving in the ocean again . . . not since that
rogue current had almost killed him.

He still didn't know what had happened. He recalled
chasing the dolphin, and then realizing he'd blundered
into a rogue current. At some point he'd started taking
on water, and from then on it was a blur. William and
Juliana had told him that they'd found him on a rock,

which he'd apparently managed to climb onto, but Cole hadn't the slightest recollection of doing so. Rather, he remembered soft arms going around him, and the feel of a slow and steady heartbeat. And while he accepted William's and Juliana's explanation on how things had happened, deep inside he felt certain that one of the sea people had rescued him—perhaps even the woman he'd seen before.

A childish giggle from somewhere near the door caught his attention.

Cole glanced that way and espied a small figure. He sighed with annoyance. Another one of the orphans had snuck into his windmill. They found him and his windmill fascinating, and just couldn't seem to leave him alone. He stood up and, following the noise, noticed a flash of movement behind an old tin store sign he'd rescued from the junk heap outside of town. He surged toward the sign, and the child—a little girl—leaped gracefully behind the cogs and gears that turned at the center of his laboratory.

Feeling like a big game hunter on the trail of a particularly wily antelope, he crept toward the gears. Another giggle rang out before the girl raced hell for leather toward the door. Before he could do no more than grasp at air, she'd swung the door open and run outside.

Juliana. He was going to have to talk with her, to tell her how disrupted his days had become. A week ago she'd asked him if he would permit the orphanage to hold its fund-raiser at Shoreham Park Manor, and while he'd agreed to the plan, he hadn't known that he'd be playing host to several orphans, who were working with Juliana and a few other ladies on planning the fund-raiser. He could barely concentrate anymore. When he wasn't mooning over her, he was either worrying about the sea people or chasing another orphan out of his windmill. Females, he mused, just seemed to have a way of inducing chaos. Indeed, his entire life had run out of control.

But he wouldn't change the situation for the world. He enjoyed Juliana's company far too much. He appreciated how she looked, and delighted in the sound of her voice, and loved the gentleness she held in her heart. Sometimes, in fact, his feelings for her frightened him. He'd never thought he'd become so enamored of a woman, and the power it gave her over him troubled him. He had placed himself at her mercy.

His desire to work on his breathing apparatus now completely subverted, he strolled out of the windmill and walked across the grounds toward Shoreham Park Manor. Even from a distance, he could hear childish shouts and laughter. Juliana had certainly proved several times over that she adored children and had a special flair for taking care of them. He wondered what sort of father he would make, for he found himself wishing that the children would give him some peace and privacy.

As he drew close to the manor, he noticed a carriage coming up the road. Immediately he identified it as Charlotte Duquet's, and uttered a deeper, more heartfelt groan. He'd ended their affair many months ago, almost a year in fact, when he'd realized that Charlotte had wanted marriage. She hadn't cared about the Strangford family bad luck, and her pursuit of him had been flattering for a time, until it had stifled him. He couldn't imagine spending the rest of his life with her; she simply wasn't his type, and when he'd told her this she'd taken it rather badly. He'd had to turn her away from the manor several times before she gave the fight up.

Christ, if he'd known the widow was sitting on the orphanage board, he never would have suggested Juliana host this year's fund-raiser. He didn't think Juliana would appreciate being forced to work with his former mistress. God willing, she'd never discover the connection between himself and Mrs. Duquet.

His step slowing with uneasy anticipation, he watched the widow's carriage pull up in front of the manor. She alighted without noticing him and made her way into the house. He finished his walk to the front door shortly afterward and went inside, too. Inside he steeled himself to meet the widow Duquet without displaying any of the distaste he felt at her presence.

Female voices reached him from the parlor. He paused outside the parlor door, hoping he might rope Gillie into joining him in the parlor, but his uncle had clearly chosen not to intrude on this situation. The same impulse grabbed hold of Cole, and he almost obeyed it and walked back outside. Still, worry about what the widow might be telling Juliana kept him in place. He called himself a coward for hesitating so much, straightened his back, and walked resolutely into the parlor.

Both women looked up as he entered. Juliana was sitting on a settee, her white skirt spread around her like an angel's halo. Mrs. Duquet, for her part, had positioned herself suggestively on a couch. Her lips curved in a languid smile. "Hello, Cole."

"Good afternoon, ladies," he managed. "Am I intruding?" Anxiously he searched Juliana's face for signs of anger or disgust, and realized she was frowning. Little lines had gathered between her brows. His mood plummeted.

"Not at all," Mrs. Duquet declared. She patted the seat next to her. "Miss Pritchard and I were just talking about the fund-raiser. Please join us. We could use a man's opinion."

The way the widow said the word *man* sounded like a caress, only he wanted to shudder. He cast a quick glance at Juliana. Her eyes had darkened, as though she'd been wounded. She looked down at her clasped hands.

Sometimes, he mused, Juliana seemed so adult to him, so mature; and at other times, she would tease and pout or, like now, become hurt very easily, as though she were just a child. A beautiful, *sensual* child, he amended, heating his blood without really trying, and needing his protection.

A string of oaths passing through his mind but not his lips, Cole sat on the settee next to Juliana. His choice earned him a quick frown from Mrs. Duquet. Silently he wondered what he had ever found attractive in the widow. She was all seduction and lies, determined to marry him no matter what the cost to others. "What sort of plans are you considering?" he asked Juliana.

Her manner subdued, she offered him a tentative smile. "I was just telling Mrs. Duquet my idea about a Fairy Garden Fete."

He lifted an eyebrow. "A fairy garden? Here, at Shoreham Park Manor?"

"This is a fete in honor of the children of the orphanage," she reminded him. "So I thought a magical theme might be nice. In any case, Aunt Pesha's gardens are very beautiful, and I thought that the townsfolk would enjoy wandering in them."

Outside of a long and pointed sigh, Mrs. Duquet said nothing.

Juliana's lower lip trembled.

He glanced sharply at Mrs. Duquet, who rolled her eyes heavenward. He wanted to berate the woman for intimidating someone like Juliana, who clearly hadn't the same level of sophistication or understanding. "A very clever idea."

"Clever if you're a ten-year-old," Mrs. Duquet muttered.

Silently damning the woman for trying to spoil Juliana's fun, he softly encouraged Juliana to continue. "Had you any other ideas?"

"Perhaps we could have a search for Fairy Birds. We'll cut bird shapes from pasteboard, and tie them to porch railings, bushes, and low branches of trees. On each bird I'll write a sentence that will assist the guest in discovering what bird is meant. For example, 'I am one of Shelley's poems' is the skylark, and 'I bring happiness to homes all around the world' is the stork. The person to have found and correctly identified the most birds wins a prize."

The widow lifted an eyebrow. "Are we to play games all day, or will we eat, too?"

"We will eat," Juliana said. "Since the children want to be included, why not dress them up as gnomes and fairies, and have them help serve dinner? The effect could be picturesque and surprising."

"Exactly what does one eat at a fairy party? Lemongrass and parsley?" Mrs. Duquet smirked at her own wittiness.

Cole shifted in his seat so that his body stood between Mrs. Duquet and Juliana, partially blocking their view of each other. "Had you a menu in mind?"

"I hadn't thought about it," Juliana admitted.

"And after dinner?" the widow prodded, craning her head around Cole's shoulder to stare at Juliana with eyes as hard as diamonds. "What do you suggest we do then?"

Juliana shrugged. "I don't know. Dancing, perhaps?"

Her voice full of sarcasm, Mrs. Duquet said, "Well, Miss Pritchard, you certainly have your fair share of ideas. I suppose we'll have to honor them, considering Cole has volunteered his home for the fund-raiser."

Juliana visibly swallowed. "I'm just one small part of the committee working to organize the fund-raiser. I want to hear everyone else's ideas, and then decide as a group which would work best."

The older woman stood, her gaze darting to Cole. "I have no doubt you'll manage to take over the committee before the fund-raiser, just as you've taken over everything else."

Cole stood as well. This, he thought, had gone on long enough. He wouldn't allow Juliana to suffer because he'd thwarted Charlotte Duquet's desire for marriage. "Mrs. Duquet—"

And yet, before he could say any more, the widow cut him off with a languid wave toward Juliana. "Oh, now, Miss Pritchard, you must forgive me. I'm old and cranky, and the things I say always sound harsher than I intended. I think your plans for a fairy dinner are delightful. And if we don't use them at the fund-raiser, perhaps you might have a fairy dinner at your, ah, *wedding*."

Juliana's shoulders slumped. She looked down at her clasped hands.

Cole tightened his lips. He could feel Juliana's embarrassment. She couldn't really respond to Mrs.

Duquet's sally about her wedding, for he hadn't asked her to become engaged yet. It was a damned awkward situation.

The widow affected a look of surprise. "Have you made any plans yet, Miss Pritchard?" she asked Juliana. "I remember your mentioning your wedding when you took tea with me and Mrs. Morris."

"I said there *might* be a wedding," Juliana clarified, her face flushed pink.

"Oh, dear. I believe I might have made a faux pas," Mrs. Duquet said, clearly enjoying herself. "Can you forgive me?"

Juliana looked agonized. Cole felt a muscle in his cheek begin to twitch. There was a quick and easy way to fix this situation: to declare his engagement to Juliana. And yet, did he really want to take that step?

Feeling as though he were teetering on the edge of a precipice, he reviewed in his mind everything that he knew about Juliana; and more importantly, how he felt about her. True, she possessed some peculiar quirks, and yes, some strange things had happened since she'd arrived at Shoreham Park Manor. Even so, did that mean he should blame Juliana for these events? Strange things always happened at Shoreham Park Manor, and before Juliana had arrived they'd always ascribed them to the Strangford family ill fortune.

Clearly she possessed many of the qualities he wanted in a wife. She'd even managed to draw out a gentle aspect of his of personality that he hadn't been aware of, and made him feel more protective and tender toward her than he'd ever expected. She was witty, and kind, and generous . . . and he couldn't imagine a day going by without her near his side. Indeed, when he looked into her yellow eyes, he saw a sunrise, and with the sunrise, everything seemed to be reborn.

Impulsively he settled an arm around Juliana's shoulders. "You've made no faux pas, Mrs. Duquet. Miss Pritchard is, in fact, my fiancée. We were planning to go into town tomorrow to shop for a token of our engagement, and post the banns."

Mrs. Duquet jerked back from him in the manner of one confronted by a deadly snake.

Cole felt a small hand slip into his. He glanced down at Juliana and lost himself for a moment in her shining yellow gaze. "You didn't tell Mrs. Duquet our good news, dearest?"

"No, I didn't," she whispered, her lips parted.

The widow's lips twisted cynically. "And when, exactly, are you marrying?"

Cole glanced at Juliana.

She squeezed his hand and smiled shyly. "Two weeks hence."

He nodded, thinking two weeks was too long.

The widow's lips twisted. "Just in time for the orphan's fund-raiser. Isn't that a rather short engagement?"

"Cole and I see no need to wait, and we have no desire for a traditional ceremony," Juliana murmured.

"Well, isn't that nice. How wonderful for the both of you. I've . . . underestimated you, Miss Pritchard. You're far more clever than I gave you credit for."

"I'm glad that's all settled, then." Cole nodded pointedly toward the hallway. "Let me walk you out, Mrs. Duquet."

Feeling slightly giddy, he released Juliana's hand, and then took Mrs. Duquet's arm. He and the widow passed through the front hall, and William opened the door for them so they might continue on outside. As they approached Mrs. Duquet's carriage, her driver jumped down from the box and stood at attention.

Throughout all of this, the widow remained silent, but now as she took her driver's hand and climbed aboard, she said, "You've been had, my dearest Cole."

"Had?" Confused, he shook his head. He just wished she would go on her way.

"You must be truly blind to not realize how she's manipulated you. She's a clever little chit, I'll give her that."

"Who? Juliana?"

Mrs. Duquet laughed very softly. "Can't you see behind her sweet smile and shy act? She's set her sights on you and now she has you. You poor man, you haven't a chance. You never did, you know."

Indignant, Cole scowled. "Please stop maligning her character. Juliana is a shy, sweet young girl with no wicked designs." *Unlike you*, he silently added.

"You surprise me, Cole. I thought you were smarter than this. Mark my words, you'll know soon enough what I'm speaking of."

"Thank you for your warning, Charlotte." Cole lifted an eyebrow and glanced at her driver. "I won't keep you any longer."

Mrs. Duquet sighed, then motioned to her footman. "Drive on, Jonathan."

Moments later, the carriage was in motion and Cole was staring at the back of Mrs. Duquet's head. *Good riddance*, he thought, watching the carriage wheels kick up dust as they disappeared down the drive. Charlotte Duquet had always had a way for kicking up dust, too. He was glad to see the last of her.

And yet, the sincerity in her voice and the silent knowledge in her eyes left him feeling slightly uneasy. Annoyed with himself and with her, he shrugged the sensation off. He wouldn't believe for a moment that Juliana had made a cully of him.

George St. Germaine walked out of the woods surrounding Buckland House holding a bouquet of wildflowers. He planned to give them to Lila, though some might consider his gift, given his purpose, foolish and impetuous. One did not convince a woman of one's worthlessness as a mate by giving her flowers. Even so, he'd been feeling very guilty lately over those purplish shadows beneath Lila's eyes, and he wanted to do something to make her smile.

And so, with an apologetic smile curving his lips and memories of their most recent moments spent together drifting through his mind, he approached the front door at Buckland House and walked inside.

"Lila," he called, determined to draw her into a conversation this time without trying to seduce her. She had a remarkably quick and amusing mind, and was knowledgeable on many subjects that women usually didn't bother with. George knew he would never grow bored with Lila for company, and he missed their long talks.

Part of him knew he was enjoying his flirtation with Lila far too much. Indeed, an impulse to tell her the truth about his identity had been grabbing hold of him lately. He often found himself wishing that the circumstances behind his meeting her had been open and honest rather than deceptive. Everything about her pleased him, and if he'd been allowed to court her as George St.

Germaine rather than Cole Strangford, he wondered where their blossoming relationship would have led.

"Lila," he called again, when no one answered.

Muted voices in the parlor caught his attention. He walked toward the parlor and noted with curiosity that the parlor door was closed, indicative of a tête-à-tête in progress. But who was participating in it?

When he intersected paths with a maidservant bound for the kitchen, he placed a hand on the maidservant's arm and forced her to pause.

"May I ask who's come to call?" he asked the girl.

Frowning, the girl shrugged. "I don't know, sir. One of Mrs. Whitham's lady friends from the village, I think."

George hadn't realized that Lila had a female friend who lived in Buckland Village. She'd always acted as though she hadn't any confidantes.

"Very well." He dismissed the maidservant with a nod.

The girl hadn't gone more than a few paces, however, when she turned around and said, "Oh, sir, did you see the letter that came for you by post today?"

"Where is it?" Instantly on alert, he knew that only Juliana would send a letter to "Cole Strangford" at Buckland House.

"On the table in the entry hall."

"Thank you, miss."

She bobbed a curtsey and continued toward the kitchen, leaving him alone. He turned and walked back to the hall. Immediately he found the letter on a salver on the table, and mouthed a silent oath at the sight of Juliana's handwriting. She'd given no return address on the letter, but he knew it had to have come from Shoreham Park Manor. The feeling that things had begun to run awry returned to him. He ripped the letter open and scanned its contents:

My dear brother, Zelda Strangford is evidently acquainted with a woman named Mrs. Howe, of Buckland Village . . .

The letter went on to describe Juliana's understanding of the acquaintance. She mentioned that Zelda Strangford had gone out of town to help a sick friend, buying them some time. It also contained several admonitions for him to be careful, followed by a description of Cole Strangford's underwater breathing device, and how she feared he might use it to discover evidence of the sea people.

George blew out a sigh. When he'd seen her letter, he'd feared it would contain much worse news than this. He already knew about the acquaintance between Zelda and Mrs. Howe, and was relieved to hear that they needn't worry about it, since Zelda had placed herself out of reach of gossip. The bit about the breathing apparatus was interesting—alarming, even—but it didn't represent an immediate threat.

Without warning, the parlor door opened.

Several people came out: Lila, Mrs. Howe, and—

George sucked in a breath. Every muscle in his body jumped to attention when he grasped the identity of the third woman.

Zelda Strangford.

The group stopped when they saw him. He gauged Lila's expression as something between hurt and confusion, while Mrs. Howe looked triumphant, and Zelda Strangford, assessing.

"Is this the man you were talking about?" Zelda asked Lila.

Unhappily Lila nodded.

"Well then, my dear, I assure you that this man is not my cousin. He is not Cole Strangford."

Lila pressed a shaking hand to her brow. Pale and tired-looking, she swayed on her feet.

George felt everything inside him go cold. He dropped the flowers he'd picked for her and rushed to her side. Slipping an arm around her shoulders, he supported her with his body. At first, she leaned on him; but then she collected herself and pulled away. Her gaze upon him was accusing, but it was the vulnerability in her eyes that damned near ripped his heart from his chest.

"Don't touch her, you rounder," Mrs. Howe demanded. "Zelda, go find Mr. Pritchard at once. We must get to the bottom of this."

Lila shook her head. When she spoke, her voice sounded faint. Still, it possessed a certain authority that only the truly foolish would dare disobey. "Mrs. Howe, I will not make a spectacle out of this . . . situation. I'm sure you'll understand if I tell you that now is not the best time for a visit between us, and that I'll call on you when I'm able."

"Mrs. Whitham, I won't leave you with this . . . this scoundrel," Mrs. Howe stoutly declared. "If he is willing to impersonate Cole Strangford, God only knows what else he will do."

"I'm going to call your father," Zelda Strangford added, and hurried out of the room.

"Cole," Lila said, her attention on George, "since I cannot convince Mrs. Howe to leave, I'm afraid we will have to seek privacy outside."

Mrs. Howe cleared her throat and said, "He is *not* Cole."

Lila's cheeks grew pink. "Sir, will you take me outside?" she asked again.

"My name is George," he said softly, his entire being filled with guilt for hurting this gentle creature. God knew he'd done nothing but upset her world since the first moment she'd seen him. "I'm so sorry, Lila. Of course I will take you outside."

With Mrs. Howe bleating like an old ewe behind them, George escorted Lila outside. Mrs. Howe appeared determined to follow them, but George paused to level a glare in the woman's direction, making her falter. Once he'd lost the town gossip, he steered Lila through the meadow. Heading for a stand of oak trees, with flowers and grass slapping at his legs and bees humming angrily at his having disturbed them, he began what was perhaps the most important conversation he'd ever have.

"I am so heartily sorry, Lila, for hurting you," he said again.

Tears gathered in her eyes, and the sight of them was like a knife in his gut. "Why, Cole? Or George? Or whoever you are?" she bit out. "Why did you abuse me in this way?"

"Oh God, Lila, I know you will never forgive me for this," he said, his voice low and shaking. Now that he stood a chance of losing her, he realized for the first time how very much she meant to him. "But I came here to Buckland House to distract you."

She began crying in earnest. Little sobs punctuated her words. "To distract me? I don't understand."

George very much wanted to tell her the truth about himself, but thoughts of Juliana and the other sea people stilled his tongue. They were all counting on him for deliverance, and he simply couldn't destroy their hopes in a selfish effort to secure the woman he loved.

For he *did* love Lila. He saw that now.

Miserable inside, he fell back on the exit strategy he, Juliana, and the Woods had concocted about William James, Cole's competitor and rival inventor. "'Tis a long story, but if you'll bear with me, I'll tell it in full."

"Please, George, promise me you'll tell the truth."

He swallowed. "I promise."

They had wandered over to the stand of oaks, and now George directed her toward a fallen log, where they both sat side by side.

"You were never the target," George swore, happy he could tell at least part of the truth. "Cole Strangford was the one we were after."

"We?"

"My sister and I."

"You have a sister?"

"I do."

"Oh."

"Do you remember how I once told you that I was an inventor?"

She nodded, her eyes swimming with tears.

"Well, Cole Strangford truly *is* an inventor, and he's working on a very special device that has interested the Royal Oceanographic Society. This device will allow a man to breathe underwater for as much as an hour. The Royal Oceanographic Society is offering a prize for the first, and best, functioning breathing apparatus."

Sniffing, she stared at him with a wounded gaze. "So?"

"Strangford's rival, William James, is also working on an underwater breathing apparatus. Mr. James hired my sister and myself to infiltrate Strangford's home and discover the particulars about Strangford's design. He wishes to win the Royal Oceanographic Society's prize, too, though he's not as scrupulous as Strangford."

"You're not very scrupulous, either," she murmured, her voice soft.

"I made a terrible mistake," he admitted.

"Why, George? Why would you do such a thing?"

"Out of friendship, and a need for money. William James is a friend of mine, and quite frankly, I'm flat broke. In any case, the scheme seemed harmless enough."

She shook her head, as if this was all too much for her. "If you were trying to find out about Strangford's invention, why did you come here, to Buckland House?"

"My sister and I heard that Cole Strangford was planning to meet you, with the possibility of asking you to be his wife. My sister went to his home in Shoreham pretending to be you. To allay your suspicions and to conform to society's requirements for gentlemanly etiquette, I came here masquerading as Cole Strangford."

"Who is that woman with you, then—the one masquerading as Zelda Strangford?"

"Her true name is Mrs. Wood, and she's an old family retainer. She assisted me in this scheme because she understood how dire my financial circumstances were."

"Why ever did you bring her?"

"For propriety's sake. I thought it would seem strange if I came here on my own."

Lila shook her head. "You thought of everything, didn't you?"

"I know how terrible you must think I am. But I repeat, I didn't mean to hurt you. I had intended to convince you that I, as Cole Strangford, would make you a poor husband, and I'd hoped you would quickly send me on my way." He sucked in a deep breath, and let it out slowly. "And yet, I found from almost the first day we'd met that you were special, Lila. You made me feel hope when I had almost given up on the world."

And it was true. Before he'd met her, his spirit had been so tired from dealing with greedy landwalkers, with whom he'd spent most of his days making deals to secure the sea people's future. Now, though, he saw that life could have its pleasures, particularly with the right mate . . . and in Lila, he had found the woman he wished to spend the rest of his life with. Abruptly he wished with all of his heart that he wouldn't have to continue to betray her after all that he'd already done. And yet, what choice had he? If he didn't keep living the lie, and doing his best to support Juliana in her effort to seduce Cole Strangford, he'd be condemning all of the sea people to an eternity in the ocean, and Lila would be forever beyond his reach.

She looked away from him and wiped her cheeks, erasing the tracks her tears had made. Silently they continued their walk along the meadow path toward the woods.

At length, she looked at him with a deeply wounded gaze. "What am I supposed to do, George? What am I supposed to think? Your little scheme which 'seemed harmless enough' has hurt me deeply."

"At least I haven't ruined your chances for marriage," he mumbled. "You would have never married Cole Strangford anyway."

"Perhaps that is so," Lila said, her attention now focused on the path they trod, "but by the same token, you've upset my life mightily. Lately I do nothing but question the plans I've made for myself. I'm not even certain a convent is the right choice for me anymore. And do you know why I ask these questions? Because I fell in love with Cole Strangford, a man who came to my house to ask for my hand in marriage."

George abruptly stopped walking.

She stopped, too, and faced him accusingly. "How dare you do this to me! You make love to me, and allow me to dream about marriage between us, when you never intended to ask me to marry you at all. It was all just a game to you, and I, a toy to play with." Turning abruptly on her heel, she started marching away from him.

Shock warred with hope and a tremulous joy inside of him. Did she say that she loved him? Had he heard her correctly? "Lila, wait!"

He grasped her by the arm, but she pulled away from him and kept walking. Desperately he hurried past her and placed himself squarely in her path. When she tried to skirt around him, he grabbed her around the waist and held her tight. "Lila, I never thought I would fall in love with you, but I did. I love you."

She thrashed in his embrace. "Let me go, George. I said I loved the man who had come to my house intending to ask for my hand in marriage. But that man doesn't exist—he was a fantasy."

"But I *am* that man."

"No, you're not. You're a scoundrel. I don't love *you*."

He released her abruptly, and she brushed past him, tears running down her cheeks.

"Lila," he pleaded. "Please stop and talk to me. I know what I did was wrong. Please tell me how I can set things aright, and win your love back."

Her steps slowed, and then stopped. She spun around to look at him. "Are you certain you want to make amends?"

"Yes," he fervently agreed. He would do anything outside of betraying his people to win her over. In the back of his mind, he was already planning the moment when they broke the gypsy's curse and he regained his natural form as a landwalker. He would then be free to spend the rest of his life with Lila. "Please tell me what I must do."

"You and I have to leave immediately for Shoreham Park Manor," she announced. "My father will join us, along with Mrs. Wood and the true Zelda Strangford. Once we arrive at the manor, we'll explain to the real Cole Strangford about the scheme you and your sister have embroiled us all in. And after we have all been honest with each other and have sorted everything out, you and I can decide what we'd like to do from there."

George swallowed. "Your proposition is a difficult one."

She shrugged, her eyes free of tears now. "'Tis your choice, George."

He could see that she wouldn't be willing to negotiate on this one with him. He also wondered if he really had any other choice. One way or another, word was going to get back to Cole Strangford that he'd been duped by two conspirators. He had to make sure he arrived at Shoreham Park Manor before the gossip, so he could extricate Juliana from the manor before she was hurt or taken by the authorities.

Indeed, now he just had to focus on saving his sister. Later, he'd allow himself to think about the implications of their failure, because as soon as Cole Strangford realized that Juliana wasn't a "proper Romany bride,'" he would no longer want her for a wife, and Juliana wouldn't stand a chance of bearing his child.

He turned to Lila and covered her hand with his own. "Give me a few hours to pack," he said, determined to write his sister a letter before he left, to inform her of this latest catastrophe and giving her time to prepare for their exit. If he posted the letter in the morning before they left, it had a good chance of reaching Juliana in a few days, whereas his journey to Shoreham with Lila and her family would take at least a full week.

Lila's expression lightened. "Are you certain?"

"I've never been more certain about anything in my life."

Twelve

❦

"JANE, CHARLES, HARRIETTE, AND JAMES; PLEASE come, quickly," Juliana directed, clapping her hands sharply to secure their attention. She'd been sitting in the parlor, following Mrs. Morris's notes regarding the organization of the fund-raiser; and now she was ready to start teaching her four "gnomes and fairies" how to serve dinner to the fund-raiser's guests. Perspiration gathered on her brow. As adorable as the children of the orphanage were, they also possessed mischievous streaks and caused immeasurable amounts of difficulty unless she kept a very close watch on them. She stood up from the writing desk, organized her notes, then turned her attention to rounding the children up.

Almost a week had passed since Cole had asked her to become his wife. Frowning, she remembered the moment she'd become his intended. How like Cole, she mused, to declare their engagement in order to protect her from Charlotte Duquet. He was a wonderful man, she mused. Lately, not an hour went by without her feeling deep regret over the fundamental, personal way she was betraying him. Often, at night when she swam in the ocean, she would curse the stars above her for giving her a man that she could never allow herself to love, though her heart demanded that she do so.

Since he'd "asked" her to become his wife, she'd divided her time between helping with the fund-raiser and planning her own wedding. Cole had allowed her free reign with both activities, preferring instead to work on his diving apparatus, and every night they found some time to sit, alone, and discuss their day's activities. The tenderness she felt for Cole brought her nothing but heartache, because she couldn't forget how she was betraying him.

Hoots and yells echoed from outside in the hallway. Wondering where the children she'd called had gone, she poked her head out of the parlor and discovered them riding down the banister. Laughing, they pretended to be riding along a sea serpent's back to the city of the sea people. Gillie had told them the tale of the sea people a week ago, and they'd loved it so much that he'd had to repeat it for them several times since.

Juliana wasn't so sure *she* liked the tale.

"Children, come off of there at once." She narrowed her eyes at the lot of them. "I need Harriette, James, Charles, and Jane at once. The rest of you must go outside, now, before something is broken."

Reluctantly they abandoned their game.

Gillie chose that moment to walk in, a few letters clutched in his hands. When he saw the children, he offered them a merry wave, and placed the letters on the hallway table. "Hello, children, are you having a good day?"

A mixed-up cacophony of answers filled the hall as they all answered him at once.

"You're listening to Miss Pritchard, I hope," he said in a mock-serious tone.

Again, children's voices echoed around the stairs. The children, Juliana knew, liked Gillie quite a lot, for he always had a story and a smile for them.

"Harriette. James. Charles. Jane. Come here," she demanded.

Halfheartedly the children slouched into the parlor, while the rest of them raced outside in a yelling and jostling mass, spilling the letters Gillie had brought in all over the place. Gillie rushed forward to pick them up at the same time she did, and they nearly knocked heads together.

"Do you need help, Miss Pritchard?" Gillie asked.

"Not today, Uncle Gillie," she told him. "I think I can manage."

He finished picking up the letters and placed them back on the salver. "I thought I saw a letter for you, Miss Pritchard. Make sure you check the pile."

Distracted by the remaining four children who had begun riding the banister again, Juliana nodded. "I will." She immediately redirected her attention to the foursome and clapped her hands together. "You four, come with me to the parlor."

An expression of relief on his face, Gillie slunk from the hallway.

Juliana shepherded the children into the parlor and sat them down on the couch near Aunt Pesha, who watched all of this with a critical eye.

"You four have agreed to be gnomes and fairies," Juliana reminded them. "I need you to practice serving food to our fund-raiser guests. To that end, I've recruited Aunt Pesha."

Aunt Pesha gave them all a regal nod of her gray head.

"We're going to go into the garden and serve Aunt Pesha," Juliana informed them.

"Miss Pritchard," the boy named James said. He was the youngest of the four. "When can we go fishing?"

The other three children groaned almost in unison.

"Stop it, James. We're tired of hearing about your fishing," Harriette said. She had nearly reached eight years old and considered herself an adult.

Charles, the one who could never sit still, snorted aloud. "I'm going to stick a big fish in your mouth to shut you up."

"Now, Charles," Juliana warned.

"But Miss Pritchard," Jane said, "James never stops talking about his fish. We can't stand it any more. If he doesn't be quiet, I won't be a fairy."

"And I won't be a gnome," Charles declared.

"And I won't be a fairy, either," Harriette added.

Juliana stifled a sigh. James had worn them all down with his constant insistence on going fishing. Apparently his father had been a fisherman before some chance disease had taken both his parents. While she felt bad for the boy, his constant whining had become irritating. "Later, James. I promise we'll fish. First we must finish our practicing."

"I want to go outside with my older brother. He always goes fishing. I want him to take me with him."

"James, do you want to be a gnome?" Juliana asked.

He nodded his head vigorously.

"Well, you can't be a gnome if you won't practice. Are you going to practice for me?"

He nodded with noticeably less enthusiasm.

"Good," Juliana declared. "Let's all go outside, then, into the gardens. Aunt Pesha, are you coming?"

"I'm coming, gel." Pesha stood on unsteady legs. "You'll be needing my help."

"Would you please direct the children on how they ought to deliver the platters of food?"

"I'd be delighted to."

Glad to have the old woman's assistance, Juliana led her little flock of gnomes and fairies outside into the gardens. Earlier, she'd had William set up a table with four chairs around it, and now she indicated that Pesha should sit at one of the chairs.

The old woman plopped into a chair and surveyed the children with a regal expression. "All right, gnomes and fairies, let me see how well you can manage."

Juliana led the children behind a small screen William had constructed out of vines and sticks to conceal the area where the food for the fund-raiser would be stored. Several small platters with domed lids sat upon a table. "All right, children, here is where you'll find the platters of food that you must bring to the guests. Each platter will be light enough for you to carry."

"What kind of food?" Harriette asked.

"I don't know yet," Juliana admitted. "Now, pick up the platter and, one at a time, walk out to Aunt Pesha. She'll explain what you must do from there."

Loud giggles interrupted her directions. Juliana glanced around the screen and noticed several children hiding behind a large bush. They had a bucket with them. Sensing that their purpose was less than noble, she shooed them away. "Please, children, try to behave, at least until I return you to the orphanage."

Laughing out loud, they scattered, two of them with

the bucket in hand. Juliana saw water slosh over the sides of the bucket and suspected they had some trick in store for one of their fellow orphans. She sighed, already exhausted by their antics, and refocused on the four who planned to serve the food. "Take a platter," she encouraged.

Their eyes wide, the children each lifted a platter and held it near their waist. Charles walked out first, followed by Harriette and then by Jane. James was the last one to go, only he wouldn't budge. Rather, he declared to Juliana in an excited voice that he was going to bring out a fish on a pole rather than a platter.

"Oh, James, just bring the platter outside and listen to what Aunt Pesha says," she told him. James obviously hadn't been the best choice for a gnome, but now that she'd started making a gnome of him, she couldn't replace him without hurting his feelings, and so she was stuck.

A flash of movement behind that same bush caught her attention. She glanced at the bush and found the same children hiding there with their bucket.

"James," a childish voice teased, "if you want to go fishing, here is a bucket of water for you."

Juliana watched as they picked up the bucket and prepared to toss it at him. "Don't you dare," she hissed at them.

Apparently her threats did little to frighten them, for they hauled the bucket backward and then propelled it forward. At the same time, James rushed toward Juliana, perhaps seeking shelter in her skirts. The rascals with the bucket moved it slightly at the last second to better aim at James's new position, and suddenly water was flying through the air.

It hit James square in the chest, then splashed backward to thoroughly douse Juliana in the face, neck, and shoulders. A single fish, which had apparently been in the bucket, flopped helplessly at her feet.

James scooped the fish up with a big smile. "I caught a fish!"

Squealing with laughter, the children scattered.

Juliana hurriedly wiped her face and upper arms with her skirt. The children had splashed her with saltwater, but they might as well have splashed her with acid. Both would have a terrible effect. She hadn't had any time to prepare herself for resisting the transformation. Her heart in her throat, she felt a familiar burning, itching sensation flood her limbs. "James, go out with Aunt Pesha," she directed.

"But Miss Pritchard, I caught a fish!"

"Go, James. Now."

His eyes large and wounded, he walked toward the gardens, stopping frequently to cast a glance at her.

Restlessness spread through her and the burning and itching intensified. She tried every trick she knew of— breathing slowly, focusing on calming images, anything she could think of—to stop the transformation, but she simply hadn't had the time to adequately focus her mind.

She was going to become one of the sea people . . . right there, at that moment, with only a flimsy screen for privacy. For one split second she contemplated running somewhere to hide, but she knew she hadn't the time, so instead she sat down in a little grassy nook near the screen and made certain no one was observing her.

Her breath coming fast, she bit her lip to prevent the cry that threatened to erupt from her and tore off her shoes and stockings. Then, the itching and burning becoming a bone-deep ache, she pulled her skirts down as far as they would go, to hide as much of her secret as possible. The sun was shining down upon her, drying up the seawater, but not quickly enough.

Inside, she felt her lungs reforming and her bones changing density. Her legs pressed against each other seemingly of their own accord and her skin became tougher, yet with a smooth and rubber quality. She stared as muscles grew one by one on her legs before her feet stretched and spread before flattening. Right before her eyes, her toes became webbed and dissolved into a silver dolphin's tail.

Even so, the transformation to sea person hadn't taken control of her body as fully as it usually did, because she was already drying. Only her lower portions seemed to be affected, and even that was reversing itself. Smothering a moan at the pain radiating from her lower limbs, she mouthed a silent prayer that everyone would stay away from her long enough for her to become a landwalker again.

Without warning, a small hand slipped into hers. Her eyes snapped open, and she stared into James's wide and fascinated gaze.

She sucked in a breath, her anxiety growing a hundredfold.

"Are you a fish, Miss Pritchard?" he whispered.

"A fish? Of course not," she whispered back in as persuasive a voice as she could muster.

"Then why do you have a fish's tail?" The boy's gaze roved downward.

She followed the direction of his stare and groaned. Her skirts had become bunched about half way up her body. Even as she watched, her lower limbs rippled with muscles that formed, then disappeared, as they hovered somewhere between legs and dolphin's tail. Quickly she pulled her skirts back down and calculated that she'd have no more than five minutes before she had fully resumed her landwalker form.

"How do you like my costume?" she asked him.

"Your costume? Why are you wearing a fish costume?"

"Why, since you all enjoy Uncle Gillie's stories about the sea people so much," she invented wildly, "I thought we could have a brief theater adaptation of one of the stories, and I'm volunteering to play the lead."

"Everyone," he shouted suddenly, making her jump, "listen! Miss Pritchard wants to have a play, and she wants to be one of the sea people."

"You're a smart little boy, aren't you, James," Juliana muttered. "Show me how smart you are by keeping quiet until I tell you otherwise."

"What was that, young man?" Aunt Pesha's voice warbled from her seat in the garden. "What did you say?"

James jumped up and down on his short legs. "Come here, everyone! Look at Miss Pritchard's costume."

Juliana waved to him in a panic. "Shh, James. I don't want everyone over here—"

"Where are you, young man?" Aunt Pesha demanded. "What are you saying? That Miss Pritchard is one of the sea people?"

The boy laughed aloud. "She is, she is, she is."

Cold with fear, Juliana checked her skirt to make sure her lower half was completely covered. Then she focused on James. "Stop it, James," she demanded sternly. "I'm not one of the sea people. I simply want to pretend to be one."

"Miss Pritchard, what are you and James doing?" Aunt Pesha called out from a distance away. "I'm coming over there."

Swallowing, Juliana smoothed her skirt and answered loudly, "James and I were just having a discussion about the theatrical production the orphans will be putting on. Stay where you are, Aunt Pesha. We'll be out in a moment."

"We want to do a story about the sea people," James said.

"Indeed." The old lady declared. "That's most irregular."

"I don't find Miss Pritchard's suggestion irregular at all," a male voice announced. Seconds later, Cole strolled into view. "The sea people may be dangerous, but they're also rather fascinating."

Juliana felt her internal temperature plummet even more. Though the sensation was mild, her legs still itched and burned; she knew she hadn't fully regained legs yet. Cole simply had to lift her skirt to discover how terribly she'd betrayed him. She stared into his blue gaze, one that had reflected such tenderness lately, and she wished with all of her heart that things had been different, that her life would have followed a different path, that she could change the future. For she knew without any doubt at all that the future which awaited her did not involve Cole.

"Miss Pritchard wants to be one of the sea people," the boy interrupted, his voice high with apparent excitement.

Juliana fought the impulse to squeeze her eyes shut and wait for the ax to fall. Rather, she threw a smile at Cole, and patted her skirt. "Sit down here, James, and be quiet. You're confusing me with all of that talk and bouncing around."

The little boy complied with a subtle yank at her skirt, as though he wished everyone to see her dolphin's tale. She managed to hold her skirt down and foil his attempt. She figured she had about three minutes left before she had legs again.

Perspiration gathered on her brow and began to drip into her eyes, stinging them.

"What's this?" the boy asked, picking up one of her stockings.

Juliana threw a quick look at Cole. He was staring at her other stocking and slippers. Embarrassed, she snatched the stocking from James. "Sometimes I like to walk around with my feet bare. The grass feels wonderfully soft."

"As long as you don't step on a bee," James observed in a knowledgeable little voice.

Cole smiled indulgently. "Miss Pritchard apparently enjoys pampering her feet."

Disgusted by how ridiculous she must appear, Juliana managed a smile in reply.

"So, you want to act out the role of a sea maiden," Cole murmured, his gaze warm.

She nodded. "Uncle Gillie has been filling the children's ears with many tales regarding the sea people. They love those stories so much that I thought this year's theatrical production could include a skit on the sea people."

"Miss Pritchard wants to be in the lead," James informed them all, his expression solemn.

At that moment, Juliana would have very much liked to stick a fish into James's mouth and silence him, however temporarily.

Head cocked, Cole's smile grew. "In the lead? How so?"

"I'm going to be one of the sea people," she reluctantly replied.

James jumped up from her skirt. "Miss Pritchard already has a costume."

"Oh?" Cole lifted an eyebrow.

"I'm having it made," Juliana said, her stomach tight. Silently she began to review the escape routes she'd planned out earlier.

"Can I see it beforehand?" Cole pressed, a smile playing about his lips. "I'd enjoy a private viewing."

"It's under here," James announced, and grasped the edge of her skirt.

"James, don't," she scolded, her voice firm. "You're behaving very badly."

"Don't you want him to see your silver tail?" the boy asked.

"I don't have a silver tail, James." Shaking her head as though amused by the silliness of youth, she focused on Cole. "I'm afraid you'll have to wait for the play to see me wearing it. It's bad luck to see a costume before the day of the event."

"I certainly don't want to tempt fate," Cole murmured.

"She does have a silver tail," James insisted. "I saw it!"

"Oh, does she?" Cole sounded amused, too, though Juliana fancied that a thread of doubt had entered his voice. "And she's wearing it now?"

Again the boy tried to grasp her skirt, evidently to prove his point.

She swatted his hands away. "James, stop it."

"Please, Miss Pritchard, show him your costume."

Juliana glanced at Cole, and forced a smile. "I must

tell you, Cole, I had no idea how difficult children can be. James is a sweetheart, but he's also so single-minded that sometimes I think he'll drive me mad."

At that moment, Aunt Pesha rounded the twig screen and examined Juliana. "Why are you sitting here behind this screen, gel?"

"James and I were having a small, private chat, and Cole joined us," Juliana patiently explained, though she wanted to scream. "We were discussing the possibility of a play regarding the sea people. What do you think, Aunt Pesha? Would the guests attending the fund-raiser enjoy such a topic?"

"Oh, they'd enjoy a drama very much," Gillie said, choosing that moment to stick his head around the screen as well. "Especially one about the sea people. Perhaps after seeing the production, someone in town will come forward and admit to seeing one of them."

Disbelief nearly made Juliana giddy. Soon, she'd have the entire household by her side, while she sat behind this flimsy screen with a dolphin's tail hidden beneath her skirt. She moved her lower half, testing to see if her tail had become legs yet, but she felt too itchy and numb to be sure *what* she had.

Cole nodded. "It's decided, then. Juliana will lead a small drama about the sea people." He held a hand out to her, offering to assist her to her feet.

Pretending not to see his hand, she busied herself with fixing a button on her bodice. She didn't want to risk standing unless she absolutely had to.

"Juliana?" he murmured. "Let me help you up."

"Just one moment." Desperately she cast about for another delaying tactic, but couldn't think of a single one.

James shook his head. His high, piping voice held both knowledge and disgust. "She can't stand up, Mr. Strangford. She has a tail. Did you ever see a fish walk around?"

"James, I wish you would stop this nonsense about a tail," Juliana scolded.

Aunt Pesha shook her head. "That boy is obsessed with fish and fishing. Has been since the first moment he arrived."

Juliana could have kissed Aunt Pesha for offering an explanation for the boy's strange claims. Lowering her voice, Juliana added, "His father was a fisherman. I think that's why he is always thinking about fish."

Cole looked at her oddly. "He's certainly determined to prove that you have a tail."

His small arms on his hips, James sulked. "No one believes me."

Juliana moved her lower half a little, and discovered that where she'd only felt one limb a moment ago, she now felt two. She nearly melted into the ground with relief. She grasped Cole's hand and, with her free hand, gathered up her skirts higher than usual, displaying a pair of very human legs.

He glanced at them as he helped her up, and his expression smoothed out. "Are you still set on having four children?"

She laughed aloud, the sound more an expression of relief than amusement. "Perhaps just three."

Out of the corner of her eye, she caught a satisfied glance pass between Pesha and Gillie. Clearly the pair of them couldn't be happier over her upcoming nuptials with Cole.

"Let's go into the parlor for some lemonade," Aunt Pesha suggested. "Gillie, take these children somewhere . . . anywhere, in fact, but in the parlor."

Sighing, Gillie nodded. "I'll tell them another story." He walked back toward where the four children were playing—James included—and gathered them around him. The little group walked toward a tree and plopped down into the shade.

Cole swooped down to pick up her abandoned stockings and slippers.

Her cheeks warm, Juliana held out a hand. "I think I'd better put those back on."

He smiled as he gave them to her. She stuffed the stockings into her apron pocket, and slipped her feet into the shoes. Then, together, they entered the manor. Juliana paused by the hallway table and glanced through the letters Gillie had brought in earlier. The old gypsy had claimed to have a letter for her, but as she looked through them, she found that they were mostly addressed to Cole, with one for Aunt Pesha.

Cole lifted an eyebrow. "Expecting a letter?"

"Uncle Gillie said earlier that he thought I had received a letter, but I guess he was wrong. There's nothing here for me."

"To the parlor, then," Cole said, and brought her into the room for a glass of much-needed lemonade.

Thirteen

❧

COLE LIFTED THE LEATHER DIVING SUIT HE'D been working on and slipped his legs into the lower portion. He paused to glance at himself in the looking glass he'd had William bring to his laboratory. It fit rather well, he decided, the trousers reaching all the way to the floor, with plenty of fabric left over to create a watertight seal within his boots. He'd waterproofed the leather with special grease and, as he shrugged the upper portion onto his shoulders, he realized that he still needed to line the suit with flannel, to keep him warm at levels deeper than he'd ever dived before.

Idly he wondered if his competitor, William James, had produced a full-body rig like his, or had used a more traditional approach and created a half-suit that ended at the waist. He'd heard via post from the University of Edinburgh that Mr. James had already petitioned for a meeting regarding his design of the diving suit. That piece of information had lent some urgency to the situation and renewed Cole's interest in completing his invention. In any case, he felt confident that his own suit had many benefits over the conventional style,

including its warmth and its pressurization properties,
allowing the diver to go down farther without suffering
so much from the painful weight of the water around
him.

"That's a fine wedding suit, Cole," Gillie observed.

Cole stiffened with surprise and spun around to espy
Gillie in the doorway. "You have a bad habit of sneaking
up on people. One of these days you're going to frighten
the life out of someone."

Returning his attention to the diving apparatus, he
snapped the buckles on the front of the suit and picked
up the helmet. Made of copper and possessing a glass
face plate, it was designed to keep the water out and his
face dry while he breathed air from the compressed oxygen tank he would strap on his back. Early morning dew
had fogged the face plate. Cole rubbed it dry with a
cloth.

"It's nine o'clock now. You only have about an hour
to put on proper clothes," Gillie reminded him.
"Reverend Deane is expecting us at the church before
ten-thirty, and the ceremony will begin at precisely ten-
thirty. We'll need some time to arrive there—separately,
of course, from Juliana."

Cole settled the diving helmet over his head. "Do you
have the license?"

"I purchased it from the parish clerk two days ago."

"Good. Everything's settled then."

"Yes, all is in place but you." Gillie walked over to
Cole and rapped on his helmet sharply. "Come back to
the house and get dressed."

Frowning, Cole took the helmet off. "I should be finished here in about ten minutes. I'll meet you inside."

Gillie shook his head. "Oh, no. I'm not falling for

that line. I'm going to make sure you have a wife before the sun sets this evening."

Cole lifted his hands in a warding-off gesture. "Did I say I didn't want to get married?"

"You don't have to say it. Your actions speak louder than words."

"Just because I'm not racing to dress in a black jacket and trousers, you think I don't want to marry Juliana?" Cole snorted. "I do want to marry her, Uncle, or I wouldn't have asked her in the first place. I'm simply trying to finish my diving suit, so I might present it to the Royal Oceanographic Society before William James does."

"I think you're getting cold feet," Gillie reflected, as though he hadn't heard Cole.

Cole sighed. "All right. I'll go inside and get dressed now, if only to appease you."

He shrugged out of the diving suit and folded it carefully before laying it in a large trunk. While Gillie watched, he locked the trunk, and then followed his uncle outside, stopping only to lock the laboratory door. He stood very close to finishing his diving suit now, and didn't want to leave it vulnerable to sabotage again. Once he'd satisfied himself that his invention was secure, he returned to his bedchamber and began to make himself presentable. As he washed and shaved, he thought about what Gillie had said. Was he regretting his impulsive proposal to Juliana?

At the time, a proposal had seemed the right thing to do. And although he and Juliana had gotten along famously over the last several weeks, validating his decision to marry her, a nagging little voice in the back of his mind kept insisting that something was amiss. Still, he'd discovered that Juliana possessed a kind and generous nature, and the deep tenderness he'd developed for her and the delight he found in her presence had soothed his worries. The thought of having her all to himself later in his bed also brought him a large degree of pleasure. There had been so much tension between them, so much teasing and alluding that he was powerless to stop the blood in his body from traveling to embarrassing areas the minute he touched her in any way.

Once he'd finished with the razor, he pulled on black trousers and a black jacket of superfine wool, and selected his finest linen shirt. His waistcoat was crafted of white velvet decorated with silk embroidered vines, and his cravat was made of white silk, as befitted the seriousness of the occasion. He put on polished black shoes, and slipped a gold watch fob into his pocket, and reflected that he hadn't dressed up this formally for many a month.

He looked around his bedchamber one last time before leaving for the church, his gaze lingering on the large tester bed in the corner of the room. Smoothing his waistcoat, the velvety fabric beneath his fingers suddenly became silken and warm in his mind as he imagined how it would feel to stroke Juliana's bare skin later that evening. She would dig her fingernails into his mattress as he pleasured her, and shiver beneath his lips and hands, and finally, when he took her, she would cry out his name, and tremble, and warm him with a gaze that possessed all of the promise of a sunrise . . .

Smiling, he turned away from the bed and headed for the front door, passing William along the way, who was directing an army of footmen and maidservants in preparing the house for the wedding breakfast. The sound of clanging pots and voices raised in industry, along with the various delicious breakfast smells and large bouquets of flowers placed in every nook and cranny, had transformed the old mansion into a place of light and happiness.

A catchy tune occurred to Cole and he began to whistle softly as he sought out Gillie in the carriageway in front of the manor. Gillie, for his part, looked very ceremonial in a similar suit of black wool superfine, although the older gypsy had enlivened his outfit with a scarlet-colored scarf at his throat rather than a cravat. Cole smiled when he saw his uncle and hopped into the gig that was awaiting them. Gillie climbed aboard, too, and moments later Cole was heading off to a new life with the woman he loved.

AUNT PESHA STUCK HER HEAD OUT OF JULIana's bedchamber and peered down the hall. She nodded once, evidently receiving a signal from a well-placed maidservant, and then pulled herself back inside before shutting the door.

"My nephew's gone to the church, gel," the older woman informed her. "We're safe now."

Juliana trailed her fingers down her wedding gown, which lay spread across her bed. The dressmaker in town had outdone herself in sewing the white satin creation, which followed a pattern designed by a famous London fashion firm. Trimmed with bobbin lace and tiny seed pearls, and gathered beneath the breasts with a white velvet ribbon, it gave Juliana the confidence she needed to face what could only be a difficult day ahead. Continually pretending to be what she wasn't had become very, very hard for her. Only the thought of her people's desperation to be free of the gypsy's dark spell kept her at Cole's side with the truth sealed permanently inside her.

"You look tense," Aunt Pesha observed. The older woman had also dressed for the occasion in a beautiful gown of pale lavender silk. Amethysts hung from her wrinkled neck and ears.

"I am," Juliana agreed. Indeed, she'd spent all night in tears over the fact that she was in love with a man she planned to betray. She'd even taken some time to contemplate telling him the whole truth, and wondered if together they could heal all of the old wounds between their families. But did she really have the right to take that chance, considering how many lives hung in the balance? In the end, she decided that she didn't.

"Don't be nervous, gel." Aunt Pesha patted her gently on the shoulder. "Everything will go smoothly. Gillie and I are both so pleased to have you become part of our family, particularly when we see what joy you've brought Cole. With you, he has a chance to enjoy all of the love and contentment that life has to offer."

And the pain and suffering of betrayal, Juliana silently added, hurting inside.

Aunt Pesha glanced at the clock on the mantel shelf. "'Tis almost a quarter after ten o'clock. We should be going if we're to arrive at the church in time."

Juliana allowed Aunt Pesha to take her hand and lead her down the staircase past the footmen and maidservants who paused to applaud her as she moved by. She smiled and inclined her head, grateful for their support. They'd been working steadily on arranging the house to her specifications. Rather than plan for a ceremony and breakfast full of pomp and ceremony, she'd designed their breakfast as an intimate, informal gathering more suited to the small number of townspeople she and Cole had invited.

At the bottom of the staircase, Mr. Wood waited for her. When she reached the floor, he stepped backward and surveyed her with moist eyes.

"My dearest daughter, you look so beautiful," he murmured, opening his arms for a hug. "I am so happy that this day has finally arrived for you."

Juliana acknowledged to herself that Mr. Wood could have had a very successful career in the theater. She moved into his embrace and offered him a hug in return. "Thank you, Father."

Out of view of Aunt Pesha, Mr. Wood winked at her.

Reminded of her duplicity, Juliana broke from his embrace and allowed him to take her arm. "We had better leave for the church." *Before I lose my courage*, she added silently.

They both rejoined Aunt Pesha, who ushered them outside to the barouche that was waiting for them. Carefully holding her gown, she climbed inside the carriage, followed by both Pesha and Mr. Wood. Soon, they were off, bouncing down the carriageway toward Shoreham, Juliana wondering if she would be able to keep from crying during the ceremony.

Down High Street her carriage rumbled, past the River Adur which spilled its waters into the ocean and Shoreham Beach, with its drift of pink and white thrift. Fishing boats bobbed gently on the river, most of them heading out into the ocean's currents. She watched out the window as the carriage turned right onto Church Street and rolled past the Thomas Macy Warehouse and the Mitchell & Sons Candle Factory before pulling to a stop in front of the church.

Several other carriages were parked nearby, suggesting that many of their guests had already arrived. Her stomach fluttering, Juliana waited for their driver to open the door, and then she descended from the carriage after Mr. Wood. Aunt Pesha followed after her, and as a threesome they entered the church.

A sea of faces turned to stare at Juliana as soon as she walked into the vestibule. The organist in the balcony began to play a stirring wedding march. Gripping Mr. Wood's arm, Juliana walked up to the front of the church, where Cole awaited her. He had dressed completely in black and white, and looked so elegant and noble that her breath caught in her throat and the fluttering in her stomach doubled.

Mr. Wood released her at Cole's side and took up post a few steps back, next to Gillie and Aunt Pesha. Cole smiled and twined his fingers through hers. She felt herself trembling and fought to remain strong in both mind and purpose. Even so, a notion that she was dreaming took hold of her and wouldn't let go. The sensation persisted even as Reverend Deane performed the marriage ceremony. When the reverend had finished making her utter promises she could never keep, she numbly signed the registry and swore an oath that a number of details—her full name, date of birth, parents' names, among other things—were true. A tender look softened Cole's eyes as he signed his own name beneath hers, and then he slid a gold band etched with flowers on her finger. To seal their newly married status, Cole kissed her very gently, his lips lingering on hers, and suddenly she wanted to throw her arms around his neck and pull him close and whisper to him the truth, and beg for his forgiveness.

Instead, she left the church as Mrs. Cole Strangford. Cries of best wishes went up as she emerged into the sunlight, and someone threw rose petals.

As husband and wife, and amid the congratulations of many voices, they climbed back into the carriage outside the church. Aunt Pesha, Gillie, and Mr. Wood boarded the other carriage. As their small cavalcade rumbled out of town to return to Shoreham Park Manor, Cole pulled Juliana close and stroked her hair gently. He seemed to know that she felt completely overwhelmed and didn't try to start a conversation outside of a few observations regarding the ceremony—that he thought it had gone very well, and how pleased he was to finally have her for his wife.

Rather than soothe her, however, each one of his declarations tore at her heart. Tears pricked her eyes, and she focused her attention on the scenery passing by rather than his gentle, understanding gaze. When they finally arrived back at the manor, and embroiled themselves in the intricacies of the wedding breakfast and the few Romany wedding traditions that she'd arranged for, she began to feel faint.

The entry hall had been cleared of its furniture and filled with tables for dining, as it was the only space in the house large enough to seat fifty guests. She and Cole sat at the head of a table decorated with great bouquets of wildflowers and wrought iron étagères that spilled fruit onto the Battenburg lace tablecloth. Gillie, Pesha, and Mr. Wood sat with them, while the rest of their guests sat at other tables decorated in a likewise manner. Maidservants and footmen ran back and forth from the dining room.

She barely nibbled on the offerings of eggs and toast, cold meats, pastries, and jam set before her; and had hardly a word for Gillie, who sat on her left. She caught Cole and Gillie exchanging several concerned glances as the morning wore into early afternoon, and though she tried to appear gay and lighthearted, she just couldn't hold up the pretense . . . not now, not when she sat next to this man who had given her his name and offered her his protection, and his home, and his love.

Just as she'd pressed a hand to her brow and wondered how much longer she and Cole would have to linger, Mrs. Morris and Mrs. Hobbs approached her and exclaimed over the beauty of both the bride and the ceremony. Juliana noticed that Mrs. Duquet had chosen not to attend. Relief washed through her.

"I had a tear in my eye when you two kissed," Mrs. Morris confessed in her straightforward manner.

Juliana summoned a smile. It quickly faltered. "Why thank you, Mrs. Morris. Cole and I are so very pleased that you could join us on this special day." She turned toward the other woman. "And you also, Mrs. Hobbs. We're very happy to have you with us this morning."

Mrs. Hobbs thanked them in reply before murmuring something about the orphanage fund-raiser and how much they appreciated her help in organizing it. Again, Juliana told her how much she'd enjoyed assisting with the project, and that most of the preparations had been completed. Now they simply had to wait for the day of the fund-raiser to arrive.

"Will you have returned from your bridal tour before the fund-raiser?" Mrs. Morris asked, her brows drawn together, clearly worried.

"We won't leave for another two weeks," Cole assured her, his voice smooth and deep.

"Oh, that's a relief." Mrs. Morris smiled. "And where will you be going?"

"We haven't decided yet," Juliana murmured. "Perhaps the Continent. Or maybe even the Spice Islands."

"Will you have enough time to plan your tour?"

"Cole and I tend to do things . . . impulsively."

"And it works very well for you," Mrs. Morris stoutly declared.

Then, noticing the well-wishers lined up behind them, the two ladies moved on.

"You've made a conquest of them," Cole whispered to her as they left. "Considering they're the ones who control most of the town's social functions, I'd say you've been accepted into the bosom of Shoreham."

Juliana nodded, aware from the tone of his voice that her friendship with Mrs. Morris and Mrs. Hobbs had pleased him. The high value that he placed on the opinion of those in town bothered her, particularly since some day, he could very well discover that he hadn't married Juliana Pritchard, and had instead wedded Juliana St. Germaine, his mortal enemy, who had duped him thoroughly and might have well emasculated him while she was at it.

A fresh wave of dizziness passed over her. "Cole," she asked huskily, "how much longer must we stay?"

He glanced down the long line of well-wishers still waiting to talk to them and admitted that they probably had another hour of small talk before they could escape.

"I'll have Gillie bring some refreshments up to my bedchamber," he added. "So we might relax alone. In fact, perhaps there's a way we can speed things up."

"I'd be grateful for anything you can do," she whispered against his ear.

He held her hand in a tight grip. "Hold on, Juliana. It will be over soon."

Slipping a hand around her waist, they stood as a pair and walked toward the first pair of guests—a wealthy banker and his wife—who were waiting to wish them well. At the same time, the small orchestral ensemble hidden behind a screen struck up a cotillion, encouraging people onto the dance floor. The atmosphere in the hall took on a merry quality that Juliana couldn't appreciate, no matter how hard she tried.

Cole exchanged a few pleasantries with the banker and his wife. Juliana also dredged up a comment or two before they moved on to the next couple. In this manner they spoke briefly with all of their guests and, much to her surprise, Juliana realized that the time spent talking to the townsfolk did go much faster when she and Cole were the ones moving around and deciding when to shuffle to the next guest, rather than sitting behind a table and waiting for the guest to take the hint and move on. At length, they finished with the last couple at the end of their receiving line, and almost everyone outside of Cole and Juliana moved onto the dance floor to enjoy a high-spirited country dance.

Cole steered her toward Gillie and Mr. Wood, who appeared deep in conversation on the edge of the dance floor, and told the two men that she and Cole were going to sneak off to their bedchamber, to "relax" from the labors of the day. Gillie grinned, slapped Cole on the back, and told him that he'd had brandy sent to their room, while Mr. Wood hugged her again and told her to take a nap and get some sleep.

Thanking the two older men, Cole swept her up into his arms in a grand romantic gesture and started toward the staircase, her white bridal gown trailing over his arms like a silken waterfall. Several of their guests saw them and sent up a cheer that followed them all the way up the staircase and onto the second floor.

When they reached the door to Cole's bedchamber, it stood slightly ajar. He kicked it open with his foot rather than release his grip on her and brought her inside. She glanced around the room with a fair bit of curiosity over what she'd discover in his inner sanctum. What she found, however, looked typical for how she'd imagined a man's bedchamber might appear: buff wallpaper with a fleur-de-lis pattern which was suitably restful, a plain varnished floor warmed by a few scatter rugs, a simple mahogany wardrobe, tester bed, and bureau cluttered with pieces of wire and metal objects, a large washstand bearing a shaving brush and razor, and wooden blinds on windows that someone had opened completely to encourage an ocean breeze to drift in.

Someone—Aunt Pesha, probably—had placed an arrangement of wild roses in full bloom on a table near the bed. Gillie must have contributed the decanter of brandy and two snifters. Overall, the bedchamber looked cozy and inviting, with a fresh neatness that couldn't help please even the fussiest of brides. Juliana, however, couldn't summon energy to do anything other than collapse on his bed.

Cole laughed softly. "The day was rather trying, no, Mrs. Strangford?"

"Unbelievably so," she agreed.

The mattress sagged beneath her as Cole sat on the edge of the bed and began to undo the buttons down her back, one by one, his touch casual rather than impatient with desire. Curious, she lifted her head to see what sort of expression he wore, and saw only concern.

"You need to relax," he informed her, "and I'm going to see that you do. We have the rest of the day to spend in my bedchamber, so there's no need to rush to anything."

She let out a long, shuddering sigh, but otherwise, remained quiet.

"First, we need to get this dress off you. It must weigh at least thirty pounds, with all of those pearls sewn on it. I don't know how you managed to remain standing."

His sympathy brought a tightness to her chest. Even so, she allowed her muscles to relax while he finished unbuttoning her gown, and then sat her up so he might slip it off her shoulders. Once he'd rid her of the heavy white satin, and a cool breeze began blowing across her body, she felt as though a tremendous weight had been lifted from her. Gratitude for his pampering—when he could have been demanding his husbandly rights—only made her feel more guilty for continuing to betray him.

He laid her gown across the chair and approached the bed again. The mattress sagged as he climbed onto the bed and positioned his knees on either side of her body. Clad only in a cotton shift, she lay still and soon felt his hands upon her back, rubbing and kneading away the soreness, bringing exquisite pleasure to the parts of her that ached from sheer exhaustion. She moaned deep in her throat and gave herself over to him.

"Juliana, if you take off your shift, I'll be able to massage your muscles more effectively," he murmured.

Needing no more encouragement than that, she dragged the shift over her head with his help, and then relaxed against the bed again. She could almost feel his gaze upon her, burning across her bare skin; and when a soft sigh escaped him and his hands cupped her bottom, she smiled, secure in the knowledge that he wanted her, but was putting her needs first.

Soon his hands were on her skin again, his touch warm yet firm. He seemed to have an uncanny knack of knowing exactly what hurt the most, and by the time he finished with her back, there wasn't an inch of skin or muscle on her that didn't tingle pleasurably. But he didn't stop there. He moved downward, to her thighs, and rubbed the muscles there before traveling lower to her calves and her feet.

She practically purred in her throat while he worked on her, and started to feel very sleepy toward the end. At some point he stopped massaging her and threw a larger blanket over her body and, sighing gratefully, she drifted off to sleep.

COLE YAWNED AND PULLED JULIANA CLOSER against his body. The sun had already begun its descent to the western horizon, and a cool breeze was coming off the ocean to sweep across his bed. He breathed in that salty air, unable to sleep but not really wanting to, either. For the last several hours he had lain next to Juliana, naked, tracing lazy circles around the luscious contours of her breasts and hips with his fingers, and burning the image of her face and form into his memory.

His own restraint and tenderness earlier had surprised him, given how badly he'd been wanting her these past weeks. He discovered he was more interested in securing her comfort and happiness than anything else, and he marveled at it. For the first time, the word "love" and Juliana's name connected themselves in his mind, and he wondered how long the connection had been there, tugging at his heart and trying to force its way into his consciousness.

He loved her.

Smiling, he fitted his body closer to hers and closed his eyes, breathing in her scent . . . something sweet and flowery and indescribable. He tried to imagine where they would be five years hence. How many children would they have frolicking around their feet?

A sudden movement brought him back from his fantasies. Juliana began tossing restlessly, her brows drawn together and a little whimper escaping her. She was having a nightmare of some sort, he realized. He pushed himself up on one elbow and brushed a few stray locks of chestnut hair back from her forehead. Should he wake her? He watched for several moments as her movements grew more urgent and another, more tortured moan emerged from deep within her. When he saw two tears slip from the corners of her eyes and trace their way down her cheeks, however, he couldn't stand to observe her suffering any longer and reached over to gently shake her shoulder.

"Juliana," he murmured. "Wake up."

Abruptly her eyes flew open and she gasped, clearly disoriented. She tried to sit up, but he held her still.

"You were having a nightmare," he said.

"A nightmare?" She looked around, the fear slowly leaking from her brilliant eyes. She blinked, and relaxed back against the mattress.

He wiped away the wetness on her cheeks. "What was it about, sweetheart?"

Blinking again, she paused. "I don't remember."

He had the odd feeling that she'd lied to him. "Are you still frightened?"

"I'm all right now," she assured him, glancing at his bare chest. A blush darkened her cheeks. Evidently she'd just realized that they were both lying on the bed completely naked. With interest, he watched her attention drop lower, to the blanket that covered his erection. The blanket had been flat against him before, but now it had tented upward in an unmistakable fashion.

Casually she pulled the blanket over her breasts.

Amused, he leaned close to her and kissed her, gently spreading her lips apart with his own and pushing his tongue into her mouth. Her lips felt hot and moist and inviting. A flush of desire passed through him when her tongue touched his tentatively.

"Juliana . . ." Cole tore his mouth from hers and buried his nose in her dark locks. The sweet, flowery smell was strong in her hair, intoxicating him. She smiled faintly, almost sadly. He ran his fingers through her curls, combing them out and encouraging them to fan across the pillow.

His breath caught in his throat. She looked so wild, so untamed. He pulled her hard against him, crushing her breasts to his chest, and felt her soft arms encircle his waist. Hungrily he kissed her again, though there was nothing gentle about it this time. He thrust his tongue into her mouth, deepening the kiss as their tongues wrestled against each other and the blanket covering her slid lower, revealing her milky-white thighs and the dark curls between them.

She moaned into his mouth and traced the lines of muscles on his back, her fingers now eagerly exploring him. Cole shifted his weight down so he could trail his lips along the ample curves of her breasts. He tasted every surface, from the delicate bones of her ribcage to the satiny undersides of breasts, and every once in a while he flicked his tongue out. Each time she arched her back, pushing against his face, clearly wanting so much more.

He had never felt so alive making love, never longed so much to possess a woman as he now longed to possess Juliana. Groaning against her perfumed skin, he slid his mouth to her nipples and kissed them gently, with just the slightest hint of pressure and moistness.

Juliana gasped, her voice trembling. "Cole . . ."

Warm waves of pleasure shot through him as her small hand found his erection and began to caress it as he'd taught her in the cave, moving her fist up and down his hot, hard length with such eagerness that he muttered incoherently with delight. Playfully he began to trace circles around her now-hardened nipples, stopping to squeeze them gently with his fingers. Juliana whimpered and rubbed the dark curls between her thighs against him, instinctively understanding how to receive even more direct pleasure from him.

But Cole wasn't about to give her release that quickly. He lifted her slightly, so that her breasts jutted toward him, and enclosed one pink nipple with his mouth. Extravagantly he ran his tongue over its sensitive surface and sucked greedily at it, drawing a groan from deep inside her, before stroking and licking her other nipple, which had hardened to a little nub.

Juliana groaned, her small hand moving faster on his erection.

Laughing, he moved his body away from hers slightly. "Greedy puss."

"I can't help it, Cole," she confessed, her voice soft and breathy with passion.

He smiled and spread her legs slowly with his hands, then dipped his head down to run his tongue along the skin of her inner thigh. She bucked against him, instinctively pushing her dark curls into his face, and he complied to a degree, flicking his tongue across her moist opening and drawing a surprised gasp from her. She opened her legs further, baring herself to him, and he licked her gently, feeling the moistness of her and knowing she was more than ready for him.

Her entire body began to tremble. When he slipped his tongue inside her, she cried out and dug her fingers into his hair. Relishing the taste of her arousal, he slipped his tongue further into her hot opening, all the way to the small piece of flesh that was proof of her virginity. Her hips moved wildly against his face, and he could feel the muscles around his tongue clenching softly. Quickly he withdrew from her.

"Oh, Cole . . . please . . ." she whispered, and he heard real pain in her voice.

"Juliana," he muttered, his own need becoming almost too painful to bear. "When I take your virginity, I'll hurt you. I'm sorry."

"I don't care," she panted, and twisted her body so that she was between his legs, and on top of him. "Make love to me now, Cole. Now."

Her softness pressing against his erection elicited a deep moan from him. He wrapped his arms around her waist and shifted their bodies until she was beneath him, her legs spread and ready for him. The tip of his shaft moist with desire, he slipped a finger inside of her and probed that delicate membrane he had to break.

Low whimpers broke from her chest. "Please, Cole . . ."

He needed to stretch her, or he would hurt her terribly. Ignoring her whimpers, he slipped another finger inside of her and slowly scissored them. Her body arched violently against his fingers, and as soon as he felt he'd done what he could, he removed them, knowing how close she stood to ultimate release.

Hurriedly he positioned himself between her legs and guided the tip of his erection to her moist opening. Then, biting down on his lip to keep himself from letting out a loud cry, he thrust forward, burying himself deep within her softness and heat. Waves of pleasure flooded him. Desperately he craved climax, but he held his body perfectly still while he nuzzled her neck.

At his thrust, she'd gone completely still. A tear slipped out from the corner of her closed eyes. He kissed it away. "I'm so sorry, sweetheart."

Several seconds passed while neither of them moved. Then, suddenly, Juliana cupped his cheek and kissed him deeply on the mouth. He needed no further encouragement, and began to plunge into her, his rhythm slow and lazy even as their lips ground against each other in passionate abandon. He moaned as all of his muscles tightened and the pleasure that had been building in his body suddenly reached a peak before relaxing in a spectacular wave.

Still, he continued thrusting, feeling her tightening all around his erection until abruptly, she let out a small wail and began shuddering with the force of her pleasure. He held her tight and stared into her face as her trembling began to subside. Then, shocked by the pleasure his new wife had given him, pleasure he hadn't known it possible for anyone to feel, he kissed the corners of her mouth, their breath mingling in pants before settling down into soft groans.

"I love you, Juliana," he whispered against her ear.

Her eyes flew open to stare at him, and he lost himself in the colors of the sunrise, and all the promises held there.

A timid knock at the door distracted him. He stiffened with disbelief. Who would *dare* to disturb him on his wedding night? He wondered if maybe he'd imagined the sound. And yet, the knock echoed again, and he knew that he was going to have to answer it.

Apologizing to Juliana, he stood up and wrapped a blanket around his midsection. He covered her up to her eyes with the counterpane and then stomped over to the door. A snarl twisting his lips, he yanked the door open and stared into Gillie's worried eyes.

"This had better involve nothing less than blood or death," he growled.

His uncle remained firm in the face of his anger. "We have some visitors that you need to meet."

"Visitors? Uncle Gillie, have you gone mad? Don't disturb me until tomorrow, at the earliest!" He slammed the door in his uncle's face and prepared to walk away when the knock echoed again.

Cursing softly, he opened the door. "Gillie—"

"Cole, listen to me," his uncle demanded softly. "These visitors claim that the woman you married is not Juliana Pritchard."

Cole felt as though the wind had been knocked out of him. He stood there, staring at his uncle and not trusting his own ears. "What do you mean, I didn't marry Juliana Pritchard? Of course I did! She's lying in my bed right now. We just . . ."

"She isn't related to the Pritchards, Cole. I have the Pritchard family downstairs in my parlor right now. You need to come."

He shook his head. Disbelief filled him. "There's been some mistake. Put these people in a bedchamber somewhere, and I'll attend to them later."

"I can't, Cole. You must come now."

He glanced back at Juliana. Her eyes were very wide, yet trusting. Love for her overwhelmed him. His gut flared with loyalty. "Juliana would never betray me," he declared.

"I'm afraid she has."

"Why are you so certain, man?"

"These people know details that only the Pritchard family could know." Gillie paused, then added in a heavy voice, "Juliana's brother is downstairs, too."

Cole felt his heart clenching in a painful way. The loyalty flaring in his gut faded away, replaced by the ashes of betrayal. His entire world seemed to be coming down around him. Suddenly, he remembered his sense that something was amiss between himself and Juliana. He recalled his lingering reluctance to marry her, and knew that his instinct had sensed the truth even if his eyes had been blinded by Juliana's beauty and sweetness.

Pressing his lips into a grim line, Cole nodded. "I'll come at once."

Gillie turned away, and Cole shut the door, saying nothing else.

"Cole? What's wrong?" Juliana lifted her head to peer at him.

Without replying, he dragged on his trousers.

She pushed herself up on an elbow. "Who was that at our door?"

Keeping his gaze averted from her, he slipped his arms into his shirt and shrugged it on.

Wrapping a sheet around her body, she climbed out of bed to face him. "Cole, why are you dressing? What's wrong? What happened?"

Her face, he saw, had become several shades paler. "We have some visitors, Juliana," he bit out. "Perhaps you ought to get dressed too, and come down to meet them. They claim that you're not really Juliana Pritchard, but someone else. Of course I'm interested to hear what they have to say."

She swayed on her feet. "Oh, no . . ."

His heart throbbing dully in his chest, he shoved his feet into boots and walked out of the bedchamber.

Fourteen

❦

JULIANA FELT A STICKY WETNESS BETWEEN HER thighs, which she knew to be her own blood. Almost dizzy with anxiety and confusion, she cleaned herself up as best as she was able, and then surveyed the bedchamber for clothes to wear. Of course she hadn't any gowns in his room other than her wedding gown, which didn't seem appropriate given the circumstances, so she put on an old pair of breeches and a shirt she found in one of his bottom drawers and hurried back to her own room to dress in one of her muslin gowns.

All the while she wondered what had brought George to Shoreham Park Manor, for she knew that their visitors could be none other than her brother and at least one of the Pritchards. Who else could possibly expose her as a fake?

Her heart aching, she knew that their mission must have been compromised beyond repair. At the very least, the Pritchards knew that George had been masquerading as Cole Strangford. Now they had no choice but to give an explanation for their deception that Cole would accept, and leave.

Unless she had conceived a child this night, they had failed. And from what she'd heard, it took more than one night to conceive. Most likely, she had failed, not only herself, but all of the sea people, and Cole, too.

Abruptly the thought of losing him hurt more than any knife she could have thrust into her gut. She shrugged into a neat, well-worn muslin gown, in her haste creating a tiny rip in one of the seams, and shoved slippers onto her feet. Seconds later she was out of her bedchamber and running down the hall, taking the stairs two at a time before skidding to a halt near the parlor door.

Inside, she heard voices. One of them was her brother's, surprising her not in the least. Her stomach turning somersaults, she walked into the parlor and surveyed the others gathered there. Cole had slouched against the fireplace mantelshelf, his face inscrutable, while her brother George sat on a settee with a pretty, older woman.

Lila Whitham, Juliana thought.

An elderly man stood next to Lila. Juliana suspected the man's identity as Mr. Pritchard. The graying woman in the corner possessed some similarity to Aunt Pesha, and Juliana guessed her to be none other than Zelda Strangford.

The Woods, for their part, sat on a couch toward the outside of the room, and Gillie stood closest to Juliana, near the doorway. Gillie looked at her with disappointment written clearly on his face as she entered.

Turning away from him, she walked quickly to her brother, who stood up. Despite their situation, she was glad to see him. Carefully she studied him to see if she could pick up any clues as to where they stood, but came away without gleaning anything.

"George . . ." she murmured, sadness and grief bringing tears to her eyes. They'd probably failed, and lost so much.

He opened his arms and drew her into a brotherly embrace. Overwhelmed, she rested her head on his shoulder for a moment, before lifting her head to gaze at him.

"I am so sorry, dear sister," he murmured, the sadness she felt reflected in his eyes.

She nodded and stepped out of his embrace.

Cole snorted, his disgust unmistakable. "What a touching family reunion."

"Now, Cole," Gillie warned, but Juliana interrupted him.

"No, Uncle Gillie," she said. "Cole has a right to feel as he does."

"Gillie isn't your uncle," Cole growled, "so don't call him so."

Juliana lifted her chin. "We're married, Cole. He *is* my uncle now."

"I married Juliana Pritchard, whom I now discover is really Anna Pritchard, who is away at finishing school in Ireland." He pushed himself away from the mantelpiece and strolled toward her. "I don't know who *you* are, but you're certainly not my *wife*."

George stood up from his settee and inserted himself between Juliana and Cole. "Don't blame Juliana for what's happened, Mr. Strangford. Blame me, instead. I'm the instigator, and Juliana was simply caught up in my scheme."

Cole's lower lip curled. He touched a strand of hair that teased her shoulders. "Oh, she's completely innocent, is she?"

A flush settled into George's cheeks.

Sensing the situation was about to take a terrible turn, Juliana suggested in a loud voice, "Why don't we all introduce ourselves, and then George, perhaps you'll explain to my husband how all of this has occurred."

"This isn't a party, Juliana. We have no need for social niceties." Shaking his head, Cole turned his back on her and faced the windows, which were about as dark and inscrutable as his eyes.

"I'm sure Juliana would like to know who she's talking to," Gillie countered in a small voice. Over the next minute or so, Gillie introduced each of them in turn, confirming Juliana's suspicions about their identities. She observed each person closely and noticed George had sat rather close to Lila, and that Lila kept looking to her brother for reassurance. Indeed, even Mr. Pritchard seemed to accept George, despite the wrong they obviously must have known he'd perpetrated against them.

After Gillie had finished, George stepped forward and mentioned the name William James. At once Cole grew very still and attentive. As George began to spin the tale regarding their supposed efforts to spy upon Cole's progress with his diving apparatus, he nodded his head slowly, as though it all made perfect sense to him.

He confirmed her impression by remarking, "I'd been wondering who'd sabotaged my diving apparatus a month ago. Obviously *she* damaged it on behalf of William James." Indicating Juliana with a sharp hand gesture, he shook his head. "Did you know that I came into your bedchamber that night, and observed you sleeping? At least I thought you were sleeping. Obviously you weren't."

Juliana nodded unhappily. "I *did* sabotage your equipment, Cole. For William James. And I knew you had come into my bedchamber that evening. I'm so sorry."

He stared at her in stony silence, her apology not having the slightest impact on him.

She turned to George. "How did the Pritchards discover your true identity?"

"Through a stroke of terrible luck," he admitted. "It turns out that Zelda Strangford is friends with a Mrs. Howe of Buckland Village. Mrs. Howe exposed my deception."

Juliana sighed. They'd worked so hard to find holes like this in their scheme, in order to close them; it just didn't seem fair that the one hole they'd missed should sink their entire mission. But it had become more than a mission to Juliana. She'd fallen in love with him, and hurt him terribly, and now she'd have nothing but grief and a sense of failure to keep her company through the years that she'd spend under the sea.

"Juliana, I must ask you a question," Gillie interrupted, his brows drawn together. "Do you possess any Romany blood at all?"

Dearly she wished to give him the answer he wanted, but she couldn't prove any claims to a gypsy heritage, so why try? "I'm sorry, Gillie, but I come from English stock."

Cole's face paled. "Then you're even more worthless to me than I'd thought. I won't gain my inheritance unless I marry a proper Romany bride, so there is no use in trying to save this situation at all."

She hung her head, unable to defend herself in any way.

Without warning, he crossed the room in three strides until he stood directly in front of her. The furrows in his forehead spoke of deep suffering. "Why did you do it, Juliana? Why did you marry me? You only had to study my diving apparatus—or destroy it, even—before leaving. And yet, you chose to rip my heart from my chest with your betrayal."

The tears that she'd been keeping choked inside welled out of her eyes and began running down her cheeks. "Oh, Cole, I never expected to marry you. I never expected to feel the way I do about you. It blind-sided me, you see. I . . . love you."

Lila Whitham uttered a tiny gasp at Juliana's declaration.

He snorted. "Love? You don't know what love is."

"I didn't know what love was until I met you." She swallowed against the knot in her throat. "Just as you said, I was supposed to stay only long enough to study your invention, and then destroy it. But I couldn't leave you, Cole. I just couldn't. I felt so alive when you were near me. You were my savior, my redemption, the one who could lead me away from loneliness that had become so much a part of my life. With your caring and gentleness, you made me feel something I never thought I could feel, and when you announced that I would become your wife, I allowed myself to live the fantasy. I fooled myself into thinking that you could be mine, and refused to listen to the wiser part of me that insisted that my future could never include you. . . ."

A great, wracking sob grabbed hold of her. She bent over with the force of it. When she straightened again, she looked into Cole's face. He appeared to be made of marble.

She turned her head away and choked back the rest of the sobs that threatened to overwhelm her.

George made a little noise. He stood, moved to her side, and put an arm around her. She felt rather than saw his surprise. "Oh, Juliana . . ." he murmured.

Mr. Pritchard tentatively cleared his throat. "Anyone have any ideas on what to do next?"

Cole scowled. "I'll petition in the morning for an annulment."

"If the constable learns that Juliana perjured herself in signing your wedding license, she'll go to Newgate," Gillie reminded him.

"We wouldn't want *that* to happen, now would we?" Cole replied sarcastically. "Newgate is for criminals."

Juliana flinched. She knew he was hurting badly, but that didn't make his harsh words any easier to hear.

"No, I'll make up some lie and tell the constable we've decided we don't suit after all," Cole continued. "We'll both have to pretend that the marriage wasn't consummated."

"*Was* the marriage consummated?" George asked.

Juliana nodded miserably, resenting the flare of hope that lightened her brother's eyes.

"Then the marriage can't be annulled," George announced. "What if Juliana is even now expecting your child, Mr. Strangford?"

Cole's expression betrayed a grudging realization that George was right. "I'm not about to abandon any child of mine. We'll remain married until Juliana is certain she isn't expecting, and then the marriage will be annulled."

Juliana felt as though she'd just been granted a reprieve from hanging. "I'm so sorry, Cole. So very sorry."

OVER THE NEXT TWO WEEKS, COLE CLOSETED himself in his laboratory, even going so far as to take his meals there. The less he saw of his perfidious "wife," the better . . . because every time he laid eyes on her, his heart ached and he wanted to put his fist through a wall. How easily she'd duped him! And what an idiot he was for falling for her tricks. Quietly and purposefully he built a fortress around his heart, one made of marble, one that she would never penetrate again. As soon as her monthly courses arrived, he vowed to hustle her out the door.

Now, as the afternoon of the fund-raiser arrived and he sat in front of his worktable making the final adjustments to his apparatus, he knew that his design was far superior to William James's, or anyone else's for that matter. He'd adapted bits and pieces of the design from a smoke helmet used by rescue workers who went into collapsed mine shafts to free trapped men, and preliminary tests had indicated that his adapted helmet, coupled with the compressed oxygen chamber, delivered a far better experience under water than even he'd expected. Tomorrow, after the fund-raiser was over, he would travel to London to demonstrate his device before the Royal Oceanographic Society, and hopefully win that lucrative contract.

A knock sounded on the door, and Gillie walked in. For once Cole was glad for his interruption. "Gillie . . . thank you for coming."

Studying Cole carefully, the older man nodded. "How are you doing, Cole?"

Keeping his gaze averted, Cole shrugged. "Not too bad, for a man who fell in love with a fraud and then had the poor sense to marry her. I suppose we must chalk my experience up to the Strangford family ill fortune."

"I feel responsible for this situation," Gillie said. "I suggested her as a potential wife, and I encouraged the two of you to marry."

"How can you blame yourself for someone else's dishonesty? You trusted, and were betrayed. While you might learn from the experience, you can't hold yourself responsible."

"I just wish there was some way you both might find your way back to each other."

Cole closed his eyes briefly, the pain of her betrayal still eating at him like acid, before fixing his attention on Gillie. "Sometimes, in the morning when I wake up, I feel a depression settling over me and I wonder, who died? Then I remember what happened, and I wish I could go back to sleep."

"She really loves you, you know."

"I can't tell the truth from the lies anymore. I don't know that I'll ever be able to." Cole looked down at his hands. "Even so, I wish things had turned out differently. *That* is the hell of it, Uncle."

Gillie cleared his throat. His voice, when he spoke, was full of false cheer. "Well, let's go try out this new invention of yours, and see how well it works."

His shoulders slumping, Cole tried to respond with the same spirit that his uncle had shown, but he knew he was just going through the motions. He stood and folded his leather diving suit into a neat bundle, while Gillie gathered up his helmet and the oxygen cylinder. Loaded down with equipment, both men left the windmill and climbed into the carriage Gillie had parked just outside.

After a quick trip into town, they stopped at the docks and paid a boy to look after their carriage. Then Cole and Gillie climbed aboard the small boat they kept at the harbor. The day was sunny and a brisk ocean breeze played about the skiff's white sail, and soon, they came to the place where Cole had first found three unidentified wrecks. He'd found several gold coins there, but as the wrecks were deep and the water murky, he'd had a great deal of difficulty salvaging with his diving bell.

His spirits rising, he donned his diving suit and water-proofed it with a pot of specially prepared grease, and drew on heavy diving boots. Cole then confirmed that the cylinder's pressure remained at twenty-three bar, and afterward Gillie helped put his helmet over his head and attach it to the suit's neck ring.

Gillie smiled. "Perhaps you'll start a new trend in bathing clothes."

"I doubt it," Cole told him, his voice muffled behind the copper helmet, but loud in his own ears. He bent backward so Gillie could strap the oxygen cylinder onto his back and attach the hose from the special fitting on his helmet to the canister. Gillie opened the valve on the top of the cylinder, and cool oxygen flooded Cole's helmet, momentarily making him dizzy.

"Are you ready?" Gillie asked him in a loud voice.

His view of his uncle restricted through a small glass faceplate, Cole nodded.

Gillie handed him an underwater oil lantern sealed in a watertight case. The air that he breathed into his diving suit fed the flame in the lantern, through a hose connected between his suit and the lantern.

"Stand on the winch, then, and I'll lower you down."

Cole complied, standing on a little wooden bar that Gillie had swung out of the ocean. Slowly his uncle turned a handle and the winch began to lower Cole into the ocean. Cole felt the water creep up his legs, then cover his waist, before finally washing up over his helmet. He sensed a minute change in pressure all around him, and knew he had gone completely underwater and was descending to the wrecks on the ocean bottom.

As always, the first couple of seconds in the water had a surreal feel to them. Everything became quiet, and the only sounds he heard—sounds from creatures he couldn't identify—were muffled. He became cold, and the sunlight faded away, and he had the sensation that he'd transported himself to an entirely different world.

The water appeared murky, but not terribly so, and Cole lifted his lantern. Its soft glow lit a small section of reefs covered with brilliant coral sea anemones and blenny or lobster in almost every crack. He swept his hand by them as he floated downward, weighted by his boots, and they scattered.

The farther down he went, the less sunlight he had from above. As his oxygen cylinder grew cold, so did the air he was breathing; and his body temperature dropped likewise. Shivering, he stared through his faceplate and could just make out the ocean bottom below him and approaching fast. Broken pieces of ship lay scattered among deep gullies and large boulders. Estimating his depth at about six fathoms, he adjusted his suit pressure by operating a specially designed valve, for too much air would cause his suit to inflate and send him flying to the surface, only to suffer a painful and sometimes fatal diving disease where the blood bubbled within the veins; whereas not enough air would leave him vulnerable to the much greater pressure of the water above him.

The winch he stood on hit bottom. He secured the winch beneath a boulder, so it wouldn't float away, and started walking along the ocean floor. The smell of copper strong in his nose, he marveled at how much easier he could maneuver, without a hose following him around like a lead rope and getting tangled in ocean debris. As far as he was concerned, the suit worked perfectly, and suddenly he couldn't wait to see how the members of the Royal Oceanographic Society would receive it.

Smiling for the first time in weeks, he rummaged around the wreck sight, fitting his body between boulders that he would have had to avoid in a suit dependent on hoses for air. Various sorts of fish, including one startled-looking eel, observed him as he picked up pieces of the ship's hull and opened a cabinet that was no longer attached to a wall. Something silver inside the cabinet glinted at him in the lantern light, and he pushed aside a layer of silt to find a silver coin.

His smile became a grin.

How long had he been diving? Almost forty-five minutes at least, he guessed. That was far longer than he'd ever managed before. His outing a complete success, he walked back to the winch seat and stood upon it before pulling sharply on the rope. A few moments later the winch seat began to rise, slowly, giving his body time to adjust to the decreasing pressure. Once he arrived back on the ocean's surface, he climbed into the skiff and stood still while Gillie unfastened and removed his helmet. After Gillie unstrapped the oxygen cylinder from his back, he set the lantern down and opened his fist for Gillie, displaying the silver coin.

Gillie whistled, long and low. He picked up the coin and examined it from all angles. "It's old, all right," he pronounced. "Probably worth a decent amount."

"More importantly, my diving suit worked perfectly," Cole said. "The oxygen cylinder is wonderfully liberating. I almost felt as though I were born to the water, so easy was it to explore the depths."

Gillie's mouth quirked. "Now you know what the sea people feel like."

"I can only imagine what it must be like to *live* beneath the sea, to swim through its currents with a dolphin's maneuverability and breath water rather than air. I think I'd rather enjoy it."

"I know you would." Gillie pulled a watch fob from his pocket. "We haven't much time before the fundraiser, Cole. We'd better return home."

Cole's good mood dissipated. He'd been dreading this evening when Juliana would last appear at his side as his wife. Soon, she would be gone. Most likely he'd never see her again, and the knowledge hurt like hell. But what alternative did he have? Keep her as a wife despite all of her betrayals, and defy the estate entailment? Put her up in town as his mistress? Neither of those options seemed worthy.

He sighed. "Let's go back."

Gillie turned the skiff toward shore while Cole shrugged out of his diving suit and folded it neatly. Neither he nor Gillie said much. A feeling of doom seemed to hang over them. After the skiff had docked alongside the harbor, Cole and Gillie collected his equipment and had the boy who'd been watching their carriage bring it around. Gillie flipped him a sovereign and in short order, they had returned to Shoreham Park Manor.

Every window in the manor blazed with light . . . and the sun hadn't even gone down yet. Cole figured that the servants must have lit every candle in every chandelier and sconce in the place. The effect was very extravagant, and very welcoming. As he passed through the entry hall and went up the staircase to his bedchamber, he saw many bouquets of hothouse flowers, reminding him of his wedding breakfast.

His heart twisted. He scowled ferociously.

Servants scurried to and fro even on the second floor, preparing rooms for their overnight guests. A few notes from a violin whispered past him as the orchestral ensemble practiced. Rich aromas of chicken and pastries wafted up the stairs as Cook prepared enough for at least one hundred people to eat. Clearly Juliana had outdone herself in preparing for this fund-raiser.

Quickly he banished her name from his mind. Thinking about her hurt too damned much, and he didn't want to torture himself unless he had to. Christ, he'd be tortured all evening with her at his side as his "wife," knowing that soon, his marriage would be dissolved and Juliana, long gone. Completely out of sorts, he marched into his bedchamber and traded his work clothes for evening clothes, stopping only long enough to snarl at William.

Purposefully he chose trousers and a jacket completely different from the ones he'd worn at her wedding. Made of deep charcoal gray superfine, they appeared only slightly less formal than his black evening clothes, and the black waistcoat and white cravat he selected more than made up for their deficiency. Aunt Pesha came upstairs to check on him just as the fund-raiser was set to begin—they were all checking on him a lot lately—and she remarked that she didn't think she'd ever seen her nephew looking more elegant or handsome.

He smiled at the compliment, even though he suspected she'd delivered it in an effort to boost his spirits. Many of the guests had already arrived, and they watched him as he descended to the fund-raiser with Aunt Pesha's hand tucked in the crook of his arm. He suspected that many of the guests were wondering where he'd put his new wife, and why he chose to escort an elderly aunt rather than the delectable piece of fluff he'd married. A moment later, he saw Juliana, and his suspicions solidified into certainty that his guests—particularly the men—must have thought him mad to prefer Pesha.

She wore a long-sleeved chemise colored a brilliant yellow that matched her eyes exactly. Gathered lace flounces decorated the gown at her wrists and along her low-cut bodice, which more than adequately displayed that she needed no padding. In fact, a single strand of pearls sporting a topaz pendant lay atop her milk-white breasts, effectively drawing attention down to her cleavage.

Cole swallowed and allowed his gaze to rove over the rest of her.

She carried a golden paisley shawl edged with fringe off her shoulders, and fluttered a fan in her right hand. Her long, chestnut hair was piled high atop her head in the Grecian fashion, accentuating her slender neck; while a yellow ribbon wound through the lustrous strands, perfectly complimenting their color. Elegant and stunning, Juliana had captured every gaze in the room.

When she caught sight of him, her deep cherry lips curled up at the corners and her eyes brightened. "Cole," she called out softly, "come and help me greet our guests."

Aunt Pesha patted his arm once before releasing him. He moved toward Juliana, who clutched his hands in her own as soon as he drew close enough, and pulled him to her side in the manner of a devoted wife. Despite himself, he felt pride at having such a stunning woman at his side.

He glanced at her with a good deal of irony. "How lovely you look this evening, Mrs. Strangford."

"Oh, Cole, I thought you'd never come down. I want you to meet Colonel Bridgers, of the Royal Navy. He's heard of your diving suit from the Royal Oceanographic Society, and he'd like to talk to you about it. I believe there's a possibility of a contract involved, should your diving apparatus prove suitable."

"I thought you preferred William James's suit," he murmured.

Her eyes darkened. "Yours is much better."

Not sure if she were serious, he lifted an eyebrow, but then she was hurrying across the room to a middle-aged gentleman in the uniform of a captain of the Royal Navy. The gentleman snapped to attention at her approach, his eyes sparkling with male admiration.

Berating himself for the jealousy that squeezed his gut, Cole nevertheless moved a little closer to Juliana.

Smiling, she introduced the two men, and then stepped back to watch as the captain and Cole indulged in a few pleasantries before the conversation turned toward the more serious subject of diving.

After a while, Juliana drifted away, and though Cole was totally absorbed in his conversation with Captain Bridgers, he still saw her sail into the crowd, chatting happily and bringing other people with like tastes together—just as any good hostess should. She stopped several times to talk to her scoundrel of a brother and Mrs. Whitham, the woman he was supposed to marry. Cole knew sympathy for Mrs. Whitham, for she had been duped just as he had, but the knowledge that she had obviously fallen in love with Juliana's brother, and he with her, tempered his sympathy.

His sense of pride for her accomplishment this evening grew as the party moved into the gardens and groups of adults wandered through the gardens she and the children had decorated, or played the games she'd arranged for, or simply conversed on the sidelines.

"Your wife is a lovely woman," Captain Bridgers remarked with a smile, surprising Cole with his unexpected, off-topic comment, until he suddenly he realized that his attention must have been wandering, because he couldn't remember the last thing the other man had said before that comment about Juliana. Abruptly he felt like a foolish, love-sick dolt.

"Yes, she is," he agreed.

The captain's eyes grew misty. "Hold on tight to her. I lost my own wife back in '05, and every morning I wake up and still expect to feel her next to me."

Silently Cole groaned. This wasn't exactly the kind of advice he wished to hear.

After a while, Captain Bridgers wandered off to converse with other members of the party who possessed more serious attitudes, and Cole mingled as well, enduring slaps on the back from a few of the gentlemen in town for netting such a catch as Juliana. Dinner was served at about eight o'clock in the evening by four little gnomes and fairies, who were accompanied by several footmen and maidservants, and many of the guests exclaimed over the quaint, entertaining nature of the picnic dinner Juliana had arranged and the exquisite manners the orphans displayed. One elderly gentleman declared the high price of the ticket to the fund-raiser well worth it, and from then on, the fund-raiser went down in the annals of town history as an unqualified success.

Cole, who'd kept his eye on Juliana throughout the evening, knew exactly the moment when she left, and he immediately sought out Gillie to discover where she'd gone. Gillie informed him that she was preparing herself for the brief drama about the sea people, which involved several of the orphans. He waited somewhat impatiently for this drama, which he learned would be held in the main hall, to begin. When Aunt Pesha appeared at the front door and asked everyone to come inside, he stood at the head of the line.

Laughing and conversing, they filed inside the main hall. At the end of the hall, next to the staircase, someone had strung an impromptu theater curtain, and once everyone had packed inside the hall, the orchestra struck up a little flourish and Aunt Pesha pulled the curtain open.

A gasp went up through the crowd.

An elaborate arrangement of papier-mâché boulders and shimmering pieces of blue tiles designed to look like a waterfall filled the impromptu theater. The backdrop was quite beautiful and had clearly required many hours to build. But the backdrop hadn't made everyone gasp.

Juliana had.

She wore a fantastic, tight-fitting gown with a flesh colored bodice and silver sheath for a skirt. Sequins embroidered in strategic locations throughout the gown gave her the appearance of a sea maiden, complete with dolphin's tail. Her chestnut hair curled unbound around her shoulders before falling to her waist, and she lounged with her "tail" to the side, like Venus in a seashell. Luminescent stockings encased her feet.

Several "water babies" frolicked beneath her, at the base of the waterfall. With a theatrical gesture she asked them to settle down, and they did so immediately, drawing a few laughs from the matrons in the audience.

Slowly, all grew quiet again, and receiving a cue from Aunt Pesha, Juliana lifted her head and began to sing in a clear, bell-like voice:

> *That in sweet sadness am I*
> *The dream that my heart seems to care for*
> *Deceives all men with a lie*
> *She calls from the waters around me*
> *And I don't dare to come nigh*
> *The sea is the tomb of the ones who heed*
> *The call of the merrymaid.*

Her voice faded away to nothing, softly, eerily, leaving the hall as silent as a tomb. An otherworldly air clung to her. Bumps rose on Cole's arms. In his mind he recalled the tale of the merrymaid, whose image was carved in a church in Cornwall. Betrayed by a faithless lover, the merrymaid threw herself off a cliff to her death, and became a sea maiden who called sailors to their deaths to extract her revenge.

Two older children marched onto stage dressed as a young woman and man, and began to act out the tale of the merrymaid. Juliana remained on her waterfall perch and narrated the story as the children acted. Cole found himself unable to look away from her. Twice he had to rub his eyes. Some instinct was nudging him at the edge of his consciousness, some realization that he needed to know but couldn't quite dredge up.

Just as the "young woman" threw herself off a cliff and to her death, to become the merrymaid, a small child dressed in a gnome's costume pushed to the front of the crowd. He carried, of all things, a small bucket of water with him. Curious, Cole watched the child, who displayed perfect manners as he fought his way to the front of the audience with the bucket of water. When he broke from the front of the line, and Juliana saw him her eyes widened. A look of horror crossed her face.

"James, no!" she gasped.

"Sea lady," the little boy cried in a high, piping voice, "you forgot your water. Don't you need your water to make a tail?" Without warning, he pulled the bucket back and tossed its contents directly upon Juliana.

Fifteen

❧

THE SECOND GASP OF THE EVENING SOUNDED
from the crowd.

Her hair wet, her eyes wide, and her mouth open in a
silent cry, Juliana stared at James. At the same time,
something very strange began to happen. The air
directly around her seemed to grow misty, as though a
steaming pot of water had been placed nearby. A low
moan escaped her. She began to thrash helplessly like a
fish that had been pulled from the sea and slammed
upon a deck.

"Oh, my God," someone said aloud. "She's having an
attack of some sort."

Cole rushed forward, reaching her at the same time
her brother George did. Cole scooped her up in his arms.

"Get a blanket," George ordered.

Cole looked at him with disbelief. "She's not cold.
Good God, she's burning up. The heat from her body is
damned near burning my palms."

"I said we need a blanket."

Aunt Pesha, perhaps sensing authority in George's
tone, hurried to do as he'd bid, and returned with a lap

blanket from the parlor. George took the blanket and threw it over her.

Cole held her tightly. An odd sort of shuddering had seized her. He felt little movements beneath her gown, as if each individual muscle was trembling at a different rate. The sensation was very unusual, and Cole felt the hairs at the back of his neck stand on end. "What's happening to her?"

"She's transforming," George said, as if this explanation would clear things up for him. "Bring her to the parlor. Quickly!"

Cole rushed into the other room and set her on the couch. George closed and locked the door behind them and raced to his sister's side. Outside, he heard Gillie telling the guests that Juliana would be just fine, that they didn't need worry.

George lifted his sister's skirt and pulled her stockings off. Cole watched in fascinated horror as the muscles in her legs rippled and reformed, changing size and moving like moles creating tunnels beneath the ground. Her skin was changing color and texture, too, going from milk-white to a silvery-gray, and becoming tough-looking.

He took an unsteady step away from her.

"You're her husband," George said to him, his face very serious. "I need you to take off those silk drawers she's wearing beneath her gown."

"What's happening to her?" Cole demanded, his mouth becoming dry. "Good God, is she . . . is she one of the . . . sea people?"

"We are both sea people," George informed him. "Now take off her drawers, and hurry. We have to get her down to the water."

Cole staggered. He rubbed a hand across his eyes.

"Mr. Strangford, Juliana needs your help," her brother prodded, his sea-blue eyes narrowed. "I'm sure she'd rather have you pawing about her intimately than me, but if you force me to, I'll take her drawers off."

Feeling like he'd wandered into a fog, Cole stumbled to the couch and kneeled by her side. The mist surrounding her now surrounded him, too. He reached under her skirt and pulled off her drawers, feeling a preternatural heat as he did so, along with the scurrying sensation of muscles realigning themselves. Even as he slipped the drawers away from her feet, she stretched mightily, her spine elongating. She whimpered, and he saw her legs seem to melt together, forming a single structure.

Chills raced down his spine. He couldn't seem to look away. "How . . . how . . ."

"That little boy splashed saltwater on her." George frowned. "My sister hadn't any time to prepare her mind to resist its effects. She couldn't halt the transformation anymore than you can halt an unexpected sneeze."

Her feet splayed out, flattening. A webbed membrane formed between her toes, growing thicker until her feet had become a dolphin's tail. Weakly she twitched her tail. Her head lolled back against the couch.

George smoothed her hair back from her forehead. "She's in terrible pain right now. The transformation is almost completed. We must get her to the ocean, where she can breathe the water as her new body is meant to."

A whimper escaped her. "Cole," she whispered, and opened her eyes to look directly at him.

He flinched. Her pupils had expanded to cover almost all of the yellow, and a thin membrane covered them, the overall effect very unsettling. "Christ Almighty."

Trembling, he picked her up, noting how her dolphin's tail curved around his body, as though she wished to caress or hang on to him.

"Is there another way out of this room?" George asked.

"The servant's entrance." Cole led the way to a small door hidden among the furniture, and soon they were slipping down the hallway toward the servant's quarters. A quick right led him to the back door. George opened it for him, and then they were outside and walking as quickly as they dared toward the ocean.

"Is she going to be all right?" Cole asked.

"If we get her to the ocean, she'll be fine. It's important for the transformation to complete after it's begun. Otherwise, she'll be sapped of strength for days to come."

Stunned and disbelieving despite what his own eyes had seen, he shook his head. "Is this some sort of parlor trick?"

"I wish it were."

"You really are one of the sea people."

"I am," George replied tersely.

"And I suppose this "William James" story was simply concealing your true purpose."

"We didn't think you'd willingly offer to sire a child with one of our own, and break the gypsy witch's curse."

"I can't believe this."

George said nothing in reply, and soon they'd reached the edge of the ocean. Cole set her down near the surf. "Now what should we do?"

He nodded toward an outcropping of boulders. "I'm going to go sit over there, on those boulders, with my back to you. You must remove her gown and any other clothes she's wearing, and put her into the water, so she can swim."

Swallowing, Cole knelt by Juliana and supported her behind the shoulders with one arm, lifting her head off the sand. He knew he should have been frightened, or at least disgusted by her. She was, after all, his mortal enemy. Legend had it that the sea people would attempt to lure all gypsies to their deaths. And yet, triumph filled him instead, along with fascination and a mixture of all of the other feelings he'd had for her, which he'd bottled up inside.

He didn't have to chase rainbows anymore.

He was holding one in his arms.

His touch as gentle as lamb's wool, he unbuttoned her bodice, untied her shift, and slipped them both from her shoulders, revealing white, coral-tipped breasts. Moonbeams bounced off her bare flesh, making her sparkle like silver in the night. Heart beating thunderously in his chest, he unfastened her waistband and untied her shift and pulled her clothes from her. She lay there, prone, vulnerable and quivering, her silver tail thrashing weakly against the sand.

The sight of her was so fantastic that Cole wanted to pinch himself to see if he were dreaming. A thousand questions about the sea people tumbled through his mind. He prayed that Juliana would be all right. And he wondered about the Sea Opal. Did George have it? Would the other man trade the opal for a chance to break the curse?

Hope flared within him. He scooped Juliana into his arms and, heedless of his fancy charcoal-gray suit, waded into the ocean. When he'd gone about waist deep, he set her into surf. She convulsed when the saltwater touched her, her tail twitching, and suddenly she swam away from him, diving into the waves before disappearing.

His heart squeezed by an emotion he couldn't name, he stared at the waves for a long time, and then returned to the shoreline where George awaited him.

"We're supposed to be enemies," Cole reflected.

George nodded. "We've always been afraid of the gypsies, considering what the gypsy witch did to us. I always found it ironic that the only way we knew to free ourselves from the curse was to try and seduce those we feared most. Unfortunately we never succeeded."

"Likewise, we've always been afraid of the sea people, the murdering thieves who stole the Sea Opal from us and then sent our leader to his death over the cliff," Cole pointed out. "We've made a point of ensuring that we never allowed one of the sea people to seduce us and produce a child of impure blood, because we were afraid your kind would rise up out of the ocean to finish the job you'd started and murder us all. Do you have the Sea Opal, by the way?"

George laughed, though the sound hadn't much humor in it. "No. We lost it a long time ago."

"That's a shame, because I was going to propose a deal. If you give me the Sea Opal, I'll keep Juliana as my wife and sire several children to dandle on my knee, and to break the curse that binds you."

The other man looked out to sea. "We don't have it, Mr. Strangford."

Cole shrugged. "How many of you are there, and where do you live?"

"We number about twenty. Many of us remain here, off the southern coast of England. Wrecks are plentiful around the Scilly Islands, and that's where we've chosen to create our small town."

"You live in shipwrecks?" Cole asked, his gaze on the waves cresting along the shore.

"We do. A few of the sea people have moved on to the Mediterranean and the South Pacific. We haven't heard from them for many years now."

"And all of this time, you've been trying to seduce my ancestors, in order to break my ancestor's curse."

Now it was George's turn to shrug. "When the chance presented itself, yes, one of the sea people attempted to seduce one of your kind. But we didn't relish those opportunities, and only very special people were chosen."

"Like Juliana."

"Exactly. Juliana, more than any of our other women, has the ability to resist the transformation from land-walker to sea person when she has time to prepare herself mentally for it. When you forced her to stand in the ocean during your 'courting ceremony,' she'd managed to prepare herself beforehand and in that way fooled you. But just now, she hadn't any time to steel herself at all, and couldn't resist the transformation."

Cole nodded his head slowly. It was all so clear now.

"So, what do you suggest we do next?" George asked after a while.

"How about you give me the Sea Opal?"

George regarded him candidly. "Juliana loves you, and knowing her as well as I do, I'd be willing to wager that she's managed to secure your love, too. Since you both love each other, why don't you stay married to her?"

"She's done nothing but lie to me and betray me," Cole reminded the other man.

"She lied and betrayed you, Mr. Strangford, because she knew that the fate of all her people depended on her seducing you and producing a child of impure blood."

"So you expect me to excuse her actions?"

"Perhaps not excuse, but at least understand them."

Cole eyed the other man closely. Something just wasn't making sense here. "If Juliana and I can live on land as a normal married couple at this point, why do your people want to break the gypsy's curse so badly? Why don't you all just come on land and stay away from saltwater?"

"I wish it were that easy," George admitted. "You see, when we assume landwalker form, and gain legs, we must still return to the ocean every day and allow our bodies to revert for a set period of time. If we don't, our skin starts to dry out and harden, and we actually suffocate. And the more days we spend in landwalker form, the longer we have to spend in the ocean each day as sea people. I once knew a man who spent six months on land, and by the end of that six months he'd had to swim in the ocean for fourteen hours every day. So you can see, after a while it simply isn't practical."

Fascinated, Cole tried to remember the wording of the spell his ancestor had used; and though he knew it once, it eluded him now. He could well imagine, however, the sea people being bound by these rules and prohibitions. "If Juliana and I manage to break the curse, though, you can all come on land without these problems."

"Indeed."

"I'm assuming you're not going to murder the last of the Strangfords in their beds when you do so."

"As long as you free us from the curse you've already

placed on us, and don't curse us to another hellish existence, you're safe."

Both men laughed. It was a good, clean sound.

At length, Cole nodded thoughtfully. Inside, however, he nearly trembled with excitement. "What about the Sea Opal? Only the jewel can reverse the Strangford family's ill fortune, and from what I've heard, you had it when you first entered the ocean. I think the Sea Opal is a fair trade for breaking the curse."

"We would have suggested this sort of deal long ago, had we any way to retrieve that bloody jewel," George insisted. "Indeed, I believe the Sea Opal is at the root of all our troubles—both your family's and mine."

"Where is it, then?"

A female voice drifted out of the darkness. "Where is what?"

Both men fell silent as Juliana rejoined them, her fins now legs again. She'd wrapped herself in the blanket. As soon as she drew close to Cole, she glanced at him from beneath her lashes.

He returned her stare, allowing his gaze to roam hungrily over her face, which the moonlight had turned silver. And he knew in that moment that he wanted her so badly that her lies meant nothing, her betrayal meant nothing as long as he could have her for his own, before his lonely life was set. He didn't care if they went to live where the warm waters flowed . . . he didn't care what crimes they committed . . . he didn't care if danger became his everyday companion.

Perhaps, though, he might not only win her, but the Sea Opal as well. The game would be a dangerous one, and her love would be the prize lost or won; and after a few seconds reflection he knew it was a game he had to play. Finding the jewel had long been his life's purpose.

"I see you're cured of your fear of the ocean," he murmured to her.

Flinching, she looked away.

He couldn't stop a smile from curving his lips. He was enjoying this. "I guess your near-drowning off the coast of Ireland hadn't been that terrible after all."

A sigh escaped her. "I can't drown. You must know that."

"And your soldier? Was he a fabrication, too?"

"He served his purpose," she responded indirectly, and he decided not to press that particular line of questioning with her brother listening in.

He looked at her for a second more, and then helplessly gave in to the impulse to pull her next to him and wrap his arms around her. Desperately they hugged, and Juliana sniffled. He knew she was crying. He had tears in his own eyes.

George cleared his throat, reminding them of his presence.

"Juliana, your brother has just made an interesting suggestion," Cole said in a tight voice, pulling away from her with only the greatest of reluctance. "He wants me to remain married to you, and produce that child that the sea people need. But I was wondering if you would help me in return."

"Help you how?" she whispered, her eyes very wide.

"Help me to retrieve the Sea Opal. Your brother claims that the sea people don't know where the opal is, but I find it hard to believe that they'd have lost such a valuable possession."

"I didn't say I was unaware of the jewel's location," George corrected him. "Rather, I told you I couldn't retrieve it. We have our own legends surrounding the Sea Opal, and they start with my ancestor Anthony St. Germaine. He's the one who originally stole the Sea Opal from your family."

"I've heard of him," Cole muttered.

"Well, after your gypsy ancestor cursed the St. Germaines to live as sea people, St. Germaine became determined that you would never get it back, so he picked a secret cave deep within the ocean to conceal the jewel in. He evidently told his relatives before he left where the cave was, and then he left with the opal, supposedly to hide it. No one ever saw him again."

Cole lifted an eyebrow. "What do you think happened to him?"

"We think he died hiding the Opal in the cave," Juliana murmured, taking up the tale. "Though we never did find his body."

"How do I know you're not lying to me?" Cole asked. "Take me to this cave."

George shook his head. "We can't. I haven't told you the rest of the tale. After St. Germaine disappeared, others went to the cave to look for him. They never came back either, though the badly decomposed body of one of his rescuers eventually surfaced nearby."

"Badly decomposed? What did this person die from? Did the body have bite marks? Was it partially eaten?"

Juliana shook her head. "The story is very vague. We don't know."

"So the cave could conceal any number of dangers." Cole thought of a giant squid he'd once witnessed when diving. It had passed below him, leaving a rush of water in its wake. He'd scrambled into the skiff damned quickly upon seeing it.

"Indeed," George agreed. "Over the decades, other men and women who thought themselves capable of handling whatever that cave held went there to retrieve the Sea Opal. Some of them left with spears and knives. They were never seen again."

"Good God." Cole rubbed his forehead. "There has to be a way to get at the bloody thing."

"If you can think of a way, please share it with us," Juliana murmured.

Disappointment brought a frown to Cole's lips. He'd always been extremely determined. He'd attacked the task of finding the Sea Opal with the same persistence as he'd shown toward his inventions, and had long ago learned to accept failure as a sign to try again in a different way. He had discovered that one simply can't quit, no matter what happened, for to surrender to failure was to allow it to triumph. And yet, now he had to face the undeniable fact after years and years of searching for the Opal, he'd finally found it, only to discover it lay forever out of his reach.

Still, he remembered his near-drowning in the rogue current. On that day, he'd damned near died chasing rainbows. But weren't some things worth dying for? Things like the Sea Opal, and things like love?

He turned to face Juliana and her brother with calm determination. "I'm going to that cave. I don't need either of you to come with me. Just tell me where it is."

Her eyes widened with surprise. She placed a restraining hand on his arm. "Cole, no. You can't. You'll die, and I won't let that happen."

"Why? Because your last chance to break the curse will die, too?"

"No, you stubborn fool. I won't let you die because I love you."

He grew warm inside. She was like a sunrise to him, a banishing of night's shadows and chill. "I'd rather go to my grave knowing I'd tried," he told her, "rather than be buried full of regrets and longing for a second chance."

George shook his head. "No."

Cole turned to Juliana. "You know me well enough to understand that I must do this, Juliana. Please trust me."

She swallowed, glancing at her brother before focusing on Cole again. "If you perish, Cole, then I might as well be dead, too. I'm going with you."

Looking at them as if they'd both gone mad, George shook his head. "I forbid it, Juliana. I won't lose you."

"The cave is fairly close to the shoreline," she told Cole, ignoring her brother. "It's located deep within an area where the shelf drops off into a gully. It's at least ten fathoms below the surface at low tide. Can you dive that far?"

"This is nonsense." George's voice rose. "Juliana, you can't take him to that cave. You'll die like the rest of them."

She shot him an annoyed look. "George, don't you see? We have to try. If we regain the Sea Opal, both our families can finally be at peace."

"Can't you at least wait until the morning? Why go racing off now? No doubt half the town is back at the house wondering, what happened to us."

"I've already waited a lifetime for the Sea Opal," Cole declared. "I'm not waiting any longer. I don't give a damn what the people in my house think."

George sighed and shook his head.

Refocusing her attention on Cole, Juliana pointed to a spot over the ocean. "It's in that direction."

Cole narrowed his eyes. "The tide is going out now. It ought to be at its lowest point in an hour or so."

"And what happens if you don't finish retrieving the Sea Opal before the tide starts coming back in?" George asked.

She shrugged. "We'll just have to work fast. How soon can you gather your diving gear?"

"I'll go and get it right now."

"I'll come with you."

Both Juliana and her brother followed Cole as he hurried up to his laboratory. Once there, he started packing up his equipment and had to endure several comments from George about their poor chances.

George poked a finger at Cole's leather diving suit. "You expect *that* to protect you from the cold water and the pressure?"

And when Cole picked up his helmet, George muttered, "How in hell can you see a thing when you have that cannonball on your head?"

But Juliana assisted him without comment and he appreciated her quiet confidence in him and his invention. In short order they had all of his equipment organized. Cole ran to the stables and roused a stable hand into preparing a carriage for him, which he drove himself back to the laboratory. He, Juliana, and her brother then loaded up the carriage; and soon, they were driving down to the docks of Shoreham.

Not a single person walked the lamp-lit streets. Cole supposed they were all up at his house eating his food and speculating on the cause of Juliana's illness. Smiling at the thought that he was actually pleased to have the entire town at his house, because it offered him privacy here at the docks, he went to his skiff and everyone climbed on board. With only the moon for a witness, they sailed out into the harbor.

Anticipation warring with worry inside him, Cole checked and rechecked his diving suit while Juliana directed George to row them to a spot about a mile off shore. When they arrived, the ocean surface as smooth as glass, Cole shrugged into his diving suit and asked George to fasten the wrist and leg cuffs.

They had a brief debate on whether or not Cole should wear his weighted boots; and in the end, decided against it, for they might require a lengthy search to find the sea cave, and that was done more easily swimming than walking along the ocean bottom in weighted boots. Instead, he left his feet bare and buckled on a much lighter weighted belt. In his belt, he shoved a knife with a very long blade.

That done, George put on his helmet before strapping the oxygen cylinder to his back. Impatiently Cole instructed the other man on how to attach the air hoses on his suit to both the lantern and the oxygen cylinder. They hadn't much time before the tide had gone out completely and would start to come back in.

After he'd suited up adequately, Cole told Juliana what she might expect from him, giving that he wasn't one of the sea people but rather an inferior landwalker who needed the protection of a diving suit. "Now, when we go beneath the water, the oxygen in my cylinder will grow cold. Since I'll be breathing the cooled oxygen, I may shiver during the dive. This is uncomfortable but expected."

"Oh, Cole . . ."

"Don't let it worry you," he insisted, and pressed a swift kiss on her lips . . . for luck.

George shook his head. "You're both mad."

Ignoring him, Cole stood on the winch. George continued to shake his head as he lowered Cole into the ocean. Seconds later Juliana splashed into the water beside him. She clutched a spear in her hand. Immediately she began to contort, her spine stretching her legs shimmering as they reformed to a silvery dolphin's tail. Somehow, in the water, her transformation seemed much more graceful than it had earlier; and when she had completed her change to half-dolphin form he knew more than a little envy over the freedom she now possessed in the ocean.

Spear in hand and looking like a Norse mermaid, she grasped his hand with her free one, and slowly the winch lowered him. He felt considerably lighter without his boots. In fact, the buoyancy of the oxygen cylinder was tugging him upward. Still, the weights in his belt and the heaviness of his helmet were enough to keep him from floating to the surface, and mentally he filed the knowledge away for possible later improvements to his diving apparatus.

After they reached the bottom, he let go of the winch rope and allowed Juliana to lead him through the water. It was very dark and murky all around him, the lantern providing light for only about two feet ahead. Fish darted away when the light touched them and, far in the distance, Cole heard the distinctive sighs of whales. The air in his suit tasted of cold copper, and he felt the water pressing in on all sides of him. Suddenly he felt very vulnerable. He shivered, and not just with the cold.

Juliana paused and observed him. Obviously she'd felt him shivering. He waved at her, indicating he was all right, and she drew him onward. He kicked his feet, which were growing numb with cold, and swam as fast as he could. At some point, she indicated with a hand gesture that he should wait for her, and she swam out of the circle of light, leaving him alone. Anxiety built in him for every moment that she didn't come back. Just when he began to think something happened to her, she returned and took his hand, her chestnut hair floating around her in a sensuous cloud.

Her eyes were very wide as she tugged him in a specific direction. He quickly realized that she'd found the cave and pulled his knife from his belt. He went with her, moving more slowly, scanning the ocean floor and ledges for the menace that had apparently taken the other sea peoples' lives.

He noticed nothing unusual.

Until they found the first body.

It didn't appear to be anything more than a skeleton, really; and covered with plankton and sea moss, it was easy to miss. But Cole, who had an eye for detail, saw it immediately and nudged Juliana toward it. Mindful that he only had so much oxygen, of which he'd already used about a quarter tank, he waved his hand around the bones to clear the silt away. Lantern held high, he observed a complete skeleton of a sea person. While the skeleton possessed arms, it had no pelvis; rather, its spine simply continued on to a tail-like structure.

Cole fought a fresh wave of uneasiness. The eye sockets glared at him, and the teeth formed a smile that seemed to mock him. Still, no bones appeared to be broken. That indicated that this person hadn't been killed by a creature that ate flesh, like a shark. No, something else was killing the sea people.

Juliana tugged at him. He refocused his attention on her, and she fearlessly began to pull him toward a dark opening in the reef. Excitement filled him. He prayed that the cave would be large enough to accommodate him and his equipment. As they paused in front of the opening, he saw that he would fit easily, and shined the lantern into its interior.

Impenetrable darkness greeted his vision.

He knew from experience that the cave could harbor any number of nasty denizens . . . eels, squid, an octopus. When Juliana started to swim into the cave, he held her back and shook his head. He didn't want her entering any further. He would deal with whatever menace awaited him on his own.

Stubbornly she lifted her chin. He didn't need to talk to her to understand that she wouldn't stay behind. He waved his hands sharply at her, trying to convey his fear for her and his anger over her refusal.

She slipped her hand from his and swam into the cave.

His heart jumping into his throat, he swam after her, the lantern held high. Immediately shadows surrounded him. He did see a few eels hiding in the crevices, and saw some odd species of seaweed, but nothing untoward leaped out at him. Ahead, he saw Juliana's tail flash silver in the darkness.

He clutched his knife in a white-knuckled grip, his attention fixed on Juliana. When she suddenly began to ascend out of sight, he thought wildly that something had grabbed hold of her and was pulling her into its den. As he followed in her currents, however, he discovered that the cave split into two channels, one of them leading upward. Juliana had chosen the vertical channel.

He shivered harder as his body temperature dropped.

Indeed, he was beginning to feel light-headed from the effects of the pressure and the continuous flow of oxygen to his body. He knew he didn't have much more time.

Kicking hard, he swam upward as well, and slowed his pace when he discovered Juliana hovering near the cave wall. She pointed up when she saw him. He followed the direction of her motion with his gaze, and saw that the ocean above them had leveled out and become glassy, as though they'd reached the surface. After making a gesture with his hands that begged her to stay put, just for a few moments, he kicked himself slowly to that glasslike surface.

Without warning, his head popped above the water, into a small chamber. Eyes wide, he grabbed the rim of the opening and lifted the lantern.

At least ten skeletons lying in various desperate poses greeted his vision.

He jerked with surprise. A half-strangled shout emerged from him and echoed around his helmet. He felt Juliana swim up next to him and, seconds before she surfaced, he grabbed her shoulders and forced her to stay under.

He wouldn't allow her to come up until he knew exactly why those sea people had died.

Squeezing her shoulder once, he released her and clasped the edge of the opening in the cave. It took quite a bit of effort to haul himself inside, given the weight of his equipment. Sitting on the edge and breathing heavily, he paused and glanced around. The cave was very dark, and made of the same local stone that a few enterprising merchants quarried just outside of Shoreham. He could detect no evidence of plant life, which didn't surprise him, given the complete lack of light.

He stood up, the stone as cold as ice beneath his toes, and swayed. The dizziness had worsened. So had his

shivering. In fact, his teeth had begun to chatter. For the
first time, he wondered if he might not make it back to
the skiff. Not only did he feel like pure hell, but the tide
was coming in. . . .

He walked a few steps around the bones, and groaned.
Nausea swirled in his stomach. He thought he might
vomit. Somehow he managed to quell the urge, and took
another step before groaning again. The oxygen cylinder
felt like a boulder upon his back. Realizing he could
search the cave more quickly without the oxygen canister riding him, he unstrapped it and set it carefully on
the floor of the cave. His hose was about five feet long,
so he'd have to pick the canister up and set it down a few
times while he explored, but that was better than having
it break his back.

It took him far longer than usual to figure out how to
take the cylinder off. His mind had grown confused, he
realized. Idly he wondered why he was using the equipment at all. He wasn't under water anymore. He flipped
the lever to stop the oxygen flow and took his helmet off.

An acrid smell wafted into his nose. He started to
choke. The dizziness he'd already been experiencing
intensified. He swayed and stumbled over his equipment, then stood there dumbly for several seconds, wondering what in hell was happening to him.

The answer came to him suddenly.

Poisonous gas!

He fell to his knees, gagging. Someone seemed to be
strangling him. He clutched his throat and staggered
toward the opening. Without really intending to he fell
toward the opening just as everything went black in his
mind.

Sixteen

❧

JULIANA SWAM BACK AND FORTH BENEATH THE opening, staying put despite her better judgment and wondering if Cole were all right. Just as she decided to join him in the sea cave, he came splashing down on top of her without his equipment. Shaking violently, he stared at her with glassy eyes.

She shouted with surprise. Panic seized her. He wasn't wearing his breathing equipment.

She hesitated, caught in indecision. Should she go into the cave and retrieve it for him, or bring him immediately to the surface?

His eyes rolled back in his head as he reached out to her, his fingers stretched into talons.

He was dying, and fast.

Trembling herself, Juliana made a decision that she hoped was the right one, and wrapped her body around his. Then, swimming as fast as she was able, she shot to the surface with Cole in tow. He felt very heavy, and his waterlogged diving suit only making him heavier, but somehow, she managed. When they broke the surface he was still trembling and his skin had turned completely blue.

"My God," George breathed. He hauled Cole over the edge of the boat. "What happened?"

"I don't know," she wailed. "Is he going to die?"

"He's suffering from some sort of toxicity reaction, and hypothermia," George informed her, his face grim. "But he won't die, as long as we get some air into him."

George grabbed the blanket the skiff's captain had been using and wrapped it around Cole. He then began to blow air into Cole's lungs, while Juliana chafed Cole's arms and legs. Suddenly, Cole's head went from side to side. He leaned over and was sick.

George spoke urgently. "Cole, what happened? What did you find in the cave?"

Cole coughed and groaned, but didn't answer.

"Did he find the Sea Opal?" he asked Juliana.

"No."

"Tell me again what happened during your descent to the cave."

Juliana explained to George exactly the steps they'd taken and the sights they'd seen, including the skeleton of one of the sea people. When she told him how Cole had fallen through the cave opening without his equipment, however, he grew still.

"Tell me again, Juliana. You say he went into the cave with his breathing apparatus on, and came out without it?"

She nodded. "He must have taken the equipment off inside the cave. And why wouldn't he? The cave must have had air in it, otherwise the water would have pushed its way up inside. . . ."

She trailed off, sudden realization grabbing hold of her.

"The air inside the cave must be poisonous," she breathed.

"My thoughts exactly." George shook his head. "Now we know why we've lost so many of our people so mysteriously."

"George, his breathing apparatus is still in the cave," she pointed out excitedly. "Why couldn't I go back there and wear his equipment while I'm searching for the sea opal?"

"You could, but you won't. It's too dangerous, dear sister. I won't let you."

"George, you must realize by now that the Sea Opal is very important to Cole. I'm afraid that if we leave it there, he'll think of nothing but that Opal until the day he dies. If I'm to have any happiness at all with him, I must get the Sea Opal."

And with that declaration, she dove back beneath the waves, her brother's shout of protest muted by the growing distance of water between them.

Determination heated her body and strengthened her limbs. Without Cole to pull along, she could move much faster and reached the cave within five minutes. Quickly she maneuvered through its dim interior and popped up into the cave.

The lantern, which still glowed feebly, glittered on the remains of almost a dozen sea people. It took every ounce of will she possessed not to scream. Beating her tail mightily, she surged upward into the cave and flopped on to shore. Over to her left and about ten feet away, she saw his helmet and oxygen cylinder. She knew it might take as long as five minutes for her dolphin's tail to transform to legs, so she shimmied along the bottom of the cave to the helmet and yanked the air hose off. Quickly she put the end of the hose into her mouth and turned the valve on the cylinder.

Pure, sweet oxygen flowed into her mouth and nasal passages. She groaned with relief and exhaled through her nose. Now she just had to remember to breathe in through the hose, and out through her nose.

While she lay on the cave floor, waiting for her tail to turn to legs, she stared around the cave. Other than the pile of bones, it appeared quite empty, its farthest corner shrouded in darkness. A sense of awe overcame her as she realized that she was probably lying next to Anthony St. Germaine himself, the man who had gotten them all into this mess.

When her tail started tingling and itching painfully, however, she forgot about Anthony St. Germaine and gave herself over to the transformation. She focused on breathing properly—in through the hose, out through the nostrils—until the pain had subsided and she could twitch her toes again.

Lifting the cylinder and carrying it with her, she walked along the cave walls, carefully studying every niche for the sparkle of a jewel. She felt certain she'd find the jewel right away, but as the minutes ticked by, she realized that her task wouldn't be so easy as she'd hoped. Her disappointment growing, she moved back to the farthest, darkest section of the cave and scanned the walls for some clue as to the Sea Opal's location.

She found nothing.

The old legends, she thought, had been wrong. Anthony St. Germaine hadn't concealed the Sea Opal in this cave. He'd placed in somewhere else. Frowning now, her hopes shattering like a goblet hurled against a stone wall, she walked back to the bones. Dear Lord, how was she going to tell Cole that the Sea Opal hadn't been in the cave? Would Cole even survive?

Tears moistened her eyes. She choked a little on the oxygen from the tank and took a tiny whiff of the air in the cave. Dizziness immediately assailed her. She swayed and sucked greedily on the cylinder, trying to banish the effects of the poisonous gas. The air in the cylinder sputtered. She took that as a sign that she'd nearly depleted her supply. She would have to go.

And yet, as she passed the bones, she noticed something sparkling out of the corner of her eye. Her entire being abruptly suffused with hope, she pushed aside the skeletons and tried not to flinch at their cold, damp feel; and when she had dug through the pile of bones to the skeleton laying on the bottom, she espied an opalescent jewel, set in a gold filigree frame, clutched in its hand.

She gasped and accidentally sucked in some more cave air. Her throat momentarily closed up and she choked, frantically drawing in oxygen from the cylinder.

The cylinder sputtered again. She discovered that it had become much harder to pull oxygen through the hose. Trembling, she tried to pull the Sea Opal from the bony hand that held it, but the skeleton's fingers were wrapped tightly around the jewel, foiling her attempt.

She started to feel light-headed and sucked hard on the hose. Only the tiniest bit of oxygen came out of the tank. With the next breath, there was none.

Her heart pounding, she abandoned the hose and held her breath. Her fingers shook as she worked on the Sea Opal, doing her best to pry it loose from the claw that grasped it. The sharp golden edges of the Sea Opal's setting cut through the skin on her fingers, making her bleed. Soon the jewel was coated in blood.

Nevertheless, despite her every effort, she couldn't get the jewel loose. Left with no other choice, she thought of other options and a feeling of nausea swept through her.

She was going to have to take the whole damned hand.

Her lungs burned and her head pounded, and the edges of her vision became black. Soon, she knew she would swoon, and then she would be dead, because in an unconscious state she would happily breathe the poisonous gas in. Miserably she pulled at his hand, trying to force the bones to crack, but Anthony St. Germaine's skeleton seemed to be made of iron and refused to bend to her will.

Helplessly she sucked in some of the cave air. Fighting the wave of dizziness that it brought, she came to the realization that she'd have to bring his entire skeleton to the surface, and allow someone with a saw to cut the jewel out of his hand.

But first she had to push all of the other skeletons off him.

Tears running down her cheeks, she swayed and her vision grew darker as she scattered the bones with her feet and hands. Someone observing her would have probably had her committed to Bedlam, she thought wildly, but she hadn't the time to really care, because in another moment she was going to die.

She took in some more cave air with another convulsive breath. Her throat burned terribly. Feeling like she'd lost all, she involuntarily breathed the gas again even as she wrapped her hand around the Sea Opal. With a mighty yank, she pulled Anthony St. Germaine up from the floor of the cave, the effort drawing a groan from her.

More poisonous gas slipped down her throat and into her lungs.

She fell, her hand now clutching the Sea Opal just like St. Germaine's. Indeed, she seemed to be holding hands with her ancestor as she crawled back to the cave opening.

Without warning, the jewel popped from St. Germaine's hand. Juliana closed her fist around it with a feeling of triumph. She took a deep breath of air. She couldn't help herself. And she fell forward, into the water, just as Cole had. Her vision darkened, and then narrowed to a single point. Her mind grew fuzzy. She blacked out.

A few seconds later she came to. Saltwater rushed around her. Something was in her hand. It hurt to clutch it. Still, for some reason she couldn't remember, she knew she had to hold on. Her arms and her legs grew numb, and started to itch. She knew she had begun the transformation, but this time it didn't hurt as much. In fact, she could barely feel it. Everything inside of her seemed to be growing lighter. It felt a little like ascending to the ocean's surface after a deep dive.

Peace filled her. The thing in her hand continued to bite into her skin, and though she commanded her hand to open and let it go, she still felt it hurting her. With more than a little surprise she realized that her body wasn't obeying any of her mind's commands. As the last of her thoughts faded away, she wondered if she were dying, or already dead.

Warmth slowly penetrated Cole's system. The black fog began to recede from his mind. After a while, he managed to open one eye, and then two, to stare up at the starlit heavens. He felt the motion of the sea beneath him, in the rocking of a boat, and wondered where he was.

"Good. You're coming around," a masculine voice said.

Cole turned to focus on George. "What . . ." He said no more, because suddenly it all came rushing back to him. "Juliana? Where is she?"

"I don't know, but I'm going to find her right now," George said, his voice determined. "I hope she didn't do anything foolish."

"God's blood, man, why are you up here coddling me when Juliana is down there all by herself?" Cole demanded, his heart contracting with anxiety.

"I wasn't coddling you, Strangford. I was keeping you alive. Of course, I could have left you here to strangle on your own vomit—you threw up water more times than I could count—but I didn't think my little sister would appreciate me letting you die after she'd worked so hard to save you. But now that I can see you'll make it—"

Cole regarded the other man angrily. "Stop blabbering, man, and find her. If *she* dies, you'll answer to me."

George said no more. Rather, he stripped down to nothing and jumped into the water. At once, a roiling mass of bubbles marred the surface of the ocean, as though a hot spring had formed right next to the boat. Cole knew he was witnessing the effects of George's transformation. After several minutes—too many, Cole thought—the bubbles died down and George disappeared.

For the next half an hour, Cole sat in the skiff by himself. As his strength returned and the effects of the poisonous gas dissipated, he managed to sit up, and then to stand, without feeling dizzy. He counted himself lucky to be alive, and knew he had Juliana to thank for his continued existence.

Juliana. How he loved her.

As the seconds ticked by and George remained beneath the waves, Cole's fear grew. He wished the boat were a little larger, so he could pace. Humbly he promised God that he would forget about the Sea Opal, and free the sea people, if only He returned Juliana to him alive. Anxiety had nearly brought his blood to the boiling point when a mass of bubbles broke the surface near the boat. He leaned over the side, his heart pounding in his chest, when George suddenly popped up with his arms around Juliana.

Cole stopped breathing when he saw her. Her eyes were closed and her lips so blue they appeared purple. Terrible certainty filled him and he trembled.

She was dead.

"Help me get her on board," George demanded.

His stomach sinking to his toes, he grabbed her under the arms and started hauling her over the side. When he saw her lower half, he groaned.

She still had legs, but they were gray, with the color and texture of dolphin's skin. Her toes, while flattened into fins, were still separated. She had transformed only half way before apparently dying.

"No," he breathed, and gathered her close against him as he pulled her out of the water. Her right arm was the last portion of her to come out of the water, and immediately he saw the Sea Opal clutched in her fist. A surprised gasp emerged from him.

With George and Cole carefully maneuvering Juliana, they managed to get her on board. Then, Cole pulled Juliana into his arms and rested his chin on her head.

Tears formed in his eyes. Unabashed, he let them fall. He had lost the only woman he would ever love, and for what? A stupid jewel that supposedly brought good luck?

George pulled himself over the edge of the skiff and flopped onto the deck, still in dolphin form. "She found the Sea Opal."

Miserably Cole shifted his weight so he might better examine the jewel. Gently he opened her fingers, noticing the cuts across her palm and how blood still flowed from the wound, and studied the ancient talisman.

The Sea Opal possessed a beauty far more potent than he'd ever guessed. Lit from within, it glowed with a rare bluish opalescence. Rainbow-colored patterns he couldn't quite perceive coiled and danced within its depths. A faint wash of red colored both the opal and its gold filigree setting, and he realized that Juliana's blood still clung to the jewel.

All thought left his mind as he stared at it and tried to absorb all aspects of its beauty. Knowledge suddenly came to him, sure and true: something lived within the depths of the Opal, some presence that had been trapped forever inside and could communicate only by changing color and swirling like the currents and eddies that washed up on shore.

"Don't stare at it too long," George admonished from somewhere to his left. "It will possess your soul."

His hand trembling, Cole stretched his arm across a seemingly impossible distance and ran a finger along its golden filigree setting. Pain blossomed in his finger. He'd cut himself. But he didn't care. Some instinct was guiding him, an instinct that had to be obeyed.

The Sea Opal, he mused. It was talking to him. Telling him what to do.

His gaze becoming unfocused, he dragged his freely bleeding finger along the Opal, allowing his blood to mix with Juliana's.

"Strangford, what's wrong with you?" her brother muttered, before breaking off and uttering a gasp. "Look at the sky!"

Peripherally Cole understood that the horizon had grown very dark in a matter of seconds. Clouds were racing across the sky with preternatural speed. They covered the moon. But his primary focus remained on the Sea Opal, and on the image that kept pushing its way into his mind: two rivers of blood, flowing into one as they reached the ocean. All of a sudden he understood that the little cut on his finger wasn't enough. Lips tight, he grabbed the Sea Opal and folded his fingers around it, making a fist. Pain blossomed in his palm. Blood began to flow from the bottom of his fist.

Opening his palm, he laid the Sea Opal on the deck and, guided by an impulse he couldn't explain, he clasped Juliana's injured hand, allowing their blood to mingle as one.

A jagged lightning bolt split the night.

"We always thought a child made by your people and mine would break the curse," George said, his voice hushed. "But it was much simpler than that."

The water around their boat began to bubble, forcing their boat to bob wildly and creating a mist that slowly surrounded them. Thunder rolled down from the heavens, and a torrential downpour flooded the ocean, but not a drop of water touched the boat. A golden glow, emanating from Cole and Juliana's locked hands, had invaded the mist around the boat, and the raindrops that touched the glow immediately evaporated.

His mental focus returning to him, Cole watched in shock and amazement as the glow grew more intense and a rainbow began to form in the mist. Juliana's half-transformed body began to shudder, and dazzling points of light raced up and down her legs, like fireflies engaged in a crazy dance. Slowly, her skin became milk-white again, her legs re-formed . . . this time, for good.

Cole stared at George and saw that he, too, was shuddering, the lights swirling around him even as his dolphin tail dissolved into legs. Awestruck, he didn't bother to wipe away the tears that were running down his cheeks.

A golden sparkle over the side of the boat caught his attention. He glanced out at the water and discovered that the entire sea was glowing softly, lit deep within by the Sea Opal's magic as those who had suffered the gypsy curse were liberated. Joy filled him and he knew that the wounds created centuries before had finally been healed.

Slowly, the mist faded away. Juliana stirred weakly in his arms.

Her brother thrashed around halfheartedly for a minute, then opened his eyes. "Good God. Is it over?" His voice shook with feeling. He sat up abruptly and looked at Cole, who sat there crying like a fool and not feeling even slightly embarrassed about it.

Cole nodded. "The curse is broken, George. You're free."

MOVEMENT BENEATH THE OCEAN STIRRED THE ocean's surface. People he didn't recognize came from nowhere to swim around the boat. They still had dolphin tails, Cole realized; but their next transformation would be their last. He gazed out at their joyous faces and in that moment regretted every second of enmity that he had ever felt for the sea people.

A babble of conversation started right there on the ocean. George told them that they were all free of the curse, and that the next time they transformed to land-walkers, they'd remain in that form forever. At once Cole invited each and every one of them to his house to stay for as long as they needed to, and watched with a brimming heart as they, too, openly wept.

Laughing, their voices raised with excitement, they headed in to shore.

Cole turned to Juliana and brushed her hair back from her forehead. She moved again, this time showing some strength. When her eyes fluttered open, she stared at him with both wonder and confusion.

"Cole, you're crying. Why?"

"You've done it, sweetheart. You brought the Sea Opal back, and together we broke the curse."

"What?" She sat up on her elbows. "The curse is broken?"

Rather than answer, he gathered her close and said, "I love you."

Her confusion evidently giving way to the same intense joy and relief he felt, she began to tremble and sob against him. "Oh, Cole, I love you, too." And in a broken voice she told him everything she held in her heart, as did he.

After a time, she pushed back from his chest and surveyed him with a gaze that matched the color of the sky on the eastern horizon . . . the color of a sunrise.

Quietly, joyfully, he stared into the promise of her eyes and allowed himself to be reborn.

Epilogue

A CROWD OF MERRYMAKERS—BOTH THE STRANG-
fords and St. Germaines—were entering the front hall of
Shoreham Park Manor. The women's sumptuous gowns
were a bright spot against the dark wood that lined the
front hall's walls, and the men's finely tailored suits
offered a civility in direct counterpoint to the distressed
oaken beams which crisscrossed the ceiling. Still, the
brilliant smiles upon every face brought the most light to
the room and, as Juliana's gaze drifted across the men
and women who had once swum beneath the sea with
her, she felt a warmth that not even the largest bonfire
could match. The warmth penetrated far deeper than
her skin, to her very heart and soul.

More than four months had passed since she and Cole
had freed the sea people from the dark spell cast centuries before among the moonlight and salt spray. During
that magical night when they'd broken the spell, the sea
people had come onto shore in little groups of three and
four. She and George had immediately shepherded them
to Shoreham Park Manor, where they'd stayed until
George began to settle them into the identities he'd cre-

ated for them years before. Now, most of her relatives and friends were comfortably established. Today, they'd returned to Shoreham Park Manor and earlier witnessed her brother George marry Lila, the gypsy woman he loved with all of his heart.

Juliana scanned the room for Cole, looking past the massive hearth and winding staircase to find him standing near a trophy case. The Sea Opal lay on black velvet within that case and almost at Cole's elbow. She shivered and placed a hand on her abdomen, taking comfort in the feel of their baby's kicks. While the jewel had brought good fortune to the Strangford family, it had also brought great evil to both the Strangfords and the St. Germaines, for it had been the reason behind the curse that had damned the families for far too long. She and Cole had spent many nights in bed talking about their best options regarding the jewel and, later in a special ceremony, they would see their final decision regarding the Sea Opal through.

Cole evidently sensed her attention on him, for his gaze rose to meet hers and he smiled, a carefree grin matched by the thick wave of black hair that fell artlessly over his forehead. He strode over to her side, parting the crowd effortlessly with his broad shoulders and looking magnificent in a black jacket and trousers of superfine wool. A gold stickpin sporting a sapphire pierced his snowy-white cravat, the blue jewel perfectly matching his eyes, which reflected sensual knowledge that made her tremble. Pleasure-filled memories of Cole's mouth on hers, of him inside her flooded over her, and her cheeks became hot.

He grinned and flicked a finger across her cheeks. "Thinking of last night, sweetheart?"

She smiled back and wrapped her arms around his waist. "How could I think of anything else?" Standing on tiptoe, she pressed a kiss against his lips, and the baby jumped between them as if expressing approval.

"Mmmm," Cole murmured and, just as she began to pull away, slipped his arms around her waist to bring her close again. He ran his tongue briefly over her lips before planting a kiss against her throat and nuzzling her ear. "I'm thinking of tonight."

Her cheeks grew even warmer, partially at the thought of the spectacle they were making in front of the entire assemblage of St. Germaines and Strangfords, but mostly at the purr of anticipation deep in his throat. She squeezed him affectionately, then forced him to release her with an insistent tug. "We're an old married couple. We have to behave respectably. George and Lila were just married; let them do the public kissing."

Cole glanced pointedly at the grandfather clock in the corner of the hall. "Make no mistake, I'm happy beyond words for George and Lila, but how much longer will the celebrating go on? I'd like to finish with the Sea Opal, so you and I can retire."

She linked her arm through his. "Let's go over and ask them if they're ready to move outside, to the cliffs."

Together, she and Cole moved toward George and Lila, who were sitting very close together on a settee. Uncle Gillie and his latest beau, a sea woman named Mary Watkins, had taken up post near the couple; and Gillie grabbed hold of Cole's sleeve as he passed, drawing both Cole and Juliana close.

Cole surveyed his uncle with a smile, his gaze lingering on the arm Gillie had placed around Mary's waist. "Will we be celebrating another wedding soon?"

Juliana watched the older couple with interest. She remembered Mary from her time spent beneath the sea. Widowed early in her marriage, Mary had spent most of her days making her home, situated in a shipwreck southeast of the Scilly Isles, more comfortable. Juliana imagined that Gillie would never again lack for comfort if he married Mary, and knew that Mary would rejoice in having a companion to care for. Silently she decided she approved of the match.

Gillie laughed and sent a sidelong glance toward Mary. "I don't know, Mrs. Watkins. What do you think?"

"I think it's a possibility," Mary admitted, her cheeks growing pink. "Gillie has a charm that's hard to resist. He may have enchanted me, only this time, I wouldn't call it a curse."

Juliana touched Mary on the arm. "If you can make an honest man of him, Mary, then the magic's all yours."

Everyone laughed. When the laughter had died down, though, Cole's expression became more serious. "Are you ready to join us on the cliffs, Uncle?"

Gillie's smile faded. "Very much so, if George and Lila are ready."

Cole nodded. "I'll ask them."

His arm still hooked through Juliana's, Cole steered them both back toward George and Lila. They had to wait for a few minutes while another couple finished giving their congratulations to the newlyweds, and when Juliana finally approached her brother she could see the fine lines of exhaustion around his eyes. Lila, too, appeared very much in need of both privacy and sleep. For months they'd been working to resettle the sea people, giving little time to themselves, and their tiredness had begun to show.

Juliana smiled faintly. "As joyous as this day has been, you both appear ready for it to end." She set a stray tendril of Lila's blond hair back into the pearl tiara Lila wore. "Lila, while you look radiant, I suspect you could use several days worth of sleep."

"She needs her bed," George agreed, "but I can promise you she won't be sleeping."

Juliana exchanged an affectionate glance with Lila. "They think of little else, no?"

Lila chuckled. "I confess my mind has been traveling in those directions, too."

"I assume you're ready to move out to the cliffs, then," Cole said, his gaze locking with George's.

George nodded. "Let's get it over with."

Cole left Juliana by George and strode over to the trophy case. He opened it and grasped the Sea Opal. The conversation that had been buzzing in the room began to die down as every gaze fixed on him. Juliana felt bumps build on her arms.

Cole lifted the jewel high, so everyone could see it, and said, "Juliana and I have a special ceremony in mind this afternoon . . . a simple but important one, which we would like you all to participate in. Please join us at the cliffs."

Murmurs replaced the absolute silence that had briefly reigned in the hall as Cole returned to Juliana's side. He took her arm and led her out of the front hall, into the chilly autumn sunshine. George and Lila fell into step after them, with Gillie and Mary the third couple in the procession and the rest of the wedding guests walking behind them.

As Juliana walked to the cliffs with the man she loved at her side, a sense of absolute rightness filled her. She knew that their decision had been the best they could make. They *had* to return the Sea Opal to the sea. Both she and Cole had agreed that they'd rather suffer the minor catastrophes that came with ill fortune than risk the evil that men were capable of in pursuit of the fabulous and magical jewel. Their love for each other, one that burned strong and true, would see them through the darkest nights.

An ocean breeze playing through her hair, Juliana paused at the edge of the cliff and looked out across the ocean. The waves rolled into the shore with foamy eagerness and, farther out, she thought she saw a dolphin's tail disappear beneath the surface. Longing and sadness filled her, for the sea that had nurtured her and allowed her to grow strong, and for the friends she'd left behind, like the dolphin who frolicked in the surf. And yet, at the same time, she knew great joy in finally resuming the form nature had intended for her, and at the prospect of spending the rest of her life at the side of a man who loved her deeply. The two feelings were almost opposites of each other, and she wondered how she could feel them both at the same time.

Swallowing, she dashed a tear from her eyes. *Goodbye, my friend*, she thought, her lingering on the place she'd seen the dolphin, before turning to meet Cole's ocean-blue gaze.

Cole grasped her hand and squeezed it once. The sympathy in his eyes told her that he must have suspected at least some of what she was feeling. She squeezed his hand back.

Without warning, he leaned close to whisper in her ear, "I love you, Juliana. You are the greatest treasure I've ever found beneath the sea."

Tears again filled her eyes. "Let's finish with the Sea Opal, so we can go home."

Cole nodded. "I want that more than anything."

Hand in hand, they waited for the rest of the wedding guests to join them at the cliffside. Then Cole moved so that he faced the guests, placing his back to the ocean. Behind him the sky was very blue, and he stood in a patch of white sea thrift, the mass of flowers reminding Juliana of a cloud.

The Sea Opal held high and the ocean crashing far below, Cole began to speak. "As you all know, our families have long been enemies. A thief once stole a jewel from the gypsies, and the gypsies cursed the thief and his people to an eternity of damnation in the ocean. But through both our families' love and courage, we've broken this dark spell, and now we are as one, and stronger for it."

Muted cheers greeted his pronouncement before everyone grew quiet again.

"Today," Cole continued, "we stand together at the place where too many of our families died all of those centuries ago. It was here that the thief murdered my ancestors, and here that the gypsies condemned Juliana's ancestors. It was here that they all went over the cliff."

The quiet reigning among the crowd grew thick and palpable. Juliana shivered.

"This jewel," Cole informed them, "lay at the root of all the trouble between our families. This Opal has brought my family good fortune, but it has also indirectly brought us all great evil and suffering. My friends, there is no place in any of our lives for the Sea Opal."

The Sea Opal shone like a beacon in Cole's hand as he held it aloft, but Juliana thought she saw a shadow pass over its surface, and suddenly she wanted nothing more than for Cole to throw it over the cliff. Immediately.

Several guests nodded in agreement with Cole. Others seemed unable to tear their attention away from the jewel.

Cole moved to the cliff's edge, his face tight with purpose. "In honor of our united families; in honor of friendship and tradition, but most of all in honor of love, I now send the Sea Opal into the sea, where hopefully it will never again bring good luck—or bad."

With that, he threw the Opal into the air. It glittered like a comet as it streaked across the sky before falling far, far below into the waves that crashed into the cliffside. Juliana stared at it until she saw it disappear into the water. A collective sigh went up among the guests.

Cole faced the crowd again. "Now we are all truly free."

Juliana rushed to his side and intertwined her arm through his. Relief far stronger than she'd expected to feel washed through her. She guessed the rest of the crowd was experiencing the same sensation, because they didn't cheer at the disappearance of the jewel . . . rather, they sagged against each other, or embraced, or cried.

George and Lila moved toward Cole and her, and they embraced. Uncle Gillie and Mary joined in, and Juliana felt her tears flowing freely like everyone else. After a while, they all began to walk back to Shoreham Park Manor, and though the sun was setting, Juliana nevertheless felt as though she were beginning a brand new day.

She tugged on Cole's arm and drew him close to her. This was a new day, she realized, one filled with light even after the sun went down. She knew that nightmares would never again find her. Smiling now, she paused to stand on tiptoe and whisper close to Cole's ear.

"Cole, darling, does your offer to teach me how to swim still stand?"

He grinned and put his arms around her waist, holding her tight. "It does, only remember: I usually swim naked."

"Let's begin our first lesson tonight," she offered, her smile becoming blissful as he swooped down to kiss her thoroughly, without the slightest regard for the crowds of encouraging wedding guests around them.

Spellbinding paranormal romance from

romance from

TRACY FOBES

Daughter of Destiny

Forbidden Garden

Heart of the Dove

My Enchanted Enemy

Touch Not the Cat

SONNET BOOKS
Published by Pocket Books

3108-01